Children of Stone

Opener of the Sky

*Thanks Bob!
Mary R Woldering
Enjoy!*

Mary R. Woldering

Copyright © 2016 Mary R. Woldering

All rights reserved

ISBN: 153743943X

ISBN 13: 9781537439433

To my parents and my family; Jackie and Ruth,
who nurtured my creative soul.
To my son Thom,
for being my editor and formatter for this volume.
To Annette Taylor,
first with me on my journey, without whom this story would never have been told
and
To the memory of Clarence H. "Buddy" Bell July 17, 1948-January 4, 2016
always a fan and friend.

Author's Note

Welcome back. I'm glad you're here again if you're a continuing reader, and glad you could join us if this is your first look into the Children of Stone series. As our story continues in just a moment, we will be looking back to around the year 2500 B.C. in Egypt and the Middle East to explore continuing story of the Children of Stone and those whose lives they affected. In this work of historical fiction, I have used many proper names for places and peoples in this story which are believed to have been used historically. I've included a glossary with this novel to explain the locations visited and terminology used throughout the book. I sincerely hope that you enjoy this story, and that the extra material provided allows you to better understand the historical setting in which this novel takes place. Enjoy!

Contents

PART ONE: VISIONS OF THE FALL **1**
    Chapter 1: How and Why 3
    Chapter 2: Sokor 13
    Chapter 3: Khmenu 31
    Chapter 4: Qustul 47
    Chapter 5: Wserkaf's Message 67

PART TWO: DJERAH **81**
    Chapter 6: Black Water in the Well 83
    Chapter 7: Peacekeepers and Plans 91
    Chapter 8: The Basket 111
    Chapter 9: One East, One West, One More 123
    Chapter 10: Truth is Hard 129
    Chapter 11: Dream Space 137
    Chapter 12: Journey up the River 155
    Chapter 13: Qustul Amani 155

PART 3: THE STORM **179**
    Chapter 14: The Link 181
    Chapter 15: The Insult 189
    Chapter 16: Djerah's Revelation 209
    Chapter 17: Actions in Haste 217
    Chapter 18: Defeat 229
    Chapter 19: Witness 263
    Chapter 20: Entry into the Camp 273
    Chapter 21: The Children's Embrace 295
    Chapter 22: Interim 303
    Chapter 23: The Fledgling 309

PART 4: RETURNINGS AND REVELATIONS **329**

Chapter 24: Regrouping	331
Chapter 25: Djerah Reborn	337
Chapter 26: Ameny	345
Chapter 27: Resolution Delayed	353
Chapter 28: The Unquiet Future	373
Chapter 29: One is Missing	383
Chapter 30: The Dark Balance	395
PART 5: WOLVES AND LIONS	**405**
Chapter 31: Wepwawet	407
Chapter 32: Lion	417
Chapter 33: Open the Sky	421
Chapter 34: Fire in the Blood	427
Chapter 35: Settling In Time	447
Chapter 36: Peace of Amani	453
Chapter 37: Flower of Life	459
EPILOGUE: OPENER OF THE SKY	**463**
GLOSSARY	**469**

Part One: Visions of the Fall

OPENER OF THE SKY

Chapter 1: How and Why

Ha-go-re! Akh-go-re Nejter Deka Nefer Sekht
my name is sung ever-present
though I am here.
I fly to you, I come
On dark but burning wings I walk on air
Open the sky to me
Ha-go-re Ta-te

The low tones of Deka's self-healing song roused Ariennu from her stupor-filled sleep. Beset by her fuzzy waking vision, Ari rolled on her right side and saw her former companion sitting cross-legged and studying her crimson painted nails as she sang the tuneful babble.

Goddess, I'm so sick, Ari shuddered. *Does she have to sing now, too? Someone make her stop!* the woman clutched her ears.

So many years earlier, when Deka had been dragged into N'ahab-Atall's wilderness camp, she sang that same song. Ari hadn't been able to hear the words that the cinnamon-skinned woman sang back then. In those days, she had been almost totally deaf. She had known by looking at the Ta-Seti woman's expression that she was singing instead of speaking. The song was the only sound Deka made for a long time.

Ari remembered their first conversation through the pain of her dry throat and aching head, even recalling the way her stern command had sounded. *You close your hole, or I'll close it for you!* her thoughts had snarled. She had struggled to follow the thought with words that she herself could not hear. "Gloas eh!" the unheard sound had emerged from her. After that, she had balled her fist and with a roar of distorted words cuffed the woman mightily. "I gloas eh for ew!" After that, Deka had fallen completely silent and dull. Only a spark of fire flashed in the dark woman's eyes like a tiny, evil dart. That had been over fifty sun cycles ago in the weed-blown, rocky sand of the eastern wilderness far to the south of Kina land.

Glancing around weakly, Ari brought herself back to the present. The russet-haired woman realized she was on a boat propelled by many rowers on a great body of rushing water. She felt the sway of the waters and the rhythmic push of the oars as the vessel sped along. The rest wasn't clear, except that it was the morning after the Sending Forth party.

Has to be the morning after. The wind blew at the flap to the cabin in which Ari was laying. She slammed her aching eyes shut in reaction to the horrid pain the light brought.

Oh, your happy little tune I see. You're enjoying this. Damn it, even my stone hurts! What did they do to me? That prince and his grandfather doubled up on me, they did. Bet the prince even shoveled his own wine-sickness on me, the nasty cur! No. Just, no, her thoughts swarmed and then gained enough strength for her to shriek aloud.

"Yaugh! You! Why did you *do* this to me? Miserable, pus-dripping kuna! Let me get up and kill you," she struggled to curl up and then lashed out, grabbing Deka's hand so she could yank her forward and clout her with her other fist. She was on the verge of throttling the woman, but a man's voice sounded outside the draped cabin door.

"You in there! Calm down. You want us to come in and calm you?"

Ari winced at the harsh sound the man's voice made, then collapsed into her part of the mat. *Guards. Dammit. It figures. I should tell them she's hurting me. Get her ugly self-beaten 'til I can work up the fist I'll shove down her throat when they're done.*

Out of one re-opened eye, Ari saw Deka, unmoved by her ranting, wave away the guard on the other side of the slit opening in the drape just as his sun-black hand began to part it.

"Oh! *Good!* Send him away, you stupid, stupid – so he won't notice me strangle you!" Ariennu squawked. "I want you *dead,* you hear me?"

Suddenly, her rage broke as she paused, panted, then rolled her eyes in delight. The events of the night that had just cascaded through her memory, but any delight was quickly replaced by nauseating sickness. *This has to be some sort of spell. Bet the old man cast it on me,* she remembered more as she worked to stop the blistering pain and nausea.

Ari rose, still weak, then inched closer to Deka.

"If this is about what I did with your precious man, then you deserved me doing it and I'll do it again the next time I get the chance." She grabbed her head in pain and fell back onto her mat. *Why do I still feel sick? It's been hours since sunrise. My stone should have been working the whole time to get the wine-sick out of me. The old man put his hand with that nasty black leather ring on my head before they took me. Goddess… Is my stone gone? Did he find a way to take it out of my head?*

She clapped her hand to her forehead in momentary panic, but felt the slight rise under her brow. The Child Stone which had been placed in her forehead so long ago was still there. Its weak signature told her it was still working to cure her of any impurities or flaws. She knew her first guess was correct. The prince had used his own spell to make her suffer both of their hangovers at the same time. He needed to be sober and well by the time the sun rose and his ships were under way.

"Prince Maatkare… your precious prince. He liked it with me, he did. I bet you he liked it with me more than he does with you. He took me with him after just *one night* and you've had him almost a month. Maybe he plans to put you out once we get to your precious Ta-Seti. Maybe he's already bored by you and wants to have *more* of me," Ari shrieked. "Now I remember. I think he even said something like that," she half-lied, knowing she was too busy enjoying herself last night to remember anything coherent either of them had said to each other.

Another thought floated through her as if the Child Stone in her head had decided to distract her. "Naibe?" Ariennu realized Naibe-Ellit wasn't on the boat with either of them. For a moment she thought the youngest of the three women hadn't been abducted.

Hmmm, King. Baby's with the King I guess. Then, she remembered Hordjedtef's voice as it ordered men to 'fetch the other one when the king sleeps.' *Well, damn him then. I guess now you'll tell me the prince is on some other boat trying Naibe on for size – if he's got anything left to try with.* She remembered they had obliterated themselves with wine and beer, then at the moment when she thought she had drunk him to the ground he had rallied and leaped at her. The rest of her memory of the evening involved them going at each other in an unparalleled and white hot frenzy until both of them blacked out. She had come to her sated senses first and stumbled around the darkened palace plaza until she was seized by the prince's guards. She thought of Deka, then of where they were headed, in growing panic. *No, this is too much. It was getting thin between me and this she-beast before. After this, there really can't be any kinship or manners between us.*

Deka found her voice at that darkest of moments, but couldn't or *wouldn't* look Ari in the eye when she spoke.

"I hear your thoughts so angry, Wise MaMa." Deka's low and lyrical voice used the name she had always called the eldest woman since the time when they *had* been friends. "You still think I am like you. I am *not*. I never was. Don't hate me because you finally see that now. I have said it to you for so many, many years," her voice hushed. "Your thoughts are right about Naibe-Ellit. Brown Eyes is on the other boat, my sister. She *is* with Prince Maatkare," the Ta-Seti woman's voice bore no hint of distress or jealousy.

"What? Don't you *sister* me. Sickness! You're sick! You know that?" Ariennu sat partway up again, animated by even more rage. "So you hand us over to that *whispering devil* – 'O Lady ArreNu' – I can hear the old man yet. Damn you! *Why*? Because I decided to have some sport last night with your murdering dog of a prince? Murdering. You should hear what a man will say when he's so drunk his tongue has thoughts of its own. I just meant to show you that you had no need to shut the rest of us off from your thoughts over him. You won't ever *own* him, even though you were acting like you did in front of his own wife and children. He doesn't really *want* you, not more than he wants me and he won't want Brown Eyes much either, once he's had a few rounds with her. I know his kind and you *ought* to by this time. His El is a desperate thing. It never gets weary and never goes down for long – he's gotta keep it wet *all* the time or the madness of the beast in him takes him over! You think I didn't recognize that? At least I *knew* what I was getting," she felt the waves of nausea hit her again.

"Goddess, my head. If you've got a ring that curses my Child Stone like princie and his grandfather have, let me come over there and snap your finger off and spit on the stump." For a moment Ariennu thought Deka might be wearing a black leathery ring just like the prince must have borrowed from the old high priest. She didn't understand what it was, but knew she couldn't look directly at it when either of the men wore it and that it nullified any strength her Child Stone gave her. She stuck her head out of the cabin and crawled over the side of the boat to retch. *Damn him too*, she suffered, feeling as though her guts were going inside out. *He should be suffering worse. He did this to me, I know it.*

Deka waited patiently for Ari to stumble back into the cabin, unmoved. "No," the Ta-Seti woman bowed her head when Ari returned. After a moment of silence she continued with her response. "How he is; his manner – it's not the reason I am with him."

"Oh, it's not the *men*, sister." Ariennu mocked, because she *knew* what Deka would say. She had said it before. The thought that she might use that excuse once again seemed even *less* palatable. "Don't even start to say it. You went to him like any desperate *kuna* I ever knew and now you think, you think…" She gasped, wiping her mouth. She was winded from nausea. "I could just strangle you."

Ariennu had never been the sort of woman to burst into tears, but now she found herself weeping in frustrated rage because she really wanted to kill Deka. On top of that, the Child Stone in her brow had noticed her anger and had begun to exude calming waves throughout her body. That sedateness, coupled with the weakness of a magically doubled hangover, nearly paralyzed her. *Aww, my stone must have allowed that bottom crawling keleb to give me the sickness because it knew I would get up and hurt her if I wasn't so sick. Dammit!* Fighting through her frustration, she continued her rant.

"You wouldn't even *have* Marai like a normal woman, but you want *that*? He's nothing but a big, hot shank to fill your belly up to the bottom of your neck and then he's on to the next hungry kuna! You're nothing to him but a honey hole. What is *wrong* with you?"

"Again," Deka sighed almost tenderly, "I never was like either of you. Even the Ntr Stones, the Children, know this."

Right. I know. I don't want to hear you now, not about them. Ari thought as she breathed out in disgust. *At least they're safe now.* She remembered that the old man *had* asked Deka to locate the *missing eight stones*. He'd asked Ari himself before the party. She fully understood why her own Child Stone, or perhaps just her instinct, had told her to give the eight far seeing ones she had guarded to Prince Wserkaf instead of continuing to hide them herself all those weeks ago. *One more thing –* She lay on her back and reached to her left for her basket of things beside the mat where she and Deka sat. Groping deep inside, she lifted up part of the woven false bottom and removed a fine linen sleeve. It was empty. The crystal wdjat she had taken in trade for the eight stones had been removed from it.

"You," her voice drained, sickened. She rubbed her eyes as if the last realization had been too much. "Deka, how *could* you?"

"His Highness had seen it in the past when Prince Wserkaf wore it. He knew it had been 'lost'. When I saw it was in your bag, I showed it to him early last evening. You were watching Brown Eyes dance. He asked me to bring it, but to keep it a secret from his grandfather. He wanted to study its energy… to see how it worked. I gave it to him. He is very strong of heart in these matters. His kingship will be a mighty one."

Ariennu saw Deka look away with a dreamy, almost girlish look in her half-shut eyes.

"You fool! He *killed* his first wife; King Menkaure's *own daughter*." Ariennu shrieked. At that instant, Deka's fingertips went up in a gesture for her to be quiet.

Ari realized she had been screaming in Kina. Her native tongue masked her words in babble until she uttered *King Menkaure*. That evoked an immediate rustle from the guards outside. She paused, panting, then continued through her teeth so the men wouldn't be able to understand her. "Even the power of all the gods in this land *combined* could not make him a king *now*. He's still alive *only* because of Hordjedtef's meddling, and you know it."

Ariennu wanted to mock and chant the words of everything she had learned, but sucked in her secret. "He told you he would choose you as god's wife when he became king?" she scoffed. "Are you twice the fool you appear to be? Did you notice he already *has* a wife? *Children* by her. Is that how you came to spread your legs so fast? On that promise made of air? Did you not even notice the women in this land make the choice of who will be king?"

"He said nothing like that to me," Deka had bowed her head.

Ari blinked her eyes again, indicating she was listening more intently.

"When I was with him the first time," Deka's eyes looked down at Ariennu again.

The elder woman shaded her eyes from the painful shaft of light from outside the curtains. It had found its way into the cabin once more. Even though she could no longer see Deka, she knew the Ta-Seti woman had told the truth.

"I learned what I was before – my lost memory returned. All that had been hidden from me came back. His noble heart woke it in me. The ignorant Bone Woman Deka has died, perhaps. I am not one merely for a man's pleasure as you or Brown Eyes are. I am already a Seti by place and Neteru by my bloodline. I know I was once Kentake, a god's mother, before all was taken from me: my life ended in the sand wastes near the place where we will go. My beloved ascended to the sky and my sweet child languished from its birth. I, too, was wounded, and lay too hurt to save it. All was dead until he resurrected the memory of it in me. My name was and is once again Nefira Sekht, the beautiful lion, his beautiful eye. Daughter of the god. I died long ago and I became a ghost, but now I return! I Go Forth By Day! *We learn* together. He is my brother in Monthu; in Ptah-ten-Atum's dark glory. I am become god again and have chosen *him* as my king. As for his wife, she too is unlike me. She is merely a commoner, a concubine whom he had honored with his home for birthing his young. To that state she will be returned."

Ariennu's head had hurt too much for her to piece together all of the things Deka was telling her. Even in pain, she felt her blood run just a little colder when she heard the words *Ptah-ten-Atum* come out of her former companion's mouth. Deka, or this *Nefira Sekht* as she wanted to be called, had been trying to say those words ever since the sorcerer had dragged her into the wilderness camp.

That name – Ptah-ten-Atum! Is that her word Ta-te? I can't believe this. The Father God of these people? Re-Atum? No. This is stupid. She cannot be one of the elder ones. Ariennu pondered through her misery.

"What are you trying to say?" she complained, still aching. Ari convinced herself the feelings Deka had over Prince Maatkare Raemkai had to be nothing more than some kind of spell of sex magic the man had used to bind her. She'd felt it herself last night. He was beautiful, powerful, wealthy, tormented, wildly animal, and even ravenous. The matter of his becoming a wolf in the middle of the ride added another layer of wonder to the entire evening. That package might engender any number of crazy ideas in a lonely woman. *Not bad*, Ari had thought. *Certainly worth a few more rounds if I wasn't so mad at Deka right now. Maybe both of us at once on him. No, Deka's just lust smacked,* Ari clucked inwardly before letting disgust overtake her again. *She was like Naibe and I were; scrapping and laying it down for fun and profit back in the old days in the sand when Marai found us. Why's she acting like this is the first one she ever had? She* has *to be under a spell*, she sniffed. *Maybe I'm more protected because I let my beautiful Marai into my heart when he was still alive. She never did, so maybe the prince could get at her heart. Something's still not right though and it's beyond any spell that man or his grandfather could cast.*

The woman smoothed her rust colored ringlets. *I know something's awfully familiar about this now. It feels like that damned darkness that followed us out of the wilderness after Marai found us and went up against N'ahab.* She remembered thinking she would see a killing that morning. It would have been at least a temporary relief to her suffering the last stages of yellow disease. She had struggled to the window of the women's hut and had seen her former cohorts trying to torment Marai.

I saw the dark thing come down. I thought it was some kind of demon coming for my soul after all the things I'd done. I could hide and wait to die back then. If it's come for me now, I don't know what I'll do other than feed her to it.

At first she had been outraged when Marai defeated them by merely walking among the men with waves of the dark energy rolling through his head and down the length of his arms like black lightning. Too weak to complain, Ari had retreated to her deathbed to await her doom, but he came to her, Deka, and round little Naibe. He was kind and gentle. He took pity on the three of them even though they deserved nothing from him. *He took me to the boat of a million stars that lay in the sand and made me lie down inside. It followed us, like a bitter old lion stalking us. Marai said it would. It attacked us when we lay together for so many years in the place of crystal and rainbow light.* Even then, Ari reflected, staring hard at Deka's face again. *She called* that *darkness Ta-Te.*

"Are you talking about the Dark? The Hidden?" Ari gasped. "You crazy fool. You think *that's* your Ta-Te? At one time you thought it was *Marai*. Now you think it's Maatkare Raemkai? You think Ptah-ten-Atum's spirit walks in *him* now?"

Ariennu didn't even *want* to think of the dark thing that invaded them because her next thought was to invariably compare that to an elder god from her own Kina land. When she visualized that force, it appeared in her thoughts as an oddly winged beast, part hawk and part bull. It stirred wind and sorcery like the god El in her own land. *El, the rising one, the phallus, the force that makes a man. The father god; the bull. Marai was a little like that too. Stupid kuna, its Marai who takes that shape. You even called him Man Sun, at first and thought you weren't worthy of him. Well he's dead and now you think… Goddess…* she collapsed, not wanting to speak to Deka about it any longer. It was too much.

OPENER OF THE SKY

Chapter 2: Sokor

Two months of a slow descent into madness followed that first morning on the boat.

At first, as Ariennu lay recovering from the wine sickness, she felt her situation was going to be temporary at worst. The argument with Deka about Maatkare infuriated her, but left her exhausted. *It doesn't matter. Stupid kuna can stay with him if he even still wants her. Be funny if after all this he picks out Naibe or me and puts her out on the shore, just the way I think he will. Can't see any man being hungry enough to need three women full time, unless what the king's ladies said about him being some kind of demon is true. Something's not right, though. This whole thing's getting a stench about it.* Ariennu rubbed the sleep from her eyes. She extended her fingertips to massage the place on her forehead where her stone lay. She knew that if she tried to contact Naibe with her thoughts, Deka would know and Maatkare might figure it out. She sulked a little. *Damned man doesn't even have a Child Stone, and yet he can read thoughts almost as well as we can.*

When Ariennu had been apart from the other two women and they had been working at different houses, she had used the Child Stones only once. *No telling what I'll stir up if I ask it something.* She decided to try, now that Deka was taking some air on the deck. *Little One…* she started. *My dark star. Can you speak to me of what will be?*

Silence.

Speak under my secrets, then. Show me you have not abandoned me, she insisted.

Calm silence followed.

Ariennu lay back to rest some more and to contemplate her fate. *I'd like the upper hand in this, please. He's an excellent match… I do see why Deka might protect that, but so much else comes with it. The wolf, the magic; skilled with a woman's body indeed, but…* she breathed, reflecting. *He's no Marai. No one will ever be. Marai was different… just a better man… a one of a kind. You could feel he loved you, that he wanted to make you happy, whatever the cost.* She thought of him lying dead, not destroyed as the old man said. *I'm here on this boat. I know now that the king isn't part of this. I just know it. He'll send men, he has to.*

She closed her eyes again, lulled by the rhythmic rowing into another healing sleep. She brushed the place on her brow and sensed the purring sensation increase.

Tell me or just show me, before Deka comes back… a secret for me. She asked the stone.

Ariennu felt her spirit lurch outward with such violence that she stifled a cry. *Yeouch! Damn. Warn me next time.* Her "body of light" twisted in the blackness of the void as if it hadn't decided if it would return or continue on its journey. She breathed out, then visualized herself in an upright position. Her arms had stretched into great brown and white speckled wings. *A hawk? Oh, funny, little one. Old man would piss himself, if he saw. That's another god-shape… Heru, I think, and that's a boy.* She couldn't recall, at the moment, a female hawk in the god groups.

She soared high, wind whistling by her feather-capped head. The gleaming Pyr Akhs rose in the horizon and nearby she saw the palace. *There. I see it now. Oh…it's earlier this morning. Maybe I can whisper something to His Majesty and he'll send a boat out to get us.* She settled on the stone rail outside the king's front window, then in a tinkling flash obscured herself with the shield of prismatic light the Children of Stone had taught her to create.

"Where are they? I want them brought to me at once!" she heard the king roar and saw him struggle to his feet while his grooms fell to their knees, his clothing in their hands. One man held out the pleated linen that formed the king's shendyt, but Menkaure swatted at the air near them and the man shrank back knowing he could be punished with instant death. Menkaure paced for a moment then noticed his own nakedness and tersely beckoned for one of his grooms to fasten and belt his clothing neatly. He beckoned the other man who held his ordinary khat to put it on him and to clasp his pectoral at his throat.

"Lady Naibe…" The king called "Lady ArreNu."

"Your Majesty." a low and timid voice suggested the king calm himself enough for the kohl to be painted around his eyes.

Ariennu saw guards returning up the stairs strong-arming the young concubines, Irika and Suenma, who had been rude to her right before the party commenced. They had been chosen by the king to entertain him after the party but when Menkaure had seen Naibe's dance his plans changed. The women froze at the door, reading the king's displeasure. The guards behind them pushed them to the floor in an attitude of worship.

"Where are they? What have you done to them?" the king demanded. Then, he continued. "Guard your words with your worthless and jealous lives."

Ariennu shuddered, almost ready to leave that scene. She had seen the king mildly happy, tired, depressed, slightly ill, and even paternal but never enraged to the point of breathlessness. The concubines were clinging to each other and crying. Menkaure slumped into his wicker day chair and had the guards bring them closer, pushing them face-down on the floor before him.

"You two know something. You will tell me everything, and if what I hear is not to my liking or if I even begin to sense you are lying to me, your throats shall feel a draft and your last words to your Father will be an apology." He pointed to Irika first. "You… You did not like my fire haired healing woman… or the young goddess-girl." He shifted in his chair uncomfortably. "You spoke ill of my young dancer as if you told a joke, but I knew your spiteful heart from the day she joined her sister here." He leaned forward, accusing. "I know you women plot to be with your Father, and to be the star in his eye. This morning Lady Naibe has gone from me when I did not give her leave and her dear sister is missing too."

The tall and lanky woman whose arm Ariennu remembered twisting when she insulted her, buried her face in her hands. Ari smirked inwardly. *I should have become a fly so I could see this closer. Look at that. I could almost laugh at the stupid kuna, scared like that. Not so proud and sure of yourself now, are you?*

The sensation of a controlling utterance at the door stirred Ari's attention. She layered extra secrecy over her hawk shadow and sensed more than saw the elongated skirt-like shendyt that swept gracefully into the room: Count Prince Hordjedtef.

And there it is. The demon himself. Damn! Ari sighed. *I see the bastard saving the day for his young pet. Wretched girl knows who has the real power in this place,* she watched the elder prince bend to the girl to comfort her and then dismiss both of them.

"Uncle, did you just dare speak for me?" Ari heard the king snarl. "I will know what became of the sojourning women who were in my house. The girls were bold enough to speak of their discomfort. I asked for them to be brought for questioning and now you release them?"

Uh-oh. Ari's vision continued. King Menkaure leapt to his feet and strode to the elder priest in such a rage that for a moment Ari hoped she would see the king liberate the Great One's head from his neck.

Be strong your Majesty…
He is the one.
He is the architect

Ari tried to get into the king's thoughts, but winced when she felt the Great One's gaze searched the outer porch as if he had sensed something.

"I've known you as my wise uncle all my life as a young prince and all through the good times and the bad with my heavy crown. I looked up to you, even passing over the advice of my brothers and my good vizier Neb, yet your heart decides it speaks as god?"

Ari knew the king blamed Hordjedtef for her and Naibe's disappearance. She watched as Menkaure pushed the elder aside and headed for the door. She saw him pause, seize the old man by the top of his collar and yank him close to his rage-darkened face. Ariennu heard his words and felt her heart suddenly drop. She knew her thought had reached the king but now she realized she should have kept it to herself.

"Just so you know, Uncle, I have also heard the cry of my sweet child's soul again through the gifts of these holy women you so callously sent packing. I am taking fine offense at what you have done." He shook the old man loose from his hand and stormed to the door about to send for his guards.

"Kind Majesty…"

Ariennu sensed the old man scrambling after the king; trying to get his attention.

"Don't." Menkaure turned from his elder. "It seems I've listened to your whispering and your spells long enough. You have been holding back and dismissing as fantasy the very truth I knew from the day my heart was torn out. The ladies, without me asking them to do so, brought my sweet one back to me. "I know this is why you sent them away. You are to protect goddess Maat, not bury her or choke her with lies." The king whirled in another pacing turn. "I will see the best rowers on my swiftest boats sent to take them up and bring them here back to my arms. They are to me more than gold."

Ariennu bowed her head, feeling an impossible blush of pride.

"But, Most High Majesty. Hear me once more and then no more if you wish," the elder protested. "These women have gained your trust and have cast spells of their own on you I fear. You know their sire was a would-be foreign usurper whom I and my second man, Prince Wserkaf, apprehended and routed. You had approved all that was done to him at one time."

Fearless wretch, Ariennu murmured in thought, *He'll turn it around and now I'll have to watch how it happened.* She saw the king pause, then think. *Goddess,* she thought quickly. *Do not listen, Majesty. Do not believe him.*

"I did, it's true." The king paused, still pacing and becoming even more agitated. "Have I piled on even more evil? Or, is it you, Uncle?"

"The fault is also mine to have taken pity on these pleasing ones, Majesty. I discovered that they cast spells on us all with their weeping and grieving, but under it, the whole time they were plotting and planning. I know the elder one whispered to you that you ought to take in her flower teas and creamed broths and not the tonics I labored to produce for you. Remember that soon enough you knew them to be weaker medicine? The younger beauty then came to you in your weakened state and further seized your godly heart." The Great One of Five straightened. "I feel there was less of love in them for you and more of vengeance."

Ariennu saw the old man's secretive gesture and the resulting twinge in the king's chest. She winced and made a cawing screech.

"Ah, Majesty, you see…" he said, rushing to Menkaure to heal him with all of the proper series of touches. She saw the elder priest look up once and noticed the reddened glare in his slit-like bird eyes. Everything dissolved around her.

The boat had stopped. Some sort of landing ritual was taking place.

"Eyes low! All attend!" A sharp voice ordered outside the rush-woven cabin walls.

Already? The King's men? Ari sat and patted her hair. *Damn! I must still look wrecked. My eye-paint's turned to mud.* Ariennu patted her body and froze, remembering her dress had been torn beyond repair by his Highness antics at the end of the party. *I'm naked. Oh thank goddess.* She found and grabbed the fabric of the dance shawl and covered her breasts. Chewing the red back into her lips she straightened expectantly as the curtain parted.

"There." A voice spoke. "In you go."

Naibe stumbled in, clutching her own dance shawl around her back, belly, and breasts. She went to her knees, breathing heavily. Her eyes were wide as plates.

"Ah... she... rah..." she rasped, scrambling on all fours to Ariennu. Ari felt her tremble as they hugged each other tightly. She had been about to tease the youngest of Marai's former companions about Maatkare, but quickly decided against it because Naibe was clearly terrified of something.

"I saw..." she started.

"He did the wolf thing when he was taking you, didn't he?" Ari asked. "He did that with me too... turned into an extra beast along with it, when he did." Her eyes rolled in delight at her own memory.

Naibe shut her eyes tightly as if doing so could stop a memory. She nodded vigorously then whimpered against Ari's naked breasts.

"I saw that, Ari, but it's not... what I..." her words failed. She continued with projected thoughts. *Once he let the wolf out, he was better. It was how he was before... and after. I tried to help him, I... It hurts.* She tucked into a ball and rocked back and forth.

"Really? He hurt you?" Ari raised one brow, amazed. She tried to make light of Naibe's comment. "Hmm. I'll say he's got a heavy plow and a strong force behind it, but I was needing a good pounding myself last night. You used to like it a little rough, too, so..."

"No, not like that. Not that part. I could meet and match what his body did with me. It was the other thing, Ari, I saw it… not the wolf, but what came behind him. There were so many. They were so dark and angry and they came into him and… and…" she sniveled.

"Spirits? Djin?"

The girl nodded, clinging to her elder.

"His thoughts. His spirit and rage. The storm. I saw it, worse than ever, Ari," Naibe confessed. "It was right in the middle of hard thunder that he got this look behind the wolf eyes… I got lost, Ari. He made me cry out for Marai and then he laughed at me and it sounded like some kind of…" she gulped.

As Naibe related her story, Ari saw the vision mirrored through her Child Stone. Prince Maatkare's clawed hands holding the young woman's hips high and firm to his as he moved with her. He grinned down at his prize, who lay senseless with pleasure, accepting and begging for more, but her lips formed the name 'Marai'.

"Ah." Maatkare had whispered. "So you dared to bring a ghost to us. But he, this Marai sees who has you now; yet another man after a handful of others? So untrue to his memory you are, my sweet ka't. And one thing more… " Ari sensed his gentle whisper and knew he was making an utterance over her. He wasn't wearing the leather *nauu* ring. He simply whispered, almost passionately. His hands released her hips and went to her throat as her head thrashed wildly. They closed and pressed almost too quickly for her to claw and fight. In an instant she was unconscious. "You are here to serve my hunger," he kissed her wildly, not slowing or stopping to see if she was still alive. "I feast on your heart as it is overwrought with the gladness of my ben doing its work deep inside you."

In moments, he finished and soon sat on his heels, bending once to gently kiss the deep blue stone pulsing in her brow. After that, he waited for her to stir. As she did and as she cried out in absolute horror he regarded her mutely, thinking. She sat to fight, but he clasped her arms.

"Shh… not so bad, now. You know that," he whispered. "You're already craving more, but me? I take. You? You give."

"The bastard," Ari hugged Naibe hard again. "You're all right now, aren't you?" she examined the young woman's throat. There was no mark. Ariennu didn't wait for an answer. She knew. *That's how he does when he's not blind drunk, then? Good thing he was out of his wits with me last night, because he would have had a fight on his hands. And he'd better not deny he killed the princess if I give that story a voice. After what I just saw through our two Child Stones, I know better.*

"I just don't understand why my sweet Khaket would let me be taken from him. Surely he's going to come for us, isn't he?" Naibe looked up into Ari's black eyes, the gold of her own brown eyes still shimmering. "We became so close last night. He was so good to me. Great One had no right to do this to us!"

"I hope His Majesty can." Ari breathed, knowing she would have to tell Naibe about her spirit journey. She didn't like to use the gifts the Children of Stone had amplified in her, other than her ability to keep secrets and to become invisible for the purpose of spying or stealing. An out-of-the-body journey was something new for her. She hesitated. "Babe, I was sick this morning, almost as bad as I used to get in the old days. So, when I was resting and letting the Child Stone cleanse me, I went back to the palace to tell His Majesty what had happened to us. I went as a small hawk, of all things. I perched on the rail and heard Majesty yelling at the old man worse than I had ever heard him. He was practically screaming. I thought he would order him killed right then, but he didn't."

"He knew something had happened to us and that wicked man had done it, didn't he?" Naibe gasped and froze in momentary thought. "I hope Menkaure Khaket ordered him to come get us."

Ariennu shook her head. "That serpent tongued old birdman. I swear he's a lizard that grew feathers. He was so sweet to him and gentle; calming him, showing such care for His Majesty. He cursed us to him. Said we were enchanters set to avenge Marai, and that he originally meant to turn us out until he decided to send us away as companions for Deka. When the prince comes back, the time of the dread prophecy will have passed."

"And then... Did you do something, Ari?"

"No. Bastard was starting to see me. I wish I had flown in there and left a load on that bald head so big he wouldn't be able to get it out of his eyes for a week. I'm not sure if he knew exactly who was listening to him. I woke up right before you came in."

Naibe's face paled. Her cheeks became a deeper rose just along the top and her eyes darkened. "He's going to die for this, Ari," she whispered. "Majesty *can't* believe him. I know it. My heart tells me he doesn't."

"I know he doesn't, and I think he knows by now that Hordjedtef pushed his own grandson into place in the royal house until the boy snapped like a bad dog. Maybe Princess Mery did make him mad and there was an accident, but the old man knew how to use his heka to push his thoughts into people's hearts. He could have covered up the entire mess. What's worse, I think Maatkare is using his own spells too; the push, like your special Ashera voice. Maybe that's why Deka…" Ari's thoughts trailed off.

Outside, the women heard sounds of men working and fastening the boat.

"We're at a shore?" Ari asked. "Already?"

"Sokor." Naibe answered. "I heard the men talking about it being our first stop. Highness has to meet someone here after sundown. One of his teachers."

City of the Dead. Ick. Why? Ari quickly had another thought. She whispered in Kina as quietly as possible. "You want to go back to the king?"

Naibe hesitated.

Ari knew His Majesty wanted to send men and boats to bring them home, but she knew he wasn't going to. *If Great One has already started to cast doubt into Majesty's heart, there's no time to waste.*

Do you have an idea? Naibe looked up.

Ariennu paused.

"I'm just hoping the Stones we both have can help us come up with something," she shrugged. It occurred to her that the Children of Stone might not want them to go back to Ineb Hedj. *If that's so… then let me make the biggest fool of myself trying.*

OPENER OF THE SKY

Prince Maatkare sent Deka to the provisions boat alone. The Ta-Seti woman brought Naibe's basket, then gave her and Ariennu instructions for the evening.

"We should wash and dress," the Ta-Seti woman whispered, her eyes downcast. "I feel you both resent me now, and you shouldn't. You least of all shouldn't, Wise MaMa. His Highness sent me to speak for him, while he attends to business with a priest here."

Ari tugged her basket closer and took the other basket, passing it to Naibe.

"Please. It will take me quite a while to keep my hand in my lap instead of around your throat," she huffed. "You want to get in my good graces again? Send for water that doesn't have river stink in it. I know there must be some, unless he plans for his men's bowels to run inside out. And don't you give me lip about it being saved for making beer either."

As if Ari's complaint had been heard, a faceless servant brought in a water jar and a smaller pitcher, set them down and then backed out.

"You need to be quiet, Wise Mama, not like some heated ka't kicked out of bed before knowing her own pleasure. I will share my water and oil because Highness has asked it of me. Then I want to say no more to you." Deka poured out the pan of water, then put the few precious drops of perfumed oil in it. When she had silently washed, patted herself dry and dressed, she pushed the bath pan to Ari and drew into herself.

In a way, Ari felt almost sorry for Deka. *You like him, I can see that. You've picked out a disrespectful one and you know he won't be tamed now. I had to show you that. He loves only himself, like most of these Kemet royals. I just knew because, until Marai found us, I was like that. You want to be his heka woman; the one who teaches him. Good luck. I just think you're going to end up being the one who gets taught.*

Deka looked at Ari; a dull expression on her face that gave no indication she had listened to any of Ari's thoughts on the matter.

Ariennu and Naibe washed and dressed silently after Deka finished, then threw the water over the side. As the sun began to set, the three women emerged from the stuffy cabin and were ushered ashore to some priest's house for a meal. As Ariennu had guessed, Maatkare chose Deka to sit beside him. Ari didn't care about the man who was their host or what his name was. She studied her area carefully and quietly, not translating or even listening to any of the dinner conversation between the prince and the priest.

Ari stared at Maatkare Raemkai as he chatted, noticing Deka sat next to her prince, oblivious to the surroundings. It was the way she had been in Little Kina Ahna when they had all lived with Marai. That much of her personality had not changed. Maatkare was much more interesting.

So good looking though. He was even fun to drink with last night before it got to be too much... watching him show off for his men. Ariennu mused, a slight smile on her lips. *Maybe not the worst idea in the world, except having to share. And whatever he did to Naibe this afternoon was uncalled for, knocking her out like that.* She paused, tucking in her thoughts when she saw the prince glance her way as if he had heard every one of them.

The signal to Naibe was a yawn. Ari leaned to a servant. "Where is your privy? My friend and I need to…"

The servant glanced at the priest who spoke to the prince. Maatkare, his eyes glimmering a little in recognition of something, motioned for an older guard to follow them. He raised a forefinger, then lowered it in a quiet gesture.

Don't be gone too long, ladies. His thoughts whispered as he brought Deka a little closer.

The shaded stall with an open half wall provided just enough room for a person to squat. After a moment, Ari rose and gestured to Naibe that it was her turn: *I'm going to cover myself and stand over you. If you just concentrate on getting to the king and not being seen, I think it'll work.* She wrapped the prismatic illusion around herself like goddess Nut's mantle, hugging Naibe up into her arms and slipping away past the guard who paced just a few feet away. As soon as she reached the causeway to the river, she let Naibe down and dropped the illusion. The two women gasped and then caught their breath, shrinking back into the shadow. Once there, they tried to get their bearings.

"Do you think he saw which way we went?" Naibe whispered.

"No, but we have to keep moving down the river. I'm sure the guard has already told… Oh Goddess… fast. The bastard knows already." Ari stopped and crouched with Naibe as guards with bobbling torches erupted from the gate to priest's house.

"Bring him out here. Stupid bastard let them run off." Prince Maatkare stormed by. He whirled as two men dragged the guard who had been set over the women out to the wall near the water in the causeway channel.

Naibe and Ariennu crouched lower, wrapping secrecy around themselves.

"Highness… They used sorcery… gone in a flash." The guard pleaded, then accepting, whispered "Have mercy…"

"I do have mercy on you. You have served me well," the prince replied, "and I have mercy on your children." The sharp sound of a blade striking hard into a body was followed by a groan. A shadow drifted over the three figures who supported the fourth, followed by a snapping sound. It meant the man's neck had been broken in a quick gesture of mercy.

Ari clapped a quick hand over Naibe's mouth to keep her from squealing aloud in horror.

"Take our unfortunate old friend to the open edge of the water. He has been given a message for Lord Sebek. What you men will know is that as he was chasing the women, he slipped at the muddy bank and the crocodiles got to him before we could." Maatkare gave orders and the required explanation to the remaining men. "I will write a message to his family of his noble deeds in my service. Be careful of the crocodiles yourselves. They can be keen on those who break the rules." He grew silent as the guard's body was carried away.

Ari faded herself into the color of the wall. She couldn't make out everything the prince was doing but it seemed to be a kind of ritual gesture followed by the spiritual howl of a wolf-dog. It grew in piercing volume overtaking Ari's heart.

Naibe's mouth opened in a silent cry.

Maatkare stopped, as if he noticed something and sniffed the air. For a moment, Ari thought she recognized the flash of shiny fang teeth in an eerie grin but realized it was an image of warning he had conjured up so that he would appear as a beast before her eyes.

I know you are near, ladies. I can smell your scents. Because you decided to run away, you now see a little more of how I am. I will find you before dawn. I hope the chase will leave me feeling less upset by that time. The prince's thought voice was calm and unruffled, just as it had been when he spoke to the unfortunate guard. He moved back up the causeway, scenting and searching for them.

As soon as Ari saw he was far enough away to appear the same size as a shabti doll, she silently grabbed Naibe and darted around the perimeter of the priest's home and into the first entrance they could find that didn't seem to be part of the building complex.

The path became a shrouded tunnel.

Ari saw two sentries at the open gate entryway. *Another temple, maybe?* She thought, hurtling by the men with Naibe in tow. The sentries stirred as if they sensed something, stared at each other, then they closed the gate behind the women who were still moving deeper inside the passageways. Ariennu relaxed, her image becoming visible. She waited with Naibe in the dust and dark, while they caught their breath.

"Killed the guard, the bastard did, just to teach us a lesson. He set the whole thing up, because he knew we were up to something. I don't even think N'ahab would have done that, goddess curse his soul." Ari spat at the ground, then pulled Naibe to the left branch of the path when they came to a division. The new hallway was close and torch lit with paintings on the walls. At intervals there were more paths and arched hollows that became other tunnels. Ari was certain they would find the way out of the other side at any moment. *A right, then another right, then a left. Um.* She paused to stroke the stone in her brow, hoping to clarify any message her Child Stone transmitted. *Where am I supposed to go? Damn. I'm going to get us lost.* She froze. *City of the Dead, Sokor. A Labyrinth, and I led us both in here.* She turned to Naibe.

"Let's just try to be calm and quiet. They will help us. They just have to."

"Um, Ari…" Naibe paused, her hand staying the older woman's hand. "You *do* know where you are going don't you?"

"I just know we have to go deeper in. I can still feel his thoughts, Babe. He's looking around down here; tracking us. He can smell us. If we keep moving in where the burial boxes are, there are enough of them and dust in the twists. I want his nose confused over what he thinks he smells. He can't stay past dawn. Sooner or later he'll have to give up on us and keep moving up the river. He'll have to leave us. Then we can get out and get down the river to Our Father Menkaure. If he's going to keep showing me how he is 'Prince Dangerous' and killing people over nothing, we're not safe. I'll curse my own soul if I ever let some man kill me, whether he was glorious on his couch or not."

"I didn't like it, Ari." Naibe admitted, just above a whisper.

"No? Really? I thought he was one wild hump! That El of his knew how to seek out every single part in my belly and womb like it was made for it. Mmm... Mmm... I wish I didn't have to get away. I'm getting another itch for it, just thinking about it working me." Ari turned every way she could, realizing the underground complex must have been huge. So far she hadn't found any two passageways that looked alike.

"With me, he put up a wall over his soul instead of becoming open to me. Devils came out of his eyes the more I sent up my loving to him. He just sucked it out and still gave nothing back. It was as if he was broken and couldn't love me like a normal man. He could give the pleasure twice over to fill in that missing part and I was screaming for it, but then I couldn't stop thinking of my Marai and how much I missed the real love he had for me... and then I couldn't breathe. I fainted."

"No I saw everything he did when you first came in. Read it off of your stone when you were crawling around the cabin floor all shocked. Bastard choked you hard enough to end you and then painted night in front of your eyes... said he would drink your heart for saying Marai's name to him." Ariennu stopped walking and sat by the wall where five corridors branched out in the dark. *Now which way?* She asked herself.

Naibe shuddered as if she wanted to gag in worry.

Ari tapped the nearly imperceptible rise in the middle of her forehead just at the top of her nose. "Come on little one... some help here. Show me those little balls of light Marai told us about that led him in the dark to your boat of wonders so long ago, if this is still real..."

"It's alright MaMa." Naibe petted Ari's shoulder.

"Still my fault we're having to run like this. We should be at the palace soaking in asses' milk, not having to get away from someone who's no better than a slave master." She saw the small lightened area in one of the corridors. "There. That way. I see those lights, I think. We have to go," Ari got to her feet and pulled Naibe up.

After a series of twists and turns and more walking, the elder woman slowed, realizing the lights might have been an illusion born of her own fatigue.

Push on if you must

Or stay

Or go this way

A voice exploded just under her brow. It was louder than the usual whisper-like singing to which she had become accustomed.

"Finally! Ouch, damn. Naibe, watch your step, there's something back here. I thought it was a wall but there's something out in front." She murmured, then felt the lid of a low stone box with some carved object on top. A stone box. *It's like my dream when I saw Marai lying dead in that black box somewhere.* She felt for the edge for a moment but realized the box in her dream had been plain and slick to the touch. This one was smooth but not as finely polished. "I can feel a draft coming over the top. Maybe it's in front of a hall that leads us out of here the back way." Ari couldn't see much in the dark until she paused and became calm enough for her eyes to switch into a kind of night vision.

In the back was a niche containing a platform for offerings. Something furred, broken and wet with gore lay in the dish. Her hands leapt up away from whatever it was as if they had been lightning struck. Atop the lid was a carved image. She felt the shape: Animal. Legs, haunches, muzzle and upright ears of Wepwawet as Guide of the Dead.

She gasped, realizing the irony of the place she had entered with the younger woman. The prince's words from late last night rang in her ears.

I'm the Lord of the Dead by the Blood of Aset… the Lord of the Dead

She remembered the revelry of the party, and the way a very drunk Maatkare cried out his howling lament about his ill-fated marriage to the king's daughter.

'Women always tryna put a collar on me', he had said. That was the moment she knew she had to get him away from the king's private area and onto his boat.

Well, damn me she thought.

Ari suddenly realized the prince was here on more than business. This was a centering and safe place for the disciples of Wepwawet who presented as a wolf or dog. *He must be from the wolf school with all of his skill with a bow, the howling, the... Oh goddess... shape shifting that's so fast no bones bend or skin stretches... he just is. I led us both to his safe space... He came here to cleanse himself? Our dinner host was his witness while we were cleaning up?*

Ariennu sensed something wasn't right in the tonality of the Children's voices. Sounds like a man imitating... like... She tensed, all of the hair on her arm rising as she heard the great wolf or dog's panting approach to the opening of the chapel. The sound of his clawed feet tip-tapped on the hardened earth floor of the path. The panting merged into an evil titter; breathing in the dark; a faint growl that grew stronger and more threatening.

> *Push on if you must*
> *Or stay*
> *Or go this way*
> *Either way leads to pain*
> *You see, I know what they sound like,*
> *Your little friends*
> *These voices in your crystal eye.*

The black-furred, hand-like paw touched her arm just before it faded into illusion.

"MaMa!" Naibe cried, panting. "He's finding us. Hide!" Naibe ran around the stone box. This time she grabbed Ari and hid in her cloaking arms. The women clung to each other, wide-eyed and silent. Before the shroud of silence covered them Ari saw the silhouette of a black wolf or dog, thin like smoke. In its place Ari thought she saw a gold armlet flashing in the slight available light of a distant torch.

Oh. He's here? She hardened her resolve, crouching and ready to fight.

In the distance the women heard a faint scampering, snapping, growling and yodel-howling. Something was circling and finding the way.

They're coming Ari. Dogs. He has power over dogs. He's sending dogs. Naibe grabbed Ariennu harder, as if it would help her gain more invisibility.

I know Baby, I know... the elder woman listened silently for a long time as the sounds circled, grew louder, and finally paused outside the room where they hid. The sounds became confused, then footsteps followed.

Maatkare stood in the doorway, golden wrist and arm bands glimmering in ambient torchlight. "I know what you tried to do," he began to pace, trying to seem thoughtful. "Maybe I would have done the same thing too if I had been in your situation. But now you've caused a good man to die because you outwitted him with your little trick." The sound of dogs growling grew louder. His thought voice growled too, half human, half dog as if he had become one of them. *Easy brothers...* he started, then spoke aloud. "Perhaps I should let them come at you. They are my trick, Red Sister. See if you like it." Maatkare's dark hand swept the air in front of him.

Ari sensed an almost-whisper.

Suddenly, black ravenous shadows emptied past him around his torso and over his shoulders; into the chamber pouncing, snarling and biting. Ariennu felt herself knocked back hard by the weight of several animals standing around and towering over her. She shrieked angrily, struggling against their weight. "Call them off! Damn you!" she swung, kicked, and shoved, but accomplished nothing.

"You're afraid... tsk, tsk... fearless Lady Ariennu... worried by some puppies."

"Am not... get them off me..."

"About to soil yourself, you naughty ka't" he chortled, toeing the threshold and gesturing. "Just a very small sample of what I can do, if you come to annoy me."

Puppies? Ari froze, her eyes clearing a little. The clawing and biting beasts had become gregarious, yipping puppies. They frolicked happily about her prone body then left, heading past the prince and out the doorway as they vanished. It had been a magnificent illusion. While Ariennu lay sprawled and gasping, the prince advanced and plucked Naibe from her hiding place behind the altar.

"I knew you both might try to run the hour I touched dry land, so I tested you." He pulled Naibe into his arms. She tried to fight but he kissed the stone in her brow, then traced his lips to her open mouth.

"Don't" Naibe whimpered a little, then relaxed in the prince's grip as if the kiss had already cast a spell "There. That's better, see…" Maatkare whispered, then turned his attention to Ariennu who was getting to her feet and smoothing her rumpled shift.

"We don't belong to you," Ari addressed him. "You have Deka. Just let us go back to His Majesty."

"I see." Maatkare countered. "So what you started in my grandfather's plaza… the heated looks out of the side of your head at me while our Crown Prince embraced you… this has become something I should ignore? And at my farewell party, we hunted each other like lions mating. There was nothing to that?" he released Naibe's chin and continued the lecture, airily lounging in the door frame. "Naughty creature. You suddenly realize your so-called 'neter stone' power, as the learned of Kemet would call it, has abandoned you, and now you try to leave me." He stepped back to beckon some of his men who had come to assist him. "I praise your courage, though your attempt was not well planned. These men will take you and our young friend back to the boat. If there's no more of this and you surrender yourself to me as the Lady Nefira Sekht has done, I promise you that you will see Our Father again in time… and perhaps you will even attend him again as his maids. Until that happens… just don't be too proud."

Chapter 3: Khmenu

After Sokor, more boats with troops and equipment joined the southbound fleet until the vessels numbered over forty. The fleet was composed of reed boats for shore excursions and light supplies. The rest of the boats were made of strapped wooden planks and were designed to carry troops, weapons and trade goods.

At the first few stops, the prince asked for food to be brought to the women. As punishment for the escape attempt he had separated them on different boats, each under heavy guard. When the prince wanted to be entertained by one of the women, he sent his two personal guards in a straw boat to collect them for the evening. As long as their behavior was without incident, they were treated in kind. Life was almost agreeable.

Whenever Ariennu was not chosen, she lay down to meditate on some sort of future. The Children of Stone seemed so broken from her life that she came to think of relying on them or any of her so-called "gifts" as folly itself. To be sure, she was glad of her ability to heal herself, her new talent of invisibility and far-seeing flight, but none of it mattered. Somehow, between Marai's death and the sorcery used by Great Hordjedtef and his grandson Maatkare, nothing seemed to work.

What's the use? Ariennu frequently asked herself. *If I try to get my thoughts to speak to Deka or Naibe, I get the same thing each time. From Deka I get this sharp silence. From Naibe I get a deep and almost crazy hurt that makes me want to do stupid things to see that she isn't lost to me.* Then she would sadly admit: *Ever since we tried to leave when we were at Sokor she's gone half mad. No, she was headed that way from the hour we learned that Marai was dead... helpless and with mostly blown wits. I-I just can't desert her like this.*

After two weeks of separation Prince Maatkare had loosened his restrictions. He allowed the women to move into a single cabin on one of the larger boats. By the end of the third week of the journey south, the fleet drew within a day of Khmenu.

Ariennu noticed that Naibe barely contained herself. She knew Wserkaf was on duty at the Greater Temple of Djehuti at this sepat and silently warned the young woman: *I don't know what you're up to, but you'd better not get Highness' attention or he'll figure on some kind of 'fix' for you.*

That 'fix' always turned out to be sex, but only as a release after he had toyed with them as if they were prisoners. Maatkare would drain Naibe's spirit. With Ariennu, he employed prisoner and torture games. Fix their attitude or teach them what disobedience or disrespect caused. He didn't kill anyone else as an example, the way he had executed the elder guard, but he zealously worked to break their spirits and to domesticate them.

All afternoon Naibe and Deka had been sorting dried herbs into gift bundles for the officials the prince might visit. The task was familiar. They prepared them just the way they had made them a lifetime ago, when they had been with Marai. The difference was that he would come aboard from time to time, look at the bundles, curse the women's carelessness and shred them, tossing the remnants about the sunny deck and slapping any of them who objected. Deka would nod and politely begin to pick up the uneven shards. Ariennu would snarl that there was nothing at all wrong... and how dare he, and Naibe would simply dissolve into childish tears which usually resulted in him choosing her for the evening.

"You heard where we are?" Naibe gestured to Ari that they should speak silently and quickly because she saw the men bringing the Ta-Seti woman in another boat. "It's Khmenu. Wseriri..."

Ari wasn't paying attention to her. "Don't start that now. If Menkaure couldn't send anyone, what makes you even dream that Wserkaf would or could get us. Have your spirits changed thoughts?"

"He'd get me..." Naibe insisted.

Ari shook her head.

Be at peace as one life ends
Another begins.
Profound truths await the patient ones
Lost in time and place.

The Children's quiet voices whispered as a kind of greeting to both women once they stood together in the cabin.

"You said that before," Ari's breath rushed out to the Child Stone in a sigh. "Do you have anything new?"

"They say the same thing to me, Ari." Naibe's expression calmed. "Things have changed though. I'm still going to send word to Wseriri. I know his thoughts will be open to the sky and the pulse of earth at this time, and he won't be protected from us while he's on duty. Highness has let us come ashore the past three evenings for supper invitations. I'll just…"

Wait. Quiet your thoughts. Deka is coming. Ari jabbed Naibe in the arm and motioned for her to go back out to greet the other woman. The moment they emerged from the cabin, Ariennu caught a glimpse of Maatkare's jewelry glinting on his folded arms in the late afternoon sun. *Damn. What's this now? Come to see Deka aboard instead of sending her with guards? Something's up.*

Ari and Naibe bent to assist their former companion as the prince boosted her up into their grasp. He stood for a moment looking half astonished and half annoyed at the three women standing in a respectful row on the narrow deck of their boat. A crafty smile slowly etched his lips. Ariennu saw his gaze fix on her for a moment.

Hmph. She scoffed silently. *What does he want?* Then she asked demurely, pretending to avert her eyes. "Shall we ready ourselves for the evening, Your Highness?"

"No." his crisp answer seemed almost too well thought out. "This is the place of Djehut, where Count Hordjedtef has rule and my tender-hearted cousin Wserkaf seeks wisdom through his duty while his senior attends Our Majesty down the river." His eyes dropped for a moment.

Ariennu sensed Naibe's breathing begin to come in short panicked gasps as she realized her thoughts had been read, interpreted, and instantly dashed. Ari hoped the young woman wouldn't scream, but knew she couldn't move to comfort her. He would pretend to see it as an alliance and a reason. She wasn't afraid of the prince, but she didn't want to give him an excuse to provoke Naibe's hysteria even further.

He grabbed the lead and tie down ropes between the vessels and swung up to the flat wooden deck as blithely as an acrobat. In the next moment he seized Naibe's hand.

"No. Don't touch me!" she snarled, pulling away with such a force that she scratched his hand.

"Ooo… little Sekht," he grabbed her forward, licked the blood from his hand, then bent to her so his lips whispered to her stone. "Eeeen-djoad, eeeen Tah-ackhgor, eeen nauuuu…"

The lightning whistled through Ari's stone. She and Deka winced, gasped, and crouched, holding their ears at the high pitched squeal in their heads. Naibe froze in place, tears streaming down her cheeks. Maatkare moved in toward the youngest woman, licked her tears mingled with the blood from his scratch, then kissed her almost gently, whispering:

"You must think I'm such a fool that I wouldn't even know how to gird myself. I know you would leap at the first chance to run for shelter in a temple again, perhaps to find your doting Prince Wserkaf… perhaps to bear to him the tale of your capture." His voice slithered and his eyes turned a glimmering wolfish yellow.

"I've decided Khmenu isn't a needed stop and have sent my words with a man." He looked over his left shoulder to see if he could catch a glimpse of men rowing to the shore with the sealed messages from King Menkaure and from his grandfather Hordjedtef.

"The priests'll have something sent back… good beer and roast meats for all before we push on. This is a sanctuary of peace and we are warriors. We have no purpose here except to quell any revolt in the surrounding area that has come up. And just in case you didn't notice it, I never *planned* a stop. I'm well aware who is here for at least another week or two.

He turned to Naibe again, pressing her and stroking her mound gently through her kala until a damp spot formed. "You really should stop this nonsense. Your Shinar sorcery doesn't work on me, and I know your stone's control word with or without the use of the hand strap. Except for your pretty eyes and the tight comfort of your sweet young clench, you are useless to me," he released her and she stumbled.

Ariennu stared at Deka, who had turned her head away.

Don't you look away from me! This is your doing, Ari's thoughts snarled.

Maatkare touched Ariennu's arm. "You tonight, however," he stepped back.

"Wha?" Ari's jaw dropped.

"I'm going to teach you manners for putting thoughts in her heart."

"But I…" Ariennu was about to say she had done nothing of the sort, but the word: "Really?" escaped her lips. "The ladder, again? Oh, I will fight you. I'm in no mood for your stupid prisoner games," she snarled.

He shrugged, turned to hop down to the straw transport scow, then beckoned to the men on the women's boat and watched them snap to attention.

"I have five fingers. I'll tuck them down one at a time, and then if you're not on this boat I'll give you a pain. While you fight, it my guards will come to get you and strap you down properly; tightly this time, not playful like before. I'll reward them with you when I've finished with you."

Ariennu shuddered. "Bring them on then. I don't care." *He won't shame me,* she thought to herself. *When I was young, I could go some rounds with quite a number of them before I got tired.* "Only two?" she spat, drawing herself taller.

Maatkare's smile grew sly as it crept out of one side of him mouth. "Brag about it, then, ka't. We'll see."

Go MaMa. Just go. Naibe's thoughts whispered gently. *We'll be alright.*

Prince Maatkare's fingers were already starting to count. Ari turned, glaring at the prince. "Your servant… comes." she airlessly mocked and moved to the edge of the deck to descend over the side. Somewhere in the distance she was aware of a catcall, and one of the men whistling.

Deka said once that we should fly away in bad times. I never wanted to do that. Me. Wise MaMa Ari. I've always been the one who's in for the fun, excitement, men, strong drink, and the good times. This with you, Maatkare, is just different. It's not about pleasure any more, it's about breaking a woman down… owning and devouring. You're just… mean and low; full of making

me be that way too, Ariennu groaned a little, hoping he had listened to every word of her thoughts.

"Mean? You of all of my pets know why I must be," he walked slowly around her, examining his men's work in tying her. "I'd like you to talk with your voice, but I had to gag you until sweet words came forth... those that beg for my kindness." Prince Maatkare hovered at Ari's left shoulder for a moment. He waved a warm and meaty joint of beef in front of her. It was so juicy that the grease ran down his forearm when he took a bite and began to gnaw it. The smell intoxicated her to the point of drooling past the gag. She had eaten a light meal in the morning and had been about to forage for some dates to whet her appetite before the prince had come to the boat. When he took her, he had her bound quickly without letting her eat or drink anything.

Prisoner game. And me so excited at first I didn't think of food. Been too long now. Thirsty. She sucked on the cloth rag a little. *Before, when it was a game...* her thoughts wandered badly. The boat had a lower cabin set below the deck. In it was a temporary cage for prisoners. His two personal guards sat at the top step to the deck, guarding. *You bring your men prisoners in this hold, too?* She tittered wickedly. *Bung them?*

The prince sighed, entertained at her words, but insulted.

She felt his knee butt the back of her leg, then noticed it had grown numb.

Ari knew Maatkare's eyes followed the line of her arms. He had ordered them bound high and fastened to a horizontal bar slightly higher than her head. Another bar was woven in front of her arms but behind her neck. A third dug into her chest just below her naked breasts so that every time she tried to take a deep breath she thought her ribs would crack. Her forced, shallow breathing alone made her feel hot and dizzy. When that sensation combined with her hunger and thirst, she felt nauseous and faint. The next bar crossed her belly and was tied to another bar crossing her back. Another pair of bars secured her thighs, front and back. The last two bars braced her legs apart at the knees and wider apart at the ankles. Rope bound her to all of the intervals where flesh, wood, and uprights met. She wasn't sure, and at that point didn't care, how everything was fixed so it was actually part of the cage.

The first time he had placed her in what he called the ladder, it had been an exciting and intense sexual session. The prince had teased, tormented, and joked with her, always stopping short of allowing her release. He would slap her rump, whisper filth, and send even nastier thought and images through her Child Stone until her skin echoed it before allowing her relief from an evening of built up frustration. No thought or words could express the experience. *Disgusting. Good. Incredible. Goddess, my insides are screaming…* she shook her head wondering how this could get more intense. *How is he…? I'm hurting damn you…*

Tonight, the binding was too tight on purpose. She was hot, tired, thirsty, and on the verge of losing consciousness. This wasn't erotic at all; it was painful.

I'm thirsty. Get bored with your game and get inside me to take it, Highness. You know you want it. Her thoughts projected.

"No. Not just yet. Oh you heat me well enough, Red Sister… but not quite enough. I need you to say you truly serve me. You know that," his husky whisper almost soothed her. She didn't see him gesture to the guards, but assumed he had given them some kind of signal. They had been seated just out of sight, but when she bent her head back as far as she could, she saw they flanked him. He unfastened the rear door of the cage and allowed them to enter.

"You have served me well… set good examples for the others in the ranks," she heard him tell each man. "The ka't will be told to pleasure you soon enough. For now, you may touch its skin; pet it, but use good self-discipline. We wouldn't want to tire it too much, would we?"

Damn you. No… Ariennu choked back the mixture of pleasure and rage as each man's fingertips stroked the skin over her ribs and cupped her sweaty breasts for a moment, then examined her belly and the opening of her mound. The prince must have signaled once more. The men suddenly stopped touching her, left through the entry door, and slithered around the cage to the other side so she saw their faces.

"I hear my hot food being brought from the galley boat. Set my table," Maatkare quipped.

A drink. I need a drink, Ari's thoughts cried as she tried to slow her breathing. The men were busying themselves with something over her head. She felt the top half of the ladder lower forward, stretching her body until her back was flat and at an angle to her already numb legs. That part of the cage was fixed with the rope once more. Agony shot through her chest and midsection as the poles bit hard against her body.

"I hear you, loud and clear. I'm going to remove your gag so you can have just a taste of beer… maybe more. But one shout from you, one instant of disrespect and there will be nothing more given you. Nod if you understand." Maatkare put his face close to Ari's ear. Despite the misery of her immobilized body, his husky whisper seduced her into agreement. Ari gasped in relief as the rag in her mouth fell away. She felt the prince grab her hair to lift her head so she was able to sip a small amount of stale beer and revel at the delicious grease he let drip into her mouth from the shank of beef.

"Your arms should be less tired in this position now, but I need to eat the soup my men brought before I take my dessert," he added.

Ari sensed him motioning to the guards again. She felt a heavy and hot weight placed on the middle of her back.

"There isn't room down here to sup, so you can be the table for my dinner," he whispered with a smirk in his voice.

"Ouch. Burns. Stop." Ariennu sucked in air, trying to struggle and failing.

"Don't move too much. The soup's very hot. Wouldn't want you to buck and spill it on yourself." The prince raised a brow and watched her for long agonizing moments, occasionally taking a long sip of the hot liquid, then beckoning one of the guards to try it.

Ariennu felt the stone carved bowl growing heavier until the weight of it caused her to lose the rest of the feeling in her back and legs. Her breath came in gasps. The world was slipping away.

Flight. Fly away from this, Ari's thoughts cried. *Children, damn all of you… useless… why? Why? True what Deka said? Is he one of us? If he has a stone or even if he doesn't, by El's power, please get him t' deliver me.*

Suddenly, as if he took notice of her thought, the prince took the bowl and set it aside.

"Fly? You? Woman, you never flew away from a damned thing and you know it. You fly *into* danger every chance you get. You crave it. When I give you some, you worry because you are losing control? Proud Ariennu. Pity."

Ari felt his hand gently stroked her cheek, noticing the roughness of the leather nauu hand piece. She never looked directly at it. Something about it swept her glance away each time she tried. She sensed that it formed an X across his palm, and if it was at all like the one his grandfather used, the strap looped around his middle finger. The tingle of impossible arousal yet misery from the strap filled every part of her. She felt a sob of ecstasy welling up in her chest. The bar under her breasts bit tighter as she panted for air. For just an instant, she wanted to die. She felt his trembling hand creep up to her fingers and knew he was almost too stimulated by her pain to speak.

"So cold your fingers are getting. Such a pity. But you fight me. You make me do this to you. You tempt my lower nature, demand to be broken by me. But, see how my hand has power over you now?" His hand with the leather appliance smoothed her cheek again. He moved behind her, caressing and gently parting her kuna gate for a moment. "See? So soft, burning for me and wet? I can make you beg for me to stop the pain and then beg for me to start it again so you will know, when you feel it, that you are still alive. I brought this food to share with you, but now, after I've enjoyed you, I'll be forced to eat alone while you watch and learn. All you have to do is speak the words that show me you submit, then I will relieve you with hours of joy. What I cannot give you tonight, I will give you another day. It will be all pleasure and only enough pain to serve as a reminder of how you can be punished if you do or speak ill to me."

"I need food and t' drink something," Ariennu hissed through her teeth. "You tease my mouth with your 'el' and I will bite it for you," she cracked her eyes, moaning in pain as the prince ordered the guards to tighten the ropes at her knees and ankles. Then the guards moved up the steps to go outside. She assumed they were allowed to watch Maatkare toy with a captive, but because it was a woman they were not allowed to see him taking her sexually.

"Now you're annoying me," he snarled, then moved behind her and seized her hips.

Ari shuddered convulsively as her body rocked forward against the bars when he entered her. She gasped, almost choking as his lips traced the side of her neck, followed by the bites. The pain of the lashings that bound her body as it strained into them with each thrust mingled with and fought her pleasure.

"No submission, means I will own your joy another way." He growled and sank his sharper teeth into her upper back; his fingertips becoming digging and gripping claws. She knew he was changing. As her thoughts drifted away from the building, but pleasant misery, she wondered: *Have your men seen you be a wolf? I bet that's why you can't let them be here…*

He growled softly, continuing.

Her sight dimmed with an agony of pleasure. She felt the blood, or at least an illusion of it, dripping over her shoulder and reveled in his tongue lapping it gently like a bee in nectar before he moved again. For a moment she felt a different and almost magnificent kind of internal power steal over her. *He won't beat me. He thinks he will do it like he broke Deka. He thinks he can suck out the energy like he did with Naibe. Not me… I keep the secrets. Not tonight. Maybe Naibe…* she thought of the younger woman and instantly tucked in the secret that somehow the young woman might try to get to shore if she hurried… *The Children. The Children are quiet. This is why, this is why. Goddess, I ache.* She sobbed inwardly, suddenly understanding why they had been silent and why she had to let the evening go forward the way the prince wanted. *I'll make you work me. I'll make you…*

Long moments passed. Ari drifted between cresting waves of pleasure that engulfed her to the tips of her fingers and toes, but her inability to move drove her senses further into a sublime but numb oblivion. She both felt and saw the shimmer of rainbow lights behind her gently closed eyes. The patterns of color swept over her body. *Lights. I see their lights shining in my thoughts. No. Little ones, don't let him rob me this way. Some other… not like this.* She felt the Children's whispers come up within her. *Why little one? Why do I have no power when I am with him? I can't turn on everything I am. I can't…*

When self is lost,
The wisdom remains

Goddess no more… Please be done… please… Every part of her body ached in a combination of numbness, exhaustion, and pleasure. She was floating. Everything had slipped away except for the brief rush of heat through her belly.

The prince sighed and rested his head on her back.

"Good..." she heard him whisper, then add: "There, you see. You *know* you liked it. You complain so much, but in the end you always love this. You'll beg for more nights like this, showing me the side no one knows... the part that craves to be so lost in joy you don't know up from down. You see, I can give that to you. I know you, now. You are sweet filth for me." What had been his clawed paw was a hand again when it reached forward, felt her face wet with sweat and angry tears, then wiped them with his fingertips. He was almost tender.

Confusion made vomit rise in her throat.

"Untie..." she spat out the taste, stunned by her own weakness. She felt him hesitate as her stomach coiled again. "Untie me, please."

He chuckled. "Blasted you hard enough to make you puke." He chortled. "You beg me so nicely, now... maybe I should leave you strapped like this for the guards when they take their turn."

"Nnnn..." Ari cried. "Leave me tied, then. I get loose, I'll kill you!" She tried to struggle, but found no energy.

Eeeeen nauuu, Red Sister. Gently, his thoughts wafted through her.

A little saliva and bile drooled from Ari's lips. *Something's not right,* she thought, as black senselessness began to envelop her again.

At first the sounds outside were faint, but grew loud enough to give both her and Maatkare pause.

Something's... Ari felt a sense of panic that had nothing to do with the terror his Highness thought he might have inspired. She knew he sensed it too. Men were shuffling beside the cabin on the right side of the boat, beckoning to the waiting guards. The ever-present slow pulse of rowing halted.

"See. There... out in the water... See them rowing like Sebek himself is chasing them. Gods she's strong. Look at her go."

"We'd better get..." a voice grew closer to the step-down into the cabin.

"Don't you dare get his Highness," said one voice. "He's in pleasure with..."

"No, this is one of the other women. He'd want to know. We *have* to."

The shuffles were followed by slight hesitation as if they were checking for sounds. Ari felt Maatkare tense and get up from her quickly, cursing under his breath. He grabbed at fabric. When she heard the rustle of the cloth, she knew he had thrown on an unbelted robe.

Highness, she sent a weary thought, *unfasten me.* She felt other words rattling thought her aching but sated body.

Eeeeen Djoad, eeeen nauuu.

"No! No more spells. Cut me loose. I can't breathe," her voice croaked. The pain from his utterance felt like hot pokers in her ears, but as it subsided she realized Prince Maatkare wasn't there. He had stomped up the short stair to the above deck.

Shouts continued.

"Look! Their boat just broke up like something hit it from underneath. Did you see that?"

"Your Highness. Look there. I think they just went under."

"Which one?" the prince demanded as Ari tried to work one of her wrists free of the crisscrossed rope that bound it to the rattan frame. She already knew which one. *Naibe.* Gritting her teeth, she twisted her hand and tucked in her fingers until was able to loosen it. *He's not thinking about thwarting me. My strength'll come back in a minute.* She tried to take a deep breath, but the pain of the bar under her breasts stifled it.

"The young one with the big eyes and bright color: the Shinar." She heard one of the guards answer.

Ariennu doubled her effort, pulling and twisting her hand.

Girl! Her thoughts went out. *I know you can swim, now swim, Baby…*

Ari felt Deka's panicked thoughts enter her own. It had been almost too long since she sensed anything other than a barrier from the Ta-Seti woman. That Ari felt her thoughts now compounded her lurking fear.

Blood. Someone bleeds, Ari sensed. *Deka knows the smell of blood. She's warning her. If Naibe gets close in, she'll be tired. She'll be quick work for any beast near the shore.* The elder woman panicked. *No. Naibe Come back!*

No. Brown Eyes. No. Death is not the way. Come back to us, Deka's thoughts echoed her own, but related that Naibe had slipped away from her and seduced a man into rowing her to the shore. Then, the raft failed and she was alone. If Maatkare caught her, he would lose face in front of his men if he didn't kill her. At Sokor, he'd played the guard's death off as an accident when it was a lesson. This time would be different, unless…

Silence.

Ariennu sensed quiet. In the far distance, she heard a call or two of men. It sounded as if they cried across the water that they didn't see her. He was probably waiting on the deck, she thought. For a moment, she thought she was about to faint and fought it. Then, Ari realized what she felt was some kind of spell. The air shimmered in front of her eyes and she sensed a further draining of her strength, followed by the jackal titter in her ears.

Damn You. Stop holding me back. I'm trying to sense her, you fiend!

Another chortle in her heart. Ariennu knew what it meant.

Good. Found her. She wriggled her right hand out of the looping and let her numb arm drop below her side for a moment. Ari's breath came in winded gasps but she rallied when she heard Maatkare angrily shriek:

"Useless wretch. I know you live for now! I should let you drown or *send* you crocodiles. Do you hear me?" then, she sensed an even darker thought. *How dare you go against me, like that? I'll suck you dry for this.*

A long silence followed. The wrapped ropes on her wrists loosened.

Suck her dry? Demon! Ari freed her other hand, then tucked her head down so that the bar across her back stopped binding. She was too short of breath and nauseated from hunger and thirst, but knew no one would get her out of the rig the prince and his guards had used if she didn't do it herself.

Ari felt Deka's thoughts cry out: *No!* As she ripped at the tightly wrapped bars and pushed them apart until the only ones left were at her ankles. When she finished freeing herself, she stumbled and fell. She heaved a little, but managed to careen up the steps and out of the cabin, completely naked. She grabbed men and clawed at their legs for support. Clambering to the rail, she lurched forward, seized Maatkare and clung to his arm. She stared into his cruel glance, suddenly struck dumb, and then felt him slap her to the deck again as if she had been an offending spider. He turned to stare at the water. Though her vision had blurred, she knew the low moon should have made a very faint shimmer on the water. She heard no distant splashing or calling out. Suddenly:

Save her. Please. I beg you… Ari sensed Deka's thought voice call from the distant boat.

Ariennu looked up from her landing place on the deck. "You go get her," she snarled. "You want me to submit to you? I'll do it. I'll do anything you want. I promise," she looked up the length of Maatkare's leg and seized a handful of his dressing robe in her hands. "If she dies…"

His stare withered down at her. The silence and cold glare told the elder woman she would not even *think* of escape again. "Get out of my sight, you splay-legged bitch, or I swear I will give the order to call them back." The prince hissed. He yanked his robe from her hands, shoved at her with his foot, and gestured.

She felt the two guards seize her upper arms, then drag her back into the cabin. They threw her down the steps, then sat at the door, watching her; their long, hooked knives out across their laps. One of them peered down as she tried to right herself, a wry and knowing grin on his face.

Oh goddess no, not now. She understood they were about to collect what the prince had promised them. She was exhausted, sore, drained of energy and starving. Lurking over everything, Ari felt engulfed with worry about Naibe. But she had just said it. *I'll do anything.* The men explained it to her without words.

Rape. I've been raped before… plenty of times, 'n forced myself on some for the fun of it. I told Marai that once, that I was hard; too hard for him to worry about trying to save or love me. Ariennu felt a pain in her chest that didn't come from the bruise the bar made on it. *Oh damn. Thoughts of him at a time like this. I can't have him in my thoughts. Maatkare has to get Naibe. I have to cave in to him. No…* She sensed Naibe's energy fading somewhere out in the deep, black river. *Her life is ending. She's let him make her weak. She's letting death take her this time.* Her thoughts called out to the younger woman. *Baby. Please live. Please come back to us. Please.*

One of the guards set his blade aside with a chuckle praising his good luck.

"Please, let me at least eat something. I'm tired. I'm starving. I'll do ya both then." Ariennu's voice rasped. She looked up, eyes bouncing and hands shaking a little. "The soup…" *Maybe if they let me eat they'll have to help Highness with something before they can… Just need time… Naibe…* she tried again, but it seemed so hopeless. *Food…*

The bowl of soup the prince had set aside had grown cool enough to develop a slight film of fat on the surface. She lunged quickly and picked up the joint of beef. Slowly, she began to gnaw it, swallowed, and felt it rise in a heave.

The guard made a face and took a step back.

"Nuh, no… I'm fine. Swallowed too fast," Ari stammered and tried again, glancing over the stone rim of the bowl from time to time. She sipped the beer one of them handed her and waited. *No noise. Oh Babe, Naibe, little one. Don't go… Let them find you.* She had hoped to hear commotion outside but all was still. She sighed, broken, set the soup aside and reached for the guard's hand.

"Um ready. Little tired, though. Try to be nice." She choked, wanting to be sick again. *Maybe*, she thought, *you won't get more than a start on me.* She let the man pull her up. *Naibe please live… Maybe he'll forget about this if Highness needs him.* She raised her leg up so the man could grab it and ease her backward against the wall for a moment, before lifting her onto his loins. She put her tired arms around his neck then nuzzled the guard's ear a little as he began.

"Nice. You have a nice… way…" she whispered. Through the exhaustion she felt the numbness returning. *It doesn't matter. I'm going invisible. I'll fade away… no one will know me ever again… There's nothing, nothing of me left but dust.*

OPENER OF THE SKY

Chapter 4: Qustul

The women's tent had been set up. Ariennu lay looking up at the place where the poles converged and took in the airy beauty of the canvas extending from the center. *Big. Better than Nahab's nasty old tents. Even better than the one Marai...* she paused, curious that the mention of his name grabbed her as if it had been part of an incantation to make him return from the Land of the Dead. *The one the Children of Stone made from thought and air when he was on their vessel.* She heard the men tidy the encampment and arrange weapons and equipment outside after the early foray. They were mumbling about something until a third man told them to hush.

Maybe these dreams about what I've become will leave me alone, now that we're outside Qustul and staying on land, she hoped.

> *Prepare, Ariennu of Tyre*
> *You will see something this night*
> *Learn something*
> *A secret to keep.*

The tiny chorus of spirit voices whispered through the stone and in to her thoughts.

Oh, something more than Highness' needs? Then why are you always replaying the moment when I finally knew I was trapped by this monster and his damned spells? Ruins my sleep. You enjoy it or something?

This afternoon, Deka rested with her.

Like the old days, eh Bone Woman? We use and get used. Another day, another pig to keep us in his pen. Good while it lasted, I guess. None of the changes made in us are any good now except that we don't age or grow ugly. If this is going to last forever... Ariennu shut her eyes and swallowed hard at the thought of such a fruitless immortality that was already, in her opinion, a curse.

As if Deka sensed Ari's continued hopelessness, the Ta-Seti woman began to hum her calming tune.

There you go with the Hagore neter whatever... Keep on singing it, sister, but you know you're not any more important to him than me or Little One. Ariennu silently reminded the woman, but more than that she tried to convince herself of that reality.

On the surface, Maatkare Raemkai disrespected all of them equally, but the elder woman knew something else was at work between him and Deka. His cruelty to her was never as sincere as it was with them. She had been the first he snared but it was more than that. He valued her differently.

Deka didn't respond.

Ari knew the biggest change had come the night Naibe tried to get away. After that, she gave up. *Go ahead,* she said to herself. *Pretend your wits are holding back your words. I'm starting not to care.*

She remembered being held in the cell while Maatkare's guards took turns with her as their promised reward. She had flown away in her heart, only thankful that they let her eat and drink a little something first. Somewhere out on the river, men were looking for Naibe, whistling, calling, and waving torches over the water. Ari was numb; having become a self-preserving animal. She couldn't think about the youngest of the women or of how her own antics with the prince and his men had been enough of a distraction that Naibe decided to escape to Khmenu, even if it failed. She went back to that moment over and over, reliving the way she tried to bury herself in the momentary glimmers of unwilling pleasure with the guards and tried to block out Deka's wounded spirit as it cried out.

Please, beloved one, for me... Find my sister.

"Too late. You *know* she has drowned by this time, the fool. Let her go to Lord Sebek then, the faithless wretch. Let him drag her to the bottom." Maatkare's voice barked back, even though he knew Deka was too far away to hear his spoken words. "This has taken too much time. Push on, by my order," his voice rose in command. The men moved to their positions and waited for the drum signal to start.

When Ariennu heard those words and felt the boat lurch forward, her emotions broke into words.

"No! You bastard. It's *your* damned fault. *You* go get her. I told you I would do what you want. I *told* you..." she screamed, struggling in the arms of the first guard who had just finished and still grappled with her, stunned that his efforts with her had meant so little.

"Then *you* join her... sick of you both." Ari heard the prince stomping across the deck over her head. For a moment, she thought he would come down the steps to pitch her overboard himself.

Calm. The children whispered. *There is no death.*

"Noooo..." Ari moaned as the first guard gripped her harder for a moment. "No more voices in my head. No," she felt the man shrug, then mutter something unsavory about her lack of interest and quit her. The other guard moved in, but paused. Ariennu felt her body trembling, but not in pleasure. *The shakes... like I've been on a bad drunk... like it was when I was getting sick. Had to be drunk to keep my guts in place. Goddess... no voices...*

"There," someone called, accompanied by other shouts. "Something floating out there..."

"Aahhh! Babe..." Ari screamed, struggling out of the second guard's grip.

Feet scampered. The boat leaned a little as rowers paused and began to obey the turn of the helm oar.

Ari collapsed into the guard's arms at first, but pushed away.

"Let me loose. I have to..."

The second man lost all interest. He found Ari's dance shawl and helped her stand while she shakily wrapped it around her hips.

By the time she stumbled back up the steps and to the rail, the prince was kneeling on a bound raft and paddling out on the dark river at heart bursting speed.

In the background amid the clamor, Ari heard Deka's thoughts plead from the rail of the boat behind them directing and begging.

Don't kill her. She's just a child... always so heart-young. You need...

Silence. Ari felt Maatkare's snarling thoughts answer the Ta-Seti woman. *Hold back from my thoughts. You don't own a thing. I let you think it... Hold back!* Out on the water, a man's howl that imitated a wolf became much less human.

Afternoon and he wants a woman, Ari's thoughts returned to the present time. She had spent much of her time in the past week curled up in a ball on her mat, drawing a blankness into herself. *I've become like Deka when she was with Nahab and the rest of us raiders. Beat us, use us, mock us, but we prevail. We grow numb. Not enough sleep, even with this rest. I don't care. At least when I do sleep I don't have nightmares about storms coming like poor Naibe does.* Ari half-snickered to herself. *Just daymares of my rage while I'm lying here contemplating your displeasure, Highness.* She reflected a little longer, sitting and pretending to nod to the dark woman's song.

Maybe this is what guilt it like. Guilt. It's this damned stone in my head that's made all these feelings grow; this guilt. I never had regrets over anything I did before it was there.

She folded the thin netting that served as a coverlet and straightened her skirt. *A trade, I guess. I loved Marai more than myself, but he died. So that's it. I got soft enough to fall in love, lost him, and remained soft enough to let regret grow in my heart. I need to stop all of that and get myself back again. I don't like being this way.*

"I understand, Wise MaMa." Deka spoke aloud. "Sometimes I'm sorry I had to accept you both. It would be easier for me if Raem were mine alone."

"Had to?" Ari rose from her mat, noticing Deka had used the prince's familiar name, a thing forbidden her and Naibe. "Then why in seventy devils didn't you speak to him so he would let us go to the king again?" Ari folded her arms.

In the nearly two months on the way to Qustul, it had never occurred to the elder woman to ask her *why*. She'd been too angry at first. Deka had been remote, but that was nothing new. She had always been distant, even when Marai had been alive. It had been just this last week of the journey, after the night they almost lost Naibe, that Ari even felt like asking her anything.

Ariennu's memory flashed again, replaying the image of Maatkare fishing the youngest woman out of the river and placing her face down over his knees as he paddled back to the prison boat. She had looked so pale when the men hauled her up to the deck.

"Dead? Goddess…" Ari bent forward, despite the guards reaching to stop her. She was cold. "Dead? You let her die?" she choked.

"You stay off her, or she will be," the prince snapped and knelt by Naibe. The guards struggled to hold Ariennu back.

"She just wanted to get away. She's not like me. She can't take this," Ari almost sobbed, struggling from the arms of the guards.

Ari was still haunted by the memory of the coldness in the prince's hard, yellow wolf-eyes gleaming from his human face. Only a hint of natural olive green color burned in them. His eyes said that if the young woman died, he would take it as a personal affront. He couldn't allow her to choose her own destiny in that way.

Startled, Ariennu stopped wrestling free of the two guards. Maatkare boosted Naibe's still form up so that her belly lay over his knees. He gestured to the guard who had just released Ari to lift the young woman's arms over her head. Oddly, Ari thought, the prince showed no anger. He seemed almost tender as he pressed on Naibe's upper back, then whispered some kind of spell that still contained the first part of the Child Stone control *Eeeen Tjoad, young honey, Eeeen Tjoad.*

She stood, shaking from the pain of the words, weeping from exhaustion, nauseated, and filled with humiliated rage. "I see what you're doing. Marai brought Naibe back once like this." She mumbled bitterly, then thought to herself. *She fought the darkness when Wserkaf visited us in the old neighborhood. It that a skill or something? Do you even* know *what you're doing? You don't have a Child Stone. How could you?*

Somehow, though, the two men were very different. Prince Maatkare possessed his own kind of instinct for healing and reviving. While she watched that night, she saw him caress Naibe's brow then touch his leather hand piece to her stone, with another utterance. The young woman flinched, then began to cough and gasp. When she opened her eyes and discovered where she was, she wept bitterly.

With a few more words, Maatkare ordered men to guide Ari to the small straw boat he used when he sent for any of them. As the men readied it, Ari sensed something from the prince that wasn't at all hard or cruel.

"How did you…" she turned to face him as he stayed with the youngest of the women.

"Stay away," he warned, then spoke firmly to Naibe, who sat choking and shivering in front of him. "Naibe. Speak." He ordered.

"I... I... Why save me? I need to be dead, if I cannot be free."

He quietly nodded, reflecting on her words.

"It's true. You need to die, but it's not your night to take that journey. It will be another night. Stand then," he stood and slowly helped Naibe rise. He wrapped his powerful arms around her, cradled her on his chest and spoke to her gently. "You hurt. I've seen it in your heart so many times. You want *so much* to be in the land that loves silence. But you see, young Inanna, your Dumuzi has sent you back to go forth to *me* now. Do not think of him again or whisper his name. Let him rest in the peace that he craves," he guided her to Ariennu.

"Feed her when she is in the cabin with you. Give her what is left of the broths I'm sending to restore her wind. Sit with her. Hold her. I will not ask for her again until we arrive in Qustul," the prince dryly addressed the elder of the two women. "And since you are on fire with a question for me, I will answer it. I *do* know how one walks between life and death; when the portal between worlds opens and when it does not. It was closed to her tonight. I knew I could bring her back. Simple as that."

Pompous ass. You might have failed, her thoughts rioted for a moment then calmed.

At first, Ari hadn't realized the prince had accepted Naibe's near drowning as an attempt at suicide, because he had couched it in the Shinar legend of Inanna going to the Underworld to retrieve her dead lover Dumuzi, the shepherd. Later, as she fed and comforted the girl and even accepted Deka's attempts at consoling her, she pondered the newly revealed depth in Maatkare's character and the way he had been strangely and seductively tender.

She came back to the present moment in the women's tent. Today, in the encampment near Qustul, he took Naibe as he promised he would.

"So, why didn't you?" she continued her question to Deka. "You *knew* we were doing well at the palace."

"You were doing *too* well. I knew Great One realized you and Little One were threats to him because King Menkaure loved you both and had begun to listen to you over him. I knew also that Raem needed to be given another chance to rule after the death of his first wife and unsuitability of his second wife. If he was not to be king in the north then I would honor him in the south which is the land of the gods. He is a warrior. I remember how to be the wife of one, to encourage his strength and virile power. I remember Ta-Te."

Ariennu felt disgusted.

"*This* again. Whoever this Ta-Te was, he never loved you. He left you for dead and still you cling to some magic fable you've made up about him ascending on a column of fiery light and saying he would return for you."

"I am here in Ta-Seti, am I not?" the dark woman re-fastened her hair in a thick braid.

Ariennu's eyes bugged slightly. She started to say something about Deka being twice as cold as Maatkare Raemkai. *Sorceress*, she muttered inwardly. *If all of this is a trick to get you to your beloved lost land, then you are well a match for him. You can stay here forever and turn our darling keeper into your new god-king, if you wish. Stones shared or not, I'm still going to get Little One and myself free of this, even if we have to wait until we are back in Ineb Hedj.* She turned her attention to her afternoon chores.

Ari knew Prince Maatkare had visited with the governor of Qustul Amani in the early morning. She had heard his men say he was going to discuss trade and then, out of courtesy, he planned to hear the elder's predictions for the coming arid season. When he returned to his encampment just after noon, he hadn't even attempted to keep his irritation secret.

Pouted and threw things like a child, he did! she laughed to herself. It had been hard for her to show no reaction to the man's tantrum. He snarled and stuck his smoldering face through the tent flap to demand Naibe's attention. The girl whimpered but stifled her regret and went to his tent.

Eh well. To work, old girl. He'll want his 'herbal' after he's achieved his 'calmness of spirit' with Baby One. I'm not hearing them, though, and she's been with him a while. Ari sat, but ignored Deka's hummed tune. Something didn't seem right. She yawned and fetched herbs from a basket, then dumped them in a stone bowl. After she powdered them together with an aromatic healing oil which she would rub into his dark and powerful shoulders.

She had just finished making the preparation and set aside the bowl when she heard Naibe-Ellit, squawk and call out in misery, followed by the prince's cursing. From the mumbling and fussing that followed it sounded as if Naibe had suddenly become nauseous and light-headed.

The prince marched her to the opening of the women's tent and flung her through it in disgust, shouting: "I gave you a week! I didn't speak a spell over you. Useless weakling!" Then he quickly sought the privacy of his tent again.

As soon as Naibe stumbled, naked and crying, through the tent flap, Ari scrambled to receive her. Deka, almost without looking up, stood regally and advanced to the opening, ushering herself to the royal tent. The ever-present guards stationed between the two tents lurked outside for a few moments, ready to report anything derogatory either of the women might utter about their general. Ariennu gathered the young woman into her arms, then cursed the guards just loudly enough to be heard.

"No. You stay out, you filthy mutts. I can hear you drooling for one of us from where I'm standing." She hugged Naibe close, then led the girl to her mat, sat with her, and began to stroke her hair to calm her. As the young woman's gasping and ragged breathing began to even out, Ari noticed the guards were still standing expectantly in the opening flap of the tent.

"What are you looking at?" She looked for one of her leather travel booties to hurl at them, even though she knew it was useless to show anger. She spat at the ground, instead. The more aggressive of the two guards, started toward her with a clear thought of rape as discipline, but his partner stayed him.

"Ho, I see." She grinned, then teased, pointing at the bulge in the man's shendyt. "You'd *like* to make me take some of the pressure off… force me…"

Both men stared at the two women, a little awed and amused. Naibe cried harder. "You know, unless Highness *makes* me do it, you get nothing. So, stop acting like you have rights."

"No I can't, MaMa. No, no more." young Naibe interrupted, burying her terrified face between Ari's naked breasts. "I thought him leaving me alone this past week would be enough, but…"

As Ari handled the girl's long and wavy black hair, she saw the red mark on Naibe's throat.

"That bastard. I'll--" the elder woman started but the second guard stepped into the tent. "Oh no you don't…" Ari dragged Naibe backward as if she was prepared to fight both men by herself. "You get him to come in here or I will get louder. I want to know why…"

"Lady Arrenu:" the guard announced. "You've been granted a short while to make the young honey calm herself and then return her to his Highness. He remains… uncomfortable," he held forward two dark bags in his hands. "When she achieves quiet, you will both wear these and return together. His Highness is troubled by the prediction and needs extra comfort. It's important."

Ariennu grumbled, nodding, yet intrigued. *Extra comfort? A dog with such a mighty knot in his prong it takes all of us to beat it down? Now, a prisoner game? Please! The sepat chief must have given him a mighty curse, not a prediction.*

"Yes, yes, I know. I will. He knows we submit. Just get out of here so I can work on her." Ariennu got up and snatched the bags from the men, then folded her arms while she waited for them to leave. She returned to the mat where Naibe lay rocking in anguish, settled beside her and gathered her into her arms.

"What did he do to you this time, Baby; choke you out again?" Ariennu didn't think Naibe would be able to bear returning to the prince in such a short while. Ari knew the prince had tried to drain her spirit again. He had been almost kind to her in the past week, but as they landed he made it clear that his good behavior toward her was over. If he expected to see her again so soon, judging from her anguish, Ari knew it would be too much for the young one.

Ariennu knew Maatkare had found a way to sink his *spiritual* fangs into her heart. Quite early, he became aware of her sorrow about Marai's death and her inability to move on. It had played into her nightmares about a darkness like a storm pursuing them and separating each of them. He read her memory of the time when Marai had been leading the women to Kemet and a sandstorm had enveloped them. He knew she had panicked and had run out into the storm with the unreasonable terror that Marai had deserted them. Maatkare found that fear and knew how to amplify the horror and feed it back through her heart. Naibe had spoken brokenly about it. Just as her deepest thunder of pleasure filled her and her body was about to explode with ecstasy he fed that horror through her, and drank deep from the energy it yielded.

Doesn't do that to me. Doesn't dare. I'd kill… Ari thought, but then realized her very agreement to submit to him, especially after a vicious argument or knowing that he would mistreat Naibe, had been enough. *Bastard knows there's a sisterhood and breaks it down between us. I stand up to him, he sucks the soul out of her and lets me see. It's no use to do anything but send her my own strength for him to take from her. At least it keeps us even,* Ari grew sad and buried her regret and fears in secrets. Just before she covered her thoughts, the prince drew any courage or resilience from her and replaced it with the thought that he owned her. What he did with Deka, Ari didn't know and really didn't want to know.

Like a bloodsucking bat on an ox, Ari thought. *Marai used to say that. It's Little One's spirit that's failing. She's becoming like a child again, the way she was before the Child Stone was given to her.* She remembered all three of them had been shells of femininity and scraps of humanity. She herself had been drunk, fat and dying of numerous tumors as well as yellow disease. Deka had been insane and functionally mute; twisted from something that broke her ribs and arms and then healed them badly, as if it hadn't understood how to repair her. Naibe had been a lascivious and drooling idiot child. She had been stocky and very short. Some kind of deformity had given her big, protruding eyes, a heavy breath, and a dreadful, sucking overbite. The Children had remade them. All had been made right with their bodies, but their characters had been less altered. Marai was still compassionate and kind to a fault. She had been the same wild and free adventuress she had been before, but oddly maternal. Deka was silent and hard as before, but her inner storms were easier to see. That eagerness had given Marai a naïve trust of the priests of Kemet and the Children of Stone as he had walked into the jaws of his own fate. With Marai gone and the Children of Stone effectively controlled by Maatkare and his grandfather Hordjedtef, everything was devolving. Ariennu had wanted to stay drunk again, even if it made her too sick to be anything but a burden. Only the thought that there might still be a way out of this growing mess kept her sober.

"No. No, no…" Ari sensed Naibe whine and struggle when she heard the men's request.

"It's alright, baby, he *knows* something's got you gripped and so do I. Certainly he won't try you again," she suggested. "I'll make *sure* he doesn't."

"I just need to rest, Mama," Naibe breathed. "I almost got away from the fear this time. I just keep forgetting to keep my thoughts out of him when he is with me. But you know how I am. The goddess in me is so drawn to broken men like him to ease their pain. It was so good to do that with the others; to know them and find their secret sweetness the way Marai and…" her voice wavered. She touched her throat, winced and flashed a naughty smirk.

"I think he —" she started, then clearly sent the thought to the elder woman: *Liked it with me this time. You know I* have *to keep trying, like Deka says, and he's said it too, in his own way.*

"Oh, he'll pay for this one day. If there are true gods and goddesses who remember our names, he will." Ari bent her head close to the young woman, whispering gently between her ear and her hand which had drawn the dark curly masses of her hair over it.

"I know," Naibe said. "I've seen the hurt he had all his life that made him this hard and I just know it's only going to get worse for him if I can't get through to him. It's why I had to try again today, but he blocked it. That's why it hurt."

"It's not your job to get through to him or *any* man and you can't convince me that your goddess Inanna, or Ashera, would want to 'fix' a man, especially not one like his Highness. As if he would even get to *start* disrespecting a goddess that much without calling for his own death. The pattern in the cloth of that man's life is the one he wove all by himself. Only *he* knows where the cross threads lie and only *he* can fix himself. If you try, he will only lash out at you. I like my way better. He uses me; and I use him. It feels good… fine in fact. You should do that too. It's better if you save your magic for a man who really *deserves* it."

"Easier for you, MaMa. The Children re-made me as a soul healer."

Ariennu laughed a little, but knew Naibe spoke the truth.

In a few minutes, after she had almost dozed in her self-calming attempts, the young woman spoke again. "Put the hood on me and take us to his tent. Best to see what he needs to have us do."

Ari placed the hood on the Naibe's head and put the other hood on herself, leaving enough of it open at the bottom so she could see the ground as they walked back across the narrow strip between the two outermost tents.

The two women stood outside the big red and yellow striped tent that late afternoon, Ari's arm slung loosely around Naibe's waist. Deka heard them and pulled aside the flap so they could enter. As she stepped inside, Ari lifted the corner of her hood and stared into the prince's glaring eyes for only a moment, then watched him pace back and forth, deep in thought. He was dressed to go out, even though it was nearly time for his evening meal.

"And who do *you* think you are, casting an eye on me before I grant you permission to do so? Times past, it would cost your head," he growled.

"Highness. Just tell us what this is about," Ariennu almost pleaded. Easing Naibe's misery and trembling had already invaded her own hard spirit. "You released Naibe to me. You see she's still shaking on her first day back with you and now you expect her to give you more? She may not yet be well. We know she almost died," Ari pressed Brown Eyes closer, protecting her.

"Hmmmph." Prince Maatkare paused and turned, studying the two women. He tapped his lower lip with his forefinger in thought. Deka had returned to sit by one side of the prince's bed, with her eyes lowered, ignoring their conversation.

I don't understand you, Ariennu thought to herself. *You knows she's getting worse. You eat her beauty and destroy her bit by bit pulling her spirit out. She's losing her will to live so fast I might not be able to get her back one day, but you don't care. You'll just toss her in the dung heap and find another. She hasn't been eating, and sometimes can't hold down what she* does *eat. Goddess...* Ari's thoughts suddenly sank.

"Well, I was *going* to make it a surprise for the good behavior you have shown recently, along with the Lady Nefira. You worked hard to bring what I need from you, but you…" he whirled and pointed his forefinger in Naibe's direction. "*Tired* too easily. But, so you won't hold me to blame…" he mocked, "I've arranged a softer bed for us and a good bath… some small bit of comfort as I prepare to go into the south to inspect the mines for a few days." His eyes became cruel slits for a moment. "The old governor owes me a favor for troubling me with his 'end of days' prophecy… of how my world is going to fly apart if I do not learn to respect the ancestors. Imagine… a mere sepat prince and one of such pale skin speaking to me thus. I should have cheerily wrung his ancient neck."

Oh goddess. Ari remembered the thought she sent out that he would 'pay for this' and tried not to react.

The prince's voice softened as he turned to the still hooded Naibe, who leaned heavily on Ariennu. "How you *are* will only help you. You already know that." He moved closer, then grazed the young woman's chin with his forefinger.

Ariennu pressed Naibe hard, hearing her whisper a slight prayer to Ashera under her breath. At the sound of her distress, Maatkare tugged the dark hood from her face. She flinched, another whimper escaping. He folded his arms across his chest, then tilted his head to one side. His lower lip jutted in a mock pout and he spoke almost tenderly. When his hand reached for her jaw and turned her head, he saw the fading mark on her neck. One of his eyebrows raised, as if he was surprised to see the mark and unaware of how it got there.

"I don't know why you're so upset. I thought to reward you *especially* for your excellent behavior toward the end. Be proud, young Honey Bottom. I'm impressed with all you can do now. You're learning to ride the chaos in both of us! You'll *learn* it well. But so you'll know I'm pleased with your work, I won't require you *or* your Red Sister tonight. You'll rest. You'll get better," his glance drifted to Ariennu, then to Deka, and softened a little more. "Tonight, I have other plans."

Protecting us, Ariennu sulked. *Sick monkey thinks he's teaching us his brand of heka. Doesn't he know women are supposed to give these gifts to men who protect and nourish their spirit the best? Is he trying to change the natural order of things? He's mad… demon-filled and mad.*

"Hoods back on, though." the prince whirled again in his pacing, cracking a slight smile. "I won't have the bearers or Old Metauhetep's men stunned by your beauty. Wuenre has already been asking for you, Red, young Rekenre too." He bowed his head in mock sincerity. "Even wrung out, you must have delighted them the other week."

Ariennu felt a wave of nausea sweep her. It wasn't disgust. It was the stifled need to shout, spit and kick several pairs of testicles on general principle. The thought of the sex excited her. The idea of being forced repulsed her.

Deka fastened her own hood obediently, then rose to go to his side.

Ariennu started to speak but silenced herself and quickly turned her attention to Naibe. As the prince waved the women from his tent, Ari lifted the edge of her hood enough to see the bearers and Maatkare's personal guard stepping to the neatly folded and stacked sedans to assemble them.

Acts like he's king already, she snorted, oddly aroused by his flippancy. *Prince Maatkare Raemkai, you've always been that way since the day we met. Even with all I know, I'd still be a happy concubine for you as long as you'd let me bend* your *bones on your precious 'ladder' myself from time to time… make you suffer and cry for 'mercy'. I'd like that a lot.*

When the sedans were ready, Ari urged Naibe to join her. Maatkare and Deka were hoisted in the one in front. She exhaled quietly as the entourage began to move back across a grassy stretch toward a darker spot on the horizon that would become the outline of the distant village of Qustul. As they jostled quietly along the path of bent grassy reeds beaten into the earth, Ariennu remembered her previous buried thought.

Babe. This sickness you have, you're with child, aren't you? She asked, but Naibe ignored her. *You know my thoughts, girl.* Ariennu shook the younger woman slightly and continued. *You noticed your moon right after Marai left us. Have you had another?*

Naibe looked down and away. She didn't want to answer.

"No? I *thought* not. Oh goddess, have mercy. Of all the wicked fortune." Ari whispered aloud. "That's perfect. Before we were pulled apart at Prince Hordjedtef's house I gave you heart fennel seeds to take each morning so your womb would be slick. You *know* the use of honey, even the Sebek's earth pessaries. When we came together at the royal palace I saw you still had plenty of it. I never *dreamed* you weren't using it. You even told me you didn't *want* a child if it wasn't Marai's, but he's *dead*. So what lie were you telling me?" she yammered on under her breath.

"Shhh MaMa… Prince Maatkare will hear us." Naibe trembled again, then spoke with her thoughts. *Two months ago I saw the child spirit playing in the king's yard, remember?*

Ari nodded.

He said he would come into my womb. I think he has. I don't want Highness to know it yet though. It's why I'm scared of what comes through me when I… It's why I had to get away to Wse at the temple when we came by Khmenu. She shook her head, dismayed.

"So. Another secret for us to keep. You think it's Wserkaf's child?" Ariennu whispered

Naibe shook her head.

"I don't know. I asked the little one to tell me whose seed took root in my belly. I asked my Child Stone and they just say I already know. But… *I don't.*"

"Well now you're growing a weapon! You've been with important men. A child by any of them would be a dangerous thing. I know the prince hasn't put you with any of his men yet like he's done with me, so it's only a chance of being sired by the divine ones."

Ariennu knew that soon as the prince discovered Naibe's condition she would be in danger. *He could have her killed. Some men don't want another man's child in their woman's belly. On the other hand, he might use a coming child for his own advantage. Then the problem will be with Deka. She will be at her death with jealousy again, the way she was when Naibe was the first to love our Marai.* Ari knew the Ta-Seti woman made no secret of her desire to create a child for Maatkare. *Naibe with child will ruin that for her, especially if she thinks* he *sired it. Wonder whose child, though.* Ariennu stared at the young woman beside her, almost afraid to ask. *Maybe this is part of the plan that the Children were trying to tell to us about.* "Be at peace as one life ends. Another begins. Profound truths await the patient ones. Lost in time and place." *We just couldn't understand it.* She turned to Naibe and cuddled her a little bit.

"We'll talk about this later… figure this out…" she smiled, happy that the gesture relaxed the young woman.

Just as the sun was setting, the prince, his personal guards and the three women arrived at a walled village. They had bypassed it the afternoon before, when the boats had first arrived and docked on the other shore. His Highness had sent a brief announcement and they moved by that he was going to the inland plain and would greet the governor in the morning.

The sedans approached this time, just before evening. Even though she was hooded, Ari sensed something was different. No guards created any sort of commotion by the walled gate. Eventually, after she heard the prince get out of his sedan and grumble a loud curse, she heard the gates swinging inward as if they had been under some magical command.

They were carried quietly through the gates, then set down. A man moved forward to greet them. Even though she couldn't understand the nuances of his dialect, Ari sensed the man's fearful respect. *He's got that one scared,* she thought, still puzzled at the lack of formal greeting. The distant scent of food wafted toward her. With the delicious odor came the sound of bowls being set out and the sound of some kind of frying meat. She scratched the side of her face under the hood. *He'd better let us take these off of our heads before we eat. This governor should be here welcoming us in and look… we have hoods. Highness never did this to us before.*

Prince Maatkare brushed past her. He spoke quietly and deliberately to the one who greeted them. Ariennu felt twitchy and hungry, eager for the prince to let them take off their hoods. Suddenly she felt his strong hand grip her upper arm and begin to lead her.

Ow! You stop…" only the knowledge that the prince was towing her with him silenced her. She had never been afraid of him, but tonight knowing he was able to read her thoughts and discover the secret she and Naibe guarded, she let him lead her and toy with her as if she had been a naughty child. Her hand held Naibe's.

When she sensed the prince had guided her from an interior passage to a smaller room on her right, Ari snatched the hood from her head then removed Naibe's hood. For a moment, she reveled in the slight wind that stirred in the passageway behind them. *A spirit?* She asked herself, turning to look behind herself at Deka and the prince. Ari saw Deka's face harden as she plucked the hood she had worn from her head. *You're afraid of something, aren't you?* Ari sent a thought then bowed her head, pleased with herself.

Deka hid her own expression by bowing her head in a submissive gesture and turning to respect the prince. When Ari turned fully around, she saw his dark shape standing in front of the door. His arms folded across his chest in what seemed to be his favorite "manly-looking" pose. The bearers and the men in his personal guard milled in the open area, inspecting the surroundings for possible traps. The early evening was calm, but something in the air felt wrong. Someone or something was watching them. Naibe moved closer to Ari, as if she knew it too.

Ariennu saw that a feather mat with folded coverlets near its foot had been rolled out on a wicker frame to form a bed to the left of the entry. Linen draping hung from a brass hook in the ceiling to keep away flies.

Nice... a real bed. Wonder what he'll expect out of me in return? It's always something, another step up for one of us. I still love his body and what he can do to mine, but sometimes... Ariennu almost cursed herself for having ever desired him because, although he disgusted her on one level, she found herself wretchedly seduced by his manner. She sniffed at the sensation of air moving outside the small room where she, the prince, and the other two women stood. She dropped her gaze in an almost demure pose, unable to resist a barb.

Maybe that little breeze means it'll rain. I know you got mad because the sepat here told you about the storm Naibe sees in her heart. Her eyes lifted, checking to see if he was paying attention. *You know it. You've been trying to harness the power in it. I wish her lightning would come out and strike you just when you think you've conquered the last of it,* Ari noticed the prince cracking a wry grin.

"Hmph! Gratitude, Red Sister? Gratitude?" Maatkare replied aloud and took another step into the room toward Deka. She lifted her hand so he could pull her closer into an embrace. The prince brushed her hand with his lips, gazing steadily into her eyes as he did.

"See now... This one has learned quickly," he remarked in a momentary but uncharacteristic devotion. Ariennu's eyes became irritated slits, but he made little of her attitude. "Through this door behind me, on the other side of the passageway you'll notice a shaded court. There's a deep tub to bathe in. Old wizard Akaru's gone into the southern hills early this year... to his retreat in New Qustul and Buhen... like the true and pampered coward he is, until he finds the 'stars' are more favorable," the prince scoffed. "He *knew* we were coming back tonight and yet he ran off, refusing to give us any courtesy, and with such a lame excuse as the stars. At least he's left some of his servants to feed us and tend to us." Maatkare stepped to one side with a magnanimous gesture. "We eat first, out in the courtyard. You two bathe first after we take our meal. Then," he ordered Ari, "sister, you get our young friend cleaned up and sweet again. The Lady Nefersekht and I will follow when you have finished and are resting for the evening."

Ari made a sneaky attempt to steal Maatkare's thoughts, by bowing her head and gently rubbing her right temple. She was dumbfounded by the prince's sudden reserved manner. *So you train us like dogs all the way up the river and suddenly we get to bathe in more than a squat pan? This isn't just you being kind, neither is your getting us to go to the water first. You're up to something. And if Naibe is--*. She noticed his eyes glimmering a little. He read her suspicions. She sighed, then tensed because she the prince had almost broken through her sheltered thoughts. *Deka's teaching him to read us better after all, damn.*

"Is what?" the prince stepped toward the russet-haired woman. One sharply angled brow raised, inquisitively.

Ariennu coughed and turned affectionately toward Naibe beside her, clapping an arm around her.

"Sick with a fever, Highness. I hope it's just from weariness and not black water fever. We passed much marsh and stand water on the way up. If she has it, then we'll all come to know it."

"Then *fix* her. And don't *lie* to me about her illnesses. I know you *all* have power to heal yourself with your Ntr stones. I've seen it when I've allowed your strength to come up a little. You know the herbs, too, so *use* them. *Sick*... she says," he turned his back and kicked an uneven place in the woven straw matting on the floor as if the young woman's illness was a planned trick. "Ask me if I believe a word that comes out of your mouth…"

"MaMa. I'm *fine* now. Tired is all," Naibe nodded. She stretched tall and seductively, but punctuated her movements with a yawn. *Be careful, Ari.* Her thoughts hushed her elder.

"Sure. I'll cure us… of you." She nodded into the young woman and led her past the prince and Deka, muttering: "You are lucky I haven't come after you while you lay drunk, cut it off, stuffed it, and used it for a wand of joy."

The prince's arm snatched out and pulled her close in a grip. The spark from the palm of his hand shivered up into her neck. His lips grazed that spot at the base of her throat again. Ari suddenly had no will to fight. She let the pleasure take her for an instant.

"Oh? You might think about it… until you remember how much you suffer for it when it's properly attached," the prince breathed. "So you disrespect me again, even though you promised me obedience to get me to save our young girlie here. Still, it amuses me to see how you thrash about so mightily at the very thought of being owned."

Ari's head snapped around to show him her displeasure, but she couldn't bury the smirk that had come to her lips. For a brief instant she forgot herself: "True, but if I had been born *here* and not in Tyre and if I'd have been by myself when we met, I'd have you trained to eat out of my hand by this time. I'd have kept you as king of *my* pleasure. But that's what Princess Meryt thought to do, didn't she?" Ariennu froze, realizing she had said far too much. Naibe gasped in horror and Deka closed her eyes, knowing Ari's talk had drifted into the forbidden.

Even though Ariennu stood facing the prince while his hand stayed her arm, she felt the growl and the hot breath of the black wolf spirit just behind her left shoulder. She turned to see if the prince had dared to create the wolf image with his men standing in the next room, but her arm instantly filled with gooseflesh. There was no man behind her. A fully formed black wolf-dog sulked behind her, head down and growling as if he was looking for her weaknesses before lunging at her. She froze.

No. Don't come at me, her thoughts cried. *Don't. Bastard.*

The animal looked up, but a human thought echoed through her.

Do you see the black dog? Do you see my dark heart? his expression warned her. The voice spoke from the opening of the door. Somehow, without her noticing it, he switched sides and shapes. The prince's face darkened a little and his eyes glimmered a radiant yellow green. The growl merged with a low voiced hyena titter issued more from his chest than from his throat. His dog teeth were visible on his lips.

Ari quickly raised her hand and breathed in, visualizing the wall of prismatic light between her left shoulder and the animal behind her. Maatkare startled a little and stepped back.

"Juice from you still, red sister? A good defense. You just *keep* on. You know I will answer it well; that you already have come to crave the pain."

She buried her own reflections and moved with Naibe out to the area where a low table had been set with a fragrant beef soup served in fine blue bowls. When she glanced back at the prince, his appearance had returned to a less threatening form. He stood with Deka by the nearly hidden pool in the low hall between pool, sleep areas, and the open plaza. She couldn't sense what he was telling the cinnamon-skinned woman, but saw her melt into his arms, helpless once again.

CHAPTER 5: WSERKAF'S MESSAGE

After their silent, joyless bath Naibe-Ellit lay resting in Ariennu's comforting arms. Deka sat in the same small room with them, anointing herself with perfumed oil and placing the peculiar gold circlet the prince had given her on her head. In a short while she planned to join the prince for their bath.

Wearing the little sun disc and the snake, I see. He wants her to play god's wife tonight for some reason, Ari mused. *So that's what's special… why we got good treatment and a bath. He's giving her some kind of status above us. Likely because I told her she wasn't so special and she complained about it to him.*

Ari knew Deka was keeping her thoughts on the matter private. The secrets made Naibe fidget visibly because of her natural empathy and inquisitiveness.

Ari, hurry her up. The young woman's thoughts urged. *I can feel her drawing my attention. She wants to tell me something but she doesn't dare.*

Shhh, Ari cautioned.

Maatkare approached the doorway and stood, indicating he was waiting for Deka to join him. She noticed and rose from her mat, naked except for a cloak. The prince turned to Naibe and Ari as if he sensed the young woman's unbeaten gentleness.

I could free your heart too, Highness… show you your soul so you could mend its hurts. Instead you will not accept it unless you steal it or hunt it like a small and fragile thing for you to eat. I see you. You are the eater of souls on the one hand like Ammit yet a guide to one's true purpose, Naibe waited for her thought to resonate.

"I see you've thought it all out, then," Maatkare Raemkai's guttural voice whispered in answer to the thought he read. "You *think* too much. Maybe *that's* what's making you sick, eh?"

"Deka should go," Naibe's eyes lowered.

Ariennu knew the young woman was exhausted as she continued speaking to the prince. "I can't bear her being here a moment longer. I'm going to burst. Not both of you at once," her light brown eyes swept up toward Maatkare. "Please,

Highness take her to bathe with you and then soothe her until you both can rest. Her thoughts are burning me. I can't bear either of your eyes looking on me tonight," she turned away from the young general's mystified expression again.

At that moment, Deka moaned with a catlike keen, as if the young woman's insult hurt her, then hurried to follow the prince to the bathing room.

Ari pressed Naibe again and moved to the bed, fluffed up the coverlet, and urged the girl to sit with her. She combed out Naibe's damp hair, humming a little as if the young woman was the child she never raised. She had given birth to five babies and dispatched countless other womb-fruit with heart seeds before she implored the Children of Stone to make her sterile. For a moment, Ariennu thought of Marai and how she had wished to create a child for him.

"You're thinking about him again, aren't you?" the red-haired woman asked. "It's making me think about him too."

Naibe nodded against the elder woman's leg. In the distance, they thought they heard Maatkare speaking gently to Deka. His deep-voiced titter floated over the empty space between the central room where they bathed and the sleeping rooms.

"I always do, MaMa," she began. "This child in my belly, though... changes so many things."

"You're two months gone. How could you let this happen? You knew..." Ari grumbled, but then she remembered no one had ever taught Naibe a thing about her body. When she had come to the thieves camp, she had been little better than a drooling idiot. During her moon time, she and Deka simply cleaned up after her and made the necessary offerings to the goddess for her. Even though the Children of Stone repaired her wits, it may have never occurred to them to see she had enough knowledge of pregnancy to end one before it started. It had been *Marai* who had convinced her to wait until he had seen the priests to bear him a child. *He* had tracked her fertility and had abstained from her when she was ripe. For Naibe, Ari knew, that had been the most grievous part of her heartache; that nothing of Marai remained of him but beautiful memory.

"I can see what the women here use if you want me to, but I don't think the heart seeds work this late without making you sick as death and then who knows what Highness will think of that."

"No, I didn't mean…" Naibe almost laughed. "I believe it *is* my spirit friend who has come into my womb. I couldn't…" her face turned away and she swallowed hard. "The goddess in me must have had other plans all along to make him come after Marai was…" her lips trembled "Was…"

Ari paused to tease out a tangle in the young woman's hair, then smoothed it. She remembered the spirit child she had seen that evening had tawny, brasslike skin color and smooth yet wavy dark hair. He was slim and agile as if he could easily learn dances and leaping. Wserkaf was a dance and sacred movement master, but it didn't mean the child was his. Naibe's dances evoked passion in all who saw her move. The child's lithe little body could easily come from either of them, or both.

"Then, if you're bound to have it, we'll have try to get away again. I don't trust what Prince Maatkare would do. He's already pushed you to the edge too many times and after you tried to swim to Khmenu, he's acted like he owns your very life itself."

Ari stopped combing, crawled to her basket and tossed the comb on top of the heap of clothing inside. When she loosened the rest of her own braids, she fluffed her hair until it sprawled and curled all around her shoulders in a dark ruddy mass.

As soon as she lay beside Naibe, Ariennu felt her thoughts transform into a strange vision. She saw Marai again when she concentrated on the memory their happy moments together. He reached out to her from a distant and dark place like a tomb. As usual, when she thought of reaching back she couldn't find him. This time, the image of Prince Wserkaf formed over her thoughts.

"Wise Mama?" Naibe whispered, almost asleep.

"Mmm?" Ariennu answered, petting the young woman gently. "Feeling any better now?"

Naibe nodded, a wistful smile moving over her face once again. "I see something. The Children want us to know something, maybe. It's coming through my stone. Want to share it with me?"

Ari didn't have time to say yes.

Naibe's soft hand wandered up to her elder sister's brow to touch the stone so that they both sensed the same vision.

"The thing I see must have happened earlier today, in the afternoon I think. It was when I was with his Highness and it's what made me cry when it came through. I made myself forget, but now…" Naibe-Ellit whispered.

"Sure," Ari breathed, snuggling with the young woman on their shared mat. They lay face to face for a moment, kissed each other's lips to soothe themselves then shared their thoughts. "Maybe they'll tell us something nice for a change… or maybe they'll say where this child in you came from."

Ariennu breathed out as the vision cleared a little. She picked out a lush interior garden with plant jars, a room to one side and a nice sesen pond full of blossoms that slumbered just beneath the surface for the night.

"Babe. I don't know about this place. It's pretty, but…"

"Oh, I know where it is, Ari. I lived here *first*." Naibe's lyrical, low voice grew so soft that Ari stared at her wondering if she was making a sound at all. Everything about this vision was different than the ones she had of Marai. In this one, a sadness overshadowed all else; even the air felt sad.

"It's Wse's house, Wseriri, but it's so sad now." She whispered.

Ari nodded.

"Something's wrong, Babe. It's not the Children giving this feeling to us. Your Wse is doing this."

Ari saw Wseriri, as Naibe called Inspector of the Ways Prince Wserkaf, sitting at the edge of his sesen pool with his feet dangling in the water.

My lady sweet goddess can you hear me? Naibe-Ellit, goddess whom I have loved. I conjure you to speak to me. Know that I felt your cry to me a quarter moon ago, but could not return it. Remember when we touched… our first time? I do. See that memory sweet one. Come to the place where it happened. See me there.

This late afternoon the women saw a slim man wearing a strange and longer dark garment with a yellow sash draped across one shoulder and down to his golden belted waist. On his head he wore a simple, dark unadorned khat. They sensed it was some kind of formal garb. He was alone.

"I see him, Babe," Ari whispered, continuing to stroke the young woman's hair. "At his pool. Did you hear him say he knew you tried to reach him a week ago?"

Ariennu felt the young woman nod, but both women sensed the quiet. There were no sounds of laughter in the house.

At that hour, in any wealthy home, servants would be cleaning and clattering to set the evening meal. Ever-present guests would be milling in the courtyard as they waited. Some of the younger maids would have been teasing and laughing as they did their last minute chores.

"Odd. It *is* quiet," Naibe remarked. "Wonder where Princess Khentie and her maids are? Maybe he just returned from his duty in Khmenu and she's still at *her* temple."

"Maybe he just found out we're not there," Ari added. "Maybe he called out for you because he's seeking *us*."

Oh... Wseriri... Naibe's eyes closed with a gentle, aching sigh. *I'm here. I cried for you so much when we were taken and again last week when I tried to go to you, but you didn't answer me.*

This time he looked up briefly, as if he heard her, then trembled. The women saw his head tilt down again and his hand go up to his face to wipe his eyes. He was weeping.

Oh beloved one, Naibe's thought reached out to him. *Why are you so sad? Is it because we're apart? You've returned from your duty to learn I am gone? She whispered into her vision. Oh, know that I miss you too.*

He looked up again, understanding whose thoughts reached out to him. Sinking into a light trance, he breathed his answer into the late afternoon air.

Naibe, my sweet one, at last I hear your voice in my heart. So many things are changing just the way you told me they must, when we were together the last time.

The women sensed him staring into the empty plaza ahead of him as if he was watching *her* image float just above the pool.

Soon all Kemet will see what has been kept secret, and still must be a secret until the time is right. It just aches my heart to know as much as I do. He bent forward, his hand tracing gently through the water. In some small way he sensed her quizzing thought.

How so? Naibe asked, wanting to command the secret from him. She smiled a little. Ari sensed her commanding 'Ashera' voice going to him. In his thoughts her voice sounded ever gentle and seductive once again. All of the days they had been apart suddenly melted away.

There have been unbearable things, tragic things, my dear, dear lady… and on the heels of something unbelievable! He whispered, but didn't have to send her the next thought.

She knew what had happened before he thought the words: *Menkaure KhaKet…*

"Oh no… not KhaKet. Dead? How could we not know it Ari? How?" Naibe's voice sounded just above a whisper and her wide eyes teared instantly.

Wserkaf began to explain.

"They came to us from the palace in the hours just before the sun rose to tell us the news," he whispered, no longer gazing out across the sesen pool. "They said that earlier that night, the king's physicians had become concerned over Our Father's recent behavior. First, they had sent word to his wife and she had summoned our brother Shepsisi and some others to be at his side. My brother was angry that his rest had been disturbed and said his majesty didn't seem worse in health, just sad. He'd been sad and less in the public eye as the stars positioned themselves for the anniversary of his fate given at Buto six years ago. Then Shepsisi saw and knew the depth of his father's suffering… how dearly he had struggled to look well. They spoke and he urged his father to continue for a little while longer, to conduct ordinary night business, then rest."

Naibe sensed Wserkaf grow silent with emotion and wanted to somehow reach through the universe to ease his suffering and to place his head on her breasts until he calmed himself.

"He… just suddenly stopped speaking and his eyes grew wide. He was dying seated in his official stateroom chair and facing the night time stars through his wide open porch. Death seized his heart in sudden distress and his soul leapt into flight. It was so quick, so peaceful that my brother stated he didn't have time to shout for the physicians already standing nearby. Our Father had just beckoned him close and with his last breath of earthly air he had smiled and whispered your name: *Naibe, my goddess, I go to you.* Did you not feel him fly to you sweet one? Did you not?" he implored.

Quiet tears rolled down Naibe's cheeks. She sobbed as Ariennu held her tighter, sharing everything she had seen.

Oh poor man. Poor sad, sad man… Was it his breaking heart that ended him? Was it truly that? She begged. *Tell me it was not because I had been taken from him.*

Ariennu had bowed her head. The moment she heard Wserkaf's words in the young woman's thoughts, she realized: *Maatkare doesn't know. Or does he? Is this why he had the tantrum? Did this sepat he visited sense something and tell him? Old man Hordjedtef must have been in the room when Majesty's death came. How could he resist sending the young general a dream?*

"I bet we'll have to keep another secret." Ariennu opened her eyes a little and saw Naibe's half open eyes flashing golden. Her stone was in the emerged position.

Mama, Naibe's thought drifted up. *Ask the Children of Stone why he doesn't know. Ask it through me.* Naibe wriggled up a little, then gently kissed the stone in her elder sister's brow.

Little ones, the russet-haired woman began reluctantly because she wanted to kiss and caress Naibe instead of reading secrets through her. Whenever the young woman's spirit energy rose, she was irresistible. Almost instantly a whispered answer returned to both women.

> *The elder king is free of the*
> *Darkness that covered him*
> *He walks the stars in joy*
> *The new must take his first steps*
> *To vanquish the wrongs*
> *To ascend in safety and full wisdom.*

"I guess Shepseskaf has to do something as king before Maatkare knows Menkaure is gone, but how in this red and black earth I can overpower that old bastard Hordjedtef's thoughts, if he decides to send them, is new to me." Ari breathed.

The voices of the Children of Stone gently answered through the thoughts of both women.

OPENER OF THE SKY

A darkness will be brought to light
Yet not accepted by most
There will be hardship
The wolf must be kept at bay

"Wolf. Even *they* called him that," Ari snickered, but realized Naibe was still linked to Wserkaf's thoughts.

"Poor Wse…" the younger woman sniveled, then turned her thoughts to the image of the man brooding at the pool. "Are you…?"

"She's gone, sweet one, yes. I'm alone in my house but it's as it should be. She is wife of her brother and king to assist him and rule at his right hand with Queen Bunefer at his left as wife of the body."

So that's why it's so quiet? Ari quietly suggested.

"Lady ArreNu? You are with Naibe? Caring for her?" the priest asked, suddenly sensing the elder woman's presence.

I am, Ari answered still thinking about the kind of upheaval the sudden death of the king must have caused and how she could keep all of this from the prince.

"I found out my senior told Prince Maatkare to take you. He isn't hurting either of you is he? I know of his penchant for being rough with his lovers. Everyone *knows* about it," a pained and mildly disgusted expression drifted over the image of his face.

Naibe whimpered a little, understanding his question, but knew it would be cruel to add to his misery since there was very little he could do. She allowed Ariennu to wrap secrecy around both of their thoughts.

Prince Wserkaf, Ari sent her own thought to the inspector. *We're not suffering too badly, but he does try to break our wills; to make us his. Best to let him think it for now, but I want to kill him half the time for all that he's taken part in!* She grumbled silently, sensing Wserkaf nodding in silent response.

Does Ka-Khet's spirit know how hard I tried, Wseriri? Do you think it? Does he know how much I wanted to help him feel love again? Bless goddess; he did not think I abandoned him the next morning, did he? She nearly sobbed aloud in Ariennu's consoling arms.

"Naibe, hush. You know I told you when we were at Sokor what I saw."

"Saw?" Wserkaf's eyes widened.

I've learned how to go places in a dream, lately. I suppose my Child Stone must have helped me. I saw Majesty was furious with old Hordjedtef that next morning, but Great One gave him a pain and told him right away it was from my tea. I'll bet the old man poisoned the king, didn't he? He knew we wouldn't be there to see it or to save him. She paused, then continued with a new thought. *Did that old bastard speak ill of us to anyone else... Blame us for it?* Ariennu whispered.

Naibe shook her head and buried it in her elder sister's breasts. She already knew the answer.

"Yes..." Wserkaf returned the answer into the air in front of him. "You've both been set for the blame, I'm afraid. That's why Maatkare *can't* know or he may just decide to mete out justice if he feels there's an advantage to it. My mentor Hordjedtef must be working something I don't understand it either, because we all *knew* he desired Maatkare Raemkai to be king, and not Shepseskaf. He's already told all who will hear him that you were both enchanters, especially you, sweet one, because of the way your dance had seduced him. My senior tried to convince Our Father that he had sent you away because of the threat and the sorcery. I think he will try to exert influence over Shepseskaf until the burial, then decide on who ought to be king. He wants Maatkare in power too, but not until he is more predictable."

"Damn him into Ammit's bowels, then!" Ariennu hissed under her breath.

"Shhh. Don't curse in anger. Just understand, Ka-Khet *did* go into the stars knowing you both meant well and he took so much happiness from you both. He wanted to remember your sacred magic, my Naibe. I saw he had even built a little shrine to you in his room." Wserkaf was silent, pausing to weep, grieving too greatly to send thoughts for a moment. His image faded.

"No. Wse. Come back. It's alright..." Naibe's thoughts whispered. Slowly, the inspector priest's image reformed as he gained control of his thoughts.

"You told him nothing ever ends, didn't you, beloved one?" His whisper to the young woman and her elder sister reached through space and time. "...Especially the part about love never ending when it is given in honesty and truth... that he could walk among the stars to be with all of his departed ones. You even whispered to him that you understood how his daughter died and how it had been Maatkare's ill temper and drunkenness, and not her own despair, didn't you? Did you tell him that because you knew he was going to die so soon?"

Ari held Naibe tight and felt her nod quietly, but hesitate.

Tell him, Babe. She breathed.

"I saw them, Wse. It made my night with him divine, in a sense. It was as if I had opened a faraway door for him because in that one glorious and beautiful night we both saw the souls of the dead gathering far, then near, like they were waiting and watching us. I took his soul into my heart and we became the fire of all the candles in the room going up into the stars," the young woman paused, reflecting. "Ari, Wse... Is it even possible?" her voice trembled.

"What, dear one?" the inspector's image drifted as if something distracted him.

"Could I have been a prophet, because I knew and saw?" she asked.

"You know you are. I think Our Father knew it. Khentie told me it too. You're that powerful. All of you women are as powerful as..." the image of Wserkaf tensed, as if he'd heard a sound somewhere in his house.

I have to go. I have something to tend to. He began to take a deep breath to rouse himself. *Please don't let Maatkare hurt her... or you, Lady ArreNu.*

I wouldn't, Ari bowed her head for a moment, hiding the idea of the misery the prince had already unleashed. The sight of Wserkaf by his pool faded into obscurity.

Ariennu whispered gently. "He's gone now, but you can give that memory to me, since I'm already hiding so much of it in here". She tapped the dark and sparkling stone in her brow, then kissed the blue lapis Child Stone in Naibe's. That allowed her thoughts to combine with Naibe's and remember it as if she herself had lived it. The king lay in her arms, stunned by the purity of the sweet love they had shared.

Be happier, my king, she felt herself whisper with Naibe's voice. Naibe, in the present time, whispered with her. *Know and believe you are a god and such a good father to all of us.*

I've tried, my sweetest child. I've tried, but been so thwarted.

You will see her again, your pretty Mery, Naibe smiled and stroked his brow. *She is here with us.*

Ari frowned, wondering what Naibe had meant by that.

I know. Soon, I think, though she would bless my time with you this night.

The King had enveloped her in his arms and caressed her breasts, showering her with increasingly passionate kisses that followed his hands until she begged for him to love her again.

Ari sensed and shared other thoughts, understanding that the idea of his death had been in both of their hearts that night.

You will live forever, my king, she felt the young woman breathe into his open mouth. *I know this.*

Ari heard her tell him she wanted him to never be afraid of the dark or of his shortening years again. She whispered together with the girl that she wanted him to face it bravely, and she knew he had never betrayed the oracle's dictates and that there had never even been any sort of curse placed on his heart.

She told you that you would not complete the hundred fifty years of fierce rule Great Khufu began and told you of a man wounded and often betrayed but still possessing a kind heart. There was no curse.

Ariennu had visited, shrouded in secrecy. She had stumbled drunkenly away to meet with her destiny at the foot of the stairs in the hands of the high priest. Ari shook her head in renewed dismay then caught the image of young Naibe showing the king the souls of all of his beloved ones reflected in her golden eyes.

He had kissed the stone in her brow, feeling its power move through him. When they shared their love again it was even more unearthly, as if the king already knew he had one foot in his own horizon. He wept when they had finished. She kissed away his tears, as if he was a lover and she was sending him off to battle. Naibe saw the hollow death in his eyes, but this time she understood and she had not been afraid of that darkness. That was how she had been taken. She had risen from the bed, tucked him in and kissed him once again. As she stood up, she was struck solidly from behind.

Deka was right. She knew it wasn't safe. She put the thought in the old man's soul that she would get the Children of Stone from us. That we could be her handmaids if Maatkare was given the control utterance, even if she got the same pain we suffer when it's spoken. That Witch! So, a choice between this demon we're with and the lair from which he crawled. We'll keep Prince Maatkare here as long as we can. Keep the truth away. When he becomes wise to it, we'll make certain he doesn't know how we hid it from him.

Naibe had drifted to sleep, exhausted by her efforts. Ariennu felt bone-weary too, and knew she would have to sleep.

Be nice if I could sleep a week and get some better strength, she thought. *Cover it up; Prisms of light around all of the secrets: Naibe being with child and the death of poor King Menkaure. At least I kept that from Wserkaf about the child. He might even* be *the father of that child.*

As she relaxed, she heard the beautiful voice of a child drifting through time and its own ages. The child-voice became deep and beautiful as a man, but also haunted and low in a serene contralto.

> *The thoughts of a new one stay hidden*
> *Until a belly swells*
> *Then she cannot hide her truth.*
> *What Maatkare Raemkai has sensed,*
> *He will know, but*
> *May consider*
> *I came of his seed.*

Someone was in the room. Ariennu wrapped another layer of silence around what she has just sensed, thinking it might be Hordjedtef coming in spirit form to see why his favorite grandchild had not received the message of the king's death.

You. Stay away from us, you heartless devil. She started, but saw the form of Marai materializing in the room where she and Naibe lay. Her heart sank. After everything they had learned tonight, this vision was too much.

You again. Ay... if you hadn't died. Ari's shoulder's slumped, then froze again because she thought she felt his touch. A spirit hand caressed her gently, lulling her, so real it was unbearable. *Goddess. Oh Marai, I can't,* she almost sobbed.

Ari. My bright and kind one. The image of Marai spoke and almost pushed through space into voiced reality. *I am alive. I did not die.*

"Wh… Stop, you." She tensed, trembling. There, in the corner of the room, he lay with his body curled as if he slept somewhere and was dreaming. Then, there was nothing.

Poor bastard doesn't even know he's dead… Second time he's said that like someone who's lost, she thought, frustrated even more over the idea that her beloved might be hanging between the land of the dead and the land of the living. Slowly, the reality of the room re-formed. *Damn, another vision. Wish it hadn't been…* she turned over and tried to sleep, but tonight sleep didn't come easily.

OPENER OF THE SKY

Part Two: Djerah

OPENER OF THE SKY

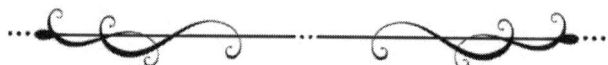

Chapter 6: Black Water in the Well

Marai sat at the well in the center of the marketplace. His hooded, silvery head rested in the crook of his elbow. With the last of his failing strength, he looked up at the stars long enough to raise his fingertips and whisper:

"Comes dawn. A new day. Time is released to go on her way." For the briefest moments, as his illusion of slowed time unraveled, he observed the stars and approaching sunrise speed up in their courses.

Reduced to gasping, but relieved, he let his head sink back into his arm then took a deep, panting breath. He thought of Ariennu, his elder wife once more. The brick walls of the small room where she and young Naibe relaxed formed in his thoughts. He knew she had sensed him.

Ay... if you hadn't died.

He sensed Ari's words. He reached forward through space and time to touch and caress her shoulder, but heard her next thought before his fingertips reached her.

Goddess. Oh Marai, I can't...

Ari... My bright and kind one... Marai's thoughts spoke with such force they almost leapt into voiced reality. *I am alive. I did not die.*

Marai knew he was too weak to stay in her world. *She didn't hear me. Maybe when I'm stronger, h*e suffered and drifted. When he looked up again, he knew he had dozed for a moment. Wserkaf was gone. Still grievously tired, he tried to picture the image of the one man from the noble priesthood who had helped him.

Wse... he thought.

At that moment, he couldn't picture the wiry-built prince who rescued him and had spent the last day working healings on him.

A dream... It must have been a dream. I'll wake up and I'll be on the roof. My beloveds will be up and getting ready for a good work day in the market.

It wasn't true. He knew everything that had happened to him: the schooling by Great Hordjedtef, the false Sed ritual, his near death and entombment for nearly three months, the resurrection assisted by Wserkaf, his learning of the women's abduction, and the death of the great King Menkaure were *not* illusions.

Marai knew he needed to go to Ta-Seti and get his wives.

What the Children of Stone wanted of me should have been simple, he thought. Just carry them here, learn of my new strengths and how to best use them, then await the next thing I might do for the betterment of men. But now… my ladies. The Children know how important they are to me.

He remembered that long ago on the beautiful night his journey with the Children of Stone began. He stood outside his cave home and sang to his beloved goddess Ashera.

Come bless me this starry night

Tonight was different and so far away from that place and time. The spirit of the dead king was moving through his beloved land. Marai felt the king's regret at his own passing, the leaving of unfinished business as it combined with his own feelings. The enormity of all that had befallen him in fifty-six years since that night of song filtered through his own psyche. He groaned, resting his head on the edge of the well.

"Oh I really am *so* tired," Marai whispered aloud and shut his eyes, hoping to clear his thoughts a little more. "Help me my goddess, help me." He felt her warmth in the form of his Naibe from so far away, but it felt faint and oddly weak. Hoping he could give himself strength along with some he sent to her, he sent the refrain of his song to her one more time:

Shine for one who begs to serve you
Return to the night…

Marai started to feel ill. Something crept toward him like a thief in the dark. The big sojourner didn't care at that moment if he was alive or dead or if men on nearly silent feet had come to kill him. Setting his head in the crook of his arm again, but protecting the sack of Child Stones at his belt, he waited. The shadowy figure hesitated, then advanced.

"So," a terse voice came from the shadow as it drew closer. "You again," it spoke a rough form of the language of the wilderness. The sound of it cut through the humid pre-dawn darkness that marked the seasons after the flood. "*Now* you find your way back," a young man with shaggy head of ear length black twists and a neat, square-cut chin beard approached him from behind. "And for no *good* reason. No one you left behind is still here, so move along."

Without fully looking up or focusing on the person behind his left shoulder, Marai knew it was Djerah, the great grandson of his half-sister Houra. He turned his head to one side, just to check and caught a glimpse of the man's beaked nose jutting into the light. Djerah's shadowy face, in just that fragment of setting moonlight, brought back too many memories of the sojourner's long dead cousin Sheb. The young stonecutter's nose grew to even more of a point when he stared down at him.

Marai first thought his and Wserkaf's talking and then their use of the Child Stones to seek his wives must have awakened the young man from a sound slumber. Then, he remembered a woman had crept from the man's apartment to meet a lover and then had returned just before Wserkaf left.

We woke you, Wse and I, but you slept through your wife betraying you. Marai grumbled to himself, truly disgusted at what he sensed. *If you knew what I suspect, you'd want me to stay and tell you everything instead of pushing me on. Such courtesy! If you weren't the only legacy of my father's clan, I wouldn't have even thought of coming back here. It's too bad I need a place to rest.*

Marai remembered an old tradition from the wilderness that could ease this awkward greeting.

He has no idea. Probably wasn't taught a thing, the sojourner chided himself. *I should just move on and sleep in someone's booth until first light.* He turned toward the young man with his palms upward while he remained seated at the well, then swept one hand to his sash to indicate to the young man that he had no weapon. The young man didn't react.

Marai understood why.

A stone. He sensed the fingers of Djerah's right hand stretched around a sizeable chunk of brick. He'd brought it with him when he came out to see who was gathering at the well at such an hour.

Good. Protect the family, though they don't deserve your care.

He saw the young man freeze, consider the gesture, then step back and look away, shivering a little.

Well. You recognized something, didn't you? he thought. The sojourner allowed the congenial flash of silver and the strange light it produced show in his eyes. *Djerah, heir of the sons of Ahu,* Marai's thought voice whispered the music of tales Djerah's elders told him as he grew up in the wilderness. *With every shred of my weary spirit, know I speak the truth and mean no harm,* Marai pushed the almost musical sound of sand crushing beneath straw or leather booted feet through his thoughts. He projected images of wide open spaces, free air, the thrill of the approach of a caravan filled with trade goods and weary travelers, all eager for water, and shaded rest.

The young man who stood slightly behind him had never known these things, but Marai knew he had heard the stories. If the thoughts he sent came through as illustrations to those often told tales, Marai knew the man might not feel so ill at ease.

Marai yawned, wondering how much longer he was going to be able to stay awake. Maybe the utterance he was supposed to whisper as part of the resurrection had been wrong. *Maybe I forgot something,* the black water of the well invited him to succumb.

Come, a sweet yet almost evil voice whispered
I sit, I wait at the still water in the Land that Loves Silence
My heart longs to calm itself
Its search gone
Its truth and the blood realized.
Its oath remembered and understood.

"Deka," Marai put his head down again, feeling waves of nausea moving through his entire frame. His tremors had come back. For an instant, the visions passed through his thoughts and overwhelmed the new reality of near collapse at the well. His hand steadied his body on the edge wide brick surround. Deka's face melted into Naibe's face and Ariennu's countenance as they became one bone face streaked with tears. "Come back to me," He whispered at the faces fading in the water.

"You have a fever," the stonecutter backed away, worried.

Marai weakly raised his hand for him to wait.

The young man moved toward him again. "The woman, Deka, from far upriver. I heard you say her name. She's not here. The others aren't either. I told you that a moment ago. I thought you had begun to rave…" Djerah explained.

"It's the poison. The priests got me to drink it as part of a ritual." Marai realized he was gasping for breath in fatigue and dizziness. "I only came back to hide another night; to sleep the rest of it off. This was the only place on this side I knew. If I can get to the roof without falling off the footholds…" The sojourner's glance focused down into the flat undisturbed black of the water in the well that had been alive with visions and voices when Wserkaf had been there earlier. He felt himself starting to sway.

"I told Etum Addi you had no business running after these madmen. You can *never* trust them. We work on their buildings and that's fine. We march with them for the militia. We draw a wage – all these are good things. To go chasing after their secret knowings and ways? That's sheer idiocy," Djerah rocked leg to leg then stretched a little as he let go of the brick. "I heard your wives complain over that plenty. They didn't want you to go either. What were you thinking? When the men came with the Inspector and got them, we all assumed you met up with them and were living over there working for them. Did you *not* find each other?"

Sheb… He scolds like Sheb. Marai gestured lamely for the man to sit with him on the edge of the well. *It's like all the years have melted away and it's Sheb talking to me of why I have to come with him and my sister to Ineb Hedj.* Marai hoped the stonecutter had inherited his sister Houra's sense of pity for helpless things and would help him get to a safe hiding place before he passed out in the courtyard. It would be dawn soon. Merchants would be trying to set up for the day.

Someone was moving around in the lower apartment. The stonecutter cast a glance backward at a young woman holding a fussing infant in her arms at their doorway.

"It's nothing, MaMa," he called affectionately and almost shyly then returned to his conversation. "My wife, Raawa, and my new son, Sheb bin Djerah."

"*That* tradition you keep well, Djerah," Marai nodded. "Good health to the boy and all of your seed." He smiled his way through an old blessing, even more disheartened by the thought that this young man didn't even realize the division in his own house. *So life goes on, h*e sighed.

"When you have no true home, all you have is tradition." The young man shrugged; his smile almost cryptic. "Men of the Sin will always wander. My grandfather used to say that."

True, Marai thought. *Father Ahu wandered our ragged young tribe of brothers and cousins and their wives from Akkad, to the Shinar; all the way to the heights and valleys of the Sangir lands and back again before finding a place on the slopes of the Sin-Ai. We'll always be a black headed people who wander looking to a prophet or plenty, warring and conquering… always divided.*

"So… Djerah is *your* name. Is your father…?" Marai began, barely able to keep coherent. He bowed his head and shut his eyes, then tried to ignore the sparkling random red and green patterns dancing before them.

Djerah squinted, shuddering as if he'd suddenly felt some eerie disturbance, then answered. "Dead? Yes, Lord of all. We're a people of widows and fatherless boys. Savta's man Sheb died before I was born. Tisehe *did* live long, as did my own father Esai, but only because the fever made them unfit for other work. In the end they became weak as old women and we cared for them until they were gone from us. I was a little one, but I remember them. Even my poor Raawa's two sisters are widows."

Marai held up his forefingers vertically… a sign for 'Wait…'

"Arrah! You must have been half-killed by those priests. You're speaking Kemet now," Djerah mused. "A moment before, I was struggling with the Kina words coming from your head." The young man continued.

Marai felt his head snap out a quick nod. He rubbed his arms, trying to stay awake a little longer. He was fading again. Djerah was still talking, but his words were as understandable in the sojourner's ears as the gibberish of chattering monkeys. He began to regret finding his young descendent and wished for a moment that he had known of a different place to stay.

"I shouldn't trust you, but if you stay out here, as overwrought as you are, anyone might seize you. There will be peacekeepers here at dawn," the young man continued.

Marai startled convulsively as the stoneworker seized and tried to lift him, albeit clumsily.

"Come on. Up you go. Damn… heavy…" the stone cutter grunted in surprise as Marai stumbled onto him. "I'll put you upstairs where you used to live overnight, but you'll need to be gone as soon as you've rested." He took a quick, deep breath, set his shoulders and back so he could support the big man, then quietly led him to the upper apartment Marai had not so long ago known as his own.

OPENER OF THE SKY

Chapter 7: Peacekeepers and Plans

Marai was asleep almost before he stretched out on the pile of rags covering the floor in the rear his former apartment. At one time, the raised brick part in the back held baskets of everyone's personal possessions and four mats: one for himself and three for his wives. The dark wool fabric, threadbare in places, had been repaired with enough tiny patches, stitched again and again, that it made the musty fabric feel soft. He didn't even notice the cloud of dust that rose from the ragging as he fell on it.

In a short while he felt his spirit rise from his sleeping body and soar up across the black river. He saw Prince Wserkaf get out of his wooden boat and whisper the words '*Until now*' over the men who had ferried them across in secrecy. For a short while, he watched the scene unfold:

The men blinked and roused themselves.

"What was that?" one asked.

"Did his Highness ever get here?" asked another.

The third looked at an empty jar of beer.

"Damned stuff must have been a higher grade to put us to sleep in the middle of the game," he inspected the board and saw that the senet pieces were still in place.

"Ay," the first shook his head. "Good thing His Highness didn't come here, after all. If he had caught us asleep…"

Marai laughed weakly in his journey and focused on his friend Prince Wserkaf. The man had done an exceptional job on his end of the utterance for the boatmen to forget, even resorting to obscuring his own hasty departure. Some servants were there to greet the Inspector at the broken gate where, in anger, Marai had taken the form of an enraged bull-man and shredded it the night before.

He sensed Prince Wserkaf speaking to them briefly as he went inside to gather some items then hurry on in the quickly-lightening dawn. By evening, the priest would be sequestered in the House of Life. Wserkaf would know, for whatever good it would do him, if Hordjedtef had poisoned the king.

Marai, in his spirit form, made a little gesture like a salute and sent a sad thought.

Peace, friend. I am well. Be wondrous; be effective today.

At some point in his slumber, the sojourner shifted. Turning over until he lay flat on his back in the darkened room, he drifted again.

Light streamed in through the remains of the old travel tent Ari had fashioned into a drape to cover Deka's window. Marai knew she wasn't there. None of the women were there. The apartment where he had lived was now an empty storage bin, full of dusty scrap and rag. By this time every morning, he knew the courtyard below should have been bustling with women cooking and men trundling out wares for sale, but the sojourner heard only guarded whispers outside. He noticed some more dusty cloth and wool ends scattered about him, as if someone had made a clumsy attempt to hide him under some of it. The sudden sound of movement outside the curtained entry door riveted his attention. Djerah glanced inside the drapery, but before Marai called out a greeting, the young man hushed him and darted inside with a clay jar.

"What's going on?" Marai yawned and stretched a little.

"Shhh. Don't talk, and above all don't go to the rail to piss. Here. Use this." The stonecutter cautioned, jamming his finger into his lips while his big guest eased himself to his feet to use the jar. Marai glanced sidelong at his host.

"Someone looking for me out there?" he asked.

"In full force," Djerah whispered. "Peacekeepers have been through here twice daily, but we told them this room was a women's private space for the families in the courtyard and that a woman with a fever was resting here. We covered you up. Yah, be merciful, they didn't check." Djerah indicated the rags on the floor as he took the jar from Marai and turned go down the steps and behind the two-level building to empty it.

Marai watched him go, musing over the god name the young man had used. *Iah is the moon god here. Yaweh-Sin is a moon god in the Sin-Ai. Makes sense he would call his god Yah. Peacekeepers doing searches, though. Wonder if the old man cracked Wserkaf's secrets. If he did, I need to get moving as soon as I can, day or night.* He stretched and began to go through the cleansing routine he had learned from the priests when he had studied across the river. *Not much left of Hordjedtef's poison today. Just a little ache. Now, I just need food.*

While Marai waited for the young man's return, the absolute quiet of the market gnawed at him. He wanted to pull back the heavy drape over the window and peer out to see how everything below looked by day since three months had passed.

Memories of his life as a merchant returned for a sorrowful moment. Nothing, not even the splendor of the Children of Stone's vessel, had compared to waking in the morning with the women smiling and laughing around him. He recalled for just a moment the joy of snuggling Naibe, Ari, and Deka before they started their day of selling spices and date candy in Etum Addi's stand below.

That life's gone and I need to be gone from here with it. Marai knew his ability to sense thoughts was once again at full strength. The markets would be closed today out of respect for the king's death. Those who lived here would be in their homes contemplating his new journey and sharing stories of his greatness. *Hordjedtef might still not know I'm alive if he's been taken up with the death of his king and all initial rituals of passage. Wserkaf won't have told anyone a thing if he still values his life.* The sojourner nodded as Djerah crept back into the upper room with a plate of bread, a crunchy piece of dried fish and a bloated skin of some 'windwater' beer.

"How long did I sleep? Is it just the next morning?" Marai guarded the volume of his voice.

Djerah shook his head, then looked over his shoulder at the sound of the rising chatter below. Deciding it was a neighbor and not a peacekeeper, the young man whispered: "You've been asleep two nights and the day in between."

"Really?" Marai's jaw sagged. *Children knocked me out for a little more repair? That was risky. Any longer and they would have thought I died and buried me again.* He understood why he was burning with hunger and reached for the food the young man had brought.

As if the young man sensed Marai's thought, he added.

"It's good you *did* wake up. Some of my family wanted me to wake you or decide you had left us and to tell the peacekeepers that you died of a plague, but I saw you didn't stink or swell in this heat. King's men have been here *too* often these two days. I haven't seen the patrols prowl like this since your women were fetched and old Etum Addi and his family were pushed out. Are you a criminal?" he squatted before his guest and tore off some of the bread he had given the sojourner for himself.

Marai sipped as little of the beer as he could tolerate, wanting to spit but not daring to be rude.

Oh, this is nasty stuff. His women don't flavor this with honey or dates to sweeten it? Guess I was spoiled with wine and sweetwater across the river. He thought of Deka's sweet honey beer. *Even in the wilderness, years ago, Houra knew how to make a decent grain beer. She should have passed on the recipe. This is awful.*

"So what do the Peacekeepers ask? I can't think they are looking for *me*," he paused when the young man didn't answer him but ate a little more of his own portion of bread. He was about to ask again, but realized Djerah was getting increasingly uncomfortable talking to him and was worried about another pass by the patrol.

"So three days later and you're not back at work?" He tried. "How did the workers get the news of the King's death?" Marai sensed Djerah *was* sociable when he wasn't feeling threatened so he decided his best tactic for getting more information would be to get the young man to talk about his own life. At that point, as he had learned first from Naibe and ironically later from Prince Hordjedtef, he could see into someone's secrets.

"They came early to us three mornings ago, just as we began the day shift. It was right before you came here. I think we were the first to hear about it," the young man's voice paused, suddenly full of emotion.

Marai saw through Djerah's memory of the moment almost instantly.

The young stonecutter, had been riding with his team on a platform that was being hoisted by a crane. As the men moved up, Marai noticed more men on the ground gathering for an announcement made by a detachment of peacekeepers and militia.

Djerah had been adjusting the sweat rag over his eyes when he saw everyone suddenly stop work. He didn't wait for the men with him. Telling them he would see what was going on, he detached the leather harness that tethered his hoist gear to the platform and slid to the nearest level below the one where he had been stationed. After a series of maneuvers, he reached the ground and joined the growing crowd as they listened to the sad news.

Marai saw that the grief of the working men was profound. Men and women milled for a moment, some crying out as if they had lost their own father.

"When they told us, I knew work would stop for a day or two. I asked to go with the king's men to the other side of the river to help spread the news. I'm to go back in the morning. For three days, no one is to open their shops except for the sellers of grain and oil." The young man continued whispering in low tones, still uncertain if he was going to be heard by anyone passing below the big upper window. "We're to go to the water only in the morning for those needs. Just this morning they came to tell us we could also fish or trap eels. I got a good sized perch and gutted it. Raawa is pressing cheese from the goat milk she strained the other day." Djerah listened for more suspicious sounds. "Today, most of us are going to the waterfront to see the boats in some of the processions, then we will get into the reeds to find eggs." He paused, remembering something. "You didn't give me an answer, either… about you being a marked man. I don't want you staying here another moment if lots are drawn on your head. I have a family."

"Well…" Marai rubbed the gathering sweat from the back of his neck, miserably aware he had not bathed in a while. The dark draped room was close and airless and the heat of the day was starting to rise. "I'll be gone at nightfall, so don't worry. My great crime, as far as they're concerned, is that I'm alive. The high priest of Djehuti wanted me dead." He finished the bread and beer the young man had given to him, but already longed for the roast duck and exquisite creamed soups with mixed green shoots, the melons and the sweetmeats he had eaten at Wserkaf's house, and the even fancier dinners he had been served when he had studied with Count Prince Hordjedtef.

"He *thought* he'd killed me, too," Marai mused. "By now, he still may not know, but soon enough he'll see I'm not so easily beaten down." The big man belched quietly to ease the workings of the beer, hoping it wouldn't cause him to suffer too greatly later. *This beer, though...* he thought, almost amused.

"And you don't have to worry, Djerah bin Esai of Ahu. I have ways of covering my tracks that he hasn't even dreamed about." Marai yawned again, knowing the bigger part of his next adventure lay ahead and almost dreading to get started in a few hours.

"Why were you wanted dead? I don't figure you killed or robbed anyone. Your wives said you were studying the mysteries and that they would soon be invited to do so, too." Djerah took the plate from Marai and set it aside, waiting to hear the answer.

"Well, they discovered I knew far more than they wanted me to know, I suppose." Marai's face grew pensive as he remembered the weeks in tutelage that he had naively assumed were civil exchanges of ideas between men of two different lands.

"So that priest who followed you here..." Djerah asked. "You know he was the same one who came to take your wives to you and bring the message to Etum Addi that got him to move to Ra-Kedet. Was Etum Addi part of this too?" The young man, a little more agitated, got up to head toward the window.

"*That* priest was a friend, but not at first. He actually ended up saving my life. He has to protect *himself* from scrutiny, now. Etum-Addi's been gone how long?" Marai asked, then thought to himself. *If I had my ladies with me that's exactly where we'd go... Ra-Kedet. If that place was still too busy with kings' men, we might go on to Kina or Keftiu. Plenty of trades to get into there.*

"My wife told me the spice man left two days after the women did and went out of here like demons were chasing him. He put our family in charge of the business here, and said he would be our supplier on the coast. Raawa and her sisters made the deal. I was across the river working with Happy Crew." Djerah peeked out of the window where Deka used to sit, trying to see if anyone had begun to move around in the plaza. "It was rough at first but we're doing better now."

"Nothing in Kemet surprises me anymore, after what I learned on the other side." Marai mused, but in another glance at the young man, he realized Djerah, despite his slight inherited gifts in sensing the unspoken, was either lying to himself or completely ignorant of his family's situation.

Doing better, eh? When I was here, Etum Addi's business was on the wings of a hawk and flying high. We both know it's something else bothering you isn't it?

The sojourner remembered one of the merchants referring to Djerah's wife as a *kuna* – Ariennu's favorite word for a promiscuous but otherwise worthless woman who was apt to peddle her flesh for advantage. *Your son was a big one for an eight moon, unripe baby. And your wife sneaks out to meet the boy's true father? Ari knew. The women helping her in the birth knew and kept silent. Ari said your Raawa complained the noise kept her awake when she was heavy with child, but she knew the woman and her family just didn't want Djerah to know about the man.*

Marai sighed. *Even Houra knew. It's why the woman railed at you about returning to work after you came to see the baby. She needed you gone before the child's real sire arrived to see his son.* Marai knew the only one who didn't know or didn't *want* to know was Djerah.

"We worked the spice until what Etum Addi left us ran out. After the tribute was paid, no one could afford to go to Ra-Kedet for more supplies and we never received any word back of him. We just went back to doing what we've always done: making baskets and totes like our savta taught us. I'm doing better paid work on the teams across the river now – not just hauling slag with the flood workers."

Marai took another polite sip of the bitter beer while the young man continued.

"My sweet wife works so hard to make the children healthy and strong, but she claims she won't move to the worker's village. Maybe one day my work will finish there, but it seems like the harder I work, the more dangerous the tasks get and the faster my earnings go. I just don't know…" he answered and began to straighten up the apartment. He tugged forward some of the ragging in which Marai had slept and nervously began to shred it into strips.

Bothers you, thinking like this and knowing I know more about you than you've said. I'd better back it off a little, Marai thought.

He remembered Houra and other women of Ahu making rough wool into lumpy yarn and rag to make burden baskets. Taking up some of the fabric he began to shred it, but fell into the work so quickly, that Djerah paused for a moment to stare.

"How do you..." the young man started to ask.

"Oh. I learned it from your Savta Houra, same as you." Marai slowed his shredding and finger-weaving from its magical pace.

The youth shifted uncomfortably again.

Marai knew Djerah still didn't like the idea of being related to him or that his great-grandmother had known him. He shook his head, sadly. "If I didn't have to go and find my ladies… if we could even have a life without scrutiny, I'd teach you the tricks I know and your people what I know about trading, that's for sure. I taught Etum Addi everything *he* knew. He was barely scraping by as you are now, when we first came here."

"So you never even *knew* the women were brought across the river," Djerah's face grew incredulous.

Marai knew the stonecutter hadn't been listening. He'd already made time line errors in his story that were as large as the sky. At first he presented himself as the son of Marai. If Djerah and his wives had gotten to know each other, they would have presented him as the *real* Marai and not some fictitious son. He laughed inwardly. *Ari, you said I was the worst liar ever and now it's going to catch me in the throat if I keep talking to this man. I'll be run off like a mad dog.* For an instant, he paused, hoping she heard his thought, but continued because he knew better.

"No. Once they got them over there, the priests told them I was dead. I think they truly thought I was for a while. I was put in a stone box and forgotten for nearly three months." He started, but saw Djerah already shaking his head *No* in dismay. The part about him being in Child Stone induced stasis hadn't even registered.

"And then those bastards made concubines of them, didn't they? To *protect* them, I'll bet they said!" Djerah turned back from the door and sat facing Marai again. "I've seen it happen with the widows of the men on the crews," he interrupted. "There was an older man on the high scaffold where I work. His family was grown and his first wife long dead. He had just taken himself a young and pretty wife. Anyway, one day he fell off. It was quick and even quicker the way she was grabbed up by one of the chief engineers! The good looking and sturdy ones with no families get picked up right away around here and mostly they are grateful of a fine and secure life."

Marai contemplated that thought about Djerah's wife and then realized another awful thing. They expected Djerah to fall that time, not some old man. *His wife wants him dead so she can gain his pension and share it with her lover. I need to warn him, but if he doesn't suspect it already, it'll just anger him.* He started to get up and go to the window himself, but Djerah stayed him.

"Moment ago, when I looked out to take the things down, I thought I saw some walkers," the stonecutter said. "If your wives are not across the river, did that priest tell you where they are?"

"Ta-Seti," Marai thought about the room he had visualized in the well water. He remembered the reddish, green-eyed imp that had begun to attack him when he and Wserkaf used the Child Stones to find them. "– with a prince who goes there to gather their issues and to show a little of the king's muscle to the distant sepats." Marai settled again and continued twisting the ragging.

"Then I hate to say it, but you might as well forget about them!" Djerah's expression and face narrowed. "It's a hard enough trip for young men and no trip at all for a woman," he scratched his head a little, muttering to himself. "I need to shear this mop I've grown soon. It gets too hot when I'm working."

"I *know* that. Which is why I need to…" Marai began to get up, about to stride out of the apartment, peacekeepers or not, but the stonecutter interrupted.

"Let me tell you, though, I went up there twice when I was newly grown. My family thought I was good with a bow and so I thought I might become a paid warrior. Thank the gods of Kemet and my ancestors I found work on the Happy Crew during the floods. After what I went through, I know anyone who takes women up there doesn't trouble themselves with bringing them back, especially not General Maatkare if he's the one who is still in charge of that division."

"General Maatkare?" Marai knew Djerah was searching his face for a reaction and stopped the sigh of dismay about to escape his chest.

"Nasty one he is, and vain, too. A prince, of course. They *all* are. Good commander, even when he was a boy, but he will kill his own men if they get unruly or oppose his orders. Odd that he would *take* women, though. The time I went with him he used any local woman who caught his eye as a pretty hostage. If there was no trouble, he paid her family. If there was…" he gestured the slitting of a throat.

The sojourner smirked in disgust, but then trembled, feeling the image of the war bull filter through his thoughts.

"Ummm… Sorry, I…" Djerah flinched, disturbed. "Didn't mean to…"

Marai knew his angst was starting to soar out of control. Beyond the perimeter of the room where they sat, he sensed the familiar darkness circling and wanting to take hold. He'd managed to gain control of it by ramming his head and shoulders through Wserkaf's perimeter wall three days earlier. Now, every time he thought of the prince and the way he might be abusing the women, he wanted to rush off into the day to find and kill him even if he was completely unprepared and unarmed. He knew he might go along the river on *this* side, creeping between buildings…

"You know the way to Ta-Seti? Is it just straight up the river? Maybe you can tell me the names of the sepats and the walking time between each," he asked, looking around almost helplessly.

Djerah paused. Marai knew the young man was anticipating the next question and already deciding on his answer to it.

"This is the journey of a madman. There'll be either thief, or king's henchmen, or militia every step of the way. You might think it's just up the river on one side or the other, but it's not that easy. There are hills and rock and boiling waters… snakes… stinging things, sickness, and villages not likely to comfort only one man making his way."

Knew that. Know you can't take me. What other choice is there but to use what's in here? And I'm not too sure that it wouldn't fail after what's already been done to me. My ladies have Child Stones. They should have been strong enough to get away from such a beast. Something else is going on. He rubbed the Child Stone under the skin of his forehead, feeling it purr as if he had given it a lover's caress. He wanted to consult the eight stones Wserkaf had returned to him, but knew he didn't dare do that in this young man's presence.

In the quiet moments we have heard your cry
We would not desert you, Man of Ai

We are always here
Within soul
Within skin.
In the quicken'd night
Bear us to our destiny
Put on the cloak of legend
Face the stirring of the darkest wind
In the opening of the sky
We rise

Gentle voices of children filled him as they often did in his moments of doubt. It had been a very long time since he'd heard a full prophetic verse from them. The sojourner knew Djerah had at least sensed *something* of the Children's words in his own soul. He even knew his Child Stone had partially emerged. The big man paused and crept to the drape in the window despite the younger man's resistance. He didn't want Djerah to see it.

Yeah. Thanks for speaking. I just wish you would make a verse about me being your sacrificial lamb? Am I? And by the way, why have you not protected my ladies?

In adversity they grow
As your metal of earth
Becomes true in flame.

So it'll be another game of senet… only the stones are in our heads and the board we move around on is the black and red earth. Hmph. Sometimes I wish… Marai thought of how his life would have been for a moment. *I would have come to Ineb Hedj with Sheb, Houra and the rest of Ahu's clan. We would have found work. I don't think we would have struggled as much as they did, unless the fever that came through took me too. I was pretty tough then… even before the Child Stone. Perhaps I would* have re-married and sired a few children before I died. I'd surely be dead by now, though.

"Did you hear something out there?" Marai noticed a befuddled look on Djerah's face. The young man had been staring at him, but dropped his gaze.

"A mark was on your forehead a minute ago. Now it's gone."

Oh, he hears the Children in his thoughts, alright. Houra had the skill and so did I. We used to talk to each other without words when she was a child. Marai's hand went to his brow. The stone was flat again. *It's a gift from our ancestors,* he stared at the stonecutter again and covered with a quick lie. *All the magic I have and I can't even tell a decent lie to save myself,* he smirked. *Ari was right about that.*

"I suppose you imagined it, then." *Well here's the answer. But if I cast a spell to make him go with me… he's trouble. I can't pay him, or even promise his family he'd come home.* He thought of Raawa and her sisters and their ultimate plan to separate from him. Then again, maybe taking him away from all of this might be merciful.

For a moment, Marai saw into Djerah's memory, visualizing him barely out of boyhood, marching with troops through stinging grasses, sitting on dismal barges and waiting for orders.

As if he already knew what Marai was thinking, Djerah drew back in a wide-eyed, horrified gasp.

"Did you lose your sense while you slept?" The young man blurted but, thinking someone might hear him outside, he quickly whispered. "I told you I can't go with you, not if you were my best beloved… which you're not! We're in *enough* trouble as it is meeting our tribute obligation, and besides, you're *not* coming back if you go. *None* of you will. If that prince so much as *thinks* you're about to take something he wants away from him, you're *done* in the land of the living. Then, he'll likely kill the women just because he *can*. Your coming up there to him will only make his life *interesting*. I'm staying here. The King's dead and soon there's going to be twice the work getting his temple finished. Yah dropped the work in my lap. It's madness to walk away while the gods are still smiling on me," his whisper grew more and more urgent.

"Then I'll just wait until dark again and be off," Marai almost wanted to grab him and explain to him that his dear wife was not faithful to his bed and that her family had likely decided on her other man as a better choice. The more he thought about the man, Marai visualized a tall but beefier fellow who was quite likely a peacekeeper moving up in the ranks. It *was* a much more profitable choice. Even though Djerah was gainfully employed, the separation while he worked across the river had already taken its toll.

Djerah quieted, having said his piece, then went to the draped doorway. When he looked back in, he added: "I'll see if I can find some bread and fish for you to take by dark. You just can't stay *here*. That's all I have to say."

"I know that," Marai backed away from the window and the door then sat heavily in the fabric scraps. He wasn't that tired. If his situation had been any different, he would have gathered the shaggy brown servant's cloak Wserkaf had given him, the eight stones, and a small basket of bread and followed Djerah down the steps of his old apartment, eager to be on his way to Ta-Seti by himself. *Boy talks too much anyway now that I got him started. At least he hasn't learned too much of me,* the sojourner mused, *or has he?*

Djerah didn't really *want* to form a bond with the sojourner. He'd allowed the man to hide in his storage area for two days, but every time he visited, thought about, or spoke to the big man something forced them into a clumsy companionship. When they met by accident that first day three passes of the moon ago, the big man said he was as the *son* of Marai Who Vanished. That legend had come from the wilderness with his family and had been discarded by everyone except his Savta who clung to it as much as she gave homage to the *malak*, or messengers of the god Sin.

Even if it's true, which I'm not sure of... the stone-burnisher thought, *I've already given him more than I owe him. Even Savta agreed his name had been banned from our lips, because he betrayed us in the hour of our greatest need.*

The young man chuckled as he trotted down the steps to his lower apartment. He felt oddly compelled to look back up at the draped doorway. *I'm sure feeling these spells he's casting... he's getting me to* care.

OPENER OF THE SKY

Djerah entered his low apartment and saw his family had left. He shook his head and came back out, realizing most of the people in his neighborhood had been led by the peacekeepers down to the water's edge to see what they could of the solemn procession across the water.

Mourning. I'm sad the king's dead. He wasn't bad except for being so drunk much of his last years. That's nothing. This man, Marai's own father, was mourning the death of his young bride for fifteen years and waiting on the old land's Asherin-Ahna to scoop him up... now that's some grief. Savta just wanted all of us to know the story of Marai, who had walked with his goddess Ashera one star-filled night when the light and singing rocked her dreams. Walked with a god, Djerah understood. *It's just a pretty way of saying a person vanished without a trace. This man said he was the vanished man's son. No. True or not, I owe him nothing more.* For a moment he thought of joining his family at the edge of the water to look at some of the procession across the water, but knew only distant glitters would be seen.

He doesn't look that much like us. Tall and big is all; half-giant. Djerah shook his head, trying to rid himself of thinking about his guest. *Something's not right though. How would he know to find my Savta if he never knew her as a boy? Why would she weep and call him her brother? Madness of age? Sun blindness, or something else? The women who had lived with him never said he was a son of anyone in particular – just plain Marai.*

His thoughts continued swarming about the big sojourner who rested up the stairs. *His eyes, though. He's using heka for sure. They're black like nearly everyone's eyes but the silver light over them makes them look ... No, he's not Marai's son... no such. He has to be the real Marai who Vanished... but that's impossible unless I'm talking to a ghost or one who himself is malak.* The stonecutter shook his head violently, not wanting any part of the foolishness. He knew the man was sending him these thoughts and he knew he had to put a stop to it.

When he scampered back up the steps and parted the drape, he saw Marai open his eyes, then take a deep breath to wake himself.

At that instant, a gentle whisper formed in Djerah's thoughts. It was something his Savta Oora used to tell him about the dreams of the life that never came to be. *She* had been Marai's wife in that fantasy, sister or not.

Twelve children...

Seven boys to grow strong and tall…
Nation builders all.
Daughters five to charm any man alive
That is another reality in a world not to be.

A lie. There was never anything between them. The legend was that Marai went mad mourning a dead woman, ran off into the wilderness and filled the bellies of wild dogs the very night my family needed him. Only my savta believed this other thing. I won't put up with this.

Djerah held up one finger, as if he was about to scold Marai, but stopped, finger in midair, realizing he had heard spirit voices in his soul.

"Hear something?" Marai almost mocked, then sat.

"I don't get you," Djerah moved backward almost to the doorway. "My gut tells me this is a fine trap you're setting for me and my family, getting my confidence and telling me stories, but you have no reason to whether you're our blood or not. We're too poor to be worth it for you. We have *nothing*. Still, you go on and on as if we were closest friends, spooking me with these funny little whisperings. They…" Djerah realized he'd said too much and grew silent.

Voices in Crystal
Children of Stone
Whispering in the Wind

The young man shivered suddenly in alarm. "I *said*, don't you use your heka on me." He glanced behind himself so that he didn't slip on the outer landing above the brick stair.

"Djerah, I don't have the time *or* the interest in *any* of what you're worried about." Marai rose to his feet and stretched, but the ceiling, as usual, was too low. He really wanted to tell the young man about the unrest brewing in his household, but decided it would be too cruel.

"Houra knew you would be able to hear wind voices. She knew you had dreams too."

"Maybe she did," Djerah grumbled. "Maybe I'm dreaming this whole knowing of you." He paused realizing Marai had just mentioned something else he shouldn't know a thing about. "I still think you've cast some kind of spell on me. Ever since you showed up at the Poors Market, I've had dreams," his voice trailed. "I thought I was just grieving over my savta's death. I thought her spirit might have been haunting my nights, too. I was about to gather some baskets to trade and go to the priests to get cleansed, but then the dreams stopped right after you and the women left. There was nothing. Then again, the exact night you came to the well, I dreamt about the *malak* all over again!" The young man continued, taking the first sorted bundles from Marai. "That's what grandfather Tisehe and Savta Oora called them. They're messengers. They're said to serve *He* on the mountain far away, whose name it is forbidden for our people to speak."

Marai listened more intently. A trembling sensation rushed through his chest just under the skin over his heart when Djerah said the word for messengers. *Malak. Houra and most of my people might have thought that. I thought the Children of Stone were the Goddess when I first heard and saw them.*

Fire and Air
In a world away
Become earth and water
Creating
Children of Stone

"Stop that!" Djerah snapped, turning again. This time Marai knew the young man was about to flee from the upper room.

"Trust me. I didn't send that verse to you. I *did* hear it, though." The sojourner knew his people often felt spirits on the heat rising from the barren earth and the whispering in the wind as they traveled. This was the way the Children of Stone, spoke the same verse to him long ago when he stood trembling and naked in their white, cloud-like room buried under the sand. *The messengers… the 'hand' of Yaweh-Sin,* he mused, *could it be? If they have come into Djerah's heart, perhaps that was why my Houra clung so desperately to her life – to hold my family in her heart until I could somehow find her; the same way I searched for the heir of Djedi and found Wserkaf. I found my Houra's heir; Children of the ones touched by the Children?* he bowed his head.

"Just sit down," he looked at the young stonecutter. "This will be hard for you to hear. You'll hear it once and then I'll go. The back and forth talk stops. The whispering under the voice stops."

The young man entered the room the rest of the way, irritated, but sat on a lump of scrap material near the big man.

Marai spoke again.

"You think Houra and her son Tisehe were just old people talking in the madness of age, but even though it scared you, you know it made you feel special… like the gods and goddesses meant for you to be so much more than the half-starved peasants your family had become." He handed another bundle of rag to the young man and continued shredding a new batch.

"So, you went into the kings' army and worked the construction crews, looking for a way to *be* that much more didn't you? Fortune was always just one step away, wasn't it?" Marai knew why Djerah avoided his eyes. The stonecutter was seeing the image of his destiny reflected in them. His stone had emerged a little, but this time he didn't care if the young man saw it.

"You know what I offer you. I'll only waste more time in talking."

A distant but gentle hum, like a thousand distant wings, softer and more of a whisper than the whine of a plague of locusts had begun to move through both of the men.

Djerah rubbed the back of his neck and squeezed his eyes shut, then rose and strode to the back of the room past Marai, who smiled because he knew exactly what the young man was feeling. The young stonecutter found a large basket of clothing which had been washed and dug a veiled cap out of it before returning to the door. Squashing it down on his head, he looked as if he was trying to ignore the sensation.

Although no words came to him, Marai knew the young man suddenly felt the mad desire to go, unquestioningly, with him all the way to Ta-Seti no matter how insane or foolish it seemed. It was the same feeling he, himself had felt on a starry night long ago.

There is something here...

Marai heard Houra's voice but knew it was speaking in Djerah's thoughts. It sounded younger and gentler than the young man remembered it, even as a baby.

Be well my young heart...
Be strong where I could not.
You will become as the eagle
You will command the sun on silver wings.
This is but the first step into the light

Djerah went back to the door and saw his family moving up the slight rise from the distant waterfront. They were hauling a big sack of grain they had taken in trade while they had watched some of the procession. After a pause, he trotted down the steps and greeted his wife with baby Sheb strapped to her breast. He nuzzled her, but noticed her tired look.

"Raawa?" he questioned, puzzled by her fatigue. "You ill?"

"Why didn't you come down? We waited for you and then there was this man with grain at the water's edge. Nan ran to get a basket so we could get it. We had no flour left."

Djerah stepped back. He saw his wife's two sisters getting the grindstones out of the lower dwelling to begin making some meal. He followed her and pulled her arm a little.

"Sweet Melon…" he called affectionately. "It was the big fellow who's been upstairs. We were talking. I forgot."

"We had no grain. It's not too bad. Nan got a basket, I said. When you work over there all the time, it's easy to forget what we need."

His shoulders slumped.

"You could come live there with me over there; your sisters too. They could find new husbands. I told you."

She silently shook her head. Djerah knew he'd made her sad. It was noisy there. The housing was small and made of thrown together brick. Everything tasted like lime dust from the building. The grit wore teeth away until one got a fever from rot that came into them. Her sisters liked it in Little Kina-Ahna. That was the other thing.

"The man Marai is leaving tonight. When he's gone and the baby sleeps, I wish to meet you upstairs. I have to go back to work in the morning." He nuzzled again and stared into her quiet black eyes. The corner of her downturned mouth twitched a little.

"Sure," her voice answered. "When he goes and baby sleeps."

OPENER OF THE SKY

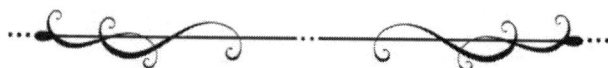

Chapter 8: The Basket

Marai crept out of what had once been his old apartment in Little Kina-Ahna as soon as he noticed Djerah's relatives had gone inside for the evening. The sojourner decided to go up to the roof to meditate and to focus on his next steps, so he wouldn't feel as scattered and upset about the coming journey. The nights were getting chilly enough for people to sleep inside again. There was even a chance he'd be alone.

He bundled his shabby brown travel cloak around himself and made his way to the roof the instant the sun dipped beneath the horizon. The last person milling below had just gone inside. No one else came up, so he went to the far side and lay down under his cloak.

Don't see me, he whispered into the air. He wanted to go to his wives one more time, but the moment he lay down he slept solidly again. Sometime later he woke with a disappointed grunt. The slightly wider sliver of the moon had risen.

Marai leapt up, gathered his belongings and started for the edge of the still-empty roof. The slot where the ladder rested was blocked by a bundle of something. When inspected it, he discovered flatbread stuffed with pitted olives and pulled roast duck. With the bread was a small jar of sweet beer.

Wserkaf. Here? While I slept?

Marai peered over the side as he sat and quickly ate. It was late enough for him to start out on his journey, but something in his heart still wanted him to pass close enough to the lower apartment for Djerah to notice he was going and perhaps come out with a changed heart. He didn't want to say goodbye because he knew he'd be tempted to send a last thought to the young man.

He's confused enough, and he's a grown man. It's his wife and family. Then, he laughed a little. *Sweet goddess in my arms! I've become Sheb and Houra of years ago trying to tease me out of my cave to come to Kemet. I'm teasing their great-grandson out of a promising career as well as a dubious marriage...* Marai thought to himself, shaking his silvery head.

He planned to walk slowly past the apartment, then send a thought to him as a final request. After that, he would move on, semi-hidden, toward the area of the

Poors Market. He would be cloaked in secrecy and shadow to keep from being seen and possibly challenged. Dotting his lips and smoothing the moisture on his chin into his beard, he bagged the beer jar and descended the steps.

Oh well, he sent a final thought. *Would have been good to have a traveling companion from the old land, but you never lived there, anyway. You know the path the army takes, but you don't track. You march where you're told to march. You don't think quickly; you follow orders out of fear.*

Marai knew he needed to move on. As he stood near the well he stared across the great river. He contemplated the journey that lay ahead for him, but noticed torches had been lit so that every single pathway and building blazed forth with lamplight.

It was just as the departed king would have wished. Great fixtures that supported and mirrored light like beacons had been erected around the gold capped tops of each of the three kings Eternal Houses. Up and down the river, other king's monuments and eternal houses blazed forth into the night sky.

You were a great king, Menkaure, Marai smiled wistfully, *but in the end you were not above the despair of a broken heart or a child's terror of the dark. Those things became your own personal darkness and paved the way for your doom. I wish we had met. Now I will know your soul only in the way sweet Naibe and Ariennu touched it and gave it some rest. I will see them soon. Perhaps in another time and world...*

Men with torches were landing in small reed boats.

Peacekeepers, damn! Marai crouched quickly behind a closed market booth, listening to what they said. *If they mention my name, this is going to be a long night.*

As he listened, he didn't hear his name. Instead, men went building to building, rapping on door frames. When someone opened a door, one of the men began to recite an announcement:

"In accordance with His sacred wishes; every lamp shall be lit at night and burn until the light of day, so that his ka will know he is so beloved and his passing into glory, a joy, yet still filled with our tears. Hail his bright spirit. We weep as his lost children. He is our father."

The heralds bowed to each household. Once they had made certain the family had enough oil, they would move to the next building.

Gradually, the lamps in all of the dwellings were lit. Unable to resist, Marai went back to the apartment steps, thinking it would indeed be a glorious sight if he went up to the roof again to see all of the lights; to see Ineb Hedj greeting Kemet's beloved king like the "so below" of all of the stars in the night sky. He wanted to sing again, the way he had always sung to his goddess in his cave at home in the distant foothills of the Mountain of Sin.

He sang on that very roof sometimes, before he went to the priests, but he knew that even if he sang a song praising Menkaure tonight, it would put everyone in this part of the village who had sworn they hadn't seen him in danger. He needed to be silent and make his departure in the opposite direction. As he quickened his step and passed the door of the lower apartment he noticed Djerah's door was open.

Raawa stood in it examining a large lidded basket. She looked up and noticed Marai, then gasped. "You still here? Djee said you were gone," her face became anxious.

Djerah emerged and noticed Marai.

"So, did *you* see her?" The young man asked him. "We told her you had gone, but she said she thought you might be near, maybe walking around. I see now..." he started but the sojourner frowned.

"Who?" Marai came closer, but glanced backward over his shoulder searching the plaza area. *Her?* he asked himself.

"An old woman came with this... said it was for one calling himself Marai." Nan came forward with the baby, who had begun to fuss.

Raawa took the child and lobbed one of her swollen breasts into his mouth.

"I told her we knew no one by this name, like Djee told us to do, but she said she understood why we would say it and asked we give it to you when we saw you." Djerah's wife began to lift the lid with her free hand, but he stayed the woman's hand, suspecting possible treachery. "She left it anyway..." Raawa continued, frowning at her young husband, her voice sounding tired and nasal.

"How long ago did this happen?" Marai asked, wondering why Wserkaf would have hired a woman to lug such a basket up the rise and post it in the doorway.

"She was here a moment ago. We thought you had left and my husband and I were seeing to the upper storeroom. Nan saw her come."

Marai felt the flash of male sexual pride cross Djerah's face and stared out of the corner of one eye at the young couple. The woman's cryptic half-smile confirmed his imagined thought. *Congratulations and good health, then,* he sent back the thought, but covered the one that followed: *Enjoy it while it lasts.*

Djerah beckoned Marai to come in for a moment. While the big man ducked under the lintel, the stonecutter lifted the basket, with a surprised grunt. It was tall enough to stand halfway his thigh with the lid on and it was heavy. He brought it indoors and Tissa, the younger widowed sister kicked the woven rush door closed so no passers-by could see what had been left for them.

Raawa put a lamp in the lower window, to respect the deceased king as the messengers had ordered, and returned to the basket at hand. The other children edged closer to see as Djerah lifted the lid.

Inside the basket was a large supply of traveling gear: folded wool and linen clothing, a large Sanghir style fringed cloak, some gold pieces to trade, as well as some good quality glass and ceramic beads and even some semi-precious stones in little leather bags. Djerah's relatives pulled out wrought bronze jewelry, large leather sandals with many thongs that went over the foot and tied at the side of the ankle in a style common to sojourners from the east. Four small tied rolls of papyrus with the shorthand version of Kemet writing and some kind of encrypted scribble that were rolled up under the clothing emerged as Raawa pawed deeper into the basket.

"Watch out… A spell…" Djerah warned as Marai picked up the scroll.

Wserkaf appearing as an old woman? Has to be… but how he had the time to break free… Marai sensed Djerah thinking something even more sinister.

"No, no spell," he assured the young man, but asked. "You read?"

"No, just counting marks," Djerah scratched his shaggy head. "The old woman said they were for you, didn't she, Nan?" he asked Raawa's wiry older sister.

"Mmm… Hmmm" a disinterested feminine voice rose from the back of the tight little room.

"Wserkaf…" Marai breathed sadly, remembering the man's ability to come and go in complete stealth when he served as Hordjedtef's eyes. Disguising himself as an old woman wouldn't have been too out of the ordinary: a ragged cloak drawn over his head, halting step, breathy but higher voice, and the power of illusion.

"By Ashera, I miss that man already, *and* he wrote it in our script. He's already taught himself the code." Marai sighed, then recited the note the priest had artfully scrawled:

> *"Go swiftly, with great wings*
> *Look ever forward, never back*
> *May all of the gods*
> *Bring you ever closer*
> *To wisdom that is Djehuti*
> *To tranquility and truth of heart that is Ma-at*
> *The great Dwty realizes the Sun*
> *After the dance in the dark storms*
> *So say I, User-Ka-ef Irimaet*
> *No more One of Five*
> *But one with you"*

Marai's hands trembled and his eyes grew moist because he knew Wserkaf wanted to be with him, taking up arms and magic tools in his fight to defeat Prince Maatkare and rescue the women if need be. Too much time had already been wasted trying to get Djerah to come with him. He studied the curious verse, again and again. Caressing the symbols gently, he turned with eyes closed, and breathed out.

> *Be with my heart along the way then…*
> *If you cannot walk with me.*

He whispered on the wind. Marai eagerly opened the second scroll and discovered a document bearing a note that it was to be read aloud to Djerah.

"Granted unto the near relations of the house of MRai, goods and pension, so that the head of this household one DjRa may have no obligation under law until the formal ascension of His Majesty King Shepseskaf has been established at the birth of the coming year. This is being granted so that said head of household will be free to guide on an upcoming journey in my absence for the purpose of obtaining in the name of Great Djehuti the stolen Ho-Ra and keys designated for the chambers at Per-A-At."

The note was followed by the formal royal cartouche with the name of Shepseskaf and beside it the simpler un-cartouched name of Wserkaf as a priest of Ra.

"Oh. What under the great stars is going on?" Djerah gasped, backing away from Marai and the basket in astonishment. "Those names. Shepseskaf is the new king? What does…" he started.

"It means you don't have to pay tribute *or* do work on the Eternal House and temples; that you can go with me after all and assist me in the journey as a representative of His Majesty." Marai paused to read Djerah's expression, then quipped: "might not be smart to say no."

"I'm being pressed into service? Seriously? I have a family." the young man took a step back into the house, flapping his arms and shaking his head in dismay. "Just like they did to Etum Addi – moving people around like they own us."

The third scroll showed a more elegantly crafted map, a list of appropriate sepats for aid, and the names of the rulers of each. At the end of the journey map Marai read the name Mtoto Metauthetep Akaru Sef, then looked at Djerah, who stared again, open-mouthed, unable to understand how such events had taken place. The young man's thoughts were too easy to read at that moment.

Savta told me this before she died. No ordinary man will come out of the sons of Ahu, Djerah thought, *and this man can just know royalty and priests intimately enough to receive a personal edict from King Shepseskaf. Raawa and her sisters and all of our children will be cared for if I go with this sojourner to Ta-Seti and help him get something?*

"With an army?" the young man asked, knowing if anything or anyone challenged the seat of power over the Two Lands, any number of princes could quickly shake up a militia of peasant irregulars and old men. "Why are they bothering with me? Keys for what?"

"No Army for now," Marai had started to pace anxiously. "I suspect some may join us later, though. I'm sorry, Djerah," he looked down at the young man, dismayed. "I've told you what it is. Come or don't. I have to leave *now*, though. I'll be at the well where you found me the other night for a few moments, clearing my thoughts. I'll just take the clothes and scrolls off the top. The rest you can all keep. I won't need them where I'm going," he seized the items, bundled them, and trudged to the courtyard well in the deepening dark.

"The peacekeepers…" Djerah's voice trailed in caution.

"Don't care…" Marai called back over his shoulder.

Djerah regarded the big sojourners back as he left. After he looked through the contents of the basket, he knew very little, other than his own reluctance, was going to keep him from stepping onto the path and heading out of town. Nothing of this made any sense to the young stone-burnisher, yet the goods were there, handily delivered in the burden basket by a mysterious old woman who had just as quickly gone out of sight as she had arrived.

Isn't this man going to Ta-Seti to get his wives back? No mention of that. The first scroll speaks of him like a god, too. He watched Raawa take out the gold and the faience beads, the chunks of turquoise and malachite, biting some of them to test them. His children had crowded close and were oohing and aahing as each new item emerged.

Marai sat at the well and stared into the still, black water one more time. He had been badly shaken by the arrival of the basket and the scrolls and didn't want the family to see how greatly it had affected him. Somehow, Wserkaf had managed to creep away from the funerary proceedings after getting the needed writs from the king and orders to Djerah's team foreman, pack the basket, garb himself as an old woman, cross the river, and then make it back to the temples, all without alerting Hordjedtef.

This is wrong, Marai bowed his head and reached into the sack of Child Stones fastened at his waist. *He can't have that much magic to him. Not a few days ago he was scared he wouldn't have time to get across the river, and now this? He must have called in favors from all of his gods. Did the king sign it, or did Wse forge the cartouche unbeknownst to the rising king?*

With his thoughts swimming in questions rather than answers, Marai removed his hand from the sack and opened the final scroll. One of the residents of the court had placed a lamp on the edge of the well for the night. He held the scroll closer to the light and made out a faint, double-coded, puzzle message of some kind.

The symbol of the Eye of God had been drawn along one edge of the roll. Marai rolled it back up again to find the reversed symbol for truth on the other side of the scroll. When the two eyes faced each other, a third image of an eight-pointed star, the symbol formed by the Child Stones blazed forth. Instinctively, more because it was the symbol of his Lady god too, Marai tapped the roll to his brow.

Almost immediately he felt Wserkaf's whisper-voice on the wind, just beneath his brow.

You were right, friend,
I am too stunned by the tragedy to act on it
You must do our work
In a far country
And I will attend here
Go quickly, Dear One
Go with the light of Maat.

The sojourner saw a moment from dawn of the first full day after the king had died. In the quiet, well-guarded *ibu* or "Pure Place" which was lit only by flickering lamps, Marai saw the thick billowing incense as the priests chanted and solemnly removed the king's organs. He re-lived the priests' looks of silent distress at how bad, cold, and choked with evil fluids his kind and noble heart had appeared. It should have been glowing and beautiful with the light of Ra. They remarked at how swollen and yellow the liver looked, then praised him for how well and valiant he must have been to battle this grave illness. *Despair choked his heart, eased by our care. It was not wine sickness*, they decided.

Then what caused the fevers? Marai saw Wserkaf step forward to pose the question. He saw the priests weeping openly at the suggestion. *The curse*, they reminded him. *It wore him down to remain so strong for his people. Do you not see that it is just as the Great One of Five stated? Can you not verify it?* Marai watched the men carefully wrap his organs in finest linen and set them in plain topped jars with characters painted on them.

You knew the truth, then didn't you? Marai reflected, sensing Wserkaf's agreement from the shadows.

Ay… no odor of wine rose from his holy ha when it was opened.

Though his training has been cursory at best, Marai recalled being taught that if wine sickness killed a man, the stench of rotting wine sugars about his corpse was nauseating. The cause was something else; something much more sinister.

Marai sensed his vision changing. He saw the Inspector sitting alone in his work room putting his signature on the document he would pass to the scribes. Whatever rage he felt over the death of the king was hammered into disciplined civility. All of his writing was coded. By instinct, the sojourner knew to trace the characters with his forefinger. When he did, he heard the translation of the code spinning through his thoughts:

"He has passed to the above."
He poisoned Our Father
"He has left us orphans

His beloved uncle Hordjedtef out of Khufu"

as he has been doing for years

"Regarded his suffering and eased it

When his moment came to embrace the stars"

He finally won.

"His end was brought by exhaustion and a broken heart"

My master knew how to pluck the strings

"In combatting the curse over which he labored to defeat.

He has finally accomplished all"

of Our Father's noble heart

"His name will live forever."

Over his worries and sadness

"Now he ascends in radiance and the new sun is born"

Be wary my Brother out of Menkaure

Cleanse your house of this elder one and his heir

"To reign anew in the bright house.

He makes all risen things sing praises.

Praise him."

A risen one and his own heir attend the will of the gods and wait your mark

Masterful... Marai thought. *I pray the Great One doesn't know what you did or that the risen one is me until you and the king are safe. I still don't see how you got through all of the time.* He stretched, cracking his shoulder and neck once and wondering when he would find a soft bed again. Marai was just about to begin a walk to the river when a squabble behind him announced a commotion in Djerah's apartment.

"I won't. I don't care. My place is here with you."

Protest answered.

"Raawa, you *know* I love you. Don't *say* that. I'd do anything to keep our family safe."

Low voiced complaining answered the young man's pleas.

"I know... I know..."

Astonishment.

"Of course it's a miracle, I just..."

Encouragement.

"I know. I miss you already, Sweet Melon. I'll be safe. I'll come back with a title to prove it to you. We won't ever have to be apart again."

Farewells ended with the shutting of a door and almost shy footsteps advancing.

"Heka," the young man mumbled. "I don't know *how* you did it, but your spell worked. I hope you're happy." the young man grumbled mightily as he joined Marai at the well.

Marai frowned, quizzing. The young man had a back pack and a walking stick.

"Did what?"

"Got that writ from the king. It's just like the one they got for Etum Addi that ordered him to go to the coast. They've pressed me in to guiding you on the military road to Ta-Seti and back. By morning we'll rest," he sat at the well heavily, staring at his feet once then noticing the door to his apartment had closed.

Marai thought of the morning when he had crossed the river to study with the priests three months earlier. Ariennu had waited at the top step of the door and had watched him go. The image of her standing there, her dark but red-kissed curls blazing like fire in the rising sunlight, had given him so much of the hope he needed when he lay entombed. *How different this is,* he thought, *Djerah's wife just proved she has a lot less affection for him. Maybe she told him she couldn't bear to see him walking away. Or maybe she didn't want him to see her smile.*

"Your wife will be protected? Her sisters too?" Marai asked, even though his second thought was that of the women dancing for joy behind the closed door.

"The gifts the old woman brought convinced her there would be much more for our family than if I stayed here and drew a wage," he shook his shaggy head. "She gave me a big hug and kiss and told me to be safe; said she'd be making offerings for my safe return. Between king and wife pushing me, I just knew I couldn't stay." The young man looked up. At that moment, the sojourner saw something dark flit over Djerah's face.

He knows, Marai looked down, chagrinned. *Dammit, he does know and he was trying to stay here to set things right. He just doesn't know it's already too late. None of those women wanted anything about him as soon as a better option showed up. Cold fish they are. Up to me to make it smooth once he starts to let the truth come forth in his heart… that there's no one, not even his children, here for his return.*

"Well," Djerah shrugged. "You rested enough? I napped after…" the young man implied a post-sex doze.

"I suppose, but there are some things I'll have to show you pretty soon. I can make this go journey faster. If you watch carefully, maybe you'll learn it too."

Houra's earlier words sounded once more and then faded on the early evening breeze.

> *Be well my young heart…*
> *Be strong where I could not.*
> *You will become as the eagle*
> *You will command the sun on silver wings.*
> *This is but the first step into the light*

Chapter 9: One East, One West, One More

"Grandfather," the tall young man in the long red shendyt greeted the small entourage that had just arrived at the gate of the palace area.

"You're here much earlier than I expected. The mothers came yesterday, but said only you had sent them early and would come later. Now here you are? What's happened? Have you seen another sign?" he looked up at the sedan in which his elder sat, shielding his eyes from the hot morning sun. He tagged beside it as the bearers brought it inside the gates.

"Fasten those," the old man in the veiled chair commanded a guard "and post your best men in the tower with bow and spear." He gestured for the bearers to lower him. As soon as they did, he stood and stepped toward the tall dark man, embracing him.

"Good to see you again, Aped. Your journey home this time was a good one?" the elder greeted his grandson warmly, his tone of caution suddenly gone.

"Good enough, but I can tell you something's not right down in the White Wall and it's wanting to follow me up the river with Inspector Wserkaf. When he journeyed to take over for me in his most recent duty, he asked me to stay extra days while he cleansed himself before starting his worship. He's never done that; never *had* to do that since I've been in training." The younger man guided his grandfather into his home, where servants bowed and began to attend to them both at once.

"It isn't right. He's done something against the code, but I sense it's something that was needed. He was still shaking and sorrowful when he arrived; given to weeping like a girl. He's not sure of himself anymore."

The old one shrugged, as if he hadn't listened. "Your mothers are settled, then? Their maids too?"

"Yes Akaru. They are in the back, discussing babies with my two goddesses." Aped, the young man urged his grandfather to a soft cushioned place by the common pool.

When his elder was settled and a servant had bought refreshment, Aped asked again: "Have you had a new vision, Akaru?"

"Vision?" the elder, called Akaru, rocked forward and slapped his crossed knee with a laugh. His earrings, four in each pale-skinned ear, jingled. "When do I *not* have a vision? Not since the Lady Mafdet healed me of the sting and opened my soul to the world of the spirit! And lately what I see has been powerful. I think I may be coming to my end here!" he chuckled.

"Grandfather," Aped sighed. "I'm sure your work is not done; not yet or I would know it myself. Are the signs in the sky right for *his* return?" the younger man worried.

Aped was always glad to host his grandfather during the opening of the raw season. That the old man sent his wives and their maids as well as many of the prettier women from Qustul was different this year. He was supposedly protecting them from General Maatkare and his troops who were little better than invading hordes. They demanded tribute and picked out the women they wanted. Sending them away protected them from a man who had little respect for the sepats or their rulers.

"The signs are right. What can I say to that? The time is coming for sure and young Prince Maatkare Raemkai is here, on top of it, ready to do his inspections and partake of his annual hunt." The elder Akaru became a little more agitated in telling. "He arrived two nights ago, then came this morning to discuss the tribute right to enjoy himself here as he usually does. Then, he asked to have his stars read. That's when I saw the signs and told him the sky would open soon and he should turn back unless he wished to die most mortally with his heart tossed to Ammit when the Sutek returns." His earrings jingled again and the elder's tawny-silver twists of hair flipped out merrily.

"And did he heed you?" Aped asked, knowing the answer but wanting to hear it spoken aloud.

"Does he *ever* hear anything that does not suit his every desire?" the elder laughed. "Of course not! He viewed it as a threat and then snapped at me that he had brought his own women this time. He expected me to have already smoothed his expedition with both Sutek *and* Nit."

"I should take it as flattery that he believes I can clap my hands and get gods and goddesses to jump. He went away mad and said he would return. I smelled a trap, dear Aped. That's why we'll post guards here for a few nights until he goes deeper into the brushland and has unknotted his tail with his women and drunk up the beer I've had delivered. I also sent him two guards for his time here," his gaze lowered for a moment.

"Guards?" the younger man couldn't contain his shock "The Wawati? The charmed ones? Why?"

"I saw other things," the elder reached for a bit of bread a servant had just brought out and dredged it in the sauce.

"What?" Aped asked.

"That much would be revealed which has been hidden for many years and that a day was coming when the mighty and the proud would be humbled. I saw change in the frame of things and in our futures… in which our great wisdoms would be hidden and forgotten by the world of learned men; the way things are, lost and eventually covered in deep water when men came to control our dark mother. This is why I said to you, 'It's time'." The elder munched the crust of bread. "I do not need to have a vision or watch the stars, especially when I pair the things I see with the tales you brought me last year." His eyes twinkled.

Aped paused, realizing that the many events in his life were suddenly moving together. "The sojourners in the marketplace?" he asked. "I had reported them and taken their incense and sweets to the Great One that day. It was a test of observations; to discover things not usually seen and report back – part of being the eyes of the Djehut."

"And you saw…" Akaru smiled and urged his grandson to continue.

"A nearly giant man with hair like the moon in full who was looking for old Djedi, but didn't know he had died some fifty years earlier. One of the women with him spirit danced with me in the manner of the ancestors. I left to report it to my teacher, but felt I somehow had seen her in my own visions. I'm sure she was of Ta-Seti. It was odd for her to be among ones who have so little, because she was so elegant… like one who should have been a goddess, but lost her way." Aped watched the man's expression mist in memory of something.

"Our mothers keep the wisdom alive. For that we protect them. It is the way it *has* been and will be. Anything departing from it, corrupts. Any goddess prideful of it, loses her place and invites a conqueror." Akaru inclined his pale head to one side as if he was dreaming or accepting another vision. "What do you remember of the legends of me? Of why I am even here in this world? Tell me what you know. It's a fine story."

"That you came from the stars, some say, not of made Earth or of MaMa. You were always pining for your star people and knew the tracks they took in the night sky. You told the great elders this and made a hole in the roof over your bed so you would wait for them to come for you," Aped began, shifting a little uncomfortably as he looked around. The plaza was quiet.

"They say one night long ago, when you had a fever, you saw the stars of the Great Bat and her milk flowing down over earth, but something let your *Star Mami* come to you. The fever almost took you, but that night you lay down and she took you to the lions. That night, *Mami Lion* came and gave you the gift of walking with them."

"And so the tale went down the river to Sneferu and to the Ancient of Days: Wise Djedi, a god of sorcerers and wizards." Akaru continued wistfully. "He came up the river with his very young student Prince Hordjedtef, who teaches you now."

The elder visualized the memory of his father Metaut pushing him forward to a very old and bent, but heavy set man. Djedi had smiled and nodded as if he knew a great secret he wasn't prepared to divulge. He remembered a slim and haughty young prince whose cruel eyes worried him even then. Akaru remembered Djedi calling a lioness out of the grass to test him. When she came out, young Metauhetep remembered she was the one who had saved him from the fever. The prince, worried they would be attacked, drew his bow.

I ran to save you, Mami Lion! He remembered how he ran and threw his arms around her neck, then nuzzled her warm fur when she happily flopped on her side. Her milk flowed and he remembered kneeling to suckle for just a quick and friendly moment. *I told you to go and take your pride into the deeper brush and not come near the world of men, because they would hunt you for your pretty pelt.*

The lions moved into the wilder brush after that. From time to time, he thought he heard her call, but he never saw her again. The thought that she was no longer with the living ones still made him tear up. Akaru cleared his throat.

Nothing was the same after that. The Ancient Djedi had told his parents that he had the marks of Akaru the Lion, son of Aker and one of the two guardians of the spirit gates. He predicted the boy would be a great and powerful one who would be able to command the very air around him, walk through flame, and talk to many wild beasts in their own voice. After that, he thought of the way he had been held close and eventually controlled by the royal families.

They protected me and educated me in the upper temples of Kemet. King Djedephre and his brother, the Count of Nekhen Prince Hordjedtef dictated that I, because I was a compliant and well educated young man, would succeed the post of sepat prince. Despite the fact that my father Metauthetep had other sons and daughters of his own body. After Djedephre died, Khafre approved the appointment and still later his son Menkaure agreed on it too.

"Because old Djedi chose me, my line succeeds me. But a time is coming when the heirs of the blood will have something to say about it," he added aloud. "My place is in study, which is why *you* study. We are not warriors, but some of the blood sons want war and want us to shake away the yoke of the black land, grow powerful, and make it ruled by the Ta-Seti kings," he said but reflected on his choice of peace.

Life has been good. There's even been no need of magic. I've been free to study and map the stars, learn the healing plants and substances, work the engineering formulae for temple building, take several wives, sire a dozen children, and govern my people with firmness and peaceful compassion. There's prosperity, even if I must rule under the heel of the Lords of the Two Lands.

He knew he would have to tell his grandson Aped what, or specifically who was coming soon, because the young priest would have to make some decisions about his own future. Much of the prophecy had been ushered in by the earlier arrival of Prince Maatkare Raemkai. Last night, he had meditated to prepare for the reading the prince would demand. He wanted to be careful, so he chose a pre-reading that might hint at what he would see in the morning. He knew the young man's dark heart and quick temper, and knew the growing disquiet in his own sepat.

Akaru had begun by calculating the position of the stars as they passed over his burnished brick observatory. As he scratched out notes and compared the positions with earlier ones and with some older historical ones, he saw something that chilled his heart. The position of these stars was different than he expected. It was as if something had moved or jiggled the positions a little bit. *Something* shimmered like a wilderness mirage up in the night sky, distorting the way the stars looked. He had seen that configuration once before when he had suffered from a fever brought on by a scorpion sting. It felt as if *something* looked in on him that night. Was it Sutek, or something much more loving? Now, it looked for him again.

*Star Mami, h*is old heart had raced. Shutting his eyes again, he breathed deep to calm himself. It wasn't any such thing. There really wasn't a 'Star Mami'. It was something else… something dreadful. It wasn't Sutek either. Sutek was dark and chaos… but this was total nothingness and absence of light. It howled after the soul of man, wanting it so it could walk as a man again. *Apep. The Hidden One is coming back. It is coming like a cloud of a storm.*

He had waited and once again he heard the same song he had heard long ago coming from the north and east:

Shine for one who begs to serve you
Return to the night…

Chapter 10: Truth is Hard

"I already know you don't trust me, Djerah, so just ask me whatever you want. My wife Ari once said I'm a dreadful liar and I'm already tired of trying to be a better one."

The stonecutter had returned to the little hillock where Marai made a nighttime shelter for both of them. It was simple: just his walking stick rammed into the earth and his cloak stretched into a tent. Nearby, residents of a small riverside community gathered to celebrate the passing of the king's soul.

The sojourner had cleared some dry grass, bundled it, and had started a dung fire in a neat brick circle near the shelter. It was evening of the first good day of walking and both men were tired and irritated. He sat cross-legged in the opening of the tent and suggested Djerah sit by him and share the bread, dates, a piece of salt fish. He tried to keep silent about the trade being a cheat. Djerah had given far too many blue beads for too little food.

The young man set the food down near the makeshift tent. At the small market near the farm where he had grown up, he had been easily swindled by supposed friends from childhood. When he told them of his mission to Ta-Seti, they had only stoked his doubts about going.

"So you *admit* you've lied to me," Djerah paused. "I know the leave given me by the king and that priest were true and they wouldn't have smoothed either of us out of Ineb Hedj if you were a marked man, so was it about something else?"

"Sit. Let's eat the fish and drink the beer and talk. I just know if I don't come forth with the truth, you won't know what has happened to you. If I don't speed things up, we'll be too late getting where I need to go." Then to himself he thought:

Here goes nothing, nothing but seeing once and for all what sort of man the Children want me to take along. Here's where I either scare him to death or start to teach him. He remembered how scared he had been the night of wonders when the Children of Stone first came to him. Even Wserkaf had been both amazed and alarmed despite his years of training in mystical things.

For a few moments, the sojourner watched the young man chewing the tough salty fish and tossing the bones into the fire. After they had eaten most of the food, Marai began.

"First, I have something to show you," he began. He quietly untied his sash, opened the little leather purse it held and greeted the gentle light that immediately issued from the eight stones inside. When he smoothed the sash flat, Marai poured the stones out and smiled as a trembling sensation swept through both men. He knew the Children were whispering something into Djerah's thoughts because of the way the young man drew back in fear. The sojourner placed the Child Stones in the eight-pointed star pattern and watched, the arcs of light formed unimpaired. As the glow spread upward, it reflected a rainbow pattern on Djerah's stern young face.

"I'm not interested in your sorcery, Bin Marai, so don't try to charm me with these pretty stones." He turned his glance away, but something in the glow lured his head back into the light spiraling upward from them.

Marai gently passed his hand through the top of the image as if he caressed a lover. As the big man's hand moved, he knew Djerah felt the same sigh of keenest pleasure well up in him. It made him fidget, embarrassed.

"If you look where I've traced it with my hand, you can see a little girl, Djerah – and she *was* so sweet when she was young. I would have done anything for her in those days," Marai pointed out the image of Houra dancing on the hillock outside his mountainous home in the wilderness. It was a scene from his own memory which had already become immortalized in the crystalline structure of the Children of Stone.

"Where is this?" Djerah stared carefully, then blinked, uncomprehending at first. "Seems familiar, like stories my savta used to tell, but…"

Marai caressed the light again, then noticed the color drain from Djerah's face as he studied the young girl with the coal colored curls woven into braids and tied with yellow ribbons. "Her face… Savta Oora?" he shook his head in disbelief when he realized he was looking at the face of his great-grandmother as a young girl in the glowing image. "But she's so *young*."

"Her name was Houra, Houra bint Ahu." Marai smiled wishing himself into that scene for just a moment. In so many ways, he wished he was back in the wilderness watching her play in far simpler times.

"How can you do these things? Make an image from so long ago just appear in light from these stones?" the stonecutter shifted, then gasped.

Marai knew Djerah saw the image of the big, rough-looking youth lifting the girl high in the air while she squealed in childish delight.

"That was me, before I was changed. You see, Houra was my half-sister. I lied to you about her being my aunt or even my great aunt," Marai's voice grew softer as he faded for a moment into the life presented in the vision. "There is no *bin Marai*, at least not yet. There is just *me*," Marai shrugged, taking in the young man's haunted expression in the flickering of the firelight and the glow of the stones.

"I knew it! My savta said the same thing and stayed on with that until she breathed no more, even though I held her and told her it wasn't possible. She scolded me as an unbeliever. Said you *were* Marai who Vanished, but we thought it the visions a dying person has. Why did you *lie* to me?" Djerah muttered to himself in disgust. "Did your priest know this about you? And what is the change you're talking about? The man in the vision looks like men in our family, but *you* don't. For all I know, you could be some wizard enchanting me into your service. This whole thing could be heka."

Marai tried to calm the young man with a hand gesture and an image of blankness and peace because at that moment Djerah had averted his eyes. The burnisher gave every indication he thought he was being bewitched.

"The priest didn't know at first, and it's a really long story which I ought to save for later," Marai clucked. "Let's just say my life got stretched out really long so I could bring little stones like these to Kemet and not die of old age on the journey. Because it did, the children had to make some repairs to my body. I was almost an old man when this journey started." He explained, sensing the young man easing a little; at least from curiosity. "In return, the priests were supposed to teach me some things. The old high priest wanted the secret of that long life from me. When he couldn't get it…"

"Damn you. You could have told me your real name. Even if I didn't believe the rest." Djerah tore at the last piece of the bread with his teeth.

"When I went over there, I never thought they would try to kill me. I thought I would come back and share the whole story with you over time. But that time is *now*," Marai swept his hand over the composition of stones as if he was divining a message.

"So what are you doing now?" Djerah studied the glow and the gestures Marai was making.

The big man grabbed Djerah's hand and waved it through the glow. "*Seeing* if one of them likes you. Close your eyes and see for yourself. It won't do anything to you."

The young man quickly shut his eyes. His hand reached over the faint glow and impulsively touched a pale whitish one that glowed like a moon. When he opened his eyes, he held it up and looked at it in the light.

"Hmm… It's changing shape as I hold it – round and now a crescent-shape like the moon."

Marai breathed a little easier. He had guessed the young man had a bigger thirst for learning than even he, himself did at one time. That curiosity alone kept him from dropping the stone and fleeing as soon as he touched it.

"I feel *something*, but I can't say what. It's like it's a small animal, still pink and blind, or a little bird. It buzzes and hums." he whispered in astonished wonder.

"The Iah stone. The moon stone," Marai remarked, recognizing it. "You would say *Yah*."

Djerah turned the stone over and over, examining it and reveling in the feeling of the pulses of energy rolling up and down his arm.

"Does it have any other heka or does it just show things from long ago?"

"I'm still learning about them and what they are. Sometimes…" Marai answered, thinking of the women again. "They seem to be alive to me… with a ka… like all of us have. They're not sorcerers' crystal, though. They're different from each other and yet sometimes they seem to be part of one great heart. They're like children… impulsive, maybe a little foolish, very loving… but sometimes they seem to act without direction. I call them Children of Stone. The priests called them Ta-Ntr stones… Stones from the land of the Gods."

"These little stones? Stones of the Gods?" Djerah roughly translated the Kemet phrase, reverently returning the stone in his hand to the pattern.

Marai looked around helplessly and set down the food. He didn't want to reveal too much at once, but now he had aroused the young man's curiosity.

"Look, Djerah…" he started, but the young man interrupted him by craning his head up to see in to new lights and images that appeared floating in the center of the eight-pointed pattern. "How can I say this? *I* don't think they are gods. Long ago, I thought they were part of my goddess Ashera. Houra may have told you I used to sing and pray to her. I don't think they are her any more or even *other* gods. I think they *are* children of a kind; maybe sort of god's *children*, but no god I have ever heard people speak of. They come from another world beyond the heavens."

"So not even *malak*? Savta's spirits of the mountain?" Djerah breathed out, as if he had been told more by private whispers. "There are more of them, aren't there? The scroll you read to us."

"A good box full of them… Sixty and six more." Marai stared into the soft light, searching for an image of where the women might be, but found no image other than empty grassland and tall cliffs along the great river. "The priests wanted all of them together so their 'power' would be complete and thought this prince could get my wife Deka, who he had seduced, to tell where they were. They made Ari and Naibe go with her to convince her, but Ari suspected a trick before the devilish plan was put into play and traded these eight to Wserkaf for his crystal eye of truth and therein…"

"Lies the problem…" Djerah finished the big man's sentence. "Well, if they *are* with Prince Maatkare…" he sipped his beer. "I can't think they are doing as well as you imagine by this time. I saw the way he treated the women he took… like prisoners if they opposed him on anything or tried to deny him their bodies."

Marai tensed, but took a deep, silent breath.

If they are truly suffering, if the Children are lying… he shook his head because the Children doing that to keep him from roaring in mad bull shape throughout all of Ta-Seti to mete out justice made too much sense.

"He's definitely the one I served under when I was a boy. You want to stay on his good side, though. He's the best I've ever seen in bow, mace, spear, and grappling, excellent in strategy too, but if he gets angry he will kill without guilt and not always quickly." The stonecutter looked around, then leaned forward to whisper: "There's no point to any of this, really. The hour he knows you are coming

133

with be their last and likely ours unless the king is sending his own troops to help us and plans to sneak up and get the ladies before the prince learns of it. He won't go up against the king."

Marai's shoulders sagged. He left the stone Djerah had touched, put the seven remaining stones back in the little bag, and finished his food. When Djerah offered him the moon colored one he held up his hand to deny it and then closed the young man's hand around it.

"Just for tonight, keep this one and see if it speaks to you some more." Marai wagged his head in dismay. "I'm too close to this. I can't hear about them or feel their energy without everything in my eyes turning red. I have to stop, before I send a devil in a shadow after him," Marai's face twisted. "I haven't seen it. The Children won't let me see it, or let my ladies have hope that I'm alive, but I feel pain and sorrow from three stars, each a different kind of suffering. He's *not* killing them – he's forcing them to *live*.

After a moment's more thought he added: "Maybe you'll be able to hear their voices for me, but not feel what I am feeling. Houra could do that with me long ago and her blood is in you," the big man got up and tied the bag of stones to his belt.

"I'm already too cross to sleep. I need to walk for a bit. You'll be safe from lurkers with the stone in your hand, so don't lose sleep listening for trouble." Marai sauntered down the hillock, into the grass, and over to the gathering of locals.

Lights were being placed around. Because Menkaure had been known to drink and celebrate to excess when he was alive, men and women were drinking and creeping off into the reeds in his honor.

Djerah watched the big man walk away, then looked at the glimmering little stone. He turned it over and over again, marveling at its ability to change form from crescent to round, just like the moon. The weight of everything he had learned during the meal suddenly descended on him and he yawned.

I still think this is the journey of fools, he thought. *Gods? Or some god beyond the sky? Not ready to die for one I know nothing about, crystal children or not. I'm sorry about his women, but he should have thought of that before he went to the priests. At least my Raawa and her sisters will be cared for,* Djerah lay back looking at the dim light glimmer in the stone. *So he is letting me hold this to see if it speaks? Why would he really do that?* The young man tucked the stone into his own sack of trade rings in the basket, but hesitated, thinking he heard something.

Djerah
Be aware
Be for Marai
Like a son.
Learn from him.

"Huh?" the stone-maker grabbed the stone and stared at it. As he did, a sedateness filled him. He lay back and slept.

Chapter 11: Dream Space

"You're trembling. Why?" Deka heard Prince Maatkare whisper gently into the side of her face, just in front of her ear so that she felt his breath waft over it. On any other night, being so close to him made her grow faint in ecstasy. Tonight, she shook uncontrollably and tears welled in her eyes.

"You were wonderful, Nefira, pure fire and frost in the water," he punctuated his words with nibbles and evil little kisses. "See when you obey me, how good I can be to you? See how you crave this; so much it makes you shake?"

"Oh..." Deka felt the word escape her throat. She remembered everything that had happened after he took her from Naibe and Ari's room. The only thing she had wanted was to be held; to be engulfed by him, but so much more had happened. She trembled as his mouth closed on hers, his tongue tracing the inside of her upper lip. He had teased and tormented her earlier, but she knew better than to cry out or beg for him even if her heart was about to burst and her womb ached for the need of him inside her. He always stopped before he allowed her release, to reflect on her pleasure, build it, and then watch her writhe in sweet torment.

I would drink your joy of me like finest wine, just a sip at a time, he had once explained, but at some point she noticed that he never lost control of his acts, even in the heat of sexual fervor. Everything about him was technique of pleasure and pain in measured amounts, but always restrained by self-control.

"Take me, beloved, please" she always whispered again and again. "Make me... fly so high..."

He paused, snickered, and teased some more.

Tonight is different, she gasped. *Something of the spirit like... Ta-te and I had done so long ago. The way I had wanted when I woke with Marai, but he didn't understand what I needed. Is this Ta-te's spirit come into my Raem? At last?*

Everything tonight had been frighteningly erotic.

After almost a month on the boats, we're in someone's palace. He told me the prince here and his family fled due to some sign in the heavens? I don't understand. Something is strange about this place and Raem knows it. Wise MaMa and Brown Eyes knew it too. It's why we couldn't be together while I dressed. The moment we came here I felt it in that little wind. I truly felt something like the earth dropping beneath my feet when we walked across the mats in the open court. It was as if this place said to me: "I have looked for you, my long lost one." Deka thought of the passage of time between everyone's arrival and this moment after the bath. Something had danced around in her thoughts while she and the prince ate their supper and again when they had bathed. Whatever it was became particularly dark and needy when she had been gently drizzling warm milky water and oil over him, then followed by gently caressing and kissing him. She remembered his hands coming up out of the water as if he sensed the darkness too. He had even gestured a protective spell.

It calls us tonight, Deka Nefira, does it not? he had seized her slim dark hand, licking the palm of it then looking up into her eyes. She had noticed the hot yellow-green glimmer in his eyes and the ever so slight elongation of his teeth. "I know you feel it too." He whispered "Don't deny that you do."

"It's something here. A memory…" she had sighed, but couldn't avoid the vision of herself as a young girl, barely grown into her breasts and dancing in a flowing red skirt on a large pattern etched in stone. *Red. The same color of the cloth I saw on some of the men. This place. Could this be the place? Is it where Ta-te ruled? Is it where I first came to be?*

"Yes. I know. It lurks. But there is something new here that never has been here before… And that would be me. If there's a spirit taunting us, it will have to overtake me first." his voice chanted nonchalantly. He had moved to the edge of the bath, hoisted himself up, then lifted her and draped a warm absorbent cloak around her shoulders. In a way, it felt like a kind of royal robe. That was when her trembling started, because those words were the ones she'd heard the Children of Stone say:

There is something new here that never has been here before

"What am I to you, beloved?" she asked, trying to get the thoughts and memories to leave her alone. "You give me honors above the others, and yet are still cold to me when we touch?"

His eyes had glimmered again, but he patted her arm quietly. At that point he had not answered her but rose to get something from the box of goods one of his men brought in. It contained two pots of cosmetic. He painted her eyes a shade of gold dust, refreshed the kohl on both of their eyes, and painted her lips a darker shade of red.

He teases me again. Now, because I asked, he will deny me, she thought but then watched as he brought out the crystal Eye of Truth she had taken from Ariennu's basket the night of the Sending Forth party.

"I know you float this on the water to see a far distance. My grandfather spoke of that to me before your red sister took it from my cousin. I told you I wanted it and you brought it to me; all by design," his eyes fluttered almost in shy reverence.

Long eyelashes, she thought, distracted, but he continued.

"Tonight we have a chance to see what it will show us," Maatkare pressed her gently and handed it to her. As she took the disc, she noticed the rainbow effect on its cut edge. The lamplight in the bathing area found the prism and illuminated it. The central or 'eye' portion clouded as if it was instantly crowded with too many images. Deka placed it on the water, half expecting it to sink, but the slight cupped shape held it above the water.

How does it float? It's too heavy to float, she watched the central eye with the prince as the images began to clear. Against the dark evening background, they both saw Inspector Wserkaf sitting near what she assumed was his own pool. She watched quietly while Maatkare taunted him about the 'eye', but wasn't listening. Outside the room in the night sky, something was still watching her.

She shook harder. *Stop this feeling,* she thought to herself. *He'll notice,* she suffered, fighting the tears. *Darkness looking up at me, too, not just down. It's not the priest,* she wept. *I hear Raem calling it tears of joy. Good. Let him think he causes my weeping. It's Marai, I know it now. His spirit is searching for me. It so much feels like the force I remember that day when he went up against N'ahab-atal and his men... he wasn't the meek shepherd or the jolly merchant then... Did he have to die to unleash Ta-te inside him? I feel the shape of the dark moving upon me, choking me. Was I wrong to think it was not he and go to Maatkare? It drives me mad... I so much need Raem like a drug to quench the fever in me.*

She heard him curse lightly about a spirit and laugh as she felt a burning crackle of energy leave him. His eyes rolled slightly back. Something red had come forth and had danced through the 'eye' in the water.

"There... Nefira, the spirit of the dead who cannot find his portals and wanders in the grey, forbidden plane. His cursed soul has come to stand beside my cousin, but I sent him a message. He will not haunt you or the Lady Naibe any longer. I've seen to it."

"Marai? Was it Marai you saw? It felt different..." Deka protested.

"Your sojourner ghost or whoever... is blocked from here. He knows I can make him suffer if he tries again," the prince looked away. For a moment Deka glanced at the floating crystal, then gasped. Something without a face but with the glowing eyes of a storm was looking back and beckoning to her. It spoke in a language from her memory and rushed through her soul, but sounded like Marai's voice.

You have returned to the land of your birth;

The land of your undoing.

It is good.

Soon, very soon

All will be made clear to you.

The one provided for you, suits you.

Use him well,

Teach him.

"Raem, best beloved," Deka began, still trembling. "I beg for you..." she crawled forward to him as he took the crystal out of the water and put it away.

"So now you are safe. I should take power over it though; make it do my bidding, make it scare you when you get too proud. I love to see you crawl to me like this," he looked over his shoulder, a smirk of cryptic delight spreading over his face.

Deka sat on her heels with her head bowed, waiting for him to take her hand and pull her to the room on the other side of the pool area where they would rest.

Use him well, the voice said. Provided for me? By whom? Ta-Te? Are you here in this place? If you are just a spirit, be my Raem and walk on Earth once more. My heart is broken with this longing, Deka's thoughts whispered back, imagining the immense darkness and power in his surrounding arms. The answer surprised her.

> *You knew my touch*
> *When you were found by the shepherd,*
> *Yet you would not teach*
> *Because you were proud.*
> *Now that you serve this one,*
> *Your pride has died.*
> *Teach him, instead.*
> *It is too late to teach the other one.*
> *I am here within soul, within skin.*
> *Know me.*

Deka felt Maatkare's arms close around her and she reveled in the feeling of his lips as he helped her stand and moved with her toward the room that had been prepared for them.

Marai sat on the ground at the edge of the hushed revelry near the water's edge. Someone in the small group of men and women who were looking across the river at the lights handed him a flask of bitter beer. He drank a very small amount "out of respect for the passing of the Great King", then approached the people, making sure he had obscured his appearance. When anyone in the gathering looked at him they saw nothing but a big, fairly plain Kemet native. After a while, some of the youths sauntered closer to see if they knew him. When he mentioned the name Djerah, they nodded that they had seen him earlier and let him sit with them. A woman came by, placed her hand on his shoulder, and smiled down at him. He thought about trailing after her for a few moments of diversion, but then:

Ariennu worked men at a campfire before I knew her, he shook his head and patted the woman's hand. *I lost her. I lost all of them. I have to get them back, Djerah or not, no distractions. I can't spend half a season walking either. I need a boat... and a dream to make it go faster than possible. Maybe I could just tell Djerah to forget about this and then fly or relocate myself so I would just be there. No, there's some reason why Djerah must go, too.*

He scooted back a little bit from the gathering around the fire pit and bowed his head, seeking answers of the stone in his brow. He patted the seven in the bag at his belt, thinking, *talk to me.*

At first, the feeling seemed too strong. Marai thought he was drowsy or dizzy, and wondered if the effects of the Sweet Horizon concoction from the temple still lingered. His spirit drew backward, up and out of his seated form. *Will someone notice? Will someone speak to me and not get a response? Will the illusion of how I look fade? Maybe I should get back to my shelter, Djerah's asleep.*

Go.

Allow.

All is watched

You shall return in the blink of an eye,

But wiser.

Marai felt the world move away from him and only the roar of something like a storm enclose him. The chorus of the voices of the Children echoed gently through his entire frame. He suddenly knew his Child Stone had sent him backward in time. He saw himself, as if he was flying separately from the events, then coming down to the celebration moments ago. Then he was talking with Djerah and handing him the small stone.

Was this the right thing to do? Should I even be taking this young man of such a fool's errand just to keep him blind to the truth in his family for a few more days?

It was a choice at the appointed time, foreseen.
Your son of heart is one.
Treat him with kindness.
Spare his life.
Guide his hand.
He walks into a greater destiny.
Remember that you were once a shepherd.
With only a song to ease your sorrow.

So it wasn't just me taking pity on him, or that he is Houra's great-grandson and my only link to the ancestors, Marai thought as his spirit soared back into courtyard at Little Kina Ahna when he saw the red imp with green eyes the prince had sent through the ether to contain him. The negative energy tingled about him as evilly as it had when he first felt it. Wserkaf defended again, just as before, and Deka wept quietly somewhere, lost in this sorcerer-prince's arms.

How much of this do you know, anyway? Is there anything I do that is not part of the original plan? Marai saw himself transforming into the raging bull at the thought of the women having been stolen from him while he lay as if dead. As he drew near, his spirit swept through the image, became part of it, felt all of the rage and anguish and then pulled away again, spinning head over heels through a brilliant void. The motion of his body formed the prismatic shell that encompassed him. He remembered it from the moments he lay dying in the black and buried stone box.

Remember the sesen.
Its petals of pink, white and blue
Rise above the water in their fragrance.
Each petal…

The voice began to crackle and fade as if something external was distorting it. Marai remembered the lesson. It was spoken to him once as he lay in the shining and iridescent pod on the Children's vessel buried in the sand. *Or was it Hordjedtef who said it?* he wondered as he tumbled through the old man's courtyard and sat once more at his feet absorbing knowledge of the great mysteries and unlocking the information from the Child Stone in his brow. The elder looked up briefly, as if he noticed Marai tumbling backward in time, and smiled. The red spark glimmered in his slit-like bird eyes. His hands rose quietly in a gesture of self-protection.

"Oh but you have no idea of the high winds of fate that are blowing even as we discourse one man to another do you?" he had said. Marai remembered him saying those words and that they had puzzled him.

He had thought the Great One was insulting him about his humble background as he usually did several times in each session. They had been speaking of choices in life. Marai had whispered that a person's life is like the lotus, patterned as the Flower of Life. One chose a petal by actions or by thought and stepped out onto it. Each step one took re-arranged the possibilities not only of his own life, but of the lives of all others in space and time. Once chosen, all other petals fell away and new ones grew along the path.

Did he recognize this moment when my soul wandered backward? Impossible. If he did, then he knows I am alive. Does he know, or have I changed things completely by coming back and seeing everything once again?

> *We can tell you this one knows*
> *Something has taken place*
> *Which he cannot control.*
> *He believes it is the death of his king*
> *The ascension of an unloved prince.*
> *His thoughts are occupied with this…*

But do you know? Marai asked. *Is this some game for you that you know the outcomes but are watching me and my ladies suffer through it? Is that why you do not protect us or warn us? Is it what you do to throw down the challenges for us and then wager on the outcomes as we suffer? Is it?*

We do not challenge you.
We do not know which choice you will take.
We know the answers and the extensions of the results to three or four densities
But cannot warn you in such manner that
Your will is no longer free to create your own wisdom.

The voices stilled in a kind of reverence as Marai revisited the porch step of his apartment where Ariennu was holding him quietly. Once again, he felt her breathing into his hair and begging him not to go to the priests… to stay and quit this foolishness. There he was, inside his old self, wanting her desperately and strongly considering changing his mind. She was hotter than fire itself that morning, and he wanted to give her his love just once more before he left, but shook his head and gave her his longest and best kiss until she swatted him and pushed him away.

"Damn you, Marai…" he heard her throaty giggle follow… "You got yourself as hard as a post, doing that. Now, get you gone before I *make* you stay."

All of the days melted into nothing. Her hand teased and stroked him until he took it away, shook his head and pecked her nose again before…

"Just come back to me…" she had said, tears in a woman who never cried over anything almost starting.

His thoughts and spirit spun beyond that moment.

If I had stayed? What would the future have held? Would I have completed the task of getting the Children of Stone to their destination some other way? He thought of being a merchant, fathering children… of thawing out the frozen parts in Deka's heart. A sigh of passion filled him. The next memories were at once beautiful and painful.

OPENER OF THE SKY

Naibe, sweet one of the goddess walking. You... all of the moments all of the hours in which we healed each other. What madness was it that I could even think of parting from you? They're hurt. I know it, he thought internally, directing his feelings toward the Child Stone in his brow. *They suffer with this man who has them, and I'm on this journey of dreams and memories. I need to go. Show my thoughts the magic and the knowledge to make it happen. I don't want to waste another instant.*

Calm.
In your anguish you have forgotten
What you call time is a thing of Earth
It is hard for us to know this.
We are flawed in this way.

The small, hushed chorus of voices reminded him. He knew. It had been nothing to them to knock him out for five and then fifty years; to take three months to cleanse him of the poison. Perhaps they had intended for him to sleep longer, since he had been so ill on waking, he thought. He felt his spirit lurch and once again he was standing in the luminous clouded place, naked and newly changed. He was wandering into the green area and sitting by a pool. The water had boiled and a stem of a plant-like thing had risen out of it with a platform containing food.

You brought me here to remember how you had created things from nothing for me! He thought. *Do you intend to make me a faster boat? Why not make me fly?*

We whisper to the heart.
At first, we created things
Because you could not.
You are stronger now.

You think I can make a flying boat. I don't even have a regular boat, Marai was about to curse, but suddenly found himself snapping back through time with such a speed that his illusion-draped peasant body flinched.

"What's the matter with you? Drunk?" some non-descript older man who had settled next to him during the singing about the king moved away, making a gesture of protection. Marai tensed, because he knew the man would have tried to tease the bag of stones from his belt.

"I – I must have dozed," Marai shook himself, amazed that no time had passed. The older man had actually been near him before he began his spiritual flight. "A dream, I suppose."

The old man nodded, laughing a little.

"Well, I have a spot in a field near here… with… my son," Marai suggested "We're journeying up the river to the next sepat to see about some work. I'd better go sleep this off." As Marai spoke, he noticed the man didn't appear quite as poor as the others in this group. *I'll just ask him,* he thought, assuming he already knew the answer.

"You wouldn't know about where I might get a boat, would you? I have some few goods I can give someone for it as long as it floats."

The man took a step back, studied Marai, touched his own lower lip and said.

"Actually…" he began, pointing to a group of dark oval shapes at the shoreline. "Over there. It floats, but leaks like a bastard. I have a new one but can't get shed of the old one. Men who can afford a wood one want it to be true for the trade. I was about to undo the planking for shoring up the new one."

Marai's jaw dropped. The Child Stones in his bag pulsed in silent agreement as if they were nodding about the transaction. "A *wood* boat? How much… I have some…" the sojourner knew a wood boat in any serviceable condition would be costly. He had been about to offer some pierced turquoise beads good for making jewelry but the man rocked back and forth on his feet and answered:

"Take it. If you and your 'boy' can get it out of here before I wake in the morning and rethink the beer I've had, it's yours. It will sink after a bit if you don't tar it, though, so be warned… won't take a hit from any of the hippos if you wrong them. I think Goddess Tauret has my name on her list, so I'd offer her something before you get in it," he laughed and pointed to the water. "See the one flipped over among the others? My last try to get the timber dry."

Marai followed the man to the water to look at the boat, mildly irritated that the man insinuated Djerah was his "blissful boy" or keleb. Then again, he didn't look old enough in his illusion to have a grown son.

The wood was evil looking and scummy. He nodded, bowed, thanked the man and hoisted it over his head with a grin. He paid no attention to the impressed gasps of the few who saw him as he moved up the rise to his tent and sleeping Djerah.

You did this? he asked the Child Stone in his own brow as he gingerly unloaded the boat from his shoulders and set it down. *Just like on the vessel in the sand when you knew I was hungry and needed clothes? I shouldn't complain, but I can already hear young Djerah complain like he's giving birth to a ram in full horn over it when he wakes up.*

> *It will float on dreams*
> *Be but first of many to*
> *One day sail the earthen sky…*
> *An ancestor of one to go*
> *Through windows of the wider places*
> *With no walls*
> *Where time as you perceive it*
> *Means naught.*

Really? These rattling pieces of rotten timber that hold water out like a winnowing basket? he thought, wondering if somehow there was a finer vessel hidden in an illusion. He let the "peasant" image fall from him as he settled on the ground near the cloak that had become a tent. *Very well. We'll see. I'd better dream up some magic then,* the big man sat, unfastened his travel boots and lay back with a sigh. In the distant part of his thoughts, as he drifted, he heard a sultry voice chanting:

"Ha-go-re! Akh-go-re Nejter Deka Nefer Sekht
my name is sung ever-present
though I am here.
I fly to you, I come
On dark but burning wings I walk on air
Open the sky to me
Ha-go-re Ta-te"

Deka? Woman of the secret flame, where are you? I saw you. I tried to tell you I did not die.

There was no response from her. The chant repeated on a loop. *On dark but burning wings I walk on air. Open the sky to me …*

"Oh what in seventy devils is this? Is that supposed to be a boat? Where did you get this nasty thing?"

Marai woke to what sounded exactly like…

"Sheb… just stop whining. I know it looks bad, but… trust me."

"Djerah," the stonecutter snapped back. "Sheb is my dead saba. You did it again."

"Well, you *complain* just like him. I already knew you would wail at me over it." Marai grumbled, shaded his eyes against the rising sun and then sat. The early mist from the river was clearing. He heard coughing and occasional retching closer to the water where other revelers had either passed out or fallen asleep.

"Look at them down there, true honor for our drunken king. Gods ease his way," Djerah shrugged, inspecting the boat's seams and mumbling. "It'll sink. You know that, don't you?" he pointed at a place where the roping was frayed and the pitch fill was cracking. "Where did you get it? Were *you* drunk?"

Marai wasn't about to talk of his spiritual journey or the communication with the Children that apparently brought the nameless donor of the boat in his direction.

"No, but you're right. I think it might take water after a while, but we can fix it as we go. It's still going to be faster than walking." *And then again, you might be surprised how much faster,* he added silently.

Somewhere in the back of his thoughts he sensed ideas beginning to flood through him about how the boat could be repaired. *I could even rebuild or outright transform it into something no man alive had seen on earth unless Yaweh-sin or Asher-ahna herself piloted it to them. Perhaps it will be like the vessel in the sand. No, maybe not.*

"You didn't *steal* this pile of dung, did you?" Djerah continued to question.

"A man was looking to get shed of it last night at the mourning revel these people were having." Marai pulled the cloak and staff that had composed the makeshift tent down and began to gather anything else into their travel gear.

"*He* stole it then," Djerah suggested. "How much did you trade for it?"

Marai snorted a little at the thought that young Djerah might have actually taken on his Saba Sheb's soul. Every word the youth spoke came out of his mouth in a denying and terse scold, just the way Sheb used to scold him about nearly everything he said or did when they lived in the wilderness.

Djerah was never like this in Little Kina Ahna, but he had a house of whining and scolding women to take him down a few notches every day he was there. Maybe he'll become the man he's supposed to be on this journey, if I don't have to knock his head a few times myself.

"The man gave it to me for the carry-off. You want to walk to Ta-Seti instead, or maybe trade all we have on a better boat?" he raised one brow, waited for Djerah to be unable to answer, then continued. "You carry the things and I'll haul the boat past this inlet. Then, we'll put it in the shallows and test it."

"At least there's long and short oars," Djerah's arms flapped. "You're really going to carry that?"

Marai took the oars out, bound them with a strip of leather that was among the supplies and made a drag for the bags and the basket Wserkaf had left them.

"You pull that and I'll take care of this," the big man took a deep breath and lifted the upside-down boat over his head. "Lead the way, I'll follow," he said. "I don't want to step in a hole and make myself lame." Marai knew he wouldn't have that sort of trouble at all, because his senses would tell him where to place his feet but he *did* want the young man to learn a little more about silent travel by giving him work. In time, he inwardly knew, there would be so much more to teach him.

Your son of heart the Children called him. He can be like a son to me now, I guess. Marai thought, remembering something the Children has whispered on the glowing vessel when they had first transformed him "those you sire, those you choose" they had told him. At that time, he didn't have a child other than his tiny daughter who died with her mother so many years ago. He wanted to have a son by Naibe and eventually Ari and Deka too if he ever managed to extricate her from the spell of lust that bound her to her captor.

I will have a son, a real son one day. You can see that can't you? Marai questioned but knew the answer. They saw many choices and yet telling him the answer would never work. If he knew, he might accidentally take a step that would alter his chosen destiny. He felt an almost imperceptible chilliness in his heart and shivered a little, then adjusted the boat he held overhead.

"No!" Akaru Metauthetep shouted and sat up on his bed. He had suddenly waked from a dream or a vision. He tucked his legs up in a cross-legged position on his bed, gripped his arms, and rocked back and forth in anguish.

His chief wife rushed in from her adjoining room and got her servant to fetch the man's grandson, Aped. Through slowly clearing eyes, the elder saw the tall young prince enter.

"Akaru? Are you well?" the younger man bent forward to check his elder's life signs. Akaru waved him away, then re-gripped his arms until he had calmed himself for a few more moments. His wife sat by him on his bed; her head on his shoulder. She patted at the base of the old man's neck to console him.

"Metau-te… you had a spirit visit you?" she asked. "Was it an evil one?"

"I assure you, Xania, you should not worry over me." Akaru looked up almost sheepishly. "You know how they speak to me and that sometimes their words are loud enough to shake me."

His grandson bent to assist, asking. "You want some tea, grandfather? Something to ease your dreaming?"

Akaru nodded, but shook himself and spoke calmly for several moments while a servant brought him the warm medicinal mixture that was usually kept at the outer edge of a central brazier in the courtyard.

"Listen carefully," he began. "Something has changed my predictions. I felt it in my dream. I must go back to Qustul Amani in four days to check my observations again. There is a shift occurring. You may not feel it, but everything is happening so fast now. He is impatient, that one, and rightly so."

Aped and Xania stared at each other, uncomprehending.

"Grandfather…" the young prince asked, "what are you talking about?"

Akaru Metauthetep took the cup the servant brought and nodded gratefully.

"Destiny, I suppose. It's why I came here early. I thought I was to protect the women from the men in the army, and that's good, but I sense my staying was now a mistake. I should have remained behind to meet the one who walks as a god. He is coming… on his way here now."

"General Maatkare thinks *he* is one," Aped guessed quickly. "If another comes, I hope he comes to teach the first one a lesson. I spoke with Great One of his grandson's interest in woman stealing; of his disrespect of the divine feminine energies. He acknowledged he would speak to him, and he stated he had already done this."

Akaru's hand went up in protest.

"No. One comes, and is not pleased with our visiting prince, but it's more than that. Besides, I know the young general's dark heart. I have always managed him well enough since he began to strut about. He knows he and his men do not take women from *our* families," the elder knew his words were becoming increasingly hollow. The descendants of his father's true bloodline wanted to rebel. He had seen all of these things in his dreams.

"So who comes?" Aped asked, sitting on the floor while Akaru's other wife came in and tended to the elder man. His own wives were awake, but the young man waved them away assuring them it was nothing and that he would come to bed soon enough.

"The one who has been killed but did not die. The one I heard singing the night the lions came when I was a boy." Akaru answered quietly, turning his face downward into his cup of tea. "It's the same giant man with hair like the moon you met in the market." Akaru's eyes sparkled as he waited for his grandson's reaction.

"We discussed him just the other night. I heard there was a usurper of the sacred ways who failed in his quest for knowledge and that Ra himself took issue… the Lady Sekhmet burnt him with her fire. Are you saying he's the same one as the man in the market?"

"I believe so. The Inspector told you that?" the elder paused, perplexed then added: "Well I suppose he would have to commit it to *some* kind of legend. Did you hear what became of the women who were with him?"

"I didn't. Great One was quite busy on my duty to him this time. Outside of his teachings, he busied himself in the palaces. It seems some private matters were keeping him there. The disciples know not to pry or be familiar when he is in such a state."

"True. I *do* remember those moods. My vision, though, was of the War Bull Montu roaring up the river. I then saw battles and fires. I'm not exactly sure how that connects, but I know it does."

Aped's eyes widened. "Do you know anything of what it meant?"

"Not really, but then I remembered the prince told me when I cast his prediction that he would not take our women, or even the lowliest of prisoners for sport this time. He boasted to me that he had brought women of high quality from Ineb Hedj and not one of them was his wife, as if his disrespect of her was supposed to impress me. He even stated he had one who had escaped from our own country and demanded to know whose daughter one called *Deka* might be." Akaru sipped and finished his tea, nodded to his wives that he was in better spirits and that he would be in to let them bless him soon.

"Pleasing One?" Aped questioned.

"I told him the same and said I did not know one with such a name as it degrades instead of lifts up, but the name hurt my heart to hear it. Then, I gave his prediction which told him his excursion was doomed. I told him to go home as soon as he could because something was coming like a storm and I did not know if it was Sutek or Sebiumeker. I really did see fires and the same battle that returned in my dream not moments ago. He thought I was lying, just to get him to go away and told me he would come back for me to make a better prediction after I had made some offerings. My heart told me I should not see them, not yet. That is why I came two weeks early. But the other man is coming here now. I think the woman from our land young Maatkare mentioned may be the very one who danced with you the year before." Akaru handed the empty cup back to his grandson and stood up with the younger man's help.

"Then I will come with you," Aped said.

"No. Do not. In fact, I would have only Xania because she is older and a few guards to bear us and tend us."

"Was there more? Did your dream *explain* anything?" Aped asked, upset.

"Eh. I've said too much again. Best say the rest than tell lies." Akaru sighed and continued.

"I have to go to my observatory and retake the calculations. Perhaps I was wrong about the dates over the years," he yawned, the tea having begun to calm him. "I saw myself step out into a place and then the sky came open and a column of light came to the ground like a golden ladder. All around me were lions and a voice that asked me to come up, to escape them, but I cried out they would never hurt me and that I could not, because I was a son of Earth now. That was how you found me."

He moved toward the room where his wives were waiting for him. "So, in the bright of morning I will go and wait for the one who comes like Montu. I will see if my calculations are correct and then I will come back to you. Stay here. Guard your own." He turned his back saying, "remember the storm is coming… that is prophecy. Soon, I'm afraid, we will all know what it means."

Chapter 12: Journey up the River

"Look at that. I told you." Djerah pointed at the water beading on the cracked pitch in the floor of the boat as soon as both he and Marai set it in the water, loaded their supplies, placed the oars and seated themselves.

"Mm," Marai grumbled, then thought to himself and to his Child Stone, *could have let us get a little further up the river before sinking us.* He continued aloud, "So let's row. If we're moving quickly enough, the water can't come in that little crack. We'll stay close enough to the shore so if we start taking on too much water we can put in and fix it."

Marai knew Djerah would have to man the rudder constantly that close to shore or they would get stuck on shoals. "You do the rudder and push us out. I'll row."

"But the water…" The young man pointed at a little rivulet starting to drip from the crack.

"Go," Marai pointed forcefully to the stern of the small wood boat that was smaller than half the size of Wserkaf's boat. Djerah took one timid step to the rear and positioned the long oar in the bronze rudder guide. Marai sat with both oars in his hands and gave the signal to push out. As the boat moved out, he took a deep breath, centered his thoughts and whispered once, "go. Even strokes. Learn the motion. Feel it through me."

Then, in a voice Djerah could hear, he said, "go. Fast. Now." He began to pull. At first his pace was even and swift, but not unusual for a strong and agile man. Gradually, Marai felt himself sink into his thoughts and the drifting feeling of power come over him in a surge of new strength. He shut his eyes and laughed a little as his speed increased. His Child Stone and the seven in the bag on his sash gave him the needed boost. Soon, he pumped a little faster.

When he focused on a V of geese flying overhead, he sent up the thought.

See that speed! The wings. Make the oars extend like the wings of birds. Almost instantly, Marai felt the surge of power flash through his arms like black lightning again. It had been so long since he had felt that strength that he almost paused to admire it.

Sweep back, forward, sweep back… he felt his arms beginning to merge with the shape of the upper oars.

His eyes closed and his thoughts soared through time and space to a dark night and rested on the sight of a young woman frantically urging the rowing of a raft.

Naibe.

He saw the raft come apart and Naibe not come up for a long time. He sensed the bitterness of the prince who held them, then heard Ari and Deka crying out for him to save her. *You will get her,* he sent a thought so strong that the man's head snapped around to look for the demon assailing him. He got another raft to get her. *Faster. Go faster or die with her.* Suddenly, the prince paddled out as if legends were already saying "at heart bursting speed." Marai sighed, but knew Naibe was safe. This had happened some time earlier, on a night near the time he woke.

Faster, his speed increased in a lurch.

"Hey. What are you…?"

Marai heard Djerah shout, roused himself slightly, and turned to look. The young man was moving the boat into the deeper water, a half-crazed look on his face.

"Out here I won't have to steer as hard. I can't keep up with you. You'll make the helm snap… How are you doing…?"

"Then just stop steering for now and come up and look to see if we're still taking water." Marai resumed his pace.

Djerah pulled the helm oar out of the water and crawled forward to look.

"What?" he cried, "it's dry. It's like the pitch has melted and reformed. D'you cast a spell on this boat?" He checked the weak seams and moved forward, but when he saw Marai's face starting to glow. The man's Childstone emerged and Djerah froze. "What's that on your forehead? I saw it before, at home…"

"Long story…" Marai called back, still rowing hard. "It's like the stones I showed you but one is inside my head. Helps me do a lot of things. Now if you are happy we're not going to sink I need you to steer. Let's stay in the middle like this and I'll see if I can get it to go even faster."

"We're about to pass Sokor, I think. You keep this up, we'll be there in under a moon's quarter."

Marai nodded and went back to rowing. He knew that the only reason Djerah didn't fall off the back of the boat while he steered was because he had the Yah stone tucked into his own leather purse. He sensed the harmony of the Child Stones, as they spoke excitedly to each other.

Why did I just now see when Naibe almost drowned trying to escape this man? he asked as he continued moving the oars. On another level, he imagined the oars had grown longer and had transformed into fins of a great fish pulling the boat forward at four times racing speed. When they flashed above the water they appeared to be normal oars in the hands of a strong and skilled rower.

Out on the river, so many of the things that had been kept from him flooded his thoughts. He saw Ariennu's degradation and wondered how she allowed a mere man to rule her like the prince did, even in sport. He felt the link the prince was forging between them and recognized it as the same manipulative spell Great Hordjedtef had woven over him that got him to abandon any of his doubts.

He's not bad looking… strong and skilled, like Djerah said, raised to be cruel in the tradition of the elder kings. Something about him though… he went back to rowing, wondering if a sail of some sort kind might help.

By night, they were far to the south. Marai and Djerah pulled the boat into a small port and traded turquoise beads for a place to beach it out of the water and turn it so they could prop it up on short oars and shelter in it.

As they sat and ate, Djerah began to ask questions.

"You're going to tell me about these spells you cast? About the stone in your forehead that makes you have the powers of a god?"

"No. Not tonight." was Marai's quick answer, but when Djerah's face filled with a disgusted expression he sighed and said, "I'll tell you they empower dreaming. You learn to dream while you're awake. I simply wanted to go faster, so the man brought me the boat. I didn't want it to sink, and I wanted to stay strong all day, so that happened. Now… I want to sleep."

"It was…" he started to say *unbelievable,* but it came out in a thought. "I just don't think I will sleep again. I touch it and it buzzes."

Marai sensed the music of the small crescent shaped stone as Djerah pulled it out of his purse and held it in his hand. He looked and saw the glimmer, then heard the voice in his own head.

So sad his plight
So twisted his future
We hold secrets
As Ariennu Wise MaMa holds them from you.
Advise him.
Teach him to embrace calm
He rocks on the brink.

Marai stared at Djerah, wondering if he had heard the message or if it was just a report of what the Stone child had learned about the young man. Djerah's lack of expression change told the sojourner that the young man had been so enchanted by the glimmering, he hadn't heard them. The message had been private.

Should I collect you, so he cannot see? I thought to ease him into this, he asked.

You should not close his eyes.
He is learning much.
Ask him to dream
Prepare him.

"It protected me when you were getting the boat last night, just like you said it would. I should have been easy prey for a thief," the young man half mumbled.

"It knows you now," Marai finished his simple meal and doused the cookfire they had built in front of the overturned boat. He yawned, but decided to show the young man one more thing. "I learned this one from my Lady Ari," he chuckled, thinking about her laughter and naughty image, the way she teased him and would hold her breasts up high in both hands. *Look at these. See how the nips are berries fat for your mouth…* and her tongue would flick out at him, beckoning him. He missed her.

"Ariennu, the Kina-Keft halfling with hair kissed by a blood moon," Djerah sighed, suddenly drowsy.

Marai knew the Child Stone in the young man's hand purred on a frequency that induced calm. He drew an imaginary square in front of them and watched the rainbow shimmer cloud it.

"See that?" he asked. "If any man or beast comes upon us while we sleep they won't see or even smell a thing." He looked and saw that Djerah had put away the stone was lying back. In moments he was asleep. *Oh well, you who thought you'd never sleep again. Enjoy.* For a moment, as he settled, Marai saw a vision of Djerah's apartment in Little Kina-Ahna. The door was open and a tall, muscular man emerged from it. He wore a white status cap. Light weaponry was strapped over his shoulder.

Peacekeeper, Marai thought at once how lucky he was that the man had stayed away while he had slept in the upper room. *That's the one she's betraying him with. Goddess mine, I hope he doesn't dream of this tonight. I don't want him knowing this until he's stronger and maybe has even seen a better woman in the distance.* He remembered the message of a moment ago and understood.

So sad his plight
So twisted his future
We hold secrets

I know, but how long until he can see it himself? Will I or anyone else be able to calm him then? Marai thought but realized the young man knew inwardly everything he needed to know. He couldn't let it overtake him. A day would come, the big man knew, when Djerah would allow himself to see everything clearly. That day he would no longer be able to dismiss his nagging doubts. For now, and for many selfish reasons, Marai hoped it wouldn't be soon.

"Uh… Marai…" Djerah woke the big man just as the sun rose. "You need to look at this," he said.

Marai's eyes popped open in a flash and he sat up, but immediately knew what had happened. The boat had changed. It was longer and of a much sturdier construction. The wood was new and not starting to rot at the roping holes. It was built for speed and even had a bracket for a mast. A mast had mysteriously arrived. It lay nearby with a yardarm and the fabric for a sail wrapped around it, all lashed tight and with good rope.

"You traded it out while I slept, didn't you? Or did you cast another spell?"

"I was talking about dreams, and you had your hand on a stone too. Are you sure *you* didn't 'cast a spell'?" Marai playfully accused the young man, still wondering why they Children were helping him now when they had done so very little for him or for the women in his life in their time of much greater need. He stopped short of asking them this time and reflected. *I know, the sesen flower and the choices. Tell me too much or help me too often and it decreases the power of my decisions. Why now though?* he mused.

A storm is coming.
The sky opens
All must be in place
At the appointed time
In readiness.

Storm. Naibe's storm. The goddess knew, he remembered the tiny and short-lived haboob, a dust djin that sought their caravan when they traveled to Ineb Hedj so long ago. She had run off and had to be rescued. That set her night terrors in motion, but gave birth to the beautiful and enchanted night when they fell into each other's arms. If she hadn't been afraid, perhaps that moment would not have happened. *And then, perhaps if I hadn't allowed myself to be put down by Hordjedtef, would*

Wserkaf have become a friend? Would I be interested in going to Ta-Seti if the women I love had never been taken from me? Mtoto Metauthetep Akaru Sef. I'm to seek him as a man who walks between worlds in Qustul, Wse said… Goddess, would the king have even died if he had not learned of Great One's treachery? And Djerah… they are right. It is *connected. It all* is.

"I don't cast spells. *You* do. I saw that protection you put up that looked like a sheet of oil on the water," The young man moved around the boat, inspecting every part of it to make sure it was no illusion and wouldn't return to the half-sinking old bundle of slats they had magically driven thus far.

"Maybe we both did it. We *were* wanting a faster boat with a sail, after all."

"Well I want a pile of gold big enough to fill the upper room where you used to live. Will they do that for me if I dream about it?"

Marai shook his head, because he knew the answer. The plan was for Djerah to be with him as descendent and student. A room full of gold and a cheating wife wasn't the best thing to come home to, just as Hordjedtef wanting to be immortal so he could rule Kemet forever was likely a bad idea. Some wishes were just wrong-headed and only granted in the short run to teach a lesson.

"Well, let's get this thing to the water and fix the sail before whoever lives in this sepat thinks we stole it. Dream of the gold if you want to once we're underway." Marai put the last of his things into the basket and flipped the heavy boat to pack it.

OPENER OF THE SKY

Chapter 13: Qustul Amani

Marai regarded the gracefully curving, massive brick walls surrounding the town. Some fisher folk were out in the reeds with nets and spears when he and Djerah scanned the edge for crocodiles or anything smaller, but vicious, then pulled their very ordinary-looking boat ashore.

"Where's this?" Marai called, but it took more tries to find the right dialect.

"Qustul Amani is here," someone called out, but cautioned, "nobody here. All gone into New City til after the dry wind."

"Looking for Prince Metauthetep, the Akaru…" he called back.

"Don't think he's here… gone up to Buhen," came the next answer. At that point someone paddled over to the caller and spoke to him. He corrected himself, "maybe here! Maybe two days here. No more."

Qustul Amani? Peaceful refuge? Marai thought. *Peace through no one being here,* he noticed the gates were made of finely carved imported cedar wood just like the gates in the walls around the palaces in Ineb Hedj. Painted rampant and fierce lion motifs adorned the walls. *Walls go around the whole place, too, not just the palace unless it's bigger than the one for the king. Armed watchtowers, too.* He paused and listened. *It's too quiet here to be such a fortress.*

"Marai…" Djerah began, "I don't think this is the right place. I don't remember this place from when I came with the army. Maybe we're supposed to go up the channel to the other one."

As the two men approached the wall and gate, Marai eyed the tense guards walking the wall and manning the towers. They were more than ready to descend on them if they looked threatening. No one hailed them or asked what business they had. They just kept walking the top of the wall and looking down at them in silence.

"No. This one feels right," Marai smiled. Something in his heart wanted to skip a little.

Old friend

OPENER OF THE SKY

Welcome

Return of the lion

"Should we go back and get weapons? All I have on me is my gutting knife. I didn't..." Djerah worried.

"No. Unless we feel this guarding is about *us*, just come with me to the gate and watch what I do. I just have a really good feeling about this place for a change... like I'm *home*," the big man whispered. Putting his hands up to his mouth, he shouted up to one of the guards in the language of Kemet.

"Looking for a man Mtoto Akaru Sef, Prince Metauthetep. Is this where I find him?"

For long moments the guard walking the top of the wall ignored him. Marai tried his own tongue. The guard paused, confused. Another guard walked toward the first one and drew his bow.

"I told you..." Djerah protested, his hand finding the grip of the knife if his belt.

"Stop that," Marai snapped, waving his hand at the young man. "They just don't know highland Kina, and neither do you." He went back to speaking Kemet and slowly shifted into the use of a few Ta-Seti phrases he had sensed from Deka.

"Good evening! May you be blessed," he tried.

The guards, joined by a third man, stared down. By this time, two men had taken aim with their bows.

"Looking for Mtoto Akaru Sef..."

"If he is inside, stranger, which I do not say he is, who comes to see him?" one of the men finally called down to him.

"I don't think he has my name, but he *does* know I'm coming. You can say its Marai bin Ahu and his kinsman Djerah bin Esai," Marai called back.

"You wait," another of the men called and disappeared from the top of the wall while the other two men remained with bows drawn. Presently, the men became relaxed and put down their weapons, but remained attentive. Marai began to pace a little, impatient.

They always do this, these important men. I had to wait for Hordjedtef when I went to study some time ago. He remembered sitting outside Great One's powdery white walls before his guards brought him through the gates for a good part of the morning. He started to sit again, knowing it might be a while.

"Let's just *go*," Djerah complained. "Maybe he's at the other Qustul. These men could just be waiting for us to drop our guard so we can be taken prisoner."

"Djerah… *think* of what you're saying," Marai sighed. "Why take so long with us when they could easily pick us off without even bothering the man if they thought we were a threat. Maybe he wasn't expecting us this soon."

Marai thought about the last five days while he waited on a response from inside the palace gates. He had made the boat move at a blinding pace, even though it grew larger and got a sail the first night. Djerah had unknowingly helped, but travel with the young man had been trying. He nagged and pestered as if Sheb had truly walked into a younger body. When he didn't worry aloud, he chatted about anything: the land they passed, people, birds that flew overhead, incidents that took place at his former work. Marai preferred little idle chatter so he could think and reflect. It was one of many reasons why he had lived apart from his tribe when his people had lived in the wilderness.

"We're running low on supplies," he had said on the second day after they tried the new striped sail. "Take out the Yah stone and whisper to it while I row. This part of the river steers well enough. Maybe they will whisper to you of someone up the way who is just *dying* to trade food and beer to us for a few beads."

Marai sensed Djerah about to say something about the mediocre quality and size of the beads, but went back to the rowing. He didn't think anything further about the trade or the need for supplies and drifted into a dreamlike state as the surging of the oars and the strokes became part of his arms once more. The Children of Stone had learned the needed movement through his efforts the day before and automatically duplicated them at a good speed. Today he felt no sweat or strain in the work. *They row through me and make it seem as if I'm pulling the wood through the water,* he laughed and began to build an even more interesting boat in his thoughts as he and the young man traveled.

A boat offloading food, wine, and beer for a small market had docked where they pulled in that night. When Djerah took out the beads, swearing they would get no more than a half ration of anything, he discovered the small turquoise beads had doubled in size.

"I didn't do it" Djerah shook his shaggy head. "That stone. I just asked. I swear…"

"Just go see if the man with all of that stuff on his raft needs some help lightening his load." Marai brushed the young stonecutter away and tried to hide the fact he was about to explode with laughter. Then, he thought of the ladies and what lay ahead.

The third morning, nothing new happened, but the Child Stone in Marai's brow and the eight other stones propelled the boat at a regularly established speed.

"Uh… Marai… You'd better come out of that daydream you are having and look at this." The young man had slipped back to where the sojourner sat. Marai opened his eyes without pausing in the automated sweep of the oars and looked to the shore where the young man was pointing. In the distance, Marai saw people running on the shore and shouting about how fast their boat was moving and that it was effortlessly maneuvering past any other boat traffic. He waved and smiled, aware that the oar continued its sweep without his hand on it.

"Wait…" Djerah frowned. "The boat is rowing itself? How?"

Part of the big man knew how, but he also knew he would never be able to put the method into spoken word. It would sound like sorcery.

"The boat has simply learned what I need," he started. "But… I agree. We might be attracting tale spinners."

"The boat learned…" Djerah puzzled, then shook his head that he didn't understand.

"Bending time and speed. Slipping through the cracks," he suggested, but the young man had gone back to man the waiting helm oar. "And you see you're not working hard as you were before, don't you?" he called, but once again Djerah, seemingly overwhelmed by the mechanics of this magical rowing, had stopped listening.

He resumed his pondering about next steps, wondering if Hordjedtef had sensed what he was doing in any way.

I doubt these people will carry this story down the river, but I think the amount of bending will come through to Hordjedtef as some kind of disturbance. He raised his hand and dropped an illusion that made the boat shimmer like the heat rising from calm water. This time, instead of a prismatic light on a flat surface, a pale sunset-colored orb enclosed the boat. Marai sensed it might look like a great bubble on the river and that it might draw even bigger crowds to see something like that speeding by. The whisper voices reassured him and made a different suggestion.

> *A vessel in which to float*
> *Cannot be seen*
> *Show the younger one*
> *Let him feel our strength.*
> *He will rise to us one day*

Rise? Marai wondered briefly, but complied. "Come here," he said. Pull the helm oar back in for a minute. The Children wanted to show you something."

Djerah sat, his expression partway between boredom and a desire to be challenged.

"Go," Marai told him. "On my count, push fore, and pull… fore and pull… think of where you want to go and let it take you."

Djerah looked at Marai's hands once and pushed gingerly only to feel the oar snatched from him, then swing back and nearly knock him off the rowing platform.

"Gods!" he muttered. "The power…" he grabbed the oar and tried to steady himself as the wooden length swung him back and forth like it was shaking a rag. "You can't be *that* strong! Slow it down!" and the rowing slowed until Djerah could grab the wood and move with it. "How is it…?" He gasped, astonished but starting to glide with the rhythmic strokes.

"I haven't asked," Marai remembered telling him and adding. "Sometimes if a gift comes it's best to take it without looking for how it works."

"Which is how you missed them trying to kill you," the young man quipped.

"And you are going to be a man of constant trouble to me now, aren't you? Just remember, not everything is as simple as you want to make it." The sojourner relaxed a little more and took the oars again, at least grateful the initial chilliness of their companionship had eased.

When a dragonfly perched on Djerah's shoulder, Marai saw the young man coax it onto his finger. He hadn't noticed the stillness inside the bubble that surrounded the boat until now. On previous days, although the wind going by them was less violent than it should have been given their speed, it had left them feeling windblown at the end of each day. Today, Marai noticed the bubble had created a calm around them. The dragonfly had become trapped when the bubble formed that morning.

"Look here, Marai, he got lost and then caught by what's around us, poor thing."

Marai felt a kinship with the creature, and of the way he had been trapped in the white bubble-like vessel in the sand… lured in and trapped. He let go of the swinging oar and stuck his hand through the pinkness of the bubble until he felt a draft of rushing air.

"Stick your hand through the membrane like I just did. It's like a real soap bubble, but it won't pop. Let the little fellow go as soon as you feel the draft."

Djerah did just that then laughed "If I stay with you long enough, I'll get this boat to fly like that for you. Just like a dragonfly. You just watch me."

"I bet you will." Marai remembered the verse he had heard float to Djerah in Houra's voice right before the journey began.

Be well my young heart…
Be strong where I could not.
You will become as the eagle
You will command the sun on silver wings.

This is but the first step into the light.

A commotion at the gate erased all of those thoughts.

A crack appeared in the gate and a curious old face peered out.

"Ah. You are finally here," the voice that came from the old face added. "If you find favor with the high kin who wears the red crown, then you must be the one I have returned to see. Are you he?"

Marai was taken aback. The man's face wasn't at all what he expected and yet at the same time it was a face he thought he had always known. *Djedi,* he thought. *The real one. He's near you or you* are *him somehow.* The sojourner started to say something in response but he couldn't get any words to come. The voice, which spoke in perfect Kemet speech was that higher sounding tenor voice that had always been in the chorus of Children's voices.

After a polite pause, the face in the gate crack continued. "I have sensed your coming for many, many years… that two would come from the north, but one would have hair of the moon and one would have hair of the sun. The young man with you, is the other of two?"

Djerah stepped forward, smoothing his dark, tightly twisted curls.

"I sense…" the elder frowned, face still in the crack but he stared at Djerah. "Oh. I see. You are a fledgling yet, not shed your plumage of doubt." his smile crinkled.

Marai wondered why the elder hadn't opened the gates to them. *Is he going to turn us around now? Does he wait for some spirit to approve of us? Fledgling? A young bird?*

"We've come a long way and at a hard speed, too," Marai insisted. "We can just trade some turquoises for a spot outside these walls, if you prefer."

"This I know," the old man grinned with unusually perfect teeth. Men came up behind them, guarding their exit. "You have come because spirit drives you up the river and have I come down from Buhen to meet you also because of this spirit.

Before I allow you to come in, I want to hear the reason from your own mouth why you come in such a rush."

Marai knew this was a test, but was getting irritated at the way all of his hurry to get here for help had suddenly ground to a stop and found a wall of stony resistance covered by a sunny smile in the man he was supposed to meet. He was a weather front on a warm day.

"I come to see a man…" Marai framed his words sternly. Djerah meanwhile threw his hands up in the air with an oath and turned to shuffle away in disgust.

"…who presumes he is a warrior god," Marai continued. "He's stolen from me and from the royal houses. I understand he sojourns near here and has three women out of Ineb Hedj in his company," Marai's eyes silvered in disgust, yet something about the man's demeanor drew him into a quieter patience. "The women are my wives."

Another thoughtful silence followed, then the old man spoke.

"I see. You would mean young Prince Maatkare Raemkai. We know him, but we are no *close* friend to him. He is a kinsman to the house of the father of Kaphre-Suph with whom we have a treaty. We are honor bound to allow him to hunt and trade in our upper region. We are expecting prepared skins and preserved meat in return." The old man paused, as if he measured each word he spoke the same way Marai had been careful with his own words. In a moment, he continued.

"You oppose Prince Maatkare because he has stolen? Stolen your women too? This is so very like his highness, but you must understand, I myself have not seen them. I sense them, and I know are *mostly* well, just as you sense it."

The gates were suddenly pulled inward by a sophisticated counterweight system. When Marai and Djerah entered, they were swung shut again and latched by a lever system behind them.

Marai focused on the full appearance of the older man who had been standing in the gate. His wiry body wore an odd shendyt – knee length in front and longer in the back. A magnificent lion-skin cloak was made so the front paws looped over each other and the tail trailed from a plain gold belt around his waist. When he turned to lead Marai into his open plaza, the sojourner saw interlocking stars stenciled carefully on the cloak in the pattern of Asar's constellation.

The old man's hair was red as the sand, but mixed with silver. It was not the typical black color of people here. It hung from his slightly balding brow, encased in a thin, gold head circlet with a lion head set on its prominence. His color, in the light, was pale and filled with freckles. When he looked up at Marai, a spark of strange recognition shone in his strange eyes. One eye was green; the other was deep brown. The sojourner was awestuck by the reality of the man as the pieces of his life and his entire journey slipped quietly into place.

Deka wanted to come to Ta-Seti to find what happened in her lost girlhood. The Children said there were three to assist. I'm first, Wserkaf must be second. Hordjedtef picked him out for reasons I can't guess yet, but they turned out to be the right ones. This man, Wse said, is the legendary lion-child ancient Djedi picked out before he died. That made him the destined third and likely more the old wizard's heir than Wse. But, what is Djerah and why are they asking me to include him? Blood? That's a thin one. For a moment, Marai felt the ire of rebellion rising. *And what this has to do with me getting my wives out of the prince's grasp and the stolen Children of Stone back to Wserkaf I have no idea.*

"I suppose I too would be unwell and eager to see an end to this, if I were you and he had taken the women I love," the elder smiled a little uncomfortably this time.

Marai knew the old man had sensed all of his inner disquiet.

"Then, pardon me, but what do you have to offer me?" *Even the Children...* Marai thought, then stopped. The old man leading them had slowed as if he heard the sojourners thoughts again.

"I can offer you men, even though I believe it's ill advised. We'd be sorely outnumbered," the Akaru answered without turning his head. "Not tonight, though. Prince Maatkare is touring the mines and the borders to the Rim of Kush. If you go for him now you won't find him. I have, however, dealt with him once on this journey of his and sent my regrets via the sepat princes on the Kush border."

Marai and Djerah trailed the old man and were followed by the guards into a simple brick palace. Other than the magical gate, there was nothing remarkable or showy in the estate. It was tiny compared to the vast palaces in Ineb-Hedj. Several shady rooms flanked a pool and few drawings adorned the whitewashed walls. Everything was meticulously clean. In the center court, woven rush mats lined the floor. There were no standing piles of refuse outside; no smells of waste. Incense and perfume abounded in the early evening breezes that did, in fact, exude peace.

A servant moved from the wings into the Akaru's open courtyard to spread more fine rush mats woven with patterns of lions, stars, and the sun in splendor out on a white limed brick table that rose from the smoothly-scrubbed floor. An older, but elegant woman slipped back and forth then told her servant to water to wash the guests' feet and hands. Cups of beer and even wine made from grapes were set out along with bread and palate-freshening green herbs. The woman took a place of honor beside the old man.

His wife, Marai mused. *He has other wives but they are not here with him. Wonder why that is?* He motioned for Djerah to sit. The young man plopped down beside him and studied the curious devotion of the servant and these formal purity rituals.

"As you have wondered, I am Mtoto Metauthetep Akaru-Sef of the Qustul Sepat and this is my chief wife Xania." There was a prosaic nod. The man pushed forward a plate of bread, greens, and sauce for his guests, gesturing for them to eat.

"I have men who want to war from New City Qustul and even in Buhen." He dabbed at sauce and passed the dish to his guests. "You might have warriors from these and other sepats waiting on only a word from me," he paused, amused by Djerah eating like a starved man. He pushed another tray toward his guests. "I tell them to be calm, though, because in my visions I have seen it will not go well at all."

He looked Marai steadily in the eye. "Do you know he always comes to us with a ten times the number of those who want a war with him? At least that? And he does not entertain prisoners for very long; toys with them a bit, then…" Akaru-Sef made a gesture of slitting his throat. "We do not wish him to come here, but we are bound by treaty." The old man lifted a dish of flat breads and sauce to them. "Our land is no longer the wondrous hunting land of his father's time, yet still he comes here under the false pretense of marshalling and inspecting on king's orders. In truth, the king needs him away from the north. His actions *do* provoke wherever he goes, but he still has value."

Marai felt as if he was in the presence a wise and benevolent man who had more of the demeanor of a priest or scholar than a warrior-king.

Peace through intellect rather than peace through might, he mused. *If he thinks Menkaure has sent us, then our journey has outrun the news. Wonder if that's the real reason we were going faster... to stay ahead of Maatkare or this one finding out? Damn the Children for this. Don't they know how this hurts me? How it hurts my ladies?* Marai felt a tingling sensation in his brow and wondered if the stone was emerging. He rubbed gently as if he was wiping a bead of sweat from it. It wasn't. A feeling of sympathy and sad longing filled him, as if the Children were trying to tell him that they had learned much from him and that outside of forcing the choices, as they had once so elegantly explained, they were doing the best they could. The Akaru was a person he needed to get to know. Marai sensed from them that he would make a great difference in the way the rescue of the women played out.

"Well..." Marai shrugged, sopping up some of the sauce with his bread. "I *do* have other news... Great Menkaure is in his Horizon about a third of a moon now. King Shepseskaf gave me the writs before I left and he expects representation from the sepats as adopted sons of him. Don't announce it yet, though, because Maatkare mustn't know this. You'll also need to make your journey north in under two moons to attend a funeral *and* an elevation... as will this Prince..."

Marai watched the look of quiet shock on the older man's face, followed by the prayer:

> *"I am the Lion-god who cometh forth with long strides.*
> *I have shot arrows, and I have wounded my prey.*
> *I am the Eye of Horus,*
> *I have arrived at the domains.*
> *Grant that the Asar Ani may come in peace."*

Mtoto Akaru Sef bowed his head, as if he wanted to weep. He had recited the fare you well and good luck in the afterlife prayer in such moving tones that both Marai and Djerah bowed their heads in temporary misery.

"I had not sensed *this* as the thing that had come upon our land," the Akaru shook his head. Marai noticed the wife reaching to soothe him by rubbing his neck. "I did not know him man-to-man very well once he ascended. We met more when he was a prince and would come up here to do commerce. I saw his daughters growing up. I *did* know of him and of his great sorrowing because he was not fierce, and of his poor children's deaths. I loved and chose his pattern of mercy. If his son is merciful, he will suffer for it too. Some in the north say kings should act as punishing gods toward their wayward citizens and not as caring men."

Underneath the old man's placid demeanor, Marai sensed a kind personal power from which came this attitude of peace. It didn't explain Akaru's initial uneasiness at the gate. He startled a little when the old man gave voice to his thoughts as if Marai had spoken aloud.

"I know you sensed evil and harshness in our land, but know it is the prince who brings it," he dipped more bread into the sauce and passed bowls of soup as the servant refreshed them. "There are warriors who are true blood of my father who wish to end young Prince Maatkare's life… more this year, even though he has stolen none of *our* women for his pleasure or taken our cattle for his food. He has actually almost behaved himself."

Their magic taming the beast? **Marai found himself thinking.** *No, the cost is still too great.*

"…And memories of his past bad acts are too long," the Akaru finished the big man's thought. "Oh I do have men who want to go up against him in spite of my forbidding it. I have set in motion another 'thing' however, because he has threatened me. Your news of the passing of our Father Menkaure has both explained and changed much. If men go and succeed in slaughtering the prince and his troops, Kemet's reprisal at the death of one of its royal sons so close to the death of the king will be unequalled. His hunting season will be over soon. He will go and discover once again his place in the new king's court."

"If there is one…" Marai blurted. He knew Wserkaf had told him that his wife and Daughter of the God despised the young prince *and* the Great One Hordjedtef. Because of her arranged title marriage to her half-brother the new king, she served as advisor of the heart. Wserkaf would become Great One and Hordjedtef would step down into long overdue retirement. Something in Marai's heart found a moment of vengeful merriment. *If she expels him because of the death of her sister, he will flee here and then be sorry he abused these people instead of forging allies to overtake the north and put the crown on his own head. He will find he has created enemies instead of allies.*

"I will go north, if I am able. Menkaure Khaket was a good man… a worthy god. He will be welcome among the stars," there was another moment of reflection, "but men are frail. Our bodies die eventually," he looked up, smiling again. "You tell me this, and tell me of the women you seek, yet neither of us truly understand why you both are still here supping with me."

Marai knew that, and knew no real information had been given except that Maatkare and the women were not likely to be at the Prince's home encampment for another week or two. All of the rush to get here had been pointless. He dabbed a piece of the bread in a kind of pale bean sauce livened with a fiery pepper that had just been brought out. Djerah did the same, then seized wine to cool his mouth. Akaru' earrings jingled as his head shook with laughter.

"You said you have not seen the women, yet you know they are not in any true danger. How do you know this?" Marai asked.

"When he arrived, they stayed on the boat, guarded. Even so, he pointed out he had rethought taking women from us because we had behaved and produced good tribute. He told me then of the one Deka; boasting of her and claiming I most assuredly *ought* to know her. He would not *allow* them out. I suppose he thought they might try to escape if their feet were on dry land. I sense they have tried twice before," he sighed. "I cautioned him that these were *women*, not animals he has captured; that he ought to respect them even better than he respected his best warriors, lest they conspire about his doom."

"And?" Marai breathed out in frustration over the need to storm wherever that prince might be whether he knew the location or not.

"He's a hard young man, and not too given to listen to good advice. The first night I told him he needed to be respectful… that I was tired of his mistreatment of women over the years because of something that happened when he was a boy. I ordered oil soap and perfume taken to his boat for them to wash." He sipped at the beer that finished the appetizers. "In the morning when he came back and I did his reading, I told him to go home because things had changed and it would be evil piled on vengeance piled on dying if he stayed. I told him of the stars in position for the descent of the storm maker. You know him as Sutek. We call him Sebiumeker and find him more like Atum." The Akaru sighed a little, "I already told you he essentially called me a liar and left saying he would prove his own truth and bring the woman who was of our land to see me in the evening. Fearing he would hurt her in front of me or do some other evil thing, I went to visit my grandson some leagues away in Buhen. He is a young priest, and my 'inside man' to what goes on in the northland. He had recently come from his duty in Khmenu two days in advance of our young prince."

"But you came back. You saw something else in the stars?" Marai asked.

"I had a vision of the woman, calling out, but could not see her face clearly, just her noble color. The other two were with her, following. I believe he takes special care of the one of Ta-Seti. He has long preferred the self-discipline and inner power of our women, even those who are peasants. It challenges him."

Marai felt more than a chill at his words. He remembered the vision of Deka and the prince in the well, and of seeing her spiritually and physically overpowered by a beautiful and sensual young man with the look of a wolf. *Has she come to her senses now that she's in her own land? Will she even* try *to escape him?* He couldn't sense that anything had changed. In his most casual thoughts, she was evidently willing to be with him. Of Ariennu and Naibe he sensed only a mild worry.

Akaru-Sef signaled that the main courses be brought out. Servants brought out more beef and roast goose, breads of varied sweetness and shapes, grain and bean delicacies, and sweet little vine fruits and nuts. It was quiet. Marai knew any entertainers or dancers were away as well as all but the chief wife. Only a few servants, guards, and cooks had returned.

He stared past all of the food into the quiet of the old man's eyes, knowing the Akaru was drawing him out; reading him the same way the priests did. In a moment's flash, their eyes locked. He found himself studying the man's balding profile, the high but backward sloping elongated forehead. Profile of the gods he had been told. His nose was narrower than typical Kemet noses, but still lobed and proud. It was the color of his skin and hair that was off. That he held any sort of title or honor in this place of deep colored men and women amazed Marai. He should have been drowned at birth with his looks.

"She told me I would find you here. Deka even told me your name, 'Akaru Sef', from her *own* vision." Marai then sent a silent thought. *Your face. Something about it strikes me, though, like something in a dream.*

"I see you looking at me and I hear your question. My face is nothing; just unusual… not like those born here, yet I was born not far from here. It is perhaps a story that bears as much long telling as the one you will not state to young Djerah;

about how you came to be healthy and unbent by age when your years are greater than my own, and what the nature of the Ntr stones is."

"I know little of them but that they are what is left of a noble race from beyond the firmament," Marai paused a little, hesitating because he still thought Djerah didn't need to hear some of this. He saw the older man frown almost imperceptibly, wrapping hot-sauced meat in his bread and eating it demurely.

After a thoughtful silence the old man spoke again.

"Deka. You and Prince Maatkare say her name is or was Deka? In our language we have such a word. It means 'one who pleases'." Akaru-Sef smiled a little wider, sipping a dark and pungent wine. "It's a child name or a pet name. It would never be her name if she were truly of this place. A grown woman is never asked to be 'pleasing' to a man or even to a company of other women. When a woman is happy, she chooses to give happiness to her lover, not to 'please', just to *be*." He offered another cup of wine to Djerah, who, unused to such strong drink, was starting to feel drowsy.

Marai caught another change of expression in the old mans' face as if he was searching for the answer to Deka's mystery himself. His eyes glimmered only once before he spoke again.

"You shared your spirit with her, but did not ask for her body. The prince who has her now takes it without asking, but that is his nature as a hunter. He *will* possess all he encounters, or he will destroy it. You will struggle to no good end for her until that day when she asks you to come to her." Then, he relaxed as if thinking about the woman was upsetting him but he was blocking out that misery. "Let me tell you of this place and its legends so you understand what is coming…"

Marai frowned, not interested, but Akaru saw that. "You wonder how what I tell you is important to you on your quest?" he asked. "Understand only that it *is* important…"

The sojourner's thoughts drifted a little as he listened to Akaru tell how the nature of the god had changed. At the same time, he contemplated and simmered over the thought that Deka might be lost to him forever.

I can't let myself think that, even though I never won her over in the first place. I still have to go to her, just to see if this prince holds her against her will as he holds Ari and Naibe. If we come apart, it makes no sense because she has the stone in her brow same as the rest of us. We're supposed to be together.

"Chaos *is* coming loose now..." Akaru-Sef began. "The seasons are dry in recent years... as if a famine comes. Soon we will go up to Buhen across the river and into the hills beyond forever if we survive. Each year we must do that when the water from the underground river dries. This year, the water may be gone for good," he sighed. "I think it's time now, especially now you are here and the king precedes me into the west."

Marai and Djerah listened to him continue the tale of how Qustul Amani should have gone dry long ago. "It has always been a gift of greenness in the wilderness, but we are a hardy people. Two days south there is better grazing land. My grandson is governor there. This year, once the new king gives his stamp, I will pass the ruler ship to him or to descendants of my father's bodily sons and live out my days with a few servants and wives down there. All I have to do after that is endure young Maatkare once a year. Maybe even that will pass when the lions abandon it and the green does not return."

Hear me, my Man Sun

Marai heard the faintest of whispers. *Deka*, he thought, then continued listening to the Akaru.

Part 3: The Storm

OPENER OF THE SKY

Chapter 14: The Link

Marai and Djerah returned to the shore after their unofficial "Welcome to Qustul Amani" meal and pulled the boat out of the water.

"I wish we could just *go* in the morning after we rested," Djerah muttered. "He isn't going to help with anything. Says we'll have warriors, thinks about it, and then says it's a bad idea."

"And go where?" Marai turned the boat over, stowed the very normal looking oars and furled sail, and stood up. "Go find this prince? I could, I suppose. I *could* have sent death ahead of me, too, but then I might have destroyed more than I needed to." He straightened up and stretched, sensing the elder's disquiet as he finished his business and trailed over to them.

"By the way Djerah, things are not always obvious or revealed. Sometimes the real meaning of a vision comes out much later," Marai thought about the killing of the thieves so many years ago and realized how much it still bothered him.

"Well that's done," The elder announced, "and no news of our prince. Stay the night while I meditate, though. In the morning I may have a fresh idea, maybe a prophecy for each of you. Our prince did not like his… maybe yours will be a better one."

"I have magical things to show you while we wait on some of this…" he waved his hands in the air as if he was clearing some muddled mess out of the air between the men. *Mess around us. Spirit tells me much of your questioning will be answered as you learn of me.* Then, he continued aloud, "come with me while I tell you more." He trailed past the men, beckoning almost shyly for them to follow.

Marai urged Djerah to quit the attitude of complaining and come with them.

"First, just call me Akaru or Akaru-Sef… It's easier for you than my many given names," he began, leading the men out of the walls of the small estate. "It's a title, but just easier…"

"What does the whole thing mean? Even your given name. It sounds like a Kemet name, not Ta-Seti," Djerah trailed along with Marai and the elder. He finished eating an extra chunk of melon and bread he snagged from the repast.

"Mtoto means 'child' and Akaru-Sef is 'Lion-god yesterday'," the old man smiled. "As for my given name, Metauthetep… it means Metaut, my father, is satisfied. I also have a throne name given by the spirit which is not spoken aloud. I was given *that* name by King Djedphre when I was presented to him by Old Djedi. That king wished me to replace my father when he went into the West. It's part of the Suph – the treaty. In return, I was educated in the school of Djehuti at Nekhen, Khmenu and in Ineb Hedj until I was well versed in everything mathematical, scientific, and spiritual that I would need to be a wise but compliant ruler here."

"So actually, *all* of your names are titles," Marai shrugged.

The three men had moved a distance from the actual walled city and walked up a slight hill in the clear, hot afternoon. A slight wind had begun to prevail from the west.

He's right about the drought, and once that comes the dust storms will be nasty, especially if they don't rain out at the end, the sojourner mused.

Come and see

Marai heard the small child's voice laughing in his thoughts. It was as gentle and loving as he remembered it had been long ago. When he had first heard it, he had been cowering in the back of his cave because the night sky had just gone brilliant with green light that came through a pink orb in the sky. Now that he thought about it, he realized that light was like the orb that had enclosed his boat when they traveled at a faster than possible speed. The voice had been Naibe's seductive voice, but it had also been his dead wife Ilara's voice.

"Come and see…" Akaru's voice mirrored the child-voice from long ago. When Marai heard it this time, he chilled, knowing that old man's voice really *was* one of the unidentified voices he had heard so long ago.

So, the Children knew about him. I knew that, because there were supposed to be three of us. This puts a seal on it, Marai thought.

He saw Akaru's eyes twinkle in childlike merriment and great pride when he looked back over his shoulder at him and Djerah as he led them along the outer wall to the western end of town. Something about the old man was just too irresistible, not of earth, and almost too peaceful.

Marai had seen the platform they approached earlier when he and Djerah came in, but he hadn't thought about it until now. It rose half-way up the exterior wall. In the center of a temple-like enclosure was a smaller square that rose higher than the wall, topped by a walk. Inside of that was a small version of an Eternal House with its four equal triangular shapes rising to a smart lime-white point.

"Yours?" Djerah asked, "I worked on the one for Menkaure during the floods," he whispered as if they approached a sacred ground. "I will tell you right now that one this size makes much more sense."

"It is also my observatory. I built a temple around it and a tomb pit under it for later," Akaru Sef beamed. "It is where I have had visions of what will come to pass." He instructed the guards who had come with them to put in the key so the bolts to the entry slid back. The men followed the sepat governor up the brick steps to the top of the observatory wall. Once again, they were aware of a steady-but-gentle breeze.

"Feel this wind, how hot and dry it is?" Akaru-Sef wet a finger in his mouth and held it up, showing how it dried instantly. "When the wind is like this, it withers our fields and with it the grazing grass. We are too low in water so soon after the flood, but down in Kemet, they won't feel it until the New Year."

"Well someone needs to tell the king to implore to his brother gods. If it's a low flood in his rising year that spells bad luck for our whole world," Djerah started.

"Which is what I told Prince Maatkare when I told him to go home. I hoped he would tell the king then *why* he went home early," the old man insisted.

"And so the fool thought you just wanted him off your land and not hunting or bothering the girls here. I've never met him, but that's the way a dog behaves." Marai scoffed.

"Ah, then you know another thing about him. The 'dog of war' affinity…" the elder snickered like a youth who told a dirty story.

"Seen in a vision, only." Marai shook his head and thought: *Dog of War has been nipping at the leg of the War Bull too long now and needs to stop.*

"Not only did he *not* believe me, he wouldn't even sit still for the rest of the truth I was giving him. The stories say there has not been a year like this since the one when I came to be, sixty-four years ago," he turned, his eyes slowly closing in some irritation.

Marai noticed how much red color was in the man's eyelashes, and how increasingly foreign to Ta-Seti he appeared.

"Young Prince Maatkare Raemkai is an educated man, grandson of one of the gods of wisdom, if you will. He isn't ignorant of the signs *or* the stars. I think he simply has come to believe he's above the gods' reproach and doesn't understand it is mostly his golden-tongued grandfather aiding him." The old man began to lead Djerah and Marai up the steps to the observation porch. "He told me he knew the stars from his own journey here. He argued the hunt would be fair enough, even challenging, but not impossible. I told him two more things: One is, when the wind shifts and goes south to east as it has so recently done, he is not to cross the desert strip between the grasses to hunt there or great evil in the way of demons will be wakened. The second is, we will be unable to supply him anything after two more weeks. We will be gone to the south until the stars that foretell this wind change." But then, Akaru Sef sighed. "Yet now, I must violate my own safety and take a boat to the royal city myself, instead of going with them."

Marai shuddered. For a moment, he saw the image of Naibe-Ellit walking in the swirling dust with eyes that did not see him. The vision played against another woman's shrill laughter in the distance. 'A storm is coming', Naibe whispered dully in the vision, as if every bit of emotion had been frightened out of her. Then, in the distance, Marai thought he heard roaring like a mighty flood of a river.

"I hear something. Is there water near here, other than the great river?" he asked.

"Now that you mention it," Djerah frowned and inclined his ear to the distant sound. "I didn't think about it until you said something, but it sounds like water running, or maybe the wind rattling dry grass."

The men looked around, then stared into the horizon. Marai felt the wind toying almost lovingly with his "tassel" hair. A feeling of peace and a strange sense of power stole over him, as if someone or something feminine in the wind recognized him.

"Ah, you hear her then. She has many names. The Lady Oya, some who live to the east call her. There, she is the wind and the storm. I like to think she is Tefnut, the gentle raining wind that feeds the flood, or Satet, the river rushing by. Many names and faces, one feminine energy. She knows you too, Marai, and whispers to you to take care because there will be more. The time for the wind demons is long past overdue."

Akaru-Sef's freckled face drew gaunt and filled with a look of mystery. "The breath of will come upon the earth and make the dunes walk. Legends say once, on the whim of a sorcerer long ago who many thought *was* Sebiumeker, you in Kemet say it is Atum himself, a whole village was covered up in a day and what is green now was once a piece of the Satet's mighty river that he buried out of anger to her. That is the water you hear… the ghost of a stream." Akaru-Sef pointed toward a distant range of buff-colored mountains. "All of that was grassland when I was a child, because the spirit of the lion blessed it. As I grow old, so does this land. If the Satet would come again, the waters would rise and there would be grassland once more." The governor turned away from the formed brick rail a little sadly. "When I go into the west, to my Amenti, it will be here my remains will lie, but none of my people will stay. They will need to bring me things of the dead from a new place if I am to live on as akh."

Marai stared hard into the horizon. A rhythm of drums sounded in his head followed by happy sounds of singing and chanting whispered into the air. *Is it the ghost of the buried village?* he asked himself, *a whole village?*

Akaru nodded as if he heard that thought and took Djerah and Marai on a tour of the rest of his Eternal House. Two chambers were full and sealed.

"My first wife is here five years, so is the woman who mothered me. Now," he cheerfully told them, "I have Xania as my chief and one more. We have many children who will be tasked to keep our resting places and honor our names, but I saw in my vision years ago that my place would be here. While I am alive, we will go to where the still water is," his grin affirmed as he broke into a quiet chanting poem.

"We will seize the cool region soon and drink at the Lake of Memory," his voice intoned.

Marai felt the trembling start in his chest and spread throughout his body. These were some of the words chanted over his head while he lay in the tomb during his trial.

"For we are perishing of thirst…" the Akaru continued as he paced out a curious design on the platform before the stone peak. It was a calculation of stars etched in relief on the brick showing Asar as the hunter again.

"For I am a child of Earth and Starry Heaven, but my race is of heaven alone," Marai felt himself whispering. It felt good to say words that he had only felt for so long… in sleep… in Wserkaf's farewell. Djerah's open-mouthed stare was followed by a taunt.

"Oh no, not magical stuff again…"

"Which, as you will learn, is only magic to those who are neither learned nor wise," Akaru broke away from his prayer for a moment.

"I will be happy as a kid in milk…" Akaru-Sef continued, sinking briefly into something like a trance just long enough for Marai to pause and stare.

After the prayer, Akaru spent most of the day Akaru walking his property with the men. He looked at the boat in which Marai and Djerah had sailed, discussed life and mundanities, and heard gossip from the city of the king. By evening, Marai knew the young man was getting twitchy.

"So… how long do we stay here?" Djerah impatiently asked from the water as he soaked in his first immersion bath.

"You and I both know he's stalling us because he's waiting on his scouts to see where Maatkare and the women are," Marai stared out into the plaza where he saw Akaru waving sage bundles and wondered what he had sensed that brought the need for that. "A day or two is my guess. Meanwhile, I'm going to get rest, get stronger, and get a sense of how I can take this snapping dog-man…" he grumbled. "I might go sooner, if I sense any further dread through these little ones tonight," Marai patted his satchel of Child Stones on his belt, then prepared to take his bath as Djerah got out of the water.

"And I have the little one you've loaned me? Wonder what it'll tell me tonight, since I'm not wishing up the speed of the boat anymore."

Marai raised a brow in surprise, then laughed. *So Djerah thinks he was making the improvements? I thought I was making them. Maybe he'll be a good choice after all. A peasant and a stonecutter. Eh? Well, I remember I was just a shepherd.*

OPENER OF THE SKY

Chapter 15: The Insult

A commotion from the village brought the men back from an early morning contemplation at the observatory. Akaru had taken the men there to discuss some of the pathways of knowledge he had acquired over the years. Djerah, not particularly interested, paced anxiously. Marai saw that, knew something was bothering him and hoped it wasn't the reality of his future in Little Kina Ahna breaking through the barricade he'd set around his heart.

The three were greeted by a delegation of men and supplies that had been sent from Maatkare's camp.

The men hurried toward the gates, but the smell instantly told them that instead of bringing good tanned skins and aged ale-beer, these emissaries had unceremoniously dumped a quantity of badly tanned skins and half-spoiled maggoty meat at the gate. It was obvious that the prince was mocking Akaru Sef's agreed contract for payment as well as attempting to bait him into a response. The guards had seized the men who delivered it and were holding them so that the old governor could rule on what should be done to them.

"His Highness sent that?" Djerah couldn't contain his shock. "What an unbelievable ass…" he spat on the ground.

Marai nudged him a little.

Just wait and see how the Akaru handles it. It's his problem this time, not ours, he sent a thought back to the young man, knowing custom dictated such shoddy work would rate at least a severe scourging of the messengers so they could take their wounded backs to show them to the man who sent them. *He'll have to send the prince a message that he's not pleased. Learn from what he does.*

At first the old man's expression didn't change. There was no outrage. Akaru's expression relayed that this was, in fact, *exactly* what he had expected to be delivered. He folded his arms and paced back and forth in front of the pallet containing the stinking load a few times.

"You have a written message for me explaining this, then?" He moved toward one of the expressionless men pinned between two guards.

Marai, who had disguised himself as an ordinary traveler, pulled Djerah aside. He urged him to move them a good distance from Akaru and the assembled men.

What are you doing? How can you change how you look just like that? The young man started, but then realized Marai didn't want to be recognized.

You know I stand out in a crowd. And forget how I do it. Just sense what they are saying. It's good practice.

Marai turned his back on the scene, then bowed his head. The first thing he sensed was Djerah objecting and claiming he couldn't do that kind of thing. Then, he saw the scroll Akaru was handed in his thoughts as if he was looking over the elder's shoulder. Akaru unrolled the message and began to read. Marai knew instantly that no official scribe had written the note. The written and drawn characters were not a schooled standard, but drawn artistically in what he sensed was Prince Maatkare's own strangely-tented but elegant characters.

Like little pointy-eared demons on some of the upstrokes… no scribe would…

Akaru read aloud.

"Beloved Lion Master… I fully understand what you are doing. My advisors tell me this is not, after all, the year of Atum's *or* Sutek's hot breath. In our voyage here, we *did* observe a plentiful rise of waters unlike the prediction of coming drought you have given. The game, poor at first as I journeyed to inspect the mines, has improved in the past two days and the beasts we take are moist-meated, not the sinew and bone of a bad year. Your foreboding has an odor about it similar to what I have left you today. Do not try to trick me into departing early as my house still rules over you, despite the amicable and friendly tones of the treaty. Yours in sovereignty, Maatkare Raemkai Grand General of Qustul, Buhen, and southward, Emissary of His Majesty Menkaure Ka-Khet Lord of the Two Lands"

Akaru-Sef quietly rolled the papyrus back into its form and slipped it into its carrying case. For a moment he meditated on an answer.

That was a challenge, Marai thought. *This prince wants to start something.*

"He writes well…" Akaru Sef addressed the man who had given the letter, motioning for his guards to release the men. "From his heart, I see." His smile was cryptic. Turning to his guards, he said "the men are not at fault for delivering their leader's words. They have been polite and have not themselves challenged us," he turned to the men. Tell your master to do as he will, then. He may stay if he wishes, but tell him I presented no trick in my observations. I am merely warning him of what I know is true." Then, he waved the men off. "Tell him, though, I will not change my own plans. We may not remain much longer to support or re-supply him for his return voyage. We desire to protect ourselves from all I have observed."

The men scampered like rats back along the trail away from the river, glancing around from time to time to see if they would be shot in the back as they left. Akaru motioned to his men to sort through the leavings on the pallet to see if anything could be salvaged and dried with natron salt. Then, he beckoned to Marai.

"He writes like his grandfather talks…" Marai mused, imagining the man's haughty and officious tone as he sat shaping his letters in his lamp-lit tent somewhere out on the grassland. "Why didn't you send the word of the king's death? He would certainly want to hurry back for the burial ceremony, then you'd be rid of him."

"Many reasons, all involving a better and less-traceable strategy." Akaru-Sef answered.

Marai noticed a strange glimmer in his host's eyes; evidence of some higher-but-secretive working.

"First, he would ask how it is I came to know this. A truthful answer would tell him someone had arrived from Ineb Hedj. He would want to know who it was."

The elder had turned away from the pile of skins so the few men who had come back from Buhen with him wouldn't hear his discourse. Marai already knew that these guards wanted to go back to Buhen, round up troops of the more rebellious warriors and follow the envoys back to the prince's encampment. Akaru finished explaining his reasons for holding back any mission.

"Second, because the time has been fairly short since Our Father has passed through to the stars, he would want to know if the news had come through another of my visions. He would likely think I had lied and might decide to make another insult to 'teach' my people something. Or, if he *did* believe me and was to stop all operations and come through here to get to the cataracts and his boats, even with men straining at the oar it would take two weeks at least. In his hurry, he might scatter the goods you seek. The women, if he has tired of them, might be assassinated as useless extra baggage. It is far wiser to let him proceed and not think that anything has changed."

The sojourner flinched at the thought that the women might be destroyed, but in the same instant he knew he was vastly underestimating their strength as he had done from the start.

He might think about ending them, but be strangely unable. Maybe Deka had this kind of plan all along, he realized. He next sensed Djerah shifting in discomfort at the elder's lack of action. The irritation rippled away from the group of men sorting through the pallet of meat and skins as a feeling of misery and disbelief. He knew that letting insults go like that came across as a sign of weakness.

"Young Djerah," the Akaru addressed the younger man. "You have to understand this prince *wants* to provoke rebellion. He's bored with the hunt and *knows* the take has been meager, despite what he wrote to me. He *wants* to show the king his might and fitness to lead, to regain his respect. I've made no secret that the old city would be abandoned against the drought. He knows that an abandoned river fortress will be matchless property from which any roving invader might launch a campaign north or south. If he seizes Qustul Amani *now*, by putting down a fight, he and the king can later stage forays deeper into Kush and the lands of the Wawat. And if he has in his service of the heart what he *insists* is one of our women… Do you yet understand why I will not give him the fight he wants, though my own blood boils with the need to release my men to *both* of you?" he bowed his head for a moment. "I'm sorry about promising men to you before I understood everything. It will get the women killed unless you take the prince first and by surprise. I'll have to meditate on another way."

Djerah sighed, threw up his hands, and spun around in disgust.

"But Shepseskaf?" Marai whispered, certain no other ears could hear him. "I doubt he would support *any* campaign with this prince. He despises him."

"I know this," Akaru Sef returned quietly. "King Shepseskaf is *himself* despised as a weakling. He is what one would call a mere stone in the road. One moves it aside, or goes 'round it without slowing down too much. Do you *yet* understand why he must not know how things have changed in the north?"

Marai left the Akaru at the observatory to meditate and went walking "to be alone with his thoughts." As he stepped out into the grassland near the walled estate, he sensed Djerah following for a while then turning to go down to the river. *Glad he's not tagging along salting me down with questions. I can think for a while.* He liked Djerah, but had seen him go from being a semi-confident young stonecutter and family man to, as the Akaru said, a fledgling eager to fly without strong enough wings. Marai wanted to get a better sense of his wives' location. For that, he needed to have no distraction.

Precious ladies, if you can sense me... he sent a thought into the universe as he wandered further from the estate. Because he was closer to the place his highness and the women had settled, he thought he might be able to break through any psychic defenses the man may have erected around his encampment. He knew he might encounter lions or other creatures in the brush, but wasn't too worried about it.

He paced forward, enjoying the sweep of hip-high straw grass opening in front of each step and then closing behind him. In the distance, he saw a stand of trees that rose mysteriously out of the grass. Nothing else grew around it but grass and a broken line of drought-withered shrubs.

Land of grass, the land of my birth, he heard Deka's voice from the encampment on the way to Ineb Hedj echoing in his thoughts.

It's where she was in love with a god but he tired of her and threw her to earth, Marai sensed Naibe's sweet-but-childlike voice repeating her own revelation about the Ta-Seti woman.

I feel Deka's spirit most of all here, he thought. *It's as if this land gives her some kind of strength.*

The wind rattled in the grass; dry branches waving in the trees sounded like water. Its feminine spirit enveloped him for a long and sensual moment. Marai remembered waking in the sleep pod with Deka, newly beautiful and elegant, wrapped around him. She tried to give him her love again, but he turned away just as he had rejected her when she was crippled and ugly.

This is my fault, isn't it? All of this. Deka wanting to come here, turning it around and refusing me, the seeking this former lover Ta-Te who maybe wasn't even a man. If I had not been so shy… Deka, if it helps at all, forgive me. Marai hastened through the grass to the trees, then sat in the shade with one arm up on his knee.

He stared back out at the distance he had come and noticed the walled village appeared as only a darkened bump on the flat and grassy horizon. *Hmm. Didn't think I wandered that far. Something's watching me, though. Lion maybe?*

It felt different than the female spirit of a moment ago.

Means something to me now. I guess I had to set her aside. Deka did need to come here. This is her place to do the work of the Children. Different journey, as she told me over and over. And Akaru is right. He did see something in the stars, I'll bet, if stars ever predict anything at all.

The sojourner began to drift into a dream. When he opened his eyes, he saw that the stand of trees where he sheltered from the sun had grown lush and green, as rich in vegetation as the room in the Children's vessel where they had brought him food when he was first transformed. The boughs of a great tree trailed down around him and dipped into gurgling water of a shaded pool.

Peace. I will have peace here, he thought, wondering if this truly *was* the place he had seen in a different time, or if it was another reality. *We'll be together, Naibe,* his own voice spoke as if it was a Child Stone voice inside his heart. It repeated a few times in fading harmonies, then quieted as he slept. After a while, a dream like a vision formed for him.

Naibe-Ellit slept with Deka. In a different, spacious tent, Ariennu dutifully oiled the prince's back and shoulders. She whispered to him of his greatness… of how she knew she must wear a blindfold because his brilliance forbade her to look on him. She begged to touch his body, to service its needs, repeating again and again that she was a dirty kuna and not worthy of him. The man laughed a little, said filthy things to her, seized her, threw her on her belly, and took her like a mad dog. It was an act. She told him a long time ago that she learned wealthy men often liked to dominate women and show power, so she had become good at such games. It lulled them into trusting. That done, she could easily rob them after they lay snoring off a "good one". *Odd,* he thought as he observed, *it doesn't feel like an act when I see her do it. Wonder if she is working him, after all, or is he ruling her? This is too real, not heat-inspiring. This is ugly.*

Ariennu. I will be there. I am so close by. I will come to you soon, he whispered into her thoughts, but didn't think she heard him.

Trees surrounded him again. It was the present time in the arid and brown grassland. He roused himself, then focused on movement in the distance.

A lion? he tensed, because he was certain he had sensed something stalking him in the grass. His hand found and tightened on the knife in his belt, hoping he didn't have to wrestle with a rogue beast. He knew he would win a fight if there was one, but he would likely be scarred and forced to delay his charge into the wilderness to get his wives while he healed himself. He crouched and grew still, obscuring his presence. If the lion came closer and found his scent, it would not be able to see him.

The tall grass rustled closer. Birds fluttered up, startled.

"Marai?" a voice called. "Are you over here in these trees?"

Akaru, Marai thought, then returned silently. *Be careful, I thought I saw a lion.*

"Oh. You *are* here," the elder man called back. "There's no lion. Remember what you were told of me by legend? If there *was* a lion, I would know it. Your heightened awareness just showed you the spirit of one near me," the elder marched steadily through the grass right in the area where Marai was certain he had seen the animal a moment ago.

The sojourner squinted and rubbed his eyes.

I know what I saw, he thought. *That was no spirit; that was a shape change.*

"Do remember, not everything is as it seems," the old man quipped. "Are your thoughts clearing any about what you plan to do?" he asked, hands clasped and his body inclined slightly forward.

Marai motioned for him to sit and extended his hand.

"Oh, I suppose I *can* sit." the elder let the sojourner help him to the ground.

Akaru Sef reminded Marai of what an older version of Wserkaf would be like, in that he had the same training against frivolous emotional display.

"I know this provokes you," Akaru began, looking into Marai's face. "That I did not act in the manner of wild highland men or even the kings in the north, returning insult for insult, but there is much you do not know of me; that I was a foundling and the fact that I rule *at all* was a gift. I felt your thoughts at my gate about my color. My light skin; the speckles on it like a plover bird; my odd color eyes." The elder began to weave his tale and talk with his hands as he did. "Old Metaut was the last king before the suph saved me and raised me. Oh, there were hushy, hushy whispers as I grew and strange things happened to me that had no explanation. Later, an old priest Djedi came and asked that I study in a Hall of Life; that I was special. He told me a lion was my mother, perhaps it was Goddess Menhit herself." The elder plucked a stem of grass and nervously picked apart the end.

Marai frowned, listening intently. Something touched his heart as the old governor related the tale. He hitched his knee up a little tighter to ease his back. "Did you ever hear the truth?"

"My father told me he killed a lioness one day but found me lying beneath her, almost fresh born... my navel string unbound but withered, as if the lion herself had given birth to me. He wondered how I had come to be... if it was possible for a lion to have a pale gold and spotty human child. Knowing I would die there, he took me home."

"I see why they allowed you to be prince and sepat chief. They need an ally, but your people respect you. If they hadn't thought you had magical powers or something of a god about you, men could have found a way to kill you." Marai thought of Hordjedtef manipulating King Menkaure to death so his grandson, a more ruthless warrior, could seize the double crown.

Wonder why these people invented such a legend if it wasn't true at least in part. It's certainly every bit as strange as Wserkaf's father insisting the god Ra had sired him. A fantastic birth is always a needed ingredient for godhood. Simple people would believe he had dropped from a lioness' womb if she hadn't eaten him.

"They could have killed me, I suppose. Even now, because of the misery this prince brings us every year since he was partially banished, there are cousins of mine who discuss who will reign after me. It is very likely King Shepseskaf will make that ruling when I go to his ascension. I'm old. I'll ask to hand this to my own grandson, Aped. He is a minor priest, but more amenable to warfare, like the other young ones. And no, I never found out a thing more about the lioness. I just know lions listen to me when I speak and there has been not attack on our people this whole time; not even when someone has been foolish."

"A lion could attack this prince any time and I would not weep too much." Marai grumbled, then paused noticing his comment had caused an almost imperceptible change in the elder's expression. It was as if he had sent an age-old admonishment to him:

Be careful what you wish up. It may have a long tail, Akaru thought to the big sojourner. Then, he abruptly returned to talk of the stars.

"There was a thing that happened long ago, before I was born. Elder Djedi told me this when I was a child. I have told it to no ordinary man, so you hear it out here and away from other men.

One of the ancient and ever-living First Ones came to the world along with a tribe of others like him. They wished to craft a man from beasts who roamed here in the grass. Some of them created the bodies of men from clay, like Khnum. Some created them of their own seed like Atum. In the end, they left, but one elected to stay behind; to watch and guide. The world of men grew strong in body, but their souls were crafted in the arms and womb of their dark mother who bore them.

They learned from her daughters. It was good, but this First One was lonely and lost. His own never returned for him until right before I came to be alive. Hearing this, I grew up observing a certain track of Asar's star, certain that group had called to me," the elder paused. "I know the pattern like these spots on my hand and you know it too," Akaru continued; "the feeling that something watches you."

Marai caught the old man reading his thoughts again, but didn't mind this time. He remembered the shimmery thing in the night sky that watched him the night he saw the Children of Stone come through in the great pink bubble. He felt it again the night he and Naibe had become lovers. Something in the particular moments always lifted them up to another reality as if it wanted to take them with it, or experience it and could not. He sensed it on the night before his journey to the priests and then again before he started here. His mouth set and twitched. *The goddess? I sang to her.*

"I used to think..." Marai started, but Akaru interrupted him.

"Certain things do not reveal themselves to a person until they are ready to know how small they really are in the great pattern of worlds beyond worlds, where time is not. It's why even wise, very wise men like Great One will ultimately be replaced and the eras of the great kings come unraveled, as I have seen. Men have invoked chaos with this pride in self. Our young prince embraces it and even boasts he can control it. The sky will open like the blossoming of a mother's sweet womb, but from it will come the storm before the great age of darkness. Some of it still isn't clear to me, though. I simply asked him to leave because his very presence begs this time to come sooner, and he will not accept that he is the Opener of the Sky."

"I guess it makes sense," Marai thought about the seven stones at his belt and the one he had lent Djerah. "Seems that if we mass up troops we might convince him."

Akaru shook his head, emitting a wry laugh. "His own death would not convince his soul. Other ways. He has to make the choice un-compelled and of his own free will."

Marai sat for a moment in silence, sorting through everything he heard. He patted the bag of stones.

"I at least have something that could show more than you know to you... clear up the mystery of your birth."

"Don't," the old man got up and Marai followed him with a half-drowsy stretch. "If you want to show me what happened in the past, I don't need to know what it is." The men sauntered back through the grass toward the walled village. The sojourner was stunned when he realized it was already the middle of the afternoon.

"How a man comes to be is never as important as what he does once he has arrived. You know this. Nor is it important to force the hand of time by trying to see what lies ahead," Akaru's voice grew suddenly stern and almost scolding.

Sesen petals and the path of choice, Marai shook his head.

"That's the prince and his kind talking, to think a person's birth *means* something. Maybe Metaut *knew* the truth about me and decided some crazy legend would be better for me to hear. Whatever it is, I'm certain he had his reasons. Thus, I became the Lion Master and my sons were of the Sons of the Lion."

The rest of the walk back was silent. Each man contemplated his own thoughts about the exchange. After Akaru led Marai to the room where his audiences were held, he bid him sit beside his chair.

"I am *no* son of a king, accidental or otherwise," Akaru-Sef chortled under his breath and reached over to slap Marai's knee. "You're so concerned about reaching this goal of freeing your wives that it makes you rage. The deaf could even hear you think. Yet, you still ask yourself how I have anything to do with this and why you must wait to go and get them simply because some strange old man asks you to wait. I can only say it's because we are both chosen by them," he pointed to the sky, then looked up with a cryptic smile. "…and this was laid out in a pattern long ago. The Ntr, as our Kemet brothers want to call them, those whose memories are in the very stones you carry, that our young prince has and that young Djerah has borrowed are the very same ones who marked me on a starlit night fifty and six years ago when I had lived just seven years. I heard their song and waited all of these years for you to make your way to me and you still cannot say who I am…" the elder's thoughts drifted.

Marai's jaw sagged. The Children had told him at the beginning that one in Kemet would teach him. It was supposed to be Djedi, he thought, but the old man died. This place was not Kemet, but was under its control for now. *Is it this old man Akaru who is the destiny, or is this another blind run after I trusted Hordjedtef and then picked out Wserkaf only to hear him tell me no?* Marai asked himself inwardly.

Destiny seemed so fragile at times, but durable as history itself. No matter how many twists and turns the river of his life took in the Children's hands, it always remained frightfully on course. Hadn't Wserkaf said the same thing to him? Deka had wanted to go home, forever and always. Her suspicious alliance with the prince brought her to this border. It may have left her trapped. If he had not taken her, no one would have found Akaru Sef. He thought for a moment, then began a slow laugh. There was yet another connection he hadn't asked about.

"Nekhen…" Marai started. "When your elder Djedi came, he brought along his student Hordjedtef."

Akaru Sef nodded, and added:

"I think I mentioned that. That first journey, Count Prince Hordjedtef Iri-Nekhen realized he had been betrayed by his sister. He had *so* looked to becoming the king of the two lands. I heard later he nearly lost his wits and had to be secluded for nearly a full year after his brother Djedephre ascended to the rule. Some thought he died, but I know he recovered and became of masterful influence to the throne, even standing in as king when the ones who ruled were away on campaign. "I knew him more as an excellent teacher," his voice trailed.

"Masterful influence," Marai repeated in disgust. "He may as well have been king for good. I think he held the power and the sway of all of the other priesthoods."

"Ah… promoting some, poisoning others."

Marai shuddered.

Poisoning. He tried…" the big man started, but Akaru held up his hand.

"He *succeeded*," he said. "Your Ntr stone could repair your body from almost anything, but it does not repair your will. He broke that. The bliss and stillness of heart you will have to regain on your own."

Marai remembered that Deka had not lost her madness or coldness, Naibe had not lost her childish fears of storms or of being abandoned. Ariennu was as stony but saucy and ribald as she had been in her thieving days. He contemplated the way he had grown confused and distracted, then broke a long silence…

"And Hordjedtef sensed *nothing* of you, as I did when I saw you?"

"We were younger then. He is only eleven years my senior. He is still well even at his age? I'm impressed. Back then, I liked him then. There was no nonsense in him. He was very, very sharp."

"And yet, you were nothing to him?" Marai grew incredulous.

"No, I don't think so. He never treated me as anything special, anyway. My guess is that elder Djedi did not speak to him of any plans for me other than this sepat seat either. He clung to his own family: his poor son Auibre… his daughter's boy now camping over the hills and making grief for us, and lately I hear he has a protégé, Prince Wserkaf. Now *there's* a man of legend for you," he paused, noticing the afternoon was advancing. "But you already know about that 'Son of Ra', don't you?" he turned his attention to his few servants beginning to prepare food for evening.

"Come with me in a while," he rose and moved out into the plaza again.

Marai followed, looking around for Djerah. He had seen him as they woke. The young man had mentioned something about walking down to check on the activities at the water, and to fish or shoot something everyone might enjoy for the evening meal since the food brought in had been spoiled.

"The young man? He has a lot to think about now," Akaru sensed Marai's thought again. "We'll see him this evening. Just come with me. So much to share with you, now that you know!!" the old man bustled the sojourner quickly.

"You see, after that night, even if my father had *wanted* to raise me as the next generation of warrior-king, it couldn't happen. He had little choice, even if there *was* nothing special about me, but you *know* that." He smiled paternally. "You speak to my soul like a friend who has always known it. Your hands and heart are open and warm, like the voices I heard that night."

Marai stepped back, thinking he sensed a sound from Djerah in the distance and turning to look for him. The elder made a gesture for him to wait until he dismissed his guards. He walked Marai back into the lower portions of the observatory where the heat of the day never penetrated. Brick steps, padded down partway, and a rope ladder descended into a burial pit. Once both men were at the bottom in the cool damp chamber, Akaru Sef flinted a lamp then urged Marai to sit on the packed earth floor with him.

"This is an even better place to talk than out in the hungry grass. Here is where we can talk and only spirits will hear us," he said, taking a deep breath and regarding Marai's face in the light for a moment. "So how is it you came upon the Ntr stones, my brother-in-this-way?" the elder asked.

Marai felt a strangeness in the man's voice.

He's doing something that makes me feel uneasy, the way Hordjedtef made me feel, just no threat… a deep scanning read, perhaps. Maybe it's because he studied under Hordjedtef. The tone of inquiry sounds the same. I'll counter... the way I did to him. Question for question.

"What do I seem like to you, when you look at me?" the sojourner asked, watching Akaru-Sef cock his head in thought for a moment, as if he heard something and almost named it. He grew silent for a little while before answering.

"I know you are not what you appear," he started. "I know you are much older than I am, but not as old as a god. I know you have traveled far from your place and that somewhere along the way *they* took you up and built you like a monument. You, of all of us, the ones they mark, are the closest to them; to what they would like to be. But, because you are made of earth, you never can be like them. You will always be drawn into living your life as a man and not the god they wished to have you become. Your friend might be one in very much more time, but he needs watching now. I saw him at the water looking at the rafts."

Marai nodded slowly. His hand drifted to the place at his belt where he kept bag of stones. He shook his head. All of the wisdom in Kemet didn't explain it so well. *Because I am made of earth. Maybe they never even understood it. This humble governor of a sepat on the River Asar, even though he was educated by and with them. He's just unlocked all of the wisdom I could have ever gained from them.*

"I didn't pick Djerah out for this journey," Marai smirked, reminiscing. "He's my sister's great-grandson, I believe I told you. The last link I have to my people. I picked out Prince Wserkaf, but both of us know his destiny, at least the way it stands as of now." He thought about Deka, Naibe, and Ariennu for just a moment. "And the women... I just don't know. Men of the sand and women..." he started to tell the Akaru that in his upbringing, life was so brutal and death so imminent that men and women never seemed to have lengthy discussions of each other's ways and over the years formed different ways as the gods had dictated.

"But you are here, and in this land we worship women as creator and maker of the earth. The men are here only to help and learn from them in reward for cherishing and protecting them and the children they make," Akaru Sef said. "Certainly Prince Hordjedtef schooled you in this way..."

"He did, but very early I knew he was cheating me on everything he taught me. I found out he wanted to get the secrets the Children of Stone had to offer and then seize them for himself. I had left them with my ladies across the river. Great

One had no reverence for *my* women as anything godly if he brought them over just to get at the Children."

Marai looked up briefly and saw Akaru-Sef's face become ghostlike, as if some terrible truth had slithered out of Marai's mouth.

"Children… you keep calling them children," Akaru whispered. "Just now that sun broke in the horizon of my thoughts. If I doubted it, I know now you really *are* the one…" the corner of his mouth twitched in nervous delight.

"One?" Marai repeated.

"Come here…" he rose and picked up the lamp he had brought. He beckoned to the sojourner, then led him to a subterranean room behind the one where they had been sitting. "Look here…" he showed a carved and painted map on a stele at the back of the room. "Here is Qustul-Amani…" he pointed. "Here, the River Asar, and there is Ineb-Hedj along it, so far away; beyond that, Per-A-At." He showed a perfectly drawn replica of how the land might look from the air when someone flew over it, perhaps during a spirit flight. "Over here is the land where they take copper and turquoises… is that where you were living so long ago?" his sandy-silvery head whipped around so quickly that his earrings jingled.

Marai stared, stunned that all of the places he knew were outlined so well on the stone.

"Sin-ai…" he breathed, beginning to get dizzy with anticipation at what he would learn next.

"Good. Then by my calculations…" Akaru brought the lamp closer and pulled a clay slab from a stack of ostraca filled with rubbed out figures on them. Quickly drawing a triangle on it, he held it up to the map. The angles and proportions matched perfectly. Over the triangle, Akaru chalked in a slightly curved arc that traveled from bottom to top of the triangle but passed in proximity to all three points.

"The stars were different the night I lay ill with scorpion fever." he tilted his head in a sheepish gesture. "Some young ones take a sting better than others, but I became very ill. They thought it might be my light color that made me suffer so. Anyway, a strange star came down and went over our village that night. I heard the elders saying that they had heard of one like it from tales of the ancient days. They told me perhaps the god Sebiumeker was said to go in a boat of a million stars and that no one has seen it since."

Boat of million stars Marai paled a little, anticipating the next truth to drop. The vessel of the Children of Stone might seem as such… but the god Sebiumeker… just the evening Ra Atum. He listened as the Akaru continued.

"It sang in a strange language for me, but now that I have heard you speak some words to young Djerah… I recognize it. My father and the elders did not. When I heard it, I ran out into the grass, and that is how I came to find the lions!"

"Ay…" Marai shook his head, breathing in the memory of that night and feeling each word rising to his lips as if it had taken on its own peculiar magic. He began to softly sing:

> *"…Return to the night…*
> *Your servant implores,*
> *Your faithful slave to kiss your feet*
> *To touch your ankle would be rapture…*
> *Into your golden fire eyes…*
> *I vanish, burnt to a cinder…*
> *Consume me, O Goddess of every joy…*
> *Until I am nothing but your will…"*

Marai felt his eyes mist as he saw Naibe-Ellit, who had become the goddess of all of his dreams, fade into Ariennu, and then into Deka. He understood that, in some way they were a triple goddess being formed.

"That is so very like what I heard…" the elder sighed, "but now it is so much more passionate, like a man who knows the truth instead of one who dreams it. You were the singer then, just as you sing now?" the elder asked.

Marai knew it was time.

"We'll need to sit down again. Right here in front of this map will do," he helped the Akaru ease himself into a sitting position on the soft earth floor, then hitched up his kilt and unfastened the pouch at his belt. "I was the singer you heard. I didn't mean to sing for anyone but Asher-Ani, but…" his words halted as he felt the impact of what he was revealing. "So much happened to me after that night, it would just be better if *they* showed you."

Akaru-Sef stared into the vague glow of the seven stones as Marai arranged them.

A moment before the energy coming from the stones he placed in the powdery earth began to enchant both of them, Marai thought he saw a slight and clouded darkness move over the Akaru's face. He blinked but saw only ecstatic tears in the elder's eyes.

"These are…" the Akaru started to say something else, but couldn't continue.

"I know… what your people call the Ntr stones… just seven of the original seventy-eight, though," Marai answered. "They called themselves Children of Stone to me. I used to think they *were* Children themselves, and had always been as Children." The sojourner moved his hands through the glow, sending a thought. *Show me my ladies. Show the answer to where I will find them.*

"Then, for a while, I thought they were the Ka and Ba, the Akh as you call it of some who once lived but were now dead." Marai continued, slowly caressing the light above the stones.

"Then, I thought, maybe they are things crafted by them; stones that could think but much better than crystals I saw some of the priests using as healing stones. I used to think they were powerless in this form; that they needed me because their ship of the stars was no longer able to fly and that some grave thing had brought them down in the sand near my place. Now, lately, I wonder if this isn't all part of some grander design to make me *think* they were helpless, because I always cared over the weak. I was a shepherd. I'm used to saving lambs from the mouths of wild dogs." he smoothed his hand over the images on the stele, realizing he had thought of his wives in that way. A wolf of a prince had seized them and was all but flaunting his catch. "*Could* it be this god Sebiumeker doing this? The one those in the north call Atum?" he asked.

"I… I don't know, really…" Akaru stared into the image the stones made, still awed that he recognized the voice of his childhood dreams coming out of the mouth of his big new friend. "But you were right to think them separate… and also wrong… each time, don't you see?"

Marai saw an image of Deka forming magically in the light of the Child stones and watched as Akaru's eyes fastened on her image. She sat in a lamp-lit tent with her eyes cast down, aimlessly twisting a strand of hair into a thin braid along the side of her head.

"So this is the one you and Djerah called Deka, the woman of Ta-Seti?" Akaru-Sef breathed out, enchanted.

"I see her face and yet…" Marai traced his fingertips along her long necked image. A weak smile filled her expression, as if she felt his touch, then faltered.

"So lovely she is, but so sad and cold. She bears a great and painful sorrow as a mother whose child was ripped from her womb," Akaru-Sef whispered.

"She told me once that she remembered birthing a child who died. Told me because I, too, suffered the loss of a wife and a baby girl. It made me mourn until the night the Children found me. It was why I sang to my goddess; to make reparations. I always felt if I had respected my wife more she would have thrived. Men of the sand need a woman to seek other women for comfort and to endure a man, not be coddled by a husband. It's wrong of my people to think that. I lost her because I never knew she needed me so much," Marai thought of Ilara again. He hadn't thought of her in a long time.

"I could love this woman here easily; make her warm if I… Could I touch her through this light as you do?" Akaru asked.

Marai nodded, knowing his thoughts about his wife who had died were unheard.

"I tried," he said. "Something else was going on with her, though. Maybe you *could* reach her in spirit," Marai watched as the man's supple and sensitive fingers extended into the gentle glowing light. He touched her brow where the stone lay as if it was an instinct. When he did, her countenance softened as if she had fallen into a dream of ecstasy, then suddenly woke and froze. Her mouth formed the words "Ta-Te?" then retreated under a quiet and dour expression.

Akaru withdrew his hands from the light and motioned for Marai to clear away the stones. He rocked back on his heels, lost in thought for a moment.

"What is it?" Marai asked, startled at how quickly Akaru had ended their exploration.

"Something," Akaru Sef mused as Marai put away the stones. "Can't say, yet, but I know I will meet this woman one day, and soon. I know we have a journey to make together."

Marai paused, then fastened the bag to his belt. That the Akaru and Deka would meet one day calmed the big man a little. *Deka told me her journey was here. Now she is in her homeland, but…*

Akaru looked toward the entry of the subterranean room where they sat.

A noise of shuffling bare feet and talking drifted down the shaft.

"I know, it's late." Akaru pressed against the earth and made his way to his feet, "but there is so much to know and in so very little time."

Marai felt a question rise in his thoughts: *Little time? You? It doesn't have to be…* but the Akaru was already climbing the ladder out of the burial pit.

OPENER OF THE SKY

Chapter 16: Djerah's Revelation

"Look at that… almost evening." Marai remarked at the position of the sun in the sky.

"You noticed," the Akaru added. "When one is thinking and learning, the day is often so short that one runs out of time before all else is done." He pointed before Marai said anything else. "Look. I see young Djerah coming up the rise, too, or… is it?"

Marai scanned the path out to the river where the fishing boats were tied and the shaduf brought water into a canal for the fields. Something covered with muck from the ditches was advancing. Some of the young men were throwing jars of water on each other to clean themselves, laughing and playing and then going to their homes after Djerah turned and thanked them. He came up to Marai and Akaru, sweaty, wet, grimy, and breathless.

"Have a good day?" Marai asked.

"Good enough," Djerah gasped, mopping his face and spreading more mud all over it. "Flies are bad out here, though. Made us *all* dance. Had to keep the mud on us to stop the bites."

"When you are clean, there's an oil for the skin to keep the welts away. Xania can get it for you." Akaru reached forward to inspect the few swellings he saw. "But you have *good* skin, so there aren't too many bad places. I could never be out near the water without my 'Stay-Off Oil'. They love my spotty old skin." He beckoned for Djerah to join them and to move toward his estate house.

"So what were you doing?" Marai felt at least happy that his younger companion had occupied himself. He knew Djerah loved physical work just as much as he did and although he had been interested in Akaru's knowledge, he wished for a moment that he had been out on the river with the young man.

"I took our boat out to check it and I saw some of the men bringing water to the fields, so I decided to help them with the lever; shore it up so it wouldn't snap. Then, I just got in and showed them some of the things we did to get the water to the builder's stones so we could cut them sharp and one thing led to another and soon I was rutting out the channel for them." He grinned widely enough to rival a hyena.

The three men got cleaned up, sat for supper, and retired early – just after dark.

Glad he's eased up a little, Marai thought to himself as he settled on the cool mat set out for his bed. His chatter kept everyone's thoughts off of all of the grim purpose of this part of the journey.

Akaru-Sef is the heir of Djedi then, chosen by him, taught by the very man who wanted so much to be the heir that he posed as him in my first visions. Marai mused as his eyes closed, *but Wserkaf is no less important, still, and not just because I turned his thoughts around and he saved me. It's something else that will reveal itself later, I guess. After all, he does have the Eye of Truth, even if he let it get away from him.*

> *It is not who holds the object made of crystal stone*
> *Be one who knows its spirit.*
> *It finds its own in time.*
> *Know that.*
> *It is important.*

Marai sensed the message the Children whispered on the breeze that soothed them in the room. His eyes closed in sleep and once again he wandered in the grey of nothingness. *The Children's vessel, but dimmer,* he thought. *Why here? Why am I seeing this now?* He drearily wondered, but the grey turned into the black and dreamless void before he was able to think about the meaning of the message:

> *You know.*
> *The pieces fall into place.*
> *Rest.*

In what seemed a moment later, Marai woke with a cold and sweating start. Djerah's rumpled mat beside him lay empty. At first he assumed the young man had risen to relieve himself, but as moments stretched out he did not return. Securing his bag of Child Stones and a blade to his belt, the silver-haired man tightened his linen kilt, stood, and then darted to the outer door of Akaru-Sef's simple palace. The household slept except for the two guards grouped around the watch fire near the wall. A half-dozing guard sprang to his feet and brandished his short spear as a warning.

"Have you seen a man…?" Marai started, but when the guard saw who it was he pointed in the direction of the observatory.

"The young man came out not long ago and went to the Akaru's thinking place."

"Is he…?" Marai didn't need to ask if Djerah was alright because he *instantly* knew the young man had put the events in his life together with a slight nudge from his borrowed Child Stone. He quickly made his way to the gates of the temple portion.

Goddess, why tonight? Marai's arms flailed. As he hurried toward the entry gates, he sensed the young man's dark mood all at once. Finding the entryway sealed, he circled the base of the lower step. A hemp ladder was slung over the side near the back so that a climber might not be seen ascending it. Tugging at it, he decided it would hold his weight and went up.

Djerah stood facing west, staring at the small gully which had been dug below. He didn't turn to notice who had made a footfall behind him.

"Djerah?" Marai ventured as took a place at the observatory rail next to the stonecutter. The young man's head whipped around. His dark, angry eyes cut through the big man once. He bit his lip in awful agony, as if he dared himself to control the coming outburst.

"Talk to me, friend," Marai felt the young man's thunder of grief and didn't need to ask him what had happened.

"My wife left me," words wrenched from his throat. "This..." he slapped the small Yah stone down on the ledge. "*This* demon-thing spoke to me. You wanted to know if it would talk to me?" Djerah's voice grew louder and shrill.

"Well it *did*, in the night. It said my family is in ruins, and now where am I? I'm off trying to make a better life for something that's already turned to dust; something that was going on under my nose and I was so busy keeping us fed that I didn't even notice!" The pale stone glimmered a little as if it sensed his emotion and had realized how painful the truth it revealed had been.

Marai grabbed the little stone to protect it from being seized and hurled to the ground below.

"I knew I should have stayed at home. I wouldn't have left if I had thought..." Djerah's eyes glistened in rage, grief, hatred, and self-pity for a suffering moment.

The sojourner placed his hand on the back of Djerah's neck, expecting him to turn and weep. Venom instead of tears poured out of the younger man.

"I came out here because I knew you'd feel it and come out here after me. You can't help yourself and *I* can't keep anything from you. You *knew* about what she was doing! The stone let me see that, too! You *knew* if I stayed I might have kept the family, but you did sorcery on me and got the king's writ on top of it. You said on the way up here you really didn't need me but these Children wanted me to come. Well damn them, damn the king, and damn you!" He rushed Marai swiftly and with his gut knife drawn. It caught the big man off guard and bent him backward over the brick railing.

Marai seized Djerah's wrists, planted his own feet and pushed back up slowly and steadily, his fingers maneuvering to the pain centers on the young man's hands. He glanced to the side to make sure their combined weight wouldn't crack the stone rail. Guards' torches below formed red-gold circles in the dark.

"Djerah, don't make me hurt you. You're always coming at me with a knife when something bothers you. Last time I broke your wrist. What do you want broken tonight?" Marai pressed deftly on the stonecutter's wrists until his hands spasmed and he released the knife. With a roar, Djerah rammed him off-balance again with his head and shoulders, but Marai lifted him firmly and shook him the way a predator shakes its prey to snap its neck. Slamming him against the floor of the observatory porch, he knocked him senseless with one slap, then went to his knees to cradle the unconscious man on his chest. The light from the torches cast eerie blood red lights on their skin.

The sojourner opened his other hand and looked at the Yah stone in his fingertips. It whined gently at first, then sang a wordless melody.

I did not need him to find out this way. He turned the little one over. *Be at peace. I'll get him calmed down and give you back, but then you need to keep him be calmer the rest of this journey.* He put the stone in his bag, ignoring the gentle rush of greeting from the other stones.

"Djerah, I wish I could have told you something you would understand, but you don't ever listen to me or hear my words." Marai attempted to console the young man, who had come to his senses enough to struggle a little.

"L-leh-meh lone," he protested through the pain of a split lip.

Marai's grip on him relaxed. He let him sit in the floor of the porch while he waited for his first emotional storm to pass. He stared into the young man's squinting eyes and evoked his thoughts as his hand touched the young man's lip to stop the stinging.

Easy. Easy now. I brought you no evil. Let me heal that, Marai sent the thought of a healed lip through his hand. Soon, he knew the pain had stopped.

Djerah exploded into a torrent of grief.

"I knew she was seeing a man," Marai began. "My wife Ari told me she thought it was so. There was talk all over the neighborhood. I just thought it would be better to get you away from there because it's not just her straying. Her sisters rallied behind her!" he tried to soothe Djerah, but that failed. "They told each other you abandoned her when you took extra work on the crews."

"So I'm twice a fool?" Djerah shook his head, wanting to mock himself. "Once to let it happen and not know; twice for coming along with you with and letting it complete."

Marai heard a sound below and turned to look through the rail down to the ground level. Akaru-Sef's guards unfastened the gate and admitted the elder, who steadily trudged up the steps to the two men and sat a few steps away on a brick bench built against the secondary wall, to catch his breath and wait for the drama to calm.

"I'm used up now, don't you see?" Djerah held up his hand to push away Marai's sympathetic grasp. "Used up! My wife and SeUpa? I've known him half my life like a cousin. We worked the same farm in the planting season at first, then he became a peacekeeper." The young man reflected for one helpless moment. "This must have been going on a long time. Now that I think about it, I wonder if little Sheb is my son, after all" Djerah turned his face to the wall until his shoulders stopped heaving.

For long moments, Marai sat absorbing the young man's words. Then…

"When you can, do come with me to your room, young man. I have ears that listen, too. Then, we will all weep together." Akaru-Sef urged the two men down from the observatory and then, standing, dismissed his guards.

After a few moments and attempts at thwarting more arguments, the three men returned to Akaru's house. He told a servant who had risen during the commotion to make up some warm soured milk with honey and calming herbs infused in it.

Marai sat silently, his hand resting on Djerah's shoulder, transmitting a little boost of peace. No one spoke until the concoction was brought.

Akaru pushed a steaming cup of it toward Djerah, ignoring his refusals.

Marai saw what he thought was the elder's heka for the first time. The man's hand went up and a gentle calmness almost like a wind issued from it. At that point, the stonecutter listened to him finally and took the milk drink, sipping slowly, then more eagerly.

"These things you see tonight were not so very surprising to you after all, were they young Djerah?" he asked. "You are angry at *yourself* because you did not face your fear that you were losing your wife and you pushed the thought away as one pushes away an evil dream. You assumed the woman would understand your efforts, but all she understood was that she had nothing but a corpse in her bed when you were there. And when you would be in the work camps you were not there at all. She went to one who *would* be there," he explained.

"How many in the Little Kina Ahna knew?" Djerah shifted his attention, giving no indication he had heard the elder's wise words. His voice had become dull and nerveless. "You say your wives knew?"

"Houra knew," Marai answered, bowing his head. He hadn't been contacted by her spirit, but the words came to his lips. "It's why she stayed with you across the river. I just had that thought."

"From your stone?" Djerah looked up, taking a larger sip of the cooling liquid.

"Perhaps you were supposed to figure it out from her manner, Djerah, but then I never discovered my own wife long ago was so sick of heart. She never brought her sorrow to me. She was always pushing me away to go out with Naim and the other young men and to go take the flocks up high to where they could eat sweet grass as sheep should, and not be like goats chewing on weeds and stems. It wasn't until I saw she wasn't eating and heard her long for release from her life in a dream that I knew something wasn't right. I pushed it away. I thought she was just afraid of birthing our child, but her spirit knew she was dying."

Djerah finished the cup and let it settle.

"You're right, you know," Djerah addressed the old man. "She was tired all the time. She fussed and didn't want me staying late in the mornings when I was with her. Sometimes, I would wake up at night thinking she was going to take the little one out to settle him. Before that, when her belly was big, I thought she was out making water as a woman will do more at night when she's big with child, but then I thought I heard voices and laughing. The night you came back I woke to her getting into bed and telling me she had been out for air," his voice trailed. "I wondered why she was so eager to have me go with you, once she knew we would have no debt or tax to earn for His Majesty." The draught of milk combined with his raw emotions had the desired effect. He yawned heartily.

"There. That will make you sleep without dreaming or having wicked dreams," Akaru smiled, satisfied. "It's what you need now. Just let the goddesses of consolation take you in their sweet arms. Let them tell you that you have lost nothing but the blindfold that was over your own eyes."

"I hope its poison," the young man grumbled, putting down the cup. "I mean, what is left for me in Ineb Hedj?" he lay down, a mournful expression easing from him as he continued to relax and drift. "If I go back, she will not have me. If I work in stone and men will tease and laugh once they know how she left," his eyes closed.

Marai wanted to tell Djerah one more time that he had mourned his dead bride and daughter for fifteen years, and fruitlessly sang to Ashera every night until the Children of Stone arrived. Then, as if by magic upon magic he was made whole and heroic enough to find love again.

Djerah will be blessed and wealthy when we return. Wse said he will see to it Djerah is placed in the School of God Imhotep. What will be done with his family will then be his choice. It'll be a new life, but the creature who watched shimmered in Marai's thoughts again. Djerah mumbled before he slept.

"Maybe one day I'll be wise like both of you. Right now, I just don't care."

CHAPTER 17: ACTIONS IN HASTE

Akaru sat in a meditative silence with Marai for a few moments. They watched the young man sleep. When the elder was certain Djerah wouldn't wake, he got up, then beckoned for the big man to follow him out to the open plaza.

"A tough and harsh blow for our young friend, eh?" the elder began.

"I knew he wouldn't take it well," Marai answered. "It's the main reason I brought him. I understand that kind of rage in the blood as if it were in my own. I thought it would be better if he was away from that family when he realized what was going on."

"That was a wise thing, then." The elder smiled but added, "it *does* surprise me that a fine young man like him doesn't have *other* women to love him – a number two wife. In Kemet *and* in Ta-Seti, you have seen we love and are loved as time and spirit permit us. Why should one be a jealous man or woman when one can always find another," Akaru shrugged.

"He could barely feed the one he had or his four children by her. She had two widowed sisters and they had between them three more children. He cared for my sister too before she went into the West. I didn't know him before I went to the priests. I just knew he was a hard worker and he was making himself old trying to be a good man. I used to see the wilderness eat men up like that by the time they were thirty. Now I see the crews will do the same thing. All a poor man ever wants is to know he can count on a woman to be strong of heart and a comfort to him when he's in his house. If she is weak, she's easy to seduce when he is away," Marai thought of Ariennu again, of her inconstancy and opportunity seeking. *Djerah's wife did the same thing, but hid her deed. Ari was at least honest and told me she tended to wander.*

"Ah," Akaru nodded, "I understand it now. So this leaves our young Djerah doubting his own worth as a lover *and* as a husband. He can't yet believe that his woman was the weak one all along." The elder, satisfied with the explanation, looked into the dimly lit sleeping passageway and moved toward it. "Watch him, though. I know his blood is up, as you said. Tonight he cries like a hurt child. Tomorrow, he will be angry."

In the morning, Djerah woke easily. Marai woke a moment later and saw that a quiet reflectiveness enveloped the young man. At the end of a light morning meal, during which pure mundanities were discussed, Akaru spoke to him.

"Young man, Djerah?" he asked and was answered with a semi-silent grunt of acknowledgement. "I want you to show me the irrigation ditch where you created a miracle in the mud yesterday. Could you?"

Djerah sighed in disgust and got to his feet to lead the elder to the river bank.

Akaru looked back over his shoulder with an almost merry wink.

In moments, Marai happily lay out all eight stones in the dark quiet of the sleeping area. Once again, the images formed like illuminated smoke.

He saw the encampment moving north toward a bordering ridge of hills and counted a large detachment of men. It wasn't as large as a full battle group, which would have contained thousands. This was a scouting and enforcement group of a few hundred troops. The sojourner had learned that princes often led forays into certain areas. If trouble the small group couldn't contain arose, the detachment would withdraw to a safe distance and then return with more troops and a killing force.

Will I be able to handle this group of men when I go? he wondered. *I have to do this at night if I do it soon. I'll talk to Akaru and get him to distract Djerah. The way he feels right now, I can't risk taking him with me. I really wish this had come forth* later, he shook his head, but knew there really wouldn't have been a better time to hear of such a tragedy.

When he shifted to a quick glance for his wives, he sensed something different near the tents. Marai stared into the image and found two men dressed in guard clothing he hadn't seen before. *These are new,* he mused. The image cleared. The men were sitting on either side of Deka outside the prince's tent. She was hand talking to them.

Mutes? he asked himself. They were very sinewy and muscled; darker skinned than the other men and much darker than most of the Kemet or Ta-Seti men he had seen.

As Deka's hands moved, the men echoed her movements; learning what she meant.

It was a mirror game. He remembered she and Naibe liked to play it with him in better times because it formed a spiritual bond between them. *Why these men? Wonder if the prince knows this. Maybe she's hoping to turn them and make an escape.*

Deka. Hear me. Open your eyes to me. He tried, but saw her head bow and turn away.

She heard his voice, but wouldn't acknowledge him. One of the men *did* sense him and looked up, teeth bared in an odd sort of growl. She stilled him by petting the back of his neck. Troubled, Marai moved his vision to a nearby tent where he sensed Ariennu and Naibe reclining.

Ari, Naibe… Marai mouthed so intently over the arrangement of stones that his eyes closed. Ari tensed. The sojourner felt her blocking him out as if she knew her thoughts were playing tricks on her. *Still thinks I'm a ghost,* he hoped his frustration didn't come through. *Will you let me into your secrets? Will you? I… am… alive… coming to you… alive. Do you hear me yet, you foolish kuna?*

Ariennu's face looked up, darkening in a moment's horror.

Foolish kuna, is it? Damn you then Marai… Oh I forgot, you damned yourself because you wouldn't listen to me. I told you we weren't as hard to kill as you thought. And you… you…

Ari. Ari. If I could put my arms through time and space and just hold you… I'm alive I tell you.

Only here in my heart. There you never died. I'm with you every day, but you have to do better than this. If you live, you have to prove it to me. You have to prove it to her, too. Ariennu indicated Naibe curling gently on her lap. Her tawny skin was light as golden ivory, her hair like waves of night. The lids of her gently closed eyes reflected a natural, unpainted grey-blue.

Naibe, open your heart. Feel my tears of joy, making me want to burst with the joy only you could share with me. He bowed his head over the stones, breathing out in a sigh he hoped she would somehow feel because he knew she couldn't hear him.

Marai. My love. Her spirit voice suddenly hushed in his heart like the warmth of a summer breeze. *I know. I never let you die in here.* Her hand pointed to her heart. *I never stopped believing...*

A sound interrupted his viewing. Laughing voices were entering. Marai quickly scooped up the stones and put them in his bag just as Akaru and a servant entered the plaza.

"Where's Djerah?" Marai hopped up, curious that the young man hadn't returned.

"We went to the ditch and the shaduf. He wanted to fish, he said, so I gave him a net and then these two fisher girls saw him and his young naked self out there on the levee and paddled a raft over to him. He sent me on back," the elder laughed. "I think he will make his own cure for a sad heart if he stays out fishing and swimming all day."

Marai frowned. Something didn't seem right.

"I don't think so. He was more upset than that. Playing with local girls is far too easy of a cure for a man who was howling his heart out just last night. Are you sure?"

"Of course I'm not sure, but he's a grown young man, not a child, my friend. You don't need to 'shepherd' him so closely. My guess is these girls will take the edge off his sorrow. He'll be sad and angry, but maybe not as much as before. In the meantime..."

And with that the elder led the big man back to the observatory to look out over the entire area and to begin to make a plan for how he might peaceably approach Maatkare so a war with Kemet would not arise. The last thing the elder wanted was trouble with the North.

"I stand on shaking ground in this place because of the suph. Unless I am ready to break the treaty, I need to place my skill in bargaining," Akaru explained. "Prince Maatkare, as I've said, provokes but stops short of a challenge, hoping I will blink and make a foolish move. I must wait until my win is certain... and we are still from almost the time of the First Ones a less strong people, no matter the boasting you may hear the young make. They take our ivories and gold, our red cloth and beer, and we get an 'almost' freedom. One day we will be a stronger people, but I will not live to see that day."

"Maybe not," Marai's smile was cryptic. "But, as you said when I arrived, the stars were different. Maybe that means the future too has changed." *And I know the women felt me, all three of them,* he thought to himself. *I can only hope that means something.*

Djerah returned in time for the evening meal, looking shy and somewhat calmer than before. He waved away any questions about the girls and went to rinse in a shallow bath, then he sat quietly to eat with the others.

Marai knew by the expression on the young man's face that outside of momentary release, nothing of substance had happened between him and the young women.

"I am glad your day bought you some ease," Akaru thanked the young man for the fish and continued. "We'll dry them for later. Will you return in the morning to catch more?"

Marai knew the comment was a two-sided witticism of fishing and fisher girls and tried not to laugh. Djerah was still quiet and reflective, but sensed the jab and smirked that he might. Then, he said no more.

After the meal had been cleared, Marai lurked a little and then did some strengthening exercises. He shot an occasional sidelong glance at the young man. Beside himself by the time the servants came to check the lamps and freshen the sheets, he asked: "Is there anything you need to talk to me about? Anything?"

"No," Djerah smirked. "I feel a little better, though. Maybe I'll fish again tomorrow."

That was *all* he said. He might have continued, but the elder approached the rolled out mats where the men were thinking of retiring early.

He brought some tea to soothe the young man, in case night demons wanted to bother him again.

Djerah shrugged, took the drink, and downed it quickly.

"Oh, I saw my better scouts in today. I didn't tell you yet" Akaru mentioned as if that most important piece of news had been an oversight. "Prince Maatkare is returning from his ten-day sojourn to the south and will soon be close enough for one to go to him. The elder glanced at them as if he expected Marai to relate a plan, then he looked at Djerah.

"Well," Djerah answered a little too quickly. "Some of the men down by the boats have met with others who fish between here and Buhen, I believe it's called. The women were…" he started. Marai noticed he was shy.

"Yes, Buhen." My grandson, Apedemeketep, and my other wives are there. Once this is settled, we'll go there for a few days before we head north."

"*They* are unhappy of this prince." Djerah's voice implied Marai and Akaru were too complacent.

Marai studied the tone of it… how the sound of the young man's voice sank lower as he spoke.

Djerah… he sent a thought.

It's alright. I'm just telling him something. I'll be fine. Spending the day with some like my own kind helped me think about it all. The young man returned, then spoke aloud, "They want to go challenge him about the bad meat he sent, about the way he's been ever since he was given full leadership. They said his father was firm but was a just man, and he is not."

The elder nodded.

"I know. Perhaps I will go with you again and speak to these men, but dark is with us." Akaru inclined his head toward his wife Xania, who was standing in the doorway to his suite. "You men sleep. We'll sort this out in the morning, eh?"

Marai and Djerah both knew the elder didn't intend any further discussion of the matter.

In the morning, Xania bent to touch Marai's arm.

"Metaut'ep is at his observatory. He wants you to come as soon as you can," Her grim voice announced. "The young man has gone. Others have gone with him."

Marai read the worry in her darting eyes and instantly grabbed for his sack of stones. This time, he didn't even check the empty mat.

You would think the Children would not allow me to sleep as if I had died when something like this happens. He started, then realized after a second blind sorting through the bag that there were only seven stones. He poured them out and knew at once that Djerah had taken the small crescent shaped Yah stone.

"Damn him!" He quickly closed his eyes, breathed out, and saw through his own stone all that had happened in the pre-dawn hours.

As soon as he decided everyone was asleep, Djerah rose and called on his 'fledgling' power, as Akaru had called it, then took the bag of eight stones. Marai saw the young man go out to the area near the central courtyard where he had seen Akaru meditating once. The stonecutter spread out the stones exactly the way Marai had placed them when he gave him the Yah stone on the way from Ineb Hedj.

Sneaky whelp. Didn't think he was even interested. I know he couldn't have been watching me that carefully. Marai remembered the protestations, the not wanting to see him use the 'heka' stones, the wonder as if he had no understanding of the vision of his great-grandmother as a girl. *So he was watching me after all. All that and he claimed to not see his wife with that man? Pshht!*

Marai's memory sorted through images of Djerah whispering into the pattern that formed above the stones as if he had woven the spell every day of his life. In the ghostly light that illuminated Djerah's face, the sojourner saw how empty the stonecutter's eyes had become. His expression was that of a resolute warrior who knew he would die soon and welcomed it. As the brief vision faded, he sensed Djerah taking the single stone and putting it in his own bag. Then, he saw the young man rise, salute the empty air, return the remaining stones and slip past sleeping guards on his way to the river.

And they slept! This is just the way it was when the Children spirited me to their vessel with the little balls of light, past Sheb, Houra, my relatives and the damned thieves who were lurking among us that night. He shook his head. *Purpose and control. Is this meant, or is some greater force moving the game pieces again?*

"He's gone to the plain to take on Prince Maatkare, that's what he's done." Marai quickly grabbed his walking sandals, tied them, threw on his cloak, and found his staff. "He lied and I fell for it. He went to the fishers and got them talked into going. He wasn't with playing with the women *all* afternoon; just a few moments. The rest of the time he was rounding men up and making plans. He told the girls and they spoke to friends from up the river. He'll get himself and every one of those adventure-happy wretches killed!"

"My beloved waits at his observatory. See him. At least do that," Xania conveyed that her husband Akaru was easily as upset over this turn of events as he was himself.

That's what he said, damn me. I should have listened to the spaces between his words. He was trying to tell me, but I didn't hear, Marai nodded and hurried toward the observatory.

The sojourner knew Djerah, even if he *had* been in the kings' militia once, wouldn't have the skill of the greenest of raiders. He and his followers would be marked and picked off easily by the prince's perimeter guards. Their deaths would *not* be swift. Ahead, Marai saw Akaru-Sef planting himself in the doorway to his observatory temple.

"Come!" the elder called, his face creased with anxiety. "Talk to me first, before you go."

"No. Time's up," the big man whirled around to leave. The elder stretched his arms forward as if he intended to stop him.

"No!" the Akaru's voice trembled in its unusual force. "Do Not."

Marai froze. For a half-instant he felt a distortion in the air as if a sudden wind had gusted but retracted just before it reached him.

"Don't follow him! You can't trail your young man without alerting the whole of His Highness' encampment. You *can't* go against his army."

Marai remembered the way the Children of Stone had helped him cross the wilderness when he first discovered their vessel by placing orbs of light in his path. In the same way, the Yah stone would likely amplify the power of moonlight if Djerah went out into the scrub before day. That light would be seen by the perimeter guards like a distant watchfire. *Stupid. Stupid...* his thoughts repeated.

"You *know* that's not true!" he turned. "If you knew anything about my life you would know I got my start whipping a band of thirty thieves. Enough talk. From what I've learned I could take those troops surrounding him, kill him, and then the rest would scatter like rats." Marai began to storm away, but Akaru hurried behind him as he cursed. "Damn him, he made things worse. And damn me for bringing him. I didn't need *any* of this…"

"Wait. If he and the boys can surprise the camp, there's *still* a chance." Akaru-Sef suggested. "You go in hard and he loses that advantage. His Highness likes strong wine as much as he likes his fine women. If young Djerah is lucky, his Highness might be drunk or with one of them." The elder urged him to stop, but Marai continued marching out of the gates.

"Surprise won't work. That prince is no wilderness thief. He's a top general with trained men," Marai slowed, then looked back to find the elder closing on him quicker than he thought a man his age would be able.

"Stop," Akaru called again. This time, Marai felt the gust of wind and the distant roar of a storm in his thoughts. It marched up his back, physically grabbed him, and slowed him down. He turned and for the briefest of moments thought he saw a golden flash in the old man's eyes. A twinkle bounced up from the elder's eyes but vanished before Marai identified it.

"Wh?" Marai asked. "Oh no, you *don't* compel me." Marai shuddered. Everything he thought about the elder Akaru was suddenly wrong: his tranquility, the way all things could be solved with good food, pleasant music, and willing fisher girls on the river. Djerah had seen through all of that and had only pretended his seduction by all of this tranquility. Marai wondered, for an instant, why he himself had been beguiled.

"You don't want me to get my wives, do you?" Marai continued walking away, forcing against the now gentler gust. "You *want* me to wait because you don't want any trouble." He shrugged, hoping his rage wouldn't propel him into the shape of a bull. "Maatkare knows that. He toys with you every time he comes here. It's you… So, not this time, friend." Marai trotted out into the field. He didn't notice the Akaru's face had changed.

The elder moved closer to him, lifting his hands again. This time Marai felt the breeze draw away his rage. The big man sensed his attempt and sent his own gentle thought in return.

I understand your regret. You tried to help him, but you failed. Let me go. Just get more men of Buhen to come behind me in the evening if you do not feel my message.

Marai shrank into the tall grass, but slowed long enough to fix his thoughts on the young man.

He thought he had nothing to lose but his life and everything to prove to himself if he comes out alive, the sojourner considered. *He broke his back for that useless woman. Maybe he didn't even really like her that much but his sense of duty to his family made him stay and work harder. So evil didn't turn to good as the song says. This is his last try then, but I did not bring him here to die.* Marai shook his head but continued striding into the grass, his rage at the new set of complications building.

What am I doing? I could kill this prince from here. I don't even have to see him. I could freeze his wicked heart, he thought. *Let me see Djerah first, though. Let me try to call him back.*

He paused, hand to his brow and eyes closed lightly.

Djerah crouched, as if he had been born a wilderness raider. A group of about thirty-five men huddled with him behind the last safe ledge before the camp. He was acting the part of the very military commander whom they stalked. He gestured for the men to keep down until the camp had been quiet for a while. They planned to rush, kill the prince and seize the women then get to safety before they were caught. Maatkare's death, Djerah told them, would give his suddenly freed troops such a sense of freedom that they would welcome the coup.

Djerah don't do this. His men do not *feel like slaves just because you did a few years ago. It won't work. He's a god to most of his men.*

Djerah opened his hand and spoke through the glimmering white stone in his palm.

Stay out of this Marai. You surprised I can hear you? His inner voice was as tart as his actual tone. *See, this stone gives me the power, now.*

You don't understand. It has *no power*, Marai protested from afar.

No power. Ha!! You're trying to lie to me again. Even so, I got tired of sitting on my hind end while you and the Lion Master held each other's hands like a couple of old women. His men are sick of him too; endlessly spouting how they should be gentle farmers and respectful hunters under the wise guidance of nature. It isn't right. I told them we came from a stock of folk who have powerful gods like Sin and El who don't need a woman's permission. Djerah's thoughts grumbled.

You'll be killed. And you don't understand how their worship works at all. They war when attacked. The bad meat was close to bringing it, but no one was hurt. The prince knows exactly how far he can push it. It's what gives him his power! Marai tried desperately to explain but knew Djerah wasn't listening. *You're outnumbered at least thirty men to one, and his men are seasoned. You'd better turn back if you expect to live.*

Djerah's thoughts interrupted.

I'm ready. I've lived enough life to suit me. Warrior's path is better than following you around.

Warrior? Fool. That's it. I'm on my way. Marai sent his anger over the distance. *You can't let the loss of your family do this to you; not like I did for my little wife who didn't even care for me much.* He anguished briefly over how the history of the men in his family was grimly repeating itself and knew no amount of talking, ethereal or in person, could change that.

You don't want to listen, and you're pretty hot now. Your ancestors would be proud, but they would also weep at the coming waste. I won't remember what you just said, but I'm on my way now, so if your real motive was to get me moving, you won, you stupid fool. Marai sighed once and touched his bow, to focus on the direction he would take.

Ho... No you don't try and talk to me. We're going in, in two hours, so you'd better show me how you can walk on air! his thoughts mocked. *You think I believe you're coming for your women out of love, so you can tell me how I feel? This is about stolen property, isn't it? It's not about love or you wouldn't have let any one of them lay an hour with that bastard once you knew.*

Marai wanted to reach out and slap the stonecutter for that comment, but felt another calm wave enveloping him from the direction of Qustul Amani.

Do not stop him, friend Marai. Akaru's voice echoed in his thoughts. *You are surprised that I have powers you have not noticed until now? It is so. I have them, but I am always loath to use them unless I must. This I tell you. As all who awaken must first die, so too must this fledgling. It is all I can say to you.*

Hordjedtef's mystery school wisdom, Marai thought. *The initiation with the mock-death of three days followed by the rising. Djerah begs for this? No. You're wrong. He's just lost his wits. There is nothing mystical about this, nothing at all. He just wants revenge. Can't you see that?*

But it is still his choice. Can you not see? Let him go. Let him be a man, the elder pleaded.

Let him be a fool.

But let him be...

Marai fought a little more, but then sat. A bellow started in the pit of his being, but he stopped it because he knew the prince would sense it. Djerah had made his choice, good or bad. At that moment, Marai felt it would be bad.

Chapter 18: Defeat

"Your Great Highness…" a voice called outside the flap of Maatkare's red, white, and yellow tent. At first, he paid little attention. Eventually:

Mmm? one slanted brow raised. *No, I don't think you want to rouse me, out there.* His fingers rose a little about to deliver a prickle of discipline to whoever it was. *Not my regulars. They know better. Not your pretty new guards, Nefira… just… shhh…* he shook his hand, smirked and waited.

"Aah! Your Highness…" the expected cry returned and the edge of Maatkare's mouth twitched again in delight. He felt Deka pause, then noticed her hand tremble just a little as she tenderly traced his brow.

He admired her. Early this morning he woke and found her stretched over his chest and lying the way one rescued from drowning might cling to a raft. He didn't let women remain in his bed often but the thought to put her out wouldn't stay. His hunger was only partly relieved. He brought her up as he sat, kissed her gently, then parked her legs on either side of his waist. She shuddered in delight but he stayed her in his lap so she faced him. He wanted her to enjoy the feel of him against her for a while longer.

"Open your eyes to me, Nefira Deka," he whispered. "You know what I want, don't you? The reflecting game your heart wants." She asked to show it to him once, but he waited for the right conditions. Waking aroused wasn't quite the right excuse. That was easy. The rest of the morning was perfect. The bright sun began to warm the tent, but a gentle breeze kept it comfortable.

Outside, noises of men milling around in the common area increased.

He ignored them, concentrating instead on the vibration of erotic might coursing through both of them.

No, not yet, his thoughts whispered. It was taking so much of his strength to resist her hot fragrance wriggling against his upright shaft. *Too fast, too fast… Shhh, easy…* He traced her brow with his fingertips to calm and slow her.

"Now you trace me. Match me like a reflection in a polished plate. Close your eyes. Sense my moves. Slow… slow… very gentle." He felt her squirm and her heart pound against his chest. Her breath came in passionate gasps. "Easy now, draw it out and make it last. Use your strength for me. Draw it inside you and make it be so much stronger."

Her stone, like a single large drop of red blood, pulsed faintly on her brow. Her eyes closed in gasping rapture. She moaned in frustration.

"Now open them, but focus on my face until all you can see is my eyes. You will not even know when I take you, because it will feel as if I have always been inside you so deep and snug."

What seemed like tenderness at first, had become a sharing and transfer of energy. He knew she was gifting him with her unconscious power now. Any barrier between them had fallen away. He owned her, but he allowed her to think she owned him.

"Touch my brow, I touch yours. Feel her blow her breath on my face so calmly." He repeated it, feeling that tremor of power rising. "Nice."

He heard the voices grow louder.

Damn. My lesson to whoever the poor bastard out there was didn't take, I see. Someone always has to interrupt me. Thought because we got back last night and I gave out extra beer, I'd get one morning without the daily dung. Too much to ask for, I see.

Just thinking of the men outside distracted him to the point of recalling something two weeks earlier that old holy man had rattled at him about the bad storms being due this year.

I deal with things. The gods, I think, are pleased. Made you run up to your grandson and take all of the pretty women, didn't I? Said it was over the alignment of stars. Hah! Lies, Akaru Metauthetep, old fool. I know what I saw in your observatory that night. I saw the way those stars lit up the crystal shaft in its core. A trick of moonlight that makes it glow like heka fire. And I have fire itself sitting here in my lap wanting to sheath me in its honey so bad that she cries for it and aches. Maatkare studied Deka's gently closed eyes, savoring the moment.

"My Lord Highness" a different man, his scribe, stood outside the closed tent flap, his voice sounding like the wing-whine of a gnat. The prince didn't want to make an example of this man too. He paused, looking over Deka's shoulder for a moment.

Curse them. They know better than to lurk around this tent… only in a dire emergency should they, and I sense nothing of the sort but this beauty going all aflutter in need of me. Prince Maatkare seized the woman and nipped at her throat almost tenderly, then harder as he felt her sigh in a little pain. She hissed in ecstasy, eliciting his own animal nature that manifested as a throaty growl.

"Do you fear me?" he grabbed her jaw and squeezed until her eyes opened.

Deka wrested her head to one side, shutting her eyes again and letting the tears of ecstatic pain flow. "I do," she gasped. "You are the dark places in my heart. I mirror our emptiness to you to show you your own darkness…" she whispered, as if she quoted the lines of an old script.

"Your Highness…" the voice of his captain of the hunt insisted. "Men are dead on both sides out there to the north…"

Men dead? Maatkare pressed Deka close for a moment, then rose with her from their place on his rumpled bed. He seized his robe and threw it on, placed his simple khat on his head, then tossed Deka her cape. With an impassive glance, the prince watched her wrap herself in it. He grabbed his mirror for a quick glance to see if *he* was presentable. Making his way to the flap, he let her out first. That was when he saw the two blood-spattered soldiers milling outside. He sealed his lips in trained hardness so he would not betray his absolute shock and embarrassment. With all of his magical energy he has not sensed a thing but interest in morning joy with the Ta-Seti woman.

What the… a rebellion and where was I? Bewitched? Second time this has happened. It's not a good look. He remembered the time on the boat when he had been delighting himself with the 'correction' of Ariennu for plotting escapes when the woman Naibe almost got herself drowned.

"Most Noble One," the scribe intoned, "not an hour ago a band of Ta-Seti and what looked like a Wawat or two raided the north side of the camp. It was only our advanced preparedness which allowed us to settle the matter with little noise. We killed many and took the rest for you to admonish. We thought, perhaps, Qustul had risen against us until we found the leader was *not* one of the Akaru's men."

"I see," Maatkare mused in puzzled wonder. *Northern perimeter? That's not far. I should have heard men fighting even through the heka web. You are a* spider, *Nefira…* his thoughts hissed.

"What did they have to say for themselves... the captives?" he asked, still perplexed. His new grooms arrived, ready to wash and shave him, but he waved them away.

"It was on the night patrol in the far north sector, the rock outcropping almost at the dust flat," the scribe related as a physician approached to see if the returning men needed aid. "Some of them jumped us but they didn't see the other flank you instructed to be on patrol. If the first had been alone, they may have taken us. We surprised them and signaled even more behind us. We took the leader, a half-blood Kemet peasant, but he will say nothing to us..."

"The leader is still alive?" Maatkare asked, a slow smile finding the edge of his lips.

"We are holding him for you, Lord, tied to the outside of the ladder stand you had us put in the hills just last night. What fortune that the gods let you know we would need it so soon." the man bowed and backed away a little while the prince stood, chin in his hand and thought about everything that had been said.

"Bring him and the others to me at the midday hour after the sun has cooked and thirsted them some. The hunt was poor yesterday," the prince hissed. "Set up my midday meal... for two, today." his glance shot in the direction of the women's tent. I would have the Ta-Seti woman attend me and share it with me while I question them." He beckoned his grooms. "Then, too, have the other women brought to watch the discipline. He'll talk, eventually, before I tear out his tongue and make him swallow it." Maatkare's mouth twisted into a peculiar grin, his eyes flashing for an instant like lightning sending its green fork of light through a storm.

Deka glanced side to side at the clot of men forming outside the prince's tent. She pushed past them as she returned to her own tent that morning. Although she and the prince had slept little, and the quitting of shared passion had been abrupt, she felt highly energized because of the scent of battle that now reached her. She had seen battle before, hunts where men had been injured, but it had never been like this. She turned once she was inside, then stared out of the tent flap to watch as the wounded arrived from the hills.

"Deka. What's going on?" she heard Naibe ask, but she didn't turn or answer her.

Some of the men's kilts were stained with blood. One man, naked and limping from a free-bleeding knife wound on his thigh leaned heavily on another man.

They need to put some moss and honey in that and bind it before the fever comes. Deka thought, *the physics know this. Why do I concern myself? Prince Maatkare emerged to talk to more of the returning men.* She knew he was angry even though he hid his rage well. She wanted to rage for him, because she had felt unusually close to him this morning. It would have been splendid, but… *Must have been a bad fight, she thought, and the north ridge? Who would come from there?*

She sensed energy pulsing in the air around her. *Is this his energy I feel? Is it a different thing? No. It's he who is watching me, the way he always has watched me. It's been so long. I remember. Men would come home bloody like this, but soon the drinking and carousing would begin. Someone would take me and then I didn't have to think about the seeing the blood any more. This is different. Something's coming. Something's looking for me that has always lurked near my heart. It almost found me in Little Kina-Ahna when the priest levied the spell on us. Wise MaMa held it off, then. She never believes how strong she is. Today is different. She's not doing it today, because she despises me. I cannot blame her. Today, it knows me.*

Deka very dimly recalled being dragged along as a fast-trick seer by the Kush fortune teller who eventually became Nahab's executioner. *I can't place his name any more. It's just as well. He had no soul, so why would he have a name? "Pepep" maybe? Like Apep? I was not Deka or Nefira then. I was Bone Woman. Nefira Sekht, Raem calls me.* She almost giggled at the thought of his odd speech impediment that made his "r" sound come out like "wr". *Nefiwra. Someone here knows my name,* her thoughts drifted as she stared outside the tent, unaware that Ariennu stood beside her, watching and sensing.

I remember more now. Almost everything has come back to me. I have so few memories left from before and in the in-between-time. It's always the same. I wake up. There's so much pain and sickness. There is a river into the trees. Is it the great river we sailed on or a smaller one? Different now. They took me and tied me up, put me on a boat. They made me scrub and wash things. I couldn't talk any more. It was hard to walk because something healed wrong. I said "De-Ka" or

"Ta" but my thoughts cried Deka, and I cried back Ta-Te. It was too hard. I stopped trying. Men with sickness to want an ugly thing like me raped me and beat me and kicked me. I would lie there and let them do what they wanted. I was invisible. I was on the shore again, thrown out as garbage and left to die. Pepep found me that time. He didn't care that I was ugly. I made trade goods for him by being 'an oracle' even though I knew I was not one of the divine. We came to N'ahab-Atall. Wise MaMa was there.

Deka paused. She looked to her side and her glance met Ariennu's hardened eyes, but the woman tore her gaze away as if she had learned too much.

The men were still milling outside. More wounded had come. Physicians were packing wounds, but Deka couldn't shake the feeling of being watched.

"What do you see out there?" Ari demanded. "Move over. My thoughts are screaming. You let me in there," the elder woman pushed her into the tent flap.

"And what *do* you feel?" Deka turned, suspicious. Naibe had risen and was making her way to the tent flap.

"Something in my heart," Naibe offered. "It makes me dizzy, light…"

"You ate," Ariennu snapped. "Are you still sick?"

"He said there was an attack on the north ridge and they took men. In a while he will have them brought here." Deka answered, her thoughts racing and conflicted.

"Oh, that," Ari's voice sank, emotionless. "I suppose he'll torture them and make us look at it. You know that. You both do. You remember N'ahab and me and how… " Ari reminded them, then added, "he'll do the leader last, save the worst for him unless he goes to his knees and begs early on."

Deka saw Ari's lips tighten, but felt the need to send her a mental reminder.

You used to be the one. It was you, Wise MaMa, who trained me, but I never hated you for it. Now you hate me because you have to let Raem train you, she scoffed. She remembered Ariennu's fists and the broken faces she could give the women who either didn't open their legs or screamed too loud and struggled too much. Though she couldn't speak well because of her deafness, she let any women or girl know they would be killed if they didn't settle. N'ahab never killed a woman for refusing, though. A resistant one was simply held down and raped by everyone in the camp until it didn't matter to her any more or until she took her own life.

The Ta-Seti woman watched Maatkare as he paced and decided what he would do. Then, he turned and fully entered his tent. This time her thoughts were of Marai. It was as if he stood near her and tried to tell her he was alive.

Like a ghost of something so big and powerful from a long, long time ago; a king perhaps. You helped me see the place by the river and how I looked. You didn't want to use us either. You were above these things of Earth until the night with Naibe-Ellit. Something broke loose in me that night. It whispered to my heart "Not for You. Not until you find a king." It whispered to me every time I thought about you – of nestling close in your arms like a child. I loved you Marai. You knew that, but then you died.

She found her mat and sat to dream about the 'now' of her life. She pretended to rest. If she did that, it would keep Ari or Naibe from asking her too much. If prisoners were being handled later, she didn't care. She would be with Maatkare. His fire would be without limit.

Prince Maatkare Raemkai… she didn't know if she had become the luckiest woman on earth or the unluckiest. If she thought Marai had been the perfection of the tawny skinned Akkad, Raem was the perfection of the brown-skinned man of Kemet. He was ravenous, demanding, and exacting. Before this journey to Ta-Seti, she had lived at his home, but barely spoke to the actual wife, Sadeh, or his three children; a boy aged two and girl likely five and a boy a year older than that.

There had been a Princess Meryt, but something bad had happened. She went mad after a miscarriage and hanged herself from their porch one afternoon. That was all the wife ever said about it and she never said it in his presence, except that this was how she became the chief wife. Talk of it would send the prince into such a fierce rage that "bad things happened" she warned, so the subject never came up.

The first night they had been together, he struck her like lightning. Later, as he sat on his heels, arms folded across his chest, he watched her lie on his bed just trembling. He had been almost tender, touching her arm; almost. *I remembered the grass and the river that night; other green eyes that had watched me like that. I understood that night that I would be his for a long time. The name came to me later: Nefersekht, Nefertfnt, Anatu the rain. Nefira… Menhit.*

Other women? They don't matter. I know his needs and understand his rights like no other, not even his ill-fated princess. This is Ta-Seti and Maatkare Raemkai has brought me here. I will reward him with my life. Her thoughts raced for a dreamy moment. *He is so much like a young, wicked god. If we could impress the king, he might still be named as an heir. Ari and Baby One had to come only because of our link to the Children of Stone.*

They will complete our path to power, but Ari hasn't said where the missing eight are. Nothing has unlocked that secret from her, not Raem's attention, not Baby One's carrying the Inspector's Child. I know. Raem knows too, but she doesn't know we do. He will employ that knowledge when he best needs to. Deka lay back and looked at her hands.

We will conquer the fat kingdoms and return a sense of purpose and order to them. She knew she had done this and been this important to someone before… in someone's strong arms. She could grow Maatkare into the perfect god-king where Marai had failed all of them by allowing himself to be killed.

Deka calmed herself a little as the three of them waited, but the thoughts Ari and Naibe exchanged invaded her privacy.

Do you feel it? Please say you do, Ari… or he has driven me mad. Naibe turned to Ari, hustling her to the other side of the tent. *I don't know why I feel it, though. Why now? Do you think it's this little one causing me to see and hear his spirit?*

I don't know about you, Ari silently answered. *I dreamed about him last night. He came and told me he was alive… alive…*

One of the new grooms had come to the tent and stood outside. He made a light baying noise that sounded almost like a cat moan. His thick, black arm reached in and beckoned.

Deka sat up, distracted from listening to the other women's thoughts. She quickly went to the opening.

Me? In to see Highness? she signed.

The groom nodded and she followed him as he led her to the prince's tent. Once inside, she saw the other groom, his twin, shaving the prince close on the face and almost clean on his head so that thick black fuzz as short as dog hair was all that remained. She stood quietly and remained reverent while the man finished, taking in the intoxicating scent of the body oil they had rubbed on him. When he dismissed the grooms, Maatkare beckoned to her to come closer.

"You understand what I require of you?" he asked, the green glitter of his eyes harder than she had ever seen it before. To her, at that moment, his dispassion made it seem as if he was addressing the air.

"To be at your side as you…" she answered, nervous, then tried again. "To show *support* of you as you question the captives."

He sat up a little more from his seemingly relaxed pose in his grooming chair, then extended one neatly manicured hand to her.

I was thinking of you while I was being prepared… the whole time." He pulled her closer, but bent her hand until she knelt to keep it from hurting. She sagged to her knees, but refused to complain.

"See, you are getting stronger. You used to show pain when I did this to you. I need you to be very, very brave today; more than I have ever asked you to be before. I need for you to show no pity whatsoever for these men when I punish them, because they have killed some of *our* men. Let your sisters cry for them if they wish. Let *them* beg for my mercy."

"I understand, beloved," she whispered; her eyes cast down.

"Gods, I desire you," he pulled her up to his mouth and kissed her hard. "If it were any other moment in time I would be inside you, you know that." He broke away from her. "Dress as if you were my Great Wife, then. I'm having them brought down earlier; not in the later day. I want to take my time with them; find out if that lion man has sent them or if I need to return to Wawat lands with a bigger force."

Deka knew exactly what the garment he requested meant. Trying not to think too much about the way he had been trembling with a combination of several kinds of lust when he gripped her, she opened the clothing chest and found a blood red shift and red printed cloak. When she put them on, she fastened her hair and donned the gold circlet with the disc he had given her before they bathed at Qustul Amani the week before.

I will be strong as I once was for my god and king Ta-Te, wherever his spirit is, she thought. I conjure it to come upon you, my love, so you do not waver in your cruelty.

When she had dressed, Deka turned and went to Maatkare, who seated her and painted the gold paint on her eyelids and deep red on her lips. *I want you.* His thoughts spoke to her. It was enough.

The guards hustled Ariennu and Naibe into the shaded opening of their tent, then tied up the side walls so the women could see everything that was about to take place.

Ari leaned toward Naibe when they saw Deka walk out beside the prince with her head held high. The elder woman's eyes filled with disdain.

"There *they* go… and look at her acting like a make-believe queen."

Maatkare settled with the Ta-Seti woman in one of the two chairs set on his audience dais. A light wind rustled through the brightly striped canopy over their heads.

"Doesn't he look like he just came down from the sun? Pretty man. Wretched though," Ariennu snorted quietly. "I might *still* take him from that proud kuna. All I have to do is *try*." She studied Maatkare's crisp indigo and white striped nemes; the gold banding of a prince pressing it onto his brow. His thin day coat illuminated every part of his finely chiseled body. A table in front of their chairs held a light meal of fruit and bread, as if they sat for a regal luncheon instead of a prisoner review.

Still excellent with a woman's body though. Makes the thunder turn you inside out all night long and when you think you're done, there's more… Mmmm, Ari's thoughts distracted her for a moment. She saw herself in Deka's place, being fed pickled melon rind.

"There," Naibe tugged Ari's arm to get her attention. She pointed to a mat stretched out on one side of the dais, on which lay a collection of bronze and leather instruments of torture. A brazier was near the mat so these things could be heated.

"Uh, yeah I see them, Babe… the tools." She put her hand over Naibe's face and thought about the old days with N'ahab's gang of thieves. *Before, when N'ahab would hurt someone, Little One never had to watch. She always stayed in the hut. She was so simple then, I don't think she would have even understood someone was getting hurt.* The Children of Stone had un-muddied her thoughts, but she was still so innocent in her that Ari felt she needed to explain.

"He *wants* us to look, the bastard. It's a test for Deka to see if she can take it, too. That's what he's doing to us. If you don't want to see it, just go away in your thoughts. As for speaking thoughts the way we do, you already know he can hear and read them, so just be careful. Maybe he'll be so wrapped up in what he's doing, that he won't notice."

"I'm not as weak as you think, MaMa. I just know something's not right about any of this," Naibe grew silent and watchful, then made another surprised whimper.

Ari looked out of the tent to see the taller of the guards, whipping and marching a bedraggled group of young men out of the dusty field beyond the camp. Some were wounded and bloodstained. Every face reflected stoniness and horror of men who knew they were about to die.

The taller of the prince's guards seized the young man on the end of the line, then systematically pushed each of the nine prisoners to their knees so that they were lined up before the dais.

"Was there not another?" she heard the prince ask. He shaded his eyes from the hot midday sun and pointed into the distance beyond the tent. "Aha! I see our newest men are bringing him in, still tied to the ladder where he belongs."

What the… Ariennu craned her body forward. *The bastard's going to rape the leader? Liar,* she snickered to herself. *You ashamed, you rutting goat? Kicked me when you tied me on that thing a moon ago and I asked you. Now I know the truth!*

"Red Sister," Maatkare beckoned to her. "Your thoughts are loud this midday, but, no, I *don't* do that. Because you insist on dreaming up such rancid juices for me to pick out, then you get out here and see if he is tied up too tight to escape. Maybe I will even have you strike him first."

No. I won't be part of this, Ariennu's thoughts shot back.

"Eeeen nauuuu, sister, for you." His hand rose with his compelling utterance.

Instant pain rushed through her Child Stone, branched to both ears and radiated through her skull. Even though she had guessed he would make her obey, she could do little about it but squall in misery.

"Damn. Hurts… please. Aahh. Stop it, curse every… oh goddess… stop…"

The new grooms from the Wawat quickly lashed the rattan outer wall onto an A-frame structure that had been anchored in the earth.

Ari's body wrenched up from her place in the open tent flap and she stumbled forward magically, as if a specter dragged her out and over to the front part of the cage where the leader of the raid was fastened. When he had been secured by the guards, the prince released her from the spell so suddenly that she fell.

He applauded in delight at the sight of her sprawling in the dirt in front of the stand.

"Very good! Get up and see the face of this man who has killed one of my best men."

Ariennu's eyes fogged in a confusion of rage and shock.

Killed? She thought. Oh. The shorter one's not here. The one who's always getting his nasty partner to back away from us at night. Lie. More likely the big one wanted a piece of one of us and didn't want to share. Probably killed him and blamed this poor wretch. Still, I have to see what kind of fool would come up on a full division, she scoffed inwardly.

The young man on the rattan grill was stripped almost naked and bleeding from half a dozen wounds. His arms were strapped over his head and his legs were braced wide. She let her eyes rise slowly, studying each place he had been tied and seeing how badly he had been hurt. *A cut on the arm and a nasty bruise over his ribs. Way he's panting it's likely broken. Ooh... arrow wound in the edge of his thigh which he's pushed through. Took courage... A swelling spear wound on the top of his foot...* Ariennu's eyes cleared and she struggled to mask her emotions because she knew at once who it was.

Goddess. Him? How? Can't know this. Can't. She felt every drop of blood in her veins turning to frost. *Djee? Here? What's he think he's doing here trying to lead this mess?* She buried her thoughts, knowing if she even gave a glimmer of recognition or shirked in delivering the opening blow, Maatkare would know about it. That would make it worse for both of them.

"Say something to him, Red, or join him there. You bragged to me long enough about how you used to work prisoners over for your thief friends when you were such a naughty young ka't. Let's see you do it now," the prince ordered. "I'm waiting," he pressed.

"You a killer?" Ariennu stammered, her voice went hoarse at the bottom of her throat. *How can I let him know I don't mean this?* She grabbed the young man's jaw firmly, drew her face close to his and barked. "Answer me or I will slap it out of you with every last tooth." Then she sent a silent thought. *If you could only hear my thoughts. Forgive me, Djee.*

"Understand. Jus… Do… fast," the young man's broken whisper answered.

Oh Goddess, the poor thing hears my thoughts. He acts as if he wants to die, she fought her shock even harder.

"I didn't ask you that. Are you a killer?" she repeated in Kina, hoping he would say something important enough for the prince to relieve her from that task.

He didn't answer.

"You'd better say something, before I ram my fist down your throat."

"What did he say?" Maatkare clapped his hands once, annoyed. "I saw his lips moving."

She released his jaw then cracked him with her fist. *Why?* Her thoughts pleaded. *Just lie. Say something, anything.*

"Storm," the young man sputtered as blood from his lip drooled onto his chin and into his unkempt beard.

Something small and white flew out of the man's mouth, when she struck him. *A tooth? Sorry!* Ari's thoughts cried out but she postured, frantic:

"Answer better than that or I'll knock another one out." She didn't want to hit him, she wanted to free him but at that moment she couldn't think of anything capable of distracting everyone long enough for her unfasten him.

"St…orm" he gasped "coming." his head sagged between his upright arms.

"Well?" Maatkare asked, coming to his feet. "What did he say?"

Storm coming? Ariennu felt her heart seizing. *That's what Babe used to cry out when she woke up from her bad dreams. Marai used to tell her he would protect her from it, but it turns out he couldn't even protect himself.*

"He said Sutek is coming. He said a *storm* is coming," she backed away a little, waiting for effect.

Naibe screamed the instant she heard that phrase but stifled her cry into a whimper.

"*Did* he now?" Maatkare trotted down from the dais. "He called *that* name?" then to Ari again: "Go on. You go and get the young honey quiet. Tell her I expect better behavior out of her."

Ariennu turned, purposely expressionless, and fled to the tent. When she arrived, she let herself go a little more, but resisted the urge to hide behind Naibe.

"It's him isn't it?" Naibe trembled and sniveled.

"Shh… don't let him see us talking." Ariennu warned, wrapping her arms around the young woman to enable a hidden conversation to go on between them. If they spoke through thoughts, Deka and the prince would pick up on the energy exchange. She knew whispering would be better. "You know who that is, don't you?"

"It's the young man from the market… Djerah," Naibe strained to see what the prince was doing but Ariennu turned her away. She had seen Deka's eyes become the size of plates at first, then harden themselves.

"Oh it is, and Deka knows it too. If she tells him, I swear… and why in all thunder and blood did he come here?" Ari lamented, struggling to keep her speech hidden under the ruse that she was calming Naibe. "Maybe someone told him about us being taken away and the poor fool thought he should come try to save us because Marai was gone. Stupid boy. Getting himself killed for nothing," Ariennu pressed her closely speaking louder for effect this time. "You sick? Don't look at this if it makes you sick." she tousled Naibe's hair, then growled over the young woman's shoulder at Maatkare. "What is he doing now? Can you see?"

"Trying to wake him up, I think," Naibe answered.

Prince Maatkare brought a cup of stale beer and threw a little of it into Djerah's face to revive him.

"Wake up, damn you. Call Sutek, will you? Why not? Talk about the storm, do you? I *know* that lion-tamer is behind this now. He sent you and your merry band of piss-trained scamps here. I'll deal with that pale-skinned old freak later, but now I want you awake to see every bit of what you caused these boys and their families." He turned and went back to his seat, lifted the glittering disc that bore the "eye" on it from his chair, then gently placed it around Deka's neck.

"That slimy kuna…" Ari muttered under her breath. "I'd like to rip that thing off her throat."

"It's Wserkaf's Eye of Truth. We knew she stole it from you." Naibe whispered, then looked at her. "Maybe *Wse* told this poor man about us when he knew it was gone. We have to find a way to get their eyes off of him until we can get him loose and he can run for it."

"Won't be able. You didn't see him up close like I did. He's hurt worse than he looks and I still had to hit him," Ariennu shuddered, checking over her shoulder to see if they were being watched. "Goddess I didn't want to but I had to make it look real. He's weak from bleeding in the sun all morning. If he ran, the first bow shot would take him out for sure."

Deka tensed, glaring at the two of them. She lifted the Wdjat gently as if she was protecting herself against a curse.

Maatkare's hand drifted to hers and brought it to his lips to kiss.

Ariennu had been keeping her thoughts away from scrutiny by whispering to Naibe, but when she saw Maatkare's odd tenderness toward Deka, her guard dropped enough for her to feel a flash of jealousy. She had wanted to get *some* kind of devotion from the prince other than the love of enthusiastic sex, but Deka's hold on him had always been secure. To her, that was incomprehensible. Ari felt his hushed thoughts moving through Deka's stone and then through theirs.

You are perfect… his thoughts sighed through hers. *You know this is what I am now and you have welcomed it. I need to see how much stronger you can be in the face of our enemies.* He turned his glance to his guards and pointed out a man at the end of the line.

"They're all so young," Naibe clung to Ariennu, as she watched the beginning of the process over Ari's shoulder. "Not a one much older than me. That one on the end can't be much more than thirteen years. He still has a boy's shoulders."

"Stay like this Babe. I'll be acting like I'm holding you. If you don't want to see this, put your head down," Ari whispered, wondering how much cruelty the girl could witness before she lost control. From time to time, she turned her head to look just so Maatkare wouldn't think she was avoiding her own witness by protecting the girl.

One of the big new grooms grabbed the youth on the end and forced him to meet the prince's eyes.

"Do you have anything to say to me?" Maatkare moved to the boy, whose brave silence answered.

"Hold him," the prince sighed in exasperation, then motioned to the groom.

The second groom joined the first. Both seized the youth, lifted him and stretched him out over the nearby brick pad, already hot from the midday sun. One held his legs, while the other tore off his coat and stretched his arms above his head. Maatkare bid the guard whose partner had been killed to fetch a clawed flail from the group of torture devices. While the man brought it, the prince removed his own sheer coat, folded it neatly and handed it to a servant so it could be placed out of the way. Then he took the flail.

In a fluid and passionless movement, Maatkare brought the lash down hard on the youth's exposed back. The sharp metal tips of the flail sliced his skin. He brought the flail down again. The young man cried out after each stroke, but each time his cries grew weaker. Maatkare paused, then bent and dipped his fingers in the blood bringing them to his mouth and licking them. "Anything?" he repeated, and dipped again. Going to Deka on the dais, he offered her the blood on his hands. She froze.

"Taste it, woman. Taste the blood of our enemies," he breathed.

Taste, taste, taste,
Taste the sweet of sacrifice... ice... ice,
Nice

Deka took his wrist between her thumb and forefinger, lifted it, then touched his fingers to her tongue. When she had licked them, she stared hard into the distance.

"See, it *is* sweet," Maatkare urged her.

Listen. The voices. Oh goddess in me she doesn't know what he's doing... Ari felt Naibe's thoughts burst through an instant after the conjuration that sounded so real. *He's sending his thoughts through her stone as if he knows how... It's a spell so she'll think the Children of Stone want this. He's turning her and she's not even fighting him,* the young woman gritted her teeth and squeezed her eyes shut, putting her fingertips up to massage her temples.

Ari let her partitioning of thought slip enough to sense Deka telling herself:

It's a game; a sport. It isn't real. Salty taste. Hmmm... The repressed emotion of her acts and the prince's power of suggestion left her breathless.

You are one with me in this sacred communion. I taste, you taste. See how sweet it is? Maatkare whispered, wrapping an arm around her. She tasted a little more of the blood.

Yes, beloved, her thoughts became oddly radiant, *we are one.*

The young man who lay on the brick pad never spoke after the flogging ceased. He whimpered, but each sound that came from him enraged the prince into bringing down a harder and more rending stroke. Ari found herself counting, cursing, and whispering:

Stop. Kill him already.

"No! Stop... I..." Naibe started but Ari's hands shot up and dropped the barrier of silence over her words before Maatkare could hear them.

You want to get us killed too?

The youth fainted from pain at the last stroke. His back, after sixteen more strokes, had turned into red exposed meat.

Maatkare stared down at his work, restive and somewhat impressed at the interesting pattern in the wounds. He walked around the unconscious prisoner slowly, then kicked his ribs furiously to see if he flinched. When he did not, he bent to see if the blood which splattered forth was fresh indicating life, or still and darkening. Satisfied with his observation, he moved to Djerah.

The stonecutter had closed his eyes and mouthed aloud. "Yah, do not forsake me."

Filled with quiet rage that the first prisoner had gone down without a word and now lay silent on the bricks, the prince returned and squatted near him to announce:

"A shame." his voice growled. His hand gesture to the throat was a sign for to the big dark Wawat groom to deftly snap the unconscious young man's neck. "But I *am* merciful," Maatkare sauntered back to Djerah again. "Your follower's wounds would have caused him great fever and a miserable death. I saluted his foolish bravery and gave him the gift of sweet oblivion. Just tell me who it is that sent you and I will deal with all of you quickly and without further misery." He paused, then added: "I'll leave one man with wounds only… give him a chance to return to the one who gave this ridiculous order so he can tell him what he saw. That could be any of you if you say his name to me…"

Ariennu felt Naibe start to send a thought to Djerah to take that option.

Don't. It's a trick. Shhh, baby, Ari distracted the young woman. *If Maatkare doesn't like what he hears he'll kill them all anyway. If Djee is silent, maybe he will live a little longer until I can… Damn him.* Ari gasped when she saw the prince pause and look in her direction.

He knew they were plotting something.

Djerah said nothing. He refused to speak as the next three men were scourged and executed. The fifth prisoner screamed he was sick of the grip the Lords of the black land had on the red and was just waiting for a force to back him.

"He's trying to be the one who lives," Ari shook her head, even though she had gone numb. "Won't work. He won't let *that* one go. He's enjoying this too much."

"Good. You spoke. Thank you," Maatkare commented, then moved to one side of the scourged and bleeding young man, but gave the signal. As the big groom wrenched the man's neck, he added, "but you said you acted alone. It wasn't what I needed to hear." He turned back to the dais, stepped up then slumped into his camp chair, more frustrated from lack of information than winded from exertion. He extended his hands to Deka again, giving her some more of the blood to taste.

What's the matter with me? Ariennu watched the beatings and the blood rite with a ghoulish fascination, but couldn't bring herself to look at Djerah. Making certain her thoughts were private, she mused, *none of this is new to me. I've done this work myself without turning a hair. It did matter once though. It still hurts me now, no matter how much brass I put up and down my spine. I see it in his face. His sharp nose and firm jaw… the deep set eyes are not that unlike Marai's face. I can see those two Akkad peasants we took and their little boys, too.* She closed her eyes for a moment, the image of a scared but feisty young woman flashing in her thoughts. *She fought us like a warrior. Then, to save her man and her boys, even after they were broken by us, she let us all hump her. I was laughing at her, drinking, giving her drink, and still mocking her and calling her a stupid kuna that must have really wanted it all along to suddenly have so little pride in herself.* Her blood chilled again in the distant memory.

"He wants me to take your place. He told me. Don't you see? Kill us. Just kill us now." The woman in Ariennu's memory begged. The force of her words never reached Ari's deaf ears but the thoughts behind them magically found her heart. It woke the elder woman from her stupor that day and she gave the peasant woman hearts seeds to keep her from getting a child from all that she put herself through. Then, that night, Ari helped them escape. Now, seeing Djerah tied up brought it all back. *I didn't do it because I was sorry for them. No. I just didn't want to be replaced. Goddess was watching me that night, I guess. That was Marai's sister. Here I am claiming no one I know missed me when I slept in the Children's pod for fifty years. I'm watching her great-grandson get taken down. Spirit wants me to get him loose? How? I'm the reason he is even* here. She understood that if the woman and her sons had died at the hands of her cohorts, there would have been no Djerah born to be tied on the ladder and suffering today.

Damn me. And if I hadn't tried to crawl up Maatkare's leg, we'd still be in Ineb Hedj. We could gotten rid of old Hordjedtef ourselves and given the Children of Stone to Wserkaf and the king as we had planned… Damn. She buried her face in her hands because at that moment she felt like screaming.

"MaMa?" Naibe sensed the turmoil and touched Ariennu's shoulder. "You're weeping? You?"

"Am I? Oh. I just thought of something." the elder woman tried to hide her emotions. "I went to a bad place in my heart with that stupid fool coming here. It'll pass. It *has* to," Ari knew the only thing she could allow herself to think about was *this* moment and of the fading hope of freeing the young man. She wrestled with her memories and hid them, then fixed her attention on Deka. "You would think she'd fight it a little more… the blood rite."

"She wants to make that change, Ari. She wants to be apart from us. You know she told us again and again she wasn't really like either of us," Naibe tried to explain. "Maybe this is what the Children of Stone *want* her to do."

"What? Let him make her his priestess, like he's already appointed himself the Lord of Death?" Ari realized she was getting louder and stopped talking for a moment, hugging the younger woman. She watched Deka seize the prince and bring his lips down to hers for a brief, passionate kiss. That gesture left the prince so intoxicated and breathless that he staggered back a step.

"Maybe she's making him *her* priest…" Naibe suggested noticing the way the back of the prince's hand went to his own lips in stunned delight and contemplation each time she released him. "Looks like he can be surprised by her, too; so maybe he's not so much in control as he is becoming controlled."

Ari noticed the prince sit heavily in his camp chair to think about everything that just happened. When he casually noticed the blood from the scourged men had spattered over his legs, Maatkare beckoned for one of the grooms to secure the remaining men and then come wash him. While the man did this, he extended his hand to hold Deka's hand as if it was *he* who needed support. After the groom finished, the prince shared some of his breakfast with her. Soon they finished eating and he pressed her hands to his face in incredible tenderness. For a few moments he drew into his own quiet meditation.

"See that MaMa… She *is* casting a spell of her own on him," Naibe quietly gasped, but Ari disagreed:

"I don't know. It still looks like it's bothering her."

Deka's calm and rigid gaze thinly masked the turmoil flitting through her eyes. She sat bolt upright at Maatkare's side with the Wdjat gleaming at her throat, but the crystal had taken on the color of blood as if it's prismatic radiance had consumed the gore they shared. The bright rainbow luminance was gone.

The prince sat straighter, renewed and ready to continue his inquiry. Four remaining captives sat on their heels. To their right Djerah, visibly weak from his wounds and loss of blood hung as if crucified on the ladder frame. Maatkare noticed one of the remaining boys weeping. He nodded, with a slow smile, and went to him.

"You," Maatkare walked around the kneeling boy, his voice sounding almost paternal. "I know your face. You've grown tall in the past year," he smoothed the tightly braided rows on the youth's head. "Still angry that your mother came to me for a few days last year? She was nice, but as you see I have others now, so you need not concern yourself." He continued, but paced a few steps, then turned back toward the boy, continuing. "Most women I choose are *glad* of this honor. If I like a woman, I praise her family and pay for any trouble her absence may have caused. So, tell me how *you* have suffered in this honor I gave her. Tell me how *you* have come to seek revenge over it. Does your mother know you have committed this crime? Did *she* send you? Do you want her to weep unconsoled when she learns what I had to do?"

Ari and Naibe watched the youth's head turn toward Djerah, as if he was making some kind of an appeal. The stonecutter struggled in his bonds and gasped for breath again, but cried out in misery.

"Uh-oh. That bruise on his side, Babe. Now I know it's a broken rib scratching at his insides," Ari hugged the young woman and whispered more earnestly. "Poor thing can't draw a good breath without it making him suffer." She tried to think of a distraction that would allow her to get the young man loose before it was too late to save him.

"She's dead!" the youth blurted out. "You killed her."

Damn. Trail of ghosts following him, Ariennu clucked to herself. *First the princess, then that guard that he killed at Sokor, now this boy's mother. How many others are there?*

"I told you, Ari. There's hundreds," Naibe answered aloud. "That's why being with him in his bed makes me weak as a sick kitten. He feeds those ghosts on the love I magnify… I see the souls of them massing near the portal every time. He nourishes them from my joy and then drinks their essence back to gain power over me." Naibe hid her face again as if her thinking about the misery the prince caused her gave it more power.

"Dead? Not *my* doing," the prince answered too quickly. "She was well when she returned home. Did she not teach you the danger of telling lies?" Maatkare suddenly raised one slanted eyebrow when he spoke to the boy again. "Oh. Her."

Ari saw the light of recognition filter over his face. "Now I remember, something about her being taken by a crocodile and yet, here you blame *me*?" He drew closer, seized the boy's chin and appeared to read his thoughts.

"I see. She went mad? Went out wading at night? How was that *me*?" he reiterated, caressing the youth's head. "How? Unless her need for me drove her to seek me in a dream. That *has* happened before…"

He paused, stroking the boy's head again.

"Oooh!" Naibe ached and hid her head in Ariennu's arm. "He did to her what he does to all of them, but her wits broke and he doesn't care?"

"It's alright… I…" but Ari's thought was interrupted by a howl of despair from the youth.

"No… ooo. Please don't kill me…"

Ari saw Deka's arms stiffen by her sides when the boy cried out, as if she felt the terror in the sound of his voice. Maatkare must have sensed her concern because he glanced back over his shoulder.

"No one has to die," his growlish voice suggested. "Just tell me *why* you came with these men and *why* they came to kill my men."

"I don't know why the others came," the boy wailed, tears starting down his face. He shivered in terror as the prince made his way to the stonecutter again.

"True?" The prince cuffed Djerah lightly under the chin so that his head bumped up.

"He knows *nothing*," the stonecutter gasped in pain. "I told them nothing; that it was Yah blessed. I told them I fought for the gods. Take me instead. I have nothing," he begged.

"Sutek, now Yah. Do you even *know* what you are doing? *Who* you are calling? I think not, you uneducated fool! Your kind wouldn't know the first name of a god unless one of the divine ones pointed to his image and spoke it to you." The prince raised a forefinger to the groom, "and know this. I am the Lord of Death." The groom snapped the boy's neck, finishing him. "His and at some point today, yours." Maatkare bounced back to the boy's body, checked him and clearly spoke a blessing over his lifeless body.

"May the Gate of Souls open for you. Safely rest in your Mother's arm; she comes to welcome her good son." He raised his face to the sun and turned to Ari, Naibe, and the remaining men who knelt between the two tents. He explained why he hadn't blessed the other men.

"This young one was a hero. He alone, so far, had a reason to come here, albeit foolish. Had it been my own mother, I might have come like this." Then, he addressed the men who were removing the dead. "Treat the poor young fool with respect. Do not cut off his hand or burn him with the traitors." Maatkare sighed, "I will send gold enough to pay for a good burial for him out of respect for his mother's memory."

"Demon!" Djerah shouted, making another valiant struggle against the ropes that tied him to the uprights.

"*And* he finds his voice for the second time. I *will* have you finish your tale before you speak no more." Maatkare rose, then turned on his heel toward the mat of grisly devices near the brazier. Next to the bloodied whip lay a short stabbing spear. He picked it up, briefly showing it around to the women and the wider circle of men assembled to witness the discipline which had already turned into several executions.

Close quarter kills, Ari sighed to herself. *Now he's going to do his own wet jobs.*

"Naibe," she whispered, making sure no one saw her lips. "There's going to be a *lot* more blood now. I thought he would have calmed down the way he was letting Deka soothe him."

Naibe shook her head. "No, I already know what happens when he gets quiet like that. It scares me even more."

The prince heated the blade on the coals for a few moments, then advanced. His groom jerked another youth to his feet. This time, without asking him any questions, Maatkare gutted him and left him screaming and clutching his bowels as he crumbled in the sand and bled out.

Naibe squealed in shock and buried her face in Ariennu's arm.

The grooms dragged the next two men up in succession. Prince Maatkare gutted one. The last youth gasped a little, knowing his life was ending. The prince extended his hand to the youth's dark, panting belly, as if he traced where the spear would go, then leapt forward and slashed the boy's throat.

"Now you see what you have done," Maatkare hissed at Djerah. "Talk to a royal son. As if of gods would listen to you? A peasant?" He turned away and walked to the mat of tools with the blade. The grooms followed and removed his blood sprayed shenti, then wrapped him in a black square robe, belting it once. "Night will come howling for your soul for that, but first…" he quickly went to the last boy, who lay dying on the brick pad, and put both hands over the slowly gurgling wound. When he beckoned to Deka, she shot straight toward him and threw one arm over his back for support.

"There, Nefira Sekht, be your sacred name," he whispered to her. He took her face in his hands and turned her glance from his face to the gaping wound on the boy's neck.

"Goddess…" Naibe murmured quietly. "Don't do it."

Ariennu's arms wrapped around the younger woman. She took a deep breath and grew cold inside.

Deka's eyes flashed up at them as if she had become irritated with their horror. She turned her gaze to the youth whose hand had just fallen away from his throat.

"See how he accepts his fate so bravely." The prince squatted by the boy, still supporting Deka. "Still alive, but see how his life goes quicker now. Give him a kiss. Guide him to his Amenti as the way opens. Taste that small bit of his soul, as you long to do. His journey will help you know and remember all," he whispered.

Deka bent close to kiss the bit of blood that had sprayed out of the boy's mouth and onto his shivering, cold lips. She felt the last tremble of the boy's lips and the stillness that followed.

Both women saw the flash of fire in her eyes when she lifted her head. A tiny drool of the young man's blood crept out of the corner of her mouth. For a moment she transformed into a dark cloaked she-beast, crouched as if guarding a meal. The fright of that image ripped the protective field from Ariennu's and Naibe's thoughts and opened them. Their stones linked and the sensation of death, the blood, and the exhilaration passed through them like a dark wave.

Power. MaMa she's getting her power from this. She's letting him in… not fighting. Naibe sent her thought and didn't care if Deka felt it. The Ta-Seti woman's glance narrowed as if she knew the thought, but no longer cared.

Ariennu held the younger woman tighter, rocking her.

Shhh. Just don't let it get to you, Babe. She sent her thought, but now she noticed a defensive glare from the prince.

Maatkare and Deka gripped each other passionately for a few moments, consuming each other's energy as they knelt by the dead prisoner. When he released her after several moments, she rose and drifted to her chair. Djerah remained. He shook his head in regret and sobbed aloud, but not in fear.

Maatkare paced a little in front of the rattan fixture, then beckoned to the tall guard, motioning for him to cut the ropes on Djerah's hands and feet.

Run. Go! Naibe's thoughts begged, even though she knew it was pointless. She hugged Ariennu, who mournfully shook her head. As they both watched the young man staggered away from the frame and fell flat in the dust.

A groom lifted and inspected the next weapon, then brought it from the mat to the prince. It was an elbow length leather glove fitted with brass ridges, rings and spiked knobs – a torture device.

Maatkare put it on moved toward the women in the tent, brandishing it, then paraded by his assembly of men who had gathered behind and to the side of the dais and the mat. A ripple of excitement moved through the crowd. It would be a last resort.

"So no one of these ten has yet given me a good reason for this attack. One defies the god-ordained rule of the black land. He is dead. Another avenges my part in the madness of his mother – and her death. It cannot be proved. Perhaps it was a thing she ate – a moldy flour that gave her a vision. The scale of truth weighs her child's heart over this pointless crime." He announced, narrating the crimes the men had committed and why they had been executed.

"Serpent's tongue. Easy to see whose seed you reckon among your ancestors," Ariennu huffed, feeling nauseous the longer she listened to the prince's words.

"So, four tens of men came and we sent all but these ten to eternity. Though they took a good number of our men and friends with them. Such a waste of life must still be answered." He began to parade in front of his men assembled behind the dais and then to the women's tent so Ariennu and Naibe could see.

"This is a gift from the Wawat allies called the Punisher's Hand." He waved the glove in front of Naibe, who tensed, repelled by the spirit of pain emanating from the dark leather. "Good tanned leather, firm padding inside, smart knobbing and knuckle bracing." He smacked his open palm with it. "I just hope he will say something I want to hear while he can still talk."

"Why should he?" Ariennu spat at the ground near his foot. "Seems like you're going to kill him anyway. If it was me I wouldn't tell you a damn thing."

Maatkare's lower lip jutted. "How soon you forget. I recall you promised me *much* one night not so long ago that you would do anything." He turned his back and returned to Deka for another moment of tender caresses.

Ari wanted to leap out of her skin, spitting and scratching. "You make me sick!" Ariennu muttered, "but you're right. You know I did it for Baby, so you would save her." She felt the younger woman squeeze her hand in gratitude.

"And that has been good for me, until now, but your fierce tongue, were it not so useful otherwise…" his naughty expression seduced her with a left-handed compliment "…needs to be ripped out of your head. You *do* seem to forget who I am," his eyes rolled, mocking, then hardened again as he began a slow stroll to Djerah.

Now he's going to kill him for sure, Ari thought to herself. *I just wish I knew why he came here and what he wanted.*

Djerah had fallen to one side in the dirt, as if he had been destroyed by the pointless deaths he had been forced to watch.

Ariennu felt Naibe raise her own shield of secrecy over the thoughts that would be exchanged herself and the young man

Why did you come? Why? Did you not understand it would be suicide? Naibe's thoughts begged.

All is gone, Djerah's pained but tentative thoughts rose.

But what about your wife? Your family? Naibe tried to console, to give the young man a reason to fight.

Gone... his thoughts grew weaker then stopped.

Maatkare released Deka and extended his forearm so a guard could secure the glove. As he trotted down from the dais he pointed to the grooms to lift the stonecutter into a kneeling position.

"Talk, damn you!" he punched Djerah's face and head four times, each in a different direction. "Why are you here?" he demanded. "Did the Akaru Metauthetep send you?!" he struck again. The spiked glove began to make a sound on the young man's face as if it pounded a wet sack.

Ariennu had seen many grisly beatings and had even cheered her men to do their worst long ago. When she had participated in the torture of the other victims, she had been able to strip them of their humanity because they were strangers. This was different. This man she knew. She stared and shook at the sight of the prince's violent frenzy.

He walked slowly around the man, sullen and controlled, but said nothing further. Between steps his fist swung and crashed down on Djerah's head or face.

What are you doing? There's no point. He can't talk... her eyes grew larger and the place in her lower throat grew harder. Through the wash of pouring blood she saw only reminders of what had been a nose, lips, and the orbit of an eye. Blood oozed from both of the man's ears. Each blow spun his head almost to the snapping point.

Goddess that's how he'll do it. Snap his neck the long way... she panted in horror.

Naibe's face had turned to open-mouthed stone. Deka stood rigid on the dais. Maatkare whirled, about to strike but thought he heard a sound.

The guards let the young man fall backward.

Ariennu saw one of Djerah's hands jerk into a rise. Hideous bubbles formed when he tried to speak.

"Ah... *now* you want to talk as you breathe your last!" Maatkare motioned for the grooms to stretch Djerah out on the brick pad, then kicked him mightily in each side. The kick in the injured side almost caused the young man to seize. The prince straddled his chest and put his ear close enough to hear the struggling man's voice. "I will give you quick peace if you tell me *why*."

A moan rose from Djerah's swollen throat and wrenched neck.

"Ie…" his mouth hissed, "O… au-mck" He sank into oblivion, unable to say another word.

"Damn. Useless. He shouldn't have made me mad like that." He raised his gloved fist a last time and was about to give a final blow when Naibe shrieked once and jerked his arm back. She had rushed out of the tent to stick her head between Maatkare's fist and Djerah's head.

"No! You will *not* kill him. I'll tell you who he is," the young woman cried, tugging the bleeding, senseless man's arm.

"Bitch! You let me be. Eeen…" Maatkare screamed in frustration. He began to utter the control words. He raised his gore and hair drenched glove to strike her face, but she turned and grabbed both of his hands, freezing his effort.

Ariennu rushed forward to grab Djerah's limp form. She saw Naibe's dark blue stone fully emerged and heard Naibe's compelling voice. Its sound was indescribably sweet and seductive on one level, but commanding on another; it was her 'hundred voices of the goddess' whisper.

Stop. Do not touch or hit. Leave us alone, your work with him is done.

So beautiful. Oh… Maatkare gasped, sitting on his heels in rapture.

The young woman's face glowed like the moon and her eyes had rolled back so that they, too, had gone white as pearls.

Ari's own eyes snapped to her right then tore themselves away in self-defense as Naibe lifted the prince from the ground, then threw him aside as if he had been an unwanted scrap. She turned, extending her strength onto the limp form of the injured man in Ari's arms. She glanced up for an instant, ready to defend herself against the prince as he uttered the control words, but saw him scrambling on all fours, panting and shaking his head in retreating rage.

He slowly got to his feet and dismissed the men who had gathered to watch the punishment, ignoring their shock that a mere 'pretty creature' could best him. As if everything had gone according to his plan, he showed no distress and barked at them to carry on with their various tasks.

Ari overheard him instruct a patrol group to go to the perimeter to scout for any remaining trouble; others busied themselves in dealing with the bodies of the dead traitors. None of that mattered. She and Naibe slowly tugged Djerah's limp for to their tent. They knew Maatkare was doing everything he could to appear undisturbed as he walked among his men in measured steps. He reassured them and congratulated them, but was completely unsure of what he had just seen in Naibe's sudden burst of strength.

The grooms started to go after Naibe for what she had done, but Maatkare held up his hand and shook his head that he would handle her later.

Deka stepped down from the dais to assist the prince, but as she did she noticed something glittering on the ground near the ladder fixture. She turned to the grooms for a moment to indicate they should quickly wash any blood and sweat off of her beloved, then quickly prepare a shallow bath with the best of oils and calming scents. That small task done, she moved back to the prince who was still muttering about the way the audience had ended.

"Heifer doesn't know what she's done!" Maatkare growled.

Deka attempted to embrace the top of his shoulders.

"*Dare* she use heka on me…" he turned toward the tent as the women pulled Djerah inside it and shouted after them.

"You two think you're showing him pity? One would think you'd *want* mercy given to him. He's dead anyway. You'll see." He panted, threw the punisher's hand off of his fist and into the dirt, then started to push Deka away.

"It's alright, beloved. You inspired awe in everyone. No one will dare wrong you again," she turned and started to kiss the prince but was distracted by the glimmer near the ladder again. "Come, let me bathe you in a little while. Let Wise MaMa and Brown Eyes see to the man if they want to. He's not important to us now," she urged, caressing Maatkare's tense shoulder and working her fingertips up the back of his sweating neck. She glanced around for his nemes. It had come off of his head as he scourged the prisoners, but none of his men had dared to pick it up. They knew to leave him alone until his rage dissipated and he asked for it.

"Let me get your adornment." she affectionately patted his arm.

He nodded quietly, bowing his head; tired.

She turned and quickly went to pick up his nemes from the place where it had fallen near the brick pad, then stepped quietly to her left to pick up the shiny thing. A swarm of energy leapt up her arm with such a lightening-like force that she almost dropped it.

No, she thought, afraid to look at it. *Oh no*. She knew exactly what it was. The wave of energy grew and began to sweep all three of the women, bringing them instant peace, followed by their concern.

Ari and Naibe had just placed Djerah in the tent on Deka's mat. They hurriedly pulled the sides of the tent down to keep the sunlight out, trying to block a visible reaction to the linking sensation. It was as if the Child Stones knew another of their own had joined them...

What? It can't be, Ari's thoughts rioted. *That thing I knocked out of his mouth is one of the eight? I thought I knocked out a tooth when I hit him.*

I know it's a little one, MaMa. It has to be. I felt it jump through me when Deka touched it, Naibe's face became almost ghostly, *but how did this poor man come to have it?*

Both women stared at the faintly gasping body on the mat between them.

"It's alright Djee," Naibe tried to speak. "He's not going to hurt you anymore. We're going to see if we can heal you." Her eyes turned away because everything on the young man's head and what had once been a sweet but angular face was reduced to red, black, broken, and swollen ruin. His nose and mouth had become little better than a ripped open cavity. She couldn't look at him. His energy was so low when she tried to sense it, that she knew he was dying.

"We *can* help him, can't we Ari?" she asked.

"I don't know," the elder woman whispered. "He looks bad... really bad." She shut her eyes for a moment, trying to sense any kind of message from her Child Stone on how to proceed.

A whooshing sensation moved through her brow. She'd felt it before when she had been falling asleep on the crystalline vessel. The second time had been when she took the shape of a hawk and flew to see the king. To a lesser extent she felt it when she obscured herself from the view of others. "Let me think," she added, feeling ill every time she tried to look at the young man's wounds. "I'm really worried. I don't know if I can. I just hope he has enough sense left to know we tried."

At peace, beyond pain
The fledgling waits
At the edge of the
Storm coming
Long ago foretold,
The warning heeded not
So seen, so it will be.

A tiny voice whispered in the women's thoughts.

"There. You heard that, too," Ari looked at Naibe to see if she was too upset to be near the wounded man. "If we can feel their voices, so can Deka. She'll tell the prince about it, I *know* she will." Ari extended her hand to test a deep purpling lump with a gash across it that stretched from one ear to the crown of his head. It brought back a more than unpleasant memory. *I took a hit like that from my own mother when she ran me off after her man raped me. Started my grown life not able to hear because of it… was cursed as a sorceress and demon bait by the very womb that birthed me.*

Then, reflecting on the mystery of how Djerah could have been given the stone, she whispered: "I know – Inspector Wserkaf must have given it to him, but why would he do that? How could he even *know* of him, and why would he send *him*?"

"So, my feckless cousin *is* behind this."

The women gasped, looked up and saw the prince standing just inside the tent opening. His arms were folded and his face glowered with disgust. He strode to Naibe in two steps, grabbed her arm and pulled at it fiercely.

"You come with me and tell me." His voice, still hoarse from shouting at the prisoners and the exertion, quietly but firmly demanded.

Ari and Naibe knew he must have decided to spy on them while Deka and his grooms prepared his bath.

"No," Naibe protested, freeing her arm from his grip. "Let me be. I'll stay here, but we'll both tell you everything we know about him."

Maatkare paused as if he was surprised that a young woman he had so easily mastered at the start of this journey had just dared to speak up to him. He watched her sag back to the young man on the mat and gently lift his head so Ariennu could put some sheeting under it.

"Water," Ariennu whispered out of the side of her mouth. "I need to see what I can do for him. There's so much swelling."

Maatkare stared dispassionately and blinked, still curious enough to look at the dark red froth emerging from the ruin that had once been a young man's face.

"He doesn't *need* water. He's past that. He'd be at peace if you hadn't stopped me. I told *you* mostly, Red. I *know* when the portals between worlds open."

"And you didn't have to take him apart like that, you bastard," she grumbled. "You healed Naibe once, are you going to tell me you can't do the same for Djee?"

"You watch your mouth. You're mad, I can see that, so I'll let it go if I hear what I want to hear from young honey here. I advise you to consider some better manners when you talk to me, or I can give you another treatment that *won't* leave you crying for more." Maatkare turned on his heel and went to the tent opening to call for good water and a towel. When he came back, he added, "besides, he's too far into his Amenti. A healing now will only make him suffer longer." He turned away, as if he didn't want to continue looking at the result of his work.

Oh you look, damn you. You see what a monster you are, Ari's thoughts hissed.

Enough, the prince glared. None of this had to happen. You know that, but you still blame me.

Naibe looked up. "I don't know if Prince Wserkaf sent him," she began. "I don't know why he should even *know* his Highness."

At that moment, while Naibe spoke with the prince, a gentle and sensuous voice whispered in Ariennu's thoughts. It was a voice she had ached to hear just once more and now that she heard it, she bowed her head in regret because she knew she would never hear it again.

Ari. Sweet Ari.
Know I will be with you soon
Know me in the storm of your strong will
Whisper to me in the storm of your heart.

She wanted to think it was Marai's voice telling her he was on the way to the encampment and that she would know him in the power of the storm, but she knew that was impossible. Maatkare would have to stretch her out on the ladder and kill her before she saw him again. At this point, she didn't think he could bear to do that to her. He still enjoyed toying with her.

"This name 'Djee', you called him on accident, Red Sister. One of you can at least tell me about the name, can't you?" he took the water, oil, and a fresh linen to Naibe.

"Djerah. His name is Djerah bin Esai, I think. None of us knew him very well. He was contracted to work the stone across the river from us so he stayed on that side most of the time. We knew his family… a wife and her widowed sisters – their seven children among them," Naibe answered, accepting the jar of water and wetting the cloth with some of it.

"Bin Esai," Maatkare set the jar of oil down beside Ariennu's leg. He straightened up, paused and looked away again. "That's Akkad style naming. He doesn't look fresh out of the wilderness. More like a half-skin. Seems familiar, now that I think of it. I think he may have even come here in the troop roundup a few seasons ago before I was at full command. You really *should* let me give him passage. If he lives, he'll have no life and no wits." He shrugged as if he had now absolved himself of any wrongdoing.

Ariennu dabbed a little at the sucking place around Djerah's mouth. She noticed he was still breathing in shallow little gasps. For an instant, she agreed.

Understand. Do it quick.

She remembered him whispering to her when she was about to hit him the first time. *I don't think he feels any pain,* she thought to herself. *He's right. It would be easy to end him... a blessing.*

"He's a kinsman of our husband. The one called Marai who your 'Great One' had killed. I don't know more about him, or even why he would know where we are or why he would wish to come," Naibe spoke.

A keening moan rose from the bleeding lump of flesh. Three heads snapped to look, thinking this was going to be the instant his spirit left his body. Maatkare looked as if he was raising his hand to impart a final blessing, but then he showed the women a small, whitish crescent shaped stone.

"He had this on him. Nefira found it." The prince shrugged, then turned to leave the tent. "I *know* what it is. When I put it with the ones I already have, perhaps it will sing the real truth to me. I was asked by my grandfather to find the rest. So that would make *seven* of these left now?"

Ariennu and Naibe exchanged quiet but distraught glances.

Seven. Fine, Ari thought to herself. *And if this one somehow managed to come here with this poor baby, then goddess knows where they are.*

Chapter 19: Witness

That Djerah had been captured and tortured was the only thing Marai allowed himself to contemplate. If he allowed other thoughts, he knew he would grow too enraged to continue his march toward the encampment. As he moved into the deep grass, he toyed once again with the idea of sending death through the air.

Too much, he thought. *The men who followed young Djerah are all dead because he got mad at his faithless wife and instead of going out and getting drunk or getting in a few small time fights to spend his anger, he takes all of the hotheads he can find? He couldn't wait. Damn this impatient blood of Ahu and our stubborn hearts. But damn my insisting on him coming in the first place so he wouldn't be there to hurt her when he found out. Why should I have cared if he hurt or killed all of those silly women? Not any of the three were worth him. So he comes with me and still tries to get himself killed.*

Marai visualized the elder's parting thoughts: Akaru Metauthetep stood in the doorway of his Qustul temple. He had pushed back on Marai with some odd form of wind heka to keep him from leaving.

He said Djerah's journey here was pre-ordained? No it was senseless. The old man didn't have any idea of what to do about Prince Maatkare. He still holds out hope for the suph his elders crafted with long dead kings. Even his own people have lost respect for him over the years.

Don't go, or *not yet, he had said* when it appeared the only intelligent thing to do was mount a force and cleanse the hunting ground where the prince was camped. That he might hurt the women or Djerah in the process was all that should have concerned him. Like Wserkaf, Akaru was torn between duty to gods, family, and country and the internal fire to abandon all of that in pursuit of a truer wisdom.

Both of these men knew I was on a journey of knowledge and that I was sent here by the Children of Stone to finish gathering the ancient wisdom tools Djedi had started collecting. It was so the Universe's wisdom could be accurately taught. I learned that we were at a point in time when the truth was being altered or denied altogether. These men knew they had been chosen to help me find these things, but so many obstacles have clouded the path I'm on, that not one of the three of us knows what's coming next. Human independence, stubbornness, time constraints, emotion. Our benefactors never thought… never had a concept of how complicated we creatures had become since the time of the First Ones, when the things they left us were scattered and hidden.

Marai shook his head and strode up into the pale gold rock of the hills. When he finished climbing hand over hand to the top of the ridge north of Maatkare's camp, he turned and saw the smoke of distant watch fires. Soon, he began to notice bloodstains, spent arrows, and dropped weapons; evidence of a lengthy and hard battle. Further away, vultures circled. The wind eddied a little, wafting the earliest odor of death.

Dozens of fools came out with him and dozens were no match for this prince's trained force. Cut them all down like it was a good day hunting. No bodies though. The men must have pulled them down to the camp for counting and putting fire to them. He ducked down behind a large rock then looked carefully into the distance. His eyes sharpened, picking a central line to correspond vertically the horizon, then hyper-focusing his vision at the crosspoint. As he visualized more lines forming, the spaces between them sharpened and enlarged. The more lines he visualized the sharper the image became, as if he was forming a flower of life and compartmentalizing every detail he saw so that it magnified and taught him all of the details he sought.

Near the camp, men were stacking bodies and sawing off left hands to pack in salt before lighting the remains. A drum of hands with the characters stating the details of the struggle would be taken home; an efficient way of counting the defeated. More bodies were being brought in from below. He knew the only ones who had been taken prisoner were those still able to walk. The helpless ones had been slaughtered where they lay.

Djerah's not among these poor devils, but I know he's not good. This prince didn't learn much from him, but Deka found the little Yah stone. They know it's one of the missing eight. Hordjedtef schooled his princeling on the control words so he can handle them with ease. He has Deka for anything else. Does she even know how much he is using her?

Marai wondered what had become of the hard-shelled but fragile creature he had once known. When he met her, she was in her lowest form; a scrawny and half-mad mute. She perched on his lap and offered herself to him as a matter of course. Horrified, because he had just killed thirty men with magically assisted strength he didn't understand, he had refused. Once again, when she first woke in the Children's crystalline pod, she offered herself to him again, but he shunned her for different reasons. She was gloriously beautiful, but he had been alone for so long that he was desperately afraid his manhood would fail her. From that moment on, *she* became the one who pushed him away. She became obsessed with finding the mysterious Ta-Te, a lover from her past who might have been a god. She had wanted *him* to be Ta-Te, but Marai denied he was, or had ever been, such a creature. Now she had sought this entity from another source: Prince Maatkare.

She was so close to solving her ancient hurts before I left; of seeing what dark force haunted her from before she was crippled. He sensed, in horrified flashes, the images of her eagerly lapping the blood from the prince's hands.

He made her take a blood bond? Why? Has she drawn the darkness she sought into herself until she becomes an eater of the dead - a bloodthirsty demon-woman like Ereshkigal? he asked himself. *If that's so, I need to abandon this slow and patient path and just be there.* He couldn't think about anything more. Leaping to his feet, he raised his hands to the sky. Slowly, the lowing noise of a forlorn bull filled his being and the dust at his feet began to swirl.

It was late afternoon when Marai overtook the camp...

Maatkare sighed, nerveless and besotted with the recent memory of everything that had happened during the day. Over the past weeks, the very presence of the woman he called Nefira Sekht Deka had begun to move him to incredible passion. If he had ever sought to master her, he began to wonder after this early afternoon, exactly who was now the master.

When he returned from the women's tent, he saw she had dismissed the grooms and servants who had prepared his bath. She didn't answer him when he compelled her to speak about the young man who lay near death nearby. Every time he started to question her about the man, she gently shushed him and soothed the concern out of his brow. Her devotion seduced him entirely. Soon, he stopped trying and he lay back to enjoy her gentle treatment.

"I know what you really want of me. I will take you soon," he blindly reached up to touch the tip of her nose with his lips. "Together we will celebrate your rebirth." Her gentle rubbing and dabbing on his chest slowed, then her caresses stopped. He opened his eyes and saw her desperately trying to compose herself. Her shoulders heaved with emotion and her hands shook so much she could no longer touch him.

"Shh. Take your time, Nefira Deka, take your time," he whispered. "It's just the chaos visiting itself on you; passing through you. Let it flow. Don't fight it, no matter how wrong or wicked it seems to you. It's the right thing for you now; the right thing for both of us. I knew your power, woman. I knew it when I saw you in my grandfather's plaza your first night across the river."

I did know, he thought. *And today, she gives birth to her truer self in the blood of our defeated foes. I remember my own rebirth; how the power felt when it first moved through me.* Maatkare gripped her hand and made it trace it over his chest, then moved it up to his mouth so he could taste the memory of the blood on her fingertips.

Little Raemkai was my dog when I was a child. I named him for me. Our name means 'the sun is my life force'. He saw himself for a moment: a little and happy princeling dancing and playing with a great black dog that was so big it almost dwarfed him. He was a gift from a sepat chief and from his size my father was certain he was part wilderness wolf. *Not a pure breed. He told me I needed a smaller red and white hound who would be a good hunter but have an even temper, but I would not give that black dog up. I loved that mutt.* He saw himself asleep with the dog protectively covering the foot of his little bed.

Deka breathed out a little, bent over Maatkare, and kissed his hand.

He froze, even though her touch thrilled him beyond endurance. The happy memory turned dark. His black dog killed one of the royal guards, then it grew wild and snappish from the taste of a man's blood.

Bastard used to tease him and kick him for no reason, that's why he did it. I wasn't there to pull him off when it finally happened. Men muzzled him and made me shoot him. He saw the brief memory of himself crying and shaking so hard he could barely nock his arrow. 'Be a man, a royal son,' they said. *Yet, as that wonderful animal died in my arms, his mighty spirit, that of a god, came into me. I snapped and bit men who came to take his body from me. I went mad for many days, as if possessed; suddenly more dog than boy.*

"Raem… beloved," Deka's fingertip's smoothed his temples. "Your eyes look far away."

"A memory," he answered as the last image of him dipping his own small hands into the dog's wound and drinking its blood replayed. *My own father knew fear of me then, and what brings me greatest joy also changed that day. They put me in quiet rooms in the temples of Wepwawet which calmed my spirit some, but it was there I learned of my true nature; that I had the power to* become *the dog.* "Now that we have shared the blood of our enemies, I need for your truth to come to more easily to me. Your sisters knew him, this leader, and you did not?" he asked one more time, propping up on his elbows. She bowed her head for a moment before she showered him with kisses.

"I did not *know* him, beyond seeing him and his family," she said. "We never spoke. He lies dying, but I cannot allow pity for a foolish man to overtake me. I don't wish to think of him, Raem, only *you*. Be with *me* now and let us leave the dead with the dead." She kissed his chest and lapped the finest sprinkle of man-fur growing there, teasing his nipples with her tongue. The chill of arousal swept him. She swung her leg over him, then moved with him in a slow, anointing glide. "Be with me unceasingly. Take me and overtake me," Deka breathed.

Maatkare welcomed her but at the same moment he took her, the dim outline of a dark aura that rested on her shoulders entered her body at the level of her heart.

I will, his thoughts whispered as he gripped her hard and eased up to take her mouth in a deep kiss. *With what began in the dawn light, we finish in the triumph of the blood.* His thoughts rushed through her soul and became part of her dark need. He paused for a moment to regard her elegant form wrapped around him and accepting him as eagerly as she had accepted the blood on his hands.

Her sigh of pleasure becalmed itself into an expression of serene wonder at the sensation of unlimited power that almost overwhelmed her, more than the way he so effortlessly filled her. That wasn't what almost unmanned the prince. The shimmer on her skin began as a glow of sweat. In the heat of pleasure between them, he watched the "glow" become red and golden flame trapped just under the surface of her skin. It was as if the Ta-Seti woman became the fire of the sun barely contained in flesh. He had sensed that energy before, but now that she had fed from the blood he offered her, it became stronger.

Gods, she drinks power from me now. As he yielded to her, the prince felt something give way in his heart. The force of it made him tremble at first, then laugh a little lasciviously, but soon it emerged as a different kind of hunger. *You will be with me now and forever,* his thoughts sighed. *You understand my need for you.*

Then, he cautioned himself: *Love. I almost want to say it to her, but I cannot. It is not possible. I won't slip and say it in the heat of any passion, not ever. I will be fierce for her, merely that.* He gripped her hips and began to slowly move them in a circular pattern. *How good her body feels!* he felt the animal detachment form inside him and struggle to show itself as if her own glimmering form had ripped it into manifested presence. Her open eyes flashed golden and red as the image of flame formed in them, then met his own green and gold eyes. If he had become wolf, she had become flame.

Underneath that flame, Maatkare saw her shape begin to change even further. He had seen the form she took before, but only in flashes and in the dark of their bed. It materialized more fully but still remained human. Her eyes cooled into a shade like his own but were slightly almond-shaped; her ears grew elongated and fangs formed. *She is beautiful,* he thought. *No others will be as close to me as she is, though I will enjoy others and often. Love? I reject it, and yet… she knows my needs, admires the thirst and hunger, and matches it with her own. Is that what it is? She is becoming mine.* Her cries of pleasure filled him and stripped him of self, elevating him. "There…" he said as she sighed and cried out again "Nefira Sekht Deka, you please me." He continued, renewed.

Ari heard the gentle lowing sound in the distance. It grew in volume and power as she felt it move down out of the hills and begin to nudge the tent walls with the first burst of wind.

"Here. Babe. Get up and help me drag him away from the flap. The wind is starting up out there," she motioned to Naibe, who was still cradling the young man's badly deformed head on her lap. Djerah needed to be out of the way and sheltered. Sand and dust coming under the edge could make a dreadful situation worse. The young woman eased Djerah's head down, rose, and pulled the mat.

Just as they placed him against the firmly staked back wall of the tent, the bright afternoon sun faded behind a growing haze of kicked-up dirt.

This isn't too strong, Ari thought as the wind grew a little then leveled off to a steady, dull roar. *Like the world's most gentle haboob.* She noticed Djerah's head and face were swelling badly and oozing a combination of old blood and watery fluid. *He's still alive. Getting hard to tell now, though.* Ariennu bent over his ruined face to check for gurgles or faint breath sounds. The bruise on his ribs had grown. Fresh blood was drooling from his mouth and little uneven rasps sounded. He was trying to cough, but couldn't. She had seen men with deep chest wounds before. Ari knew he would, at some point, drown in his own blood.

Naibe had made a coverlet for him out of two of her shifts.

Ari dabbed water on his weeping wounds, even though she didn't think any of their care would make a difference.

Djerah lay still. At regular intervals, he trembled a little as if he breathed his last.

"I'm sorry I made Highness stop. I wasn't thinking about how you would suffer," Naibe whispered to the dying young man. "I just couldn't let him kill you that way. I had to try." She went silent for a moment and then used her Ashera voice to compel him: *Please, Djerah, feel no pain. Speak to your heart and let us know if you are ready to leave the land of the living. MaMa and I will pray for you. We will weep for you; mourn you.* She tried to make their old neighbor feel better about letting his life go. *You were so very brave to try to save us. I thank you so much.*

Ariennu got a fresh cloth and mixed a few drops of boiled wine and water mixture onto the area where his shattered jawbone jutted out of an ugly laceration. It had been his mouth. The fluid bubbled, then settled and dripped into his deeply purpled neck. She knew that even if he couldn't swallow the fluid, she could keep that place moist.

A lowing sound in the distance grew nearer and louder; a cross between the bellow of a bull and the roar of wind. A gust buffeted the tent for a moment.

"Hear that?" Ari asked. "Spirit's coming for this poor baby," her shoulders sagged, defeated. An unexplained anguish descended on her as if the sum of her adventures in life compared to the young man's innocence was, at this moment, unbearable. "Oh you damned gods of death! You take *me* down to your valley of dust and let him be healed instead. I've done everything I need to do. I've loved. I've lost. This young one was just getting started. It's not even fair."

Naibe's eyes lit, shiny with her own tears, because she fully understood. That Ariennu, who had always been in control of her emotions, was so upset made it worse for her.

"MaMa, don't be sad. We have to be brave for Djerah. I *do* hear it, though. You *know* it's a bull roaring. Maybe Marai's soul is coming to take him, since his sister was Djee's savta. Maybe they'll *both* be coming," She gently blew her breath out on the young man's ruined face.

Naibe hadn't realized her hand was so close to the young man's hand. She tensed when it moved against hers as if he was trying to grasp and squeeze it. The clear liquid of tears mixed with blood pooled at the broken orbit of one of his blind eyes.

"And don't *you* cry either," Naibe whispered, then asked: "Do you want to live Djerah? Do you?"

"Pfft. I hope he has better sense," Ari hissed and stood up. "If he *does* live, what kind of life will he have? Blind? Likely deaf and unable to speak. The seat of knowledge in his heart will be lost to him. We'd have to feed him through a reed straw if he even gained the power to suck on it." The elder woman's thoughts turned to the man who had caused all of the damage. "Damned bastard!" her voice rose to a scream when she thought of the way Maatkare, in a complete and unquenched rage, had mauled the young man's face until there was nothing left but shattered bone and spongey tissue. "You left him hanging between life and death; on the brink of Sheol like this and now you celebrate?" She paused in her tirade to notice a deep, almost animal, moan. It sustained and rose to a scream of ecstasy. Deka – followed by his whispers of encouragement.

"Damn you! Both in there feasting on each other like it's your cursed wedding night. Your men are even out here laughing and wagering how many times you're going to bang her gong before you run dry." Ariennu jumped to her feet and went to her basket. She opened the lid and grabbed one of her walking sandals.

"Shut Up! Shut Up! Shut Up! I should jump over there and fling a shoe at that ass plowing her, I should. You *both* deserve death, not this poor child here." Ari went to the flap to peel part of it open, sandal in one hand.

"Mama, *I* stopped him. It's *my* fault Djee is suffering like this," Naibe hushed, but the sound of the wind grew louder and the force of it began to rattle the sides of the tent.

Ari peeked outside the tent through a hole she opened in the bound front flap. The dust had grown thicker and started to swirl throughout the camp. Men scrambled into their tents, taking all flammable items inside. Three men with their heads wrapped in rags doused the central cook fire with water. They cursed mightily and leapt away from the cinder filled smoked that billowed and swirled around them. As soon as they were satisfied flame wouldn't re-ignite or spread to any of the tents, they too rushed into shelter. Suddenly, the sound and dust was on everyone, muffling the sounds of breathless joy from the royal tent.

I should hope it blows your tent over and shows you to your men, but you'd probably jump up and wave your nasty el around at them. Kemet royal pride be damned. Ariennu secured the flap and went back to Naibe and the still body of the young man.

"Did he just…?" Ari noticed how still he had become. The wind gradually subsided.

"I think he's the same," Naibe answered, then added. "Look, Ari," she raised her hand. "This is how I know." Djerah's hand gripped hers with all of his fading strength. "He keeps trying to thought talk, but I won't let him. He wants to tell us something."

"Wonder what?" she asked.

At that moment, he suffered a little more; a moan escaped him.

No pain, no pain… Naibe ordered, gripping and squeezing his hand in hers. Neither woman noticed the shadow, tall and great, that suddenly stood between the tents.

OPENER OF THE SKY

Chapter 20: Entry into the Camp

He strode into the camp behind the waning drafts of wind he had conjured. All the way up the river, Marai had dreamed about roaring into the encampment in the bull form of Bakha Montu. He rethought the fantasy of ripping down tents and laying waste to everything in his path, because he knew Naibe and Ariennu were in one of the tents tending to a fatally injured Djerah. Deka was in the royal tent with the prince. Sadly enough, he already knew she did *not* wish to be rescued.

> *Contemplate, Man of Ai*
> *See the destiny before you*
> *To measure the steps*
> *In greatest care*
> *Is more awesome than the charge of the wrathful beast.*

The Children of Stone had repeated those words to him while he sat on the ridge overlooking the encampment. Whenever he shrugged their whispers away, they repeated the verse more clearly.

So. Approach them as if I were a god, eh? He almost laughed to himself. *The Children want me to show power, might, and strength, but not wrath. Why should I even listen to them? They haven't helped me that much so far. This royal devil needs his death to come to him now.* The sojourner stood between the tents with his arms folded.

> *You have only self-deceived*
> *What stalls you is your doubt*
> *If you must not wait*
> *Go between moments that*
> *Wait for you.*

The chorus of childlike voices whispered their sing-song phrases in Marai's heart. They sounded stronger and included the almost-warble of Metauthetep's voice as if the Akaru's own message sought a path through his thoughts. It, too, held back the strength of his avenging storm.

Between moments. Marai remembered he had paused time when Prince Wserkaf helped him recover from the poison and then released it when the inspector had to leave him.

I raised the moon higher with the Yah stone that Djerah took. I prayed to the goddess in my sweet Naibe that there would be enough time to know all that I needed and somehow it just happened. He sped time up on his journey to Qustul. He shook his silver head, knowing that he needed to decide quickly. He was still too angry to be careful.

"Then time will have to stop entirely for everyone here, because I *cannot* go forth, until my wrath eases." He whispered aloud, then stood with his legs wide. He bowed his head as if it had suddenly become fully horned and put out both hands. With his deep breath, he felt a surge of dark lightning begin in his brow, leap down to his heart, and then pulse up from the back of his head to leap through his fingertips. At that moment, everything slowed, then reversed slightly as if it jumped into midair with a popping sound before it ground to a stop. As soon as everything paused motionless, Marai darted into the encampment and glanced around to see how well the spell had worked.

Men who had taken shelter in their tents stood frozen and staring through small finger-made openings. He turned and found himself staring at Ariennu's messy reddish curls. Her eyes were uncustomarily rimmed in red as if she had wanted to cry but couldn't allow herself the luxury.

Ari. Sweetness. I'm here now. *Everything's going to be all right.* He knew every thought he had sent her resonated in her stone but because of the alteration of time came through as confused child-whispers. She looked upset. He wanted to enter the tent right away to see the extent of Djerah's injuries, but he turned to the royal tent instead.

If I go now and see him, I will show no mercy. Deka might be killed when I take that devil she's with. Maybe altering the moments around me will stop the chances of that. He moved toward the royal tent past two huddled guards with their faces protected against the sand. One of them had turned to react to either a noise or the lack of sound.

Marai started to open the tent, but froze at the gentle purring of sound inside his thoughts.

Breathe.

Release.

Too angry. I know. It would be so easy to just kill him and carry Deka away, but it's what a coward does. I want to fight him and kill him as a warrior so he will have my face etched into his eternal damnation.

He stood by the opening of the tent and whispered, *I am here. I have always been here within skin, within soul. I am an illusion in your heart.*

The sojourner quickly decided he would remove the prince's weapons while he was frozen, secure him, and then separate out Deka and the Children of Stone as well as Wserkaf's Wdjat. He would not kill the prince unless the man broke free of the spell and attacked him.

As he took one last step toward the tent he noticed two big, dark men clad in simple shenti and cap. They approached, paused, and stared at him. They backed up, then crouched like startled animals.

"For you time moves not," Marai paraphrased, shocked into rattling out the words of his enchantment one more time.

Neither man was affected by his words.

Marai thought he heard a defensive growl coming from one of them, then recognized the men from a vision.

These men were with Deka in my dream. He paused, but they began to draw their blades.

Mutes, he sensed. *Deka must have been teaching them hand talk… but why? And why do they not freeze like other men? They should understand my spirit voice.*

Mama Menhit their thoughts echoed in unison, but didn't sound like thoughts he read from other people.

Menhit? Lioness God, the slaughterer? Marai quickly analyzed what he'd heard coming from their thoughts. *Do they think she is Menhit?*

"You see me. Do you hear me?" he asked, but the men continued to slowly creep up as they watched him. "Menhit. Mama Menhit," he tried aloud, then *Menhit. Mama Menhit.* He tried with his thoughts, then swept his right hand toward the tent. The spell for the time alteration had just popped into his thoughts and had been more of a contemplation than a spell. He didn't know how long it would last or if the prince would suddenly free himself and be able to come storming out unbound.

I should have just jumped in there and stuck him. This was a bad idea.

Protect, the pair repeated, but when the sojourner looked directly into their eyes he noticed something odd. He couldn't quite place the blackness of their eyes, but in just an instant they changed and flashed gold before returning to a normal appearance. Each man moved in unison with the other as if they were trained to work together. Their ebony skin rippled a muscular purple in the afternoon light. In a fighting situation, they would be excellent, if they knew what they were doing at all.

They aren't warriors. They protect, but don't speak or reason. Some kind of defect… and the eyes. He knew he had seen that glimmering transparent eye somewhere, but no answer entered his thoughts. He tried to communicate again.

Deka. The woman's name is Deka… the one with the prince. She is one of my wives, he felt an odd sort of calm steal over him and paused while the guards stood studying him. The two guards had no curiosity whatsoever that the rest of the camp was frozen. They remained focused on the sojourner as if he had suddenly become the only creature they were able to see.

But I'm not so angry now. Why? If I stop time, it stops anger? He frowned, wondering if the Children of Stone had broken through his thoughts and stemmed his rage. *Are there limits to the things they can help me do? Am I limited?* he wondered, then sent a thought internally to his own Child Stone:

You don't understand. I need to be angry. I need everything I was given that morning when I took the lives of the thieves.

The chorus of voices filtering through his stone whispered an all-too-quick response.

Rage without thought is no longer advised.

Before, you did not know your strength
So it was taught you.
We learned your regret of that day.
Though death fills your thoughts,
Do wise, yet unexpected things
The woman Deka is the point of this meeting.
The prince is not.

Unexpected, Marai stepped back. He had to agree. If the women, and especially Deka, could be broken free of this man's influence, such an act would be punishment enough. He would face returning to Ineb Hedj with his reputation brought under scrutiny and a scandal preceding him. It would be a longer lasting and much more effective punishment than killing him or physically beating him. *Deka is there of her desire because she does not know I live. If I show her… Menhit. Lioness.* He turned away from the tent flap for an instant, wondering what he would say to her when she *did* see him.

I wonder if this prince has any idea what he might have inspired by getting her to taste the prisoner's blood. If Naibe can be Ashera and I brought Bakha by my rage, she very well could be reflecting Menhit, the mother of Heka. I wonder if he knows, Marai shook his head and sent further thoughts to the grooms.

You won't harm me. I will not mistreat the one who is Deka. I want to see her, but I will be civil to her and to the prince… He sent the men a thought. As if his request had been magical, the men stood still, regarded each other for a moment, and then put away their swords and took off running.

What? They shouldn't have scattered just because I said I wasn't going to hurt her. Something else going on here with these men. Marai moved around the two men who had been huddled outside the royal tent. He waved his hand in front of their frozen faces to see if his spell remained secure. As he did, he thought he sensed passion coming from the tent.

Hmm. And if they are… Marai snickered like a naughty youth. He truly hoped he had spoiled their tryst when he stopped time. *Somehow I don't think I have, though.* He shrugged and entered.

Maatkare and Deka lay on the prince's bed; their eyes gently closed and fluttering as if they dreamed. *They must have been resting afterwards – the sweetest rest.* He recalled almost painfully the way he and Naibe would lie exhausted in each other's arms or the way Ari would toy with the hornlike locks of his hair after an afternoon of love. Marai drew closer for a moment, trying to get a better look at the sleeping couple, but he was distracted by the stack of bloodied but neatly folded clothing. Except for the rumpled bed linens beneath them, everything was neat and precisely placed. The prince's arm was slung over Deka's side and back; her leg draped over him.

Kill him, Marai's thoughts grumbled. *Kill him and make her stop this foolishness and come with us.* Then… *No. Perhaps I should just wake her slightly and make her think I have entered her dreams.* He raised one finger.

Only you will know, sweet Deka. You will see that I live.

Deka lazily turned her head and opened one eye. She sought the face of the prince, noticed he slept, then looked up into Marai's face. Her eye widened in fear when she realized she couldn't move.

I'm here, sweet Deka. The big man sent his thoughts into her stone, knowing there would be no barrier. She would hear him clearly. *I'm no dream this time; I'm no ghost in the well.*

He saw her struggle; her speechless mouth formed the word 'Raem' as if she asked for his help.

I know you believed me dead and you were looking for a way to come to Ta-Seti, but you're here. You did it now, after trying so hard.

She struggled again but only moved her head the tiniest bit. Her Child Stone emerged in self-defense.

Shhhh, Marai put his fingers to his lips and turned away to leave, but then turned back unable to resist a slight scold.

You know what you did was wrong; to lose yourself for a man. No woman who knows her own power has to do that. You knew your strength. Your Ta-te didn't take that from you, but this one here will try.

"W…" her lips asked *why* as her power over Marai's utterance grew stronger. He knew she would gain control of herself in moments and be able to free Maatkare.

"Dream." he whispered a lie aloud. "A powerful dream, nothing more," and left the tent, but chuckled to himself. *And His Highness is going to be pretty mad once she gets him loose.*

The sensation of Djerah's suffering assaulted him the moment he stepped toward the women's tent. Marai knew the young man's life was fading beyond any chance of a cure, so he quickly sent him encouragement.

I am here, Djerah, cling a little longer to your life. Allow me the moment to try. Behind him, a din of alarm rose from the royal tent.

"But Raem, his ghost is *here*… out of my dream. I *know* what I saw."

"Here. Woman, stand still to me."

Quiet followed. Then:

"Your Ntr stone has risen. Something is working a spell on you. Let me speak over it."

Marai froze and turned back. He knew two things: Prince Maatkare was going to use the control utterance to get Deka to stop yammering about visions. If he did, the pain of the psychic assault might affect his time altering spell. He would have to face the prince *before* he saw Djerah. Marai placed the back of his hand against his own stone, shut his eyes and concentrated as he sensed:

Eeeen Nauuu…

Marai felt the impact of the words prickle through the stone in his brow. He hurried to the dais and sat at the foot of the brick platform and listened to Deka suffer in protest, reacting to the power of the incantation.

"Shhh. There. Easy, I'm done. But you have to tell me now, Nefira, *now*…"

"I couldn't move in my dream. I couldn't wake up."

Marai heard whimpering and his gentle reassurance go on for a while. Certain time was still frozen outside the tent, he decided to release the rest of the camp except for the women's tent.

"As it was before the storm," Marai breathed. "None will think my presence is out of place or strange… but Djerah, Ari, and Naibe are held still in their place."

The mysterious grooms returned from wherever they had gone. All in them encampment began to bustle around with their tasks. Some voices exclaimed:

"What was that?"

"Wasn't there a storm coming a moment ago?"

"What happened? I don't see anything, do you?"

"No, it happened. See the grass over there bent flat?"

More cursing and shuffling sounded in the tent.

Marai wasn't interested in the particulars of the conversation, but he had begun to feel highly amused at the chaos his spell had caused. This time, so far, the Children of Stone were right. He enjoyed making a man who felt powerful and in control of everything in his world suddenly find something had escaped him. It would be fun to watch him squirm.

In a few moments, the prince emerged with Deka on his arm. She froze, and stumbled on weak knees.

"Oh, no…" she gasped. "Not…"

Maatkare's eyes widened, first in disbelief and then in a peculiar sort of mirth. He loosed Deka's arm for a moment and raised a hand to dispel any lingering illusion before him. Marai winced in distaste as he felt the prickling sensation on his arm and leg again and blocked it.

"You dare enter my space, uninvited?" the prince asked. "Are you mad?"

"Well I am not *happy*, but…" Marai waved his fingertips and the swirl of the wind whooshed lightly in the palm of his right hand. He almost laughed at the tiny leftover from the swirl of dust he caused.

Maatkare stared, carefully stripping his face of any surprised expression. Fully understanding that the image of Marai was no ghost or illusion, the prince scooped Deka up into one arm and towed her up to the dais. After they both stepped up onto the platform, he gave her a peck on the tip of her nose and sat her quietly in the folding chair next to his own.

"You may stay seated, but you *will* remain below me," he nonchalantly added, then turned his back for a moment.

Marai smiled out of the corner of his mouth as he recalled the trained courtesy and charm that all royal sons extended. The back turning was designed to show any guest that he had no fear of being jumped. After a moment, he turned to face the sojourner again and sat. Marai sensed the prince's thoughts going to Deka, who had quickly retreated into stunned and quiet reserve. *No need for worry, Nefira. I'll take care of this,* then *we'll talk.*

Her downcast eyes darted side to side. They told Marai everything about her tale of confusion and humiliation.

"So, Marai bin Ahu is it?" the prince began, the look of irritation breaking through his nonchalant expression. "You've come far. From the Land that Loves Silence, I see." He paused for effect, letting his unruffled response sink in. Marai knew the prince was doing everything he could to act as if he had actually *expected* this visit, but his anxiety showed ever so slightly when his left hand strayed to Deka's fingertips to calm and reassure her.

"It *does* seem I went there, stayed some moons, and came back. It *wasn't* pleasant." Marai fought off the urge to swat the crooked smirk off of the prince's face. He remembered the agony of the Sweet Horizon mixture he had swallowed. It had been intended to end him, but put him into a deep sleep filled with prophetic-yet-jumbled nightmares. His recovery had been even more painful.

Marai found himself studying the man to determine what his strengths and weaknesses were, but more than that, what his appeal to Deka was. *Medium color for a Kemet man; darker than Old Hordjedtef, though. He has an excellent build. He'd have to have one to be a master of weapons and an unquestioned leader of so many men. He's vain about it, though. Likes to show off his skills on the field and in his bed.* Marai laughed to himself, instantly feeling any shred of respect he might have had for the man vanish. *Has an el most men might envy and he can lay a woman down like a god, but can he* love *one? I doubt his kind knows what that word even means.* He shook his head. *All that and still shorter than I am.*

"I guess I'm not so easily killed as some would like me to be," Marai added aloud.

He felt the ache of unrequited affection enter his stone and his heart when he stared at the woman seated beside the prince. Even so, he knew she had changed.

Deka, he sent a quick thought. *I told you I understood. Now, stop suffering.*

It is you, then? Truly you, out of heka? No ghost or dream? Her thoughts timidly returned, but she winced knowing Maatkare had pried into those thoughts.

Marai kept his eyes down as if he didn't notice anything change, but glanced up long enough to see the pulse of red at her brow before he looked back at the prince. She was in absolute torment.

Deka. Easy, he consoled. The twitch in Maatkare's shoulder showed the sojourner he would have to do more to partition his thoughts. The prince sensed him sending messages to the woman at his side and that knowledge made him act cagey.

Marai sensed that all of the impulsivity and madness this Maatkare was rumored to have was very likely true. The only thing that separated the man from raving insanity was his cold intelligence and trained control. *The training as a priest and as a warrior saved this one's soul. If I can poke him enough, make him lose control, he can still be bested. He'll get sloppy. He delays me seeing others, but the longer he does, the more I will learn him. My frozen time...*

I see you, he thought, and allowed the prince to hear his analysis. *Your vanity shows in the way you come out and display your body, your fitness, and your wealth to me. All about you; brows plucked to look like wings of a descending hawk; your Khat embroidered with gold; your eyes that menace. You've worked so hard on your look.*

"So?" the prince cleared his throat. "You're some sort of sorcerer then? You can return from the realm of death? I would like to know *how* you do that," he inspected his pearly polished nails in a gesture that intimated disinterest.

"I can't tell you."

"Can't, or won't?" the prince asked.

Marai knew his eyes had started to glimmer in an angry silver overlay that mimicked the color of his Child Stone. The prince was testing him and testing Deka at the same time.

"I was gifted by what your people call the Ntr, your Highness," Marai sat forward, elbows uncomfortably on his knees. "I haven't had the time or inclination to question it. I just accept that I am no longer an ordinary man."

"Sometimes a gift comes with a hidden cost or a higher expectation," Maatkare mused then began again. "I *had* heard of you when I was at home; that you were some gifted outlander who had lived long but had not aged a bit. I didn't question my esteemed grandfather as to why he thought to destroy you, or to even deal with you in the first place. As Great One, his decisions remain a mystery to all but himself and the great, wise Djehut."

Marai shifted again. The idea that parrying with this prince was a mistake had begun to creep into his thoughts again.

"If you indeed know how to heal yourself from death and he finds this out, he will likely piss himself over it until he discovers your secret. Could it be that when all of the stones are in one place the answer will be revealed to whoever holds them? Grandfather told me you were instructed to deliver them to the priests. *I* am a fully elevated priest as well as a warrior, but I have decided while young I would pursue the warrior's path. At this moment I have all but seven of them."

Maatkare frowned at the light of the low sun. He shaded his eyes from the rays that had found his face. With a simple gesture, he signaled for men who had discovered he was conducting another audience to move the chairs further under the awning and to fetch three cups of beer. "Does he actually *know* you live?" He turned to Deka whose eyes were still downcast. "He told me that you most certainly did *not* live. When we sensed you, we assumed it was a haunting and blocked your spirit's access."

"I feel quite sure he knows I'm alive by now," Marai looked down. *And that blocking explains why I could not speak to my wives before this, you wretched little cur.*

"Look," Marai was on his feet suddenly, ready to go to the tent where he sensed Ari, Naibe, and Djerah were still frozen. "I know you view me as your enemy, so let's just stop this serpent-tongued chatter and let me get to my other wives and my man who's been hurt while I can still save his life."

"Not… yet…" Maatkare commanded. "*You* sit down again while I learn the truth behind your man storming us earlier," his hand grasped Deka's hand and squeezed it a little, "which he learned was not smart the *hard* way." Maatkare continued "…he and the fools following him. The women have spoken to me already that my cousin Wserkaf is a player in this adventure of yours." His glance lowered, but Marai felt the sensation of constant thought-energy. "So interesting that such a disciplined man would turn against his own blood and family to tell you where your things were." One of his eyebrows raised in a self-satisfied but inquisitive expression.

"His Eye of Truth, which he usually wore, is also here. He wants it back," Marai mumbled, then sat with such force that the cane chair creaked mightily under his weight.

"You mean the Eye of Truth which he *allowed* to be taken from him by the woman Ariennu. Had he truly *valued* that gift which his own mother gave him, he would not have given it up so lightly. Rumor has it he was under an enchantment, however. Grandfather and I *both* thought he was above such mortal temptations, but then I heard the tale he had bounced up your youngest one's skirt quite a few times until Princess Khentie resented the crowd and put her out." He smirked, as if he enjoyed watching Marai squirm, as he told the tale. "I found her a worthy bedmate until this one here began to exert herself a little more," he pointed to Deka. His thoughts shifted back to Marai and he waited, stopping to savor the beer and nod about its quality when it was presented. He gave Deka some of it and then offered the sojourner the third cup.

Marai fought the urge to slap the cup out of the prince's hand and then let enough dark lightning loose to sanitize the entire camp. He took a deep, but invisible calming breath and reached for the drink, knowing the time stop over Djerah's life and suffering had begun to slip. Thoughts of Djerah suffering in the women's tent flooded his heart with such power that Marai winced in a kind of shared misery. The stonecutter was choking and sucking at nothing but the fluids that filled his lungs.

I am here for you, Djee. Be strong. Seize your life. Don't let it go.

Maatkare continued speaking. "So, your mission was to bring the Ntr stones to the priests. If I am *not* the one you like, name him. We are all in the same royal brotherhood. I promise you upon my own damnation to the belly of Ammit that I would get them to whichever priest… in time."

Marai knew the prince was delaying and ignoring his interest in the other tent, but understood the exchange was making the young general uncomfortable when he noticed the mouth twitch under the dismissive smile and his hand straying to Deka's hand again.

"I will, of course, be within my rights to *carefully* examine them," Maatkare paused, trying to study Marai's discomfort a little longer. "Something else makes you sweat in misery, though." his fingers drummed on the armrest of his folding chair. "I believe it's the suffering of the one the women called Djee? You sense it, as do I, but I'm afraid he's finished. Even if you had gone straight to their tent before you met with me, you would have accomplished nothing. I had no choice, you see. When a man or group of men come hot into my camp there can be only one answer, and that's death. Even if that man is a kinsman the answer is always the same. Death. It's young Naibe's fault that he still lives and suffers so much. I would have ended him but for her pulling him away before the killing blow."

Marai sighed, nerveless. *Everything is true*, he thought. *Naibe should have let the prince release Djerah.* He ached for her. *She thought the Children of Stone might save him, but there's too much injury. He'll never be right unless we can get him all the way into the wilderness and inside the Children's vessel and he will certainly die we can make that journey.* He looked into the princes' eyes once more and pushed the image of Naibe and Ariennu through his thoughts.

Maatkare smirked again, haughty but clearly tiring of the conversation.

"As for you taking the women back. That's complicated," he glanced briefly at Deka; self-assurance on his face. "As your concubines, you being deemed a criminal, they were caught in the same unfortunate fate."

"Wrong," Marai grumbled about to leap on the prince over the insult. "They were successful at the market; they made things and sold them. They *had* a means of surviving me. They were denied their work."

Maatkare pursed his full lower lip and steadied his gaze into Marai's open, but irritated expression again.

"Hmm. I heard them mention that; spice sales and candied fruit? Red Sister selling unlicensed women's medicine and yet no record of them as guest workers ever existed or came to our eyes until the Inspector was sent on mission. My grandfather mentioned to me that their employer had recently left town rather than face additional tribute charges for using unregulated workers."

"We paid tribute and even made gifts. What concern of His Majesty's was that?" Marai bent further forward in an attempt to keep his hands in his lap.

"Manners, Sojourner Marai. Hear the *rest* of my story."

Marai shut his eyes and shook his head slightly. *I'm listening and counting the moments 'til I can open hand you, you pompous fool.*

"Are you now? Death wish, then?" the prince spoke his own thoughts in response and seamlessly went on with his explanation.

"My grandfather had your 'widows' gathered to face justice as potential spies for some interest, but when he saw they were both good to behold and apparently skilled in the gentler arts, he offered them to our wondrous Menkaure as possible servants. Soon enough, though, some amount of treachery was discovered. I had already chosen this lovely one, so she asked that I take them with her rather than banish them into the wilderness." The prince took up Deka's hand again and kissed it, then pulled her close for a kiss on the mouth. "Forgive my rudeness… but she *is* lovely isn't she? Hard to resist when one knows how to handle a woman properly." The prince looked at Marai with one eye while he kissed.

The sojourner knew that look was an implied insult about his lack of bed skills, but he quickly dismissed it.

"As for my being a criminal, my Lord Highness…" Marai spoke with all of the sarcastic gentleness he could still muster. "My crime was merely that of bringing the Children of Stone to Kemet and in return seeking the unlocking of the knowledge they placed in me."

"And *that* fell apart. You are now no better than an outcast. Your man greets death and now you have come to take the women *back* from me?" Maatkare smirked, apparently enjoying the spiritual dagger he was turning.

"I have. And when I have them, I'll be no more trouble to anyone else in your hierarchy. I have learned over *many years* not to linger where I am unwanted," Marai sat forward again, head bowed and elbows on his thighs. *This isn't going to work*, he felt his face darken in rage, but knew he had begun to project the image of the black face, the pale hide and the white-silver hair with extending horns – an image of the bull. *There, you decorated beast, see just a little of me start to come forth.*

Through his own reddened stare, he saw Maatkare tense as if something bothered his arms and migrated to form as a lowing sound in his ears. He released Deka for a moment and tucked his middle fingers into his palm to form a defensive gesture against the negative energy he felt.

Sorcery. Damned sacrilege *is what it is.* The prince's eyes glimmered a little as Marai felt him scramble for the spiritual upper hand over someone who was evidently invoking a major god in the blink of an eye. *Try to come at me as Atum. You dare!*

Marai knew he had found the way in, but the prince's thoughts still opened for him:

Heka. Finally, it comes. Serves me right for poking him. I'm getting tired of the day anyway, but he tempts me. Maatkare cleared his throat and spat slightly, indicating he had deflected the psychic assault.

"Bakha Montu, not Atum, or so your grandfather told me," Marai corrected, noticing the greenish glimmer in his younger foe's eyes and that the points of side teeth now indented his lower pout. *Wolf-dog,* he thought. *Wrong match for a bull, but a nasty fight if he keeps low to the leg.*

"Still... I have cared for these women, under the knowledge that they were gifts to me, and to eventually become esteemed servants and concubines if they weathered this journey. I could give you two of them back, maybe… if you pay me for their care." The prince turned his left hand from the self-protective gesture and opened it with a magical flourish, revealing the pale, crescent-shaped stone, then sent one of Deka's grooms into his tent. While he waited, he held the stone up to the sun that filtered through the afternoon haze. A ray of light formed and cascaded down to Marai in the chair at the bottom of the dais.

The sojourner's heart sank. The little 'Yah' stone verified everything he had sensed earlier about the battle, the capture, torture, and death when he felt its gentle glimmer. He saw how Deka's face, emotionless at first, had grown haunted as she watched; how it seemed to find its own beautiful but dreadful peace. He saw the way she resisted the taste of the blood, but eventually began to welcome the ritual. Marai bowed his shining head when he felt Naibe's distress that caused her to drag

Djerah from death. He was unashamed of the tears of rage and frustration that ran down his cheeks.

"You're angry." Maatkare guessed Marai had seen everything in the stone. "You've seen through this little stone like an eye of memory, haven't you?" he sat up in his seat a little, checking Marai's demeanor. "You want to kill me, but I think the Ntr in these pieces don't want you to. I see this war going on behind your eyes and now you weep like broken-hearted child."

Marai wanted the prince dead. He didn't want any spectacular bloodshed. Allowing him the dignity of a fight, even an unfair one, like the one the Children of Stone had given the thieves in the wilderness was too good for this prince. The sojourner wanted to look up in moments, see Deka by herself, know Maatkare was suddenly without substance and that demons had dragged away his screaming soul.

Maatkare turned the stone over in his hand, studying it once more. Fascinated, he almost lost himself in the trance-like feeling its soothing glow projected over him. He held it up to the light, seeing if the sun could amplify its power.

"I know this thing has its own strange heka and is a companion to the others I have already as well as seven more," he looked straight at Marai with eyes so calm they seemed almost asleep. "If I were to send the two women back to you, provided they still *want* to go back to a life of no promise and likely as exiles, would you be willing to instruct me in their use?"

Marai's heart leapt out of the pit into which it had fallen a moment before. *He's bright, but still woefully stupid if he thinks heka is all I am capable of.* The opportunity for revenge suddenly stared him in the face and the prince had just dared ask for the tools to inflict it on himself.

The groom returned from the royal tent. He carried a beautiful ebony box inlaid with ivory, red, gold leaf and turquoise paste work. Sighs from the Children of Stone flooded Marai's heart, even before the prince opened the box.

When he did, Marai knew the small white Yah stone in Maatkare's hand must have twitched sharply because his hand jumped and he dropped it in the box with the others. Sorrow, tenderness, and soothing chased by a thousand thoughts swarmed over each other, like bees in a hive, lamenting the distress of one of their own as its story was transmitted. While Marai welcomed the sensation, his senses told him the prince had hardened his own heart instinctively.

Go to his thoughts. Shame him, Marai suggested.

In an instant the Children took the lead and the prince's psyche was filled with an outpouring of the women's sighs. They roamed his soul, circling like demons, and tried to draw it out.

Exiles. I doubt that, Marai thought to himself. *Obvious he doesn't know what's happened in Ineb Hedj; that his influence may be all but…* he checked his thoughts against the questioning glance the prince gave him.

We are always part of you, Man of Ai
Even parted, we are soul and spirit of you

The children in the box, together with the Yah and even those secretly in the bag at his waist chorused. He knew what they were telling him to do.

I'm sorry, little ones. This is it, then. I have to say goodbye for now, even though I haven't greeted most of you in so very long. No more, Marai told his stone and through it, the rest of the stones. Although every instinct told him to disobey, he quieted his rage, unfastened the pouch at his belt and emptied the seven stones into the palm of his hand.

"There. These are the other ones you and Great One have sought," he felt the ache, as the seven remaining stones sensed the presence of the others in the nearby box. The building harmonic chorus of the stones swept through both men. Marai patted them gently, placed his hands on them and felt the light and warmth travel up his arms. He quietly emptied the stones into the box with the others laying his hands on all of the Children of Stone at once, waiting to see if they objected.

I have to feel your sweet music one more time. He smiled, but felt Deka gasp slightly. He knew she understood what he was doing. Just in case, he glanced into her eyes and sent her the silent message.

Take care of them. Be the link I need between us, the trust I won't forsake. You know you and I are bound as long as we both shall live.

The prince's eyes narrowed; shocked that Marai was prepared to let the remaining stones go so easily. He shot a glance at the woman beside him and waited for a trap to spring.

We are now for each other,

the Children repeated to each other and to Marai.

"I'll let you use them, learn their knowledge, *if* they wish to teach it to you. You can't force them to do it. Not even *I* can do that. Just give me what I need." He removed his hands from the box and returned to his seat even though he didn't want to sit below the prince or look at his evil-sweet expression another instant. The dark energy had returned to gnaw at his thoughts just as strongly as if the prince had sent a silent and provoking utterance.

Man-Sun. Wait. Don't leave me. I…

A quiet and tentative prayer of a voice entered his thoughts. Deka was in anguish.

Shhh. No, I forgive you, woman. Just understand what I am asking of you. He sent back the thought to her semi-privately, hoping the glamour of the Children of Stone would keep Maatkare distracted enough to miss what he had sent her.

"I'll tell you this, though," Marai added. "You may take them now and you may try to use them for a while, but they cannot and will never *belong* to you. You will find their 'power' limited, even once you understand them. They are only *keys* to the mysteries. They will lead you to these hiding places if, and only if, they decide you are worthy. Otherwise, they can and will destroy all that you hold dear. Once these places are found, you must work with them as *they* intend, not as you may like. Make no mistake, Highness. You have already ignored their many warnings."

Maatkare's expression reflected his interest, layered over by astonishment that a sojourner was actually speaking from below him as if he was equal or superior.

"The storm?" the prince dismissed with a snicker. "Oh, I don't think so. Or was it *you* running up here to challenge me, balls blazing, and then not finding you had enough to do so?" He snapped the box containing the Children of Stone shut and waited for an answer.

After a moment of choosing his next words carefully, the sojourner answered

"If it had been my *own* will, you would have died in agony before you ever saw my face and your esteemed grandfather have suffered a worse fate the hour I learned what had happened. Deka knows this, but may deny it in her heart. So does Ari and Naibe. That either of you are still breathing is only on the whim of these Ntr." Marai frowned, then closed his eyes. He felt Djerah's intense pain cease and subside into numb shock as the young man slipped from life at an increasing speed.

Then…

Houra, Marai sensed his sister's spirit nearby. *As a little girl.* Her smiling half-shy scamper flitted behind him to the tent and back. She poked at him, showing off the toy he'd made for her over seventy years ago. The ghost of the little girl shrugged, then slipped back to the tent.

He knew why. *She's come to guide her great-grandson and here I am dealing with a devil I'd be better shed of.*

"On your return to Ineb Hedj, Prince Wserkaf will take them from you," Marai announced. He looked helplessly in the direction of the tent. Little Houra flirted and waved at him.

"Oh," Maatkare mused, then suddenly snickered as if he knew how badly the sojourner wanted to get up and that he wasn't going to permit it. "I see how this works," his pointed teeth flashed. "It's numbers. Threes. You chose three women. One of them, thinking you dead, chose me. Another picked my ever fickle elder cousin. I have absolutely *no doubt* they will gain some confidence in me in time. I believe I too am being chosen," he nodded knowingly at Deka.

"So you think you know?" Marai began to get to his feet, despite the prince's objection. "That it's a choice the same way kings are chosen? If you think that, then maybe you also know that the Akaru of Qustul was chosen by the Children of Stone *many* years ago on the very same night I was chosen and that plans were made for one more of Great Djedi's choosing. Your grandfather believed *he* was the one as Djedi had trained him and he cared for him in his death. He still believes it is true and has not stopped in his efforts to get them. Why do you think he even told you of them?"

"Sit back down," Maatkare ordered. "I have *not* given you permission to go. How do I know these stones have more power than their use as focusing tools? I've seen some things and sensed a few others. Show me something new," the prince changed his mind again and warned, "I don't want to see a court entertainer's illusion. I want to see something *impressive*. I want to know for *myself* why grandfather considers you or any of this worth so much of his trouble." The prince quickly peeked into the glimmering box one more time, stood and beckoned his guards.

"Then allow me to go see the others, before I decide to go in spite of you. I have a man to snatch from the jaws of death"

"You think…" Maatkare growled, starting to scramble to his feet.

Marai stared down at the prince without sitting.

"I *know*. I doubt you can stop me without calling all of your men and then it will just be bloodier than you like," he sent the image of his single-handed defeat of the group of N'ahab's thieves in the wilderness on his first day away from the Children of Stone's vessel. "I could have decided to see my ladies and young Djerah before I saw you, but I gave in to the wish of the Children's wish to at least announce myself." He turned toward the tent, but heard a scuffle and the "thap" sound of an arrow striking the folds in his cloak. It clattered to the brick surface of the dais.

"Damn You!" Prince Maatkare cursed under his breath. "That should have hit you true."

"Don't bother wasting another, then," Marai snapped his head around to see the prince examining his swiftly handled bow and Deka whispering frantically for him to let Marai see the others.

"You want to see something impressive?" He moved toward the opposing tent, starting to gesture the final release of time for the three people inside. "You give me a few moments alone with them, then *you* bring the Children… *and* Deka. You'll see, hear, and learn more than you might *ever* deserve to know. Until then, don't bother me and *above* all don't try to kill me again."

Turning away from the prince, he moved quickly toward the women's tent empty-handed. He didn't look at the prince or Deka but felt her inner trembling and that the prince grumbled for her to behave herself.

I let you think you took this one, sojourner Marai; and I can see what my grandfather saw and dreaded in you. But we're not done. This is just day one, and I have a lot of life left where I can walk nicely beside you and look for the soft spots… a lot of life.

At that point the image of the skulking hound, obedient to a superior, but watchful master formed in Marai's thoughts. It was a threat and a promise.

"We'll see. Highness, we'll see…" his hand reached forward to the flap of the women's tent and parted it.

OPENER OF THE SKY

Chapter 21: The Children's Embrace

"Oh Marai, oh my sweet…" Ariennu leapt into Marai's arms from her frozen place at the tent flap the moment his hand pulled the cloth open. She clung to him, sag-kneed and weeping, arms clawing at him as if she was drowning. "Oh please goddess, don't let this be another dream."

"I'm here, Ari, I'm here. I'm *real*. It's really me," his embrace lifted her from the ground for a moment. As he set her down and stared warmly into her heart, he knew so much about her had changed.

Ari? Has she shrunk? She looks so hard and sad now. It's like we never shared love, or had any of those sweet times in Little Kina Ahna before I left. She's no longer soft when I hold her… goes stiff like she wants my touch but… doesn't. Marai kissed her eyes lightly, tangled his hands in her wildly scrambled hair and wished that one touch between them would be enough to sweep away everything that had happened to her in the past four months. Her eyes had grown old and wizened again. The brand of a beaten and temporarily subdued life showed in her Child-Stone-rejuvenated face, but that look showed him she had remained defiant, almost to the last.

Marai wanted to press her to him forever; to return her fire and to once again make her into the joyous, smart-mouthed concubine she had been, but at this moment they both knew there were more urgent needs. He felt her pull away to show him the back of the tent. Naibe-Ellit sat there. She cradled the young man's bleeding, bound head higher than his chest and crooned a gentle lullaby in her multi-layered command voice.

Her too… broken. Little goddess knows *I'm here, but she doesn't even look up at me. Why?* he crept toward her and in another instant, knelt beside her. All he had wanted to do was touch her eyes and lips so gently, but the sight of Djerah in her arms sucked the joy out of his return.

The young man's once swarthy and pleasing face didn't even look human. His shattered jaw and eye sockets appeared held together by a few shreds of unbroken skin that eased into a swollen purple and black mass that oozed blood and fluid. From the condition of his face, Marai knew Djerah was blind. A hole by his flattened nose and a gash above the lip bubbled shallowly as the stonecutter's struggle to rasp air in and out of his failing lungs grew weaker.

Marai tore his eyes away. When he touched Naibe's arm, he instantly re-lived the long, agonizing moments of the prince slamming at Djerah again and again with the mace-like glove for no *sane* reason. Maatkare had simply wanted to spend his rage and frustration on something. Torturing and killing the youths had not been enough to satisfy his hunger for brutality. The sojourner wanted to magically trade Djerah's suffering to the prince and to rob him of his good health for his crime, but he knew it wasn't possible.

"Why did he come?" Naibe half-sobbed, her eyes still ensorcelled by the Djerah's pain. She focused so deeply on the easing of his suffering that she didn't acknowledge Marai's presence. He edged behind her to firmly rub her tired shoulders, then stared down at the tragic, beaten form of the young man again.

"I stopped Prince Maatkare, but now I don't know if it was the right thing to do. Djee suffers so much. His Highness hurts people. He hurts them *bad* because he likes to take their life force from them; but in the end, when he is satisfied and full, he releases them so there is no more pain. It's just his way," Naibe whispered dully, still not acknowledging Marai's presence. "I couldn't let him do it. I couldn't…" One tear started down her round cheek. Her chest lifted and fell in panting misery.

Marai kissed the back of Naibe's neck through the dark thickness of her hair and read the memory of the way she grabbed the prince and flung him more than the length of a man, then dragged Djerah away to safety. She had suddenly and without warning accessed all of her the warlike aspect.

"He just kept beating him and beating him and beating, but Djee hung on." Ariennu scooted over to be with Naibe and Marai. She tentatively put her arm around his back acting as if she thought he might vanish, then lay her head on Naibe's shoulder. "And that bloodthirsty kuna Deka was smiling the whole time. She's *not* the same woman any of us knew. It's madness. She thinks he'll make her into a god's wife."

"Shhh… Shhh… Ari, I know. It's been so hard with me gone and you having to be the strong and brave one." He knew she had buried everything inside her heart the same way she had done in the bad days before they were ever together.

"I'm here now. You can let it go. You can rest," Marai whispered by her ear. "I came to his tent first, just to make it safer for the rest of us."

"She *was* something like that before she was with us in the wilderness and she kept saying she would be reborn only when her feet were on the ground in Ta-Seti. She wants her throne back and thinks Highness will get it for her. Goddess, Marai. It's *both* of them. He made her drink the blood of the prisoners and she didn't even fight it. She *wanted* it. She wanted *more* of it each time," Ari babbled out the story that Marai had already sensed.

"Ari. Let those thoughts go. I need you *here* right now. *Djerah* needs you," he breathed out gently and touched the places on Djerah's face and head, to sense the scope of his wounds. The young man had begun a series of weak panting breaths. The cycle of death was entering its final loop. Marai knew he couldn't delay and stroked the stonecutter's blood-spattered chest to send warmth to it until the panting eased a little.

"Djerah, Djerah I'm here now," he whispered.

The young man moaned and appeared to struggle away as if he fought the healing touch and *wished* to die.

"I wish I had left him in Ineb Hedj. I wish to the *goddess*..." Marai bowed his head and looked away, biting his lips. He'd never seen wounds so severe on someone who was still alive. He didn't want him to suffer, and he wanted him to recover, but couldn't think of anything more to do for him at that moment than warm and calm him with his hands. He touched the young man's face.

"Marai is here," Naibe consoled him even though she hadn't looked directly at the sojourner the entire time he had been in the tent.

"I'm here, Djerah. I will heal you if it *can* be done," Marai's voice trembled because he didn't think anyone *could* heal the young man. "If the goddess says no, then I'll ease the hurts so you go to her in peace."

Marai rose to help Ariennu tie up the right side of the tent so more air and light could be admitted. It was near the end of the day. He noticed Maatkare and Deka had secluded themselves in his tent again, but sensed they were talking about and already examining the Children of Stone like children who had been presented with new toys. At any moment, the sojourner guessed, curiosity would overcome his royal foe. He would emerge to interrupt whatever healing they had started. For now, he tied the strap on the tent wall firmly and spoke over to the men working outside. A physician and assistant still tended a few of Maatkare's men, patching them up from injuries received in the morning battle.

Don't see me, he sent a thought toward all of the men in the open area.

"The prince has the Child Stones, Ari." he turned; a grim tone in his voice. "I can't use any but the ones the three of us have in our heads. Djerah's beyond medicine though. The prince was very likely right."

"By great El, I've come to hate him, the foul snake." Ariennu hissed as she tied the rope that held up the flaps and dully stared at the two new grooms seated outside his tent entry. "And those new guards…"

"Ariennu," Marai took a step toward her when he had tied his part. He clutched her tenderly, but firmly to his chest for a moment. "Don't. Whatever you're feeling can't get in the way, now. You know it's not even true, either. Go be mad at him later. Goddess knows *I* certainly want to hurt him, but we have to clear our thoughts of all the dark feelings if we're to help Djerah *at all*. The Children didn't understand our rage at each other and even our lust and the way it can twist even good intentions at first, but they do now. It's why I couldn't just drop him and his grandfather the hour I came to my senses back in Ineb Hedj," he felt the woman nod into his chest, but knew her thoughts still drifted.

"You said he had the stones. I know he has the one Djerah brought and the box with the others and the Wdjat. I suppose Prince Wserkaf gave you the others, too?"

"No. Your prince has *all* of them now. I gave all of them to him. I was thinking of how to get them all back and stay on the task they gave me years ago, but then the Children told me it really *didn't* matter in the short passage of days who had them. They've learned how to link and manipulate events in our world through being inside us," he stared dully and almost deflated at the gilt-trimmed white, red, and yellow tent, then turned back toward Naibe and Djerah.

"What? Him?" Ari stopped him for a moment. "He *can't* have the Children. It's too dangerous with the heka he knows… and with Deka protecting him. She's teaching him, too, but I know she can't be in *love* with him. It's not her nature. Must be heart-blind. And he can't *love* anything but himself. Bed sport is all it is. The man has some crazy skills; and he's not bad on the eye, but when you get with him, you see he really *doesn't* have a soul. He's full of ghosts and devils, just like Baby told me. He will suck yours out of you through the clench and make a meal on part of it then add it to his collection. I thought I was tough enough to take it" Ari gasped, winded at her own recitation. "I used him plenty. I just never thought I'd…" she stumbled, emotional. "Maybe I should have just been looking for a way to kill him," she shuddered, rubbing her arms as if every erotic memory had suddenly become dirty and disgusting.

"Shh, Ari. Just stop beating yourself," Marai dismissed her. "You do what you do. You've always liked men and you've damned any of them who tried to tie you down, even me at first. You needed to forget when you thought I was gone. But Djerah needs us now. We'll sort the rest of this out later."

Ariennu nodded as if she quietly understood, then tilted her head back and pecked at Marai's nose once as if she was thanking him for his mercy.

"Love you, woman," he whispered, but knew she had been flooded with the memory of Maatkare's treatment of her. "Know that. Now, let's go see about this." He pressed her once then led her to Naibe-Ellit and Djerah at the back of the tent.

Naibe sat quietly, steeped in a trancelike attitude that told him nothing else mattered but the failing life of the young man in her arms. Any other time, Marai knew she would have leapt to greet him, cried, kissed every inch of him, then begged to be held and touched in return. He would have gone weak at the feel of her nuzzling deep into his strong arms. Her goddess nature wasn't just about the sensuous side of her being. He knew she had given her all to stop Maatkare from delivering the 'mercy' blow. Now she was entirely focused on giving the young stonecutter life, even if he had to take it from her. It haunted him. *One day, dear gods, one day, I hope not soon, or I will need to break time forever.*

She whispered sweet promises to the young man that soon he would feel so much better. Her gentle hand which she had wrapped in a piece of cloth dabbed some of the fluids that oozed from his wounds.

Marai looked into her eyes once when she glanced up, but only briefly. She was hiding something from him. The happy and passionate, but strong young girl was gone. In her place a woman of unearthly beauty and grace smiled winsomely and knowingly up at him, then turned her gaze back to Djerah. She stroked his chest rhythmically, as if that would regulate his failing breath and heart.

The sojourner wanted to go to her… to pamper her and love her, but knew it would have to wait. He reached out to help Ariennu kneel by Naibe, then slipped behind both of them so the young woman could lean on him to rest a little. He buried his face in her hair, trying to see if there was anything left of her warmth or if the prince had drained all of it away as he had with Ari. The scent of her neck invaded him and lifted him out of his momentary feeling of helplessness.

I see you my sweetest Marai. I know you are really here, really alive. Yet my heart is so heavy, my eyes can't look at you.

Naibe. Sweet goddess, why do you suffer? his thoughts asked her.

The hushed whisper of one of the passionate Ashera poems she used to recite to him as they made love, filled his thoughts. He heard them echo through his memories of all of her passion in her multi-layered magical voice:

> *I am lifted beyond the sky to heaven…*
> *I open for you,*
> *To take in all of you.*
> *You rule me completely until I have died a small*
> *Death of joy.*
> *I am not me and you are not you,*
> *No self or time exists in this new place,*
> *We have built with our love.*
> *All is no more but divine bull of the sky and cow of the Earth…*
> *I am lifted beyond the sky to heaven… oh yes…*
> *I feel the sweet pulse of your seed bursting hot in me…*
> *And I am transported…*

My belly fills with stars…
Stars bursting out of my mouth and lifting me higher.
I die, I drift, I float, I know…

He felt her words stir in the bottom of his heart and stick in his breathless chest. An agony of desire and at the same time a keen misery that he had been gone too long welled up in him. His hands froze and his heart exploded with the rush of so many dreams and wishes covered by so many heartaches of how he had not been with her to learn at the same moment she had learned.

"What?!!" he choked, barely able to speak. "Naibe?"

Naibe-Ellit looked up and back. Her solemn eyes brightened a little and a smile tentatively started to curl her lips.

For Marai, nothing else mattered, not even Djerah dying in front of him. He knew she hadn't looked at him at first because he would have sensed it instantly. His mouth found hers and devoured it as his hand slipped down to caress her rounded belly. She yielded for a glorious moment but then drew away.

Ariennu sensed their thoughts and grew miserable.

"So you figured that out, eh?" she started. "It's not yours, Marai. There's no way it can be. I told her how to get rid of it when we found out, but she wanted it to be yours so bad she kept it. She got her moon weeks after you left, just a day or two of it, though. We made the offerings to goddess for her to speedily get a child when you came home. Then, when we got pulled apart, I told her to take the seeds. She told me she didn't have it in her heart to do that anymore; that maybe a child from another could help her forget. Outside *this* nasty bastard here, there was…" she started to indicate Maatkare, but saw Marai wasn't paying attention.

Marai grinned all over himself, leaning around her right arm.

"Oh Naibe-Ellit, my goddess. Naibe, Naibe…" Marai's open mouth traced her face, eyes and lips. He didn't want to hear about whose child it *might* be. He *knew* the child was his and in that instant knew exactly when it had happened.

"When this is over I'm going to sail us down the river to Per-A-At and kiss that man myself," he wanted to run and scream for joy. Of *course* it was his child.

"Wserkaf's prank when he first met us. He used his wdjat and the sun to redirect our charm energy and scramble our thoughts." He waited for her to nod, but she had returned her glance to Djerah. "You almost died that day, my sweet one. During the blurring of our thoughts from his spell, I knew we had been together."

"Well, I wanted to die that afternoon because of what I saw, Marai. Even though being with you was my every desire," Naibe whispered. "The darkness came for us like an evil shadow and I saw you lying dead, and there was Deka's grinning face in the middle of all of it. The horrible storm darkness that sits on her shoulders called *my* name," her head bowed. "See how it is *now*? It *was* prophecy. Maybe it was *this* poor one I saw lying dead," she indicated Djerah, whose breath still rasped unsteadily. "Oh, see him take his last breaths?" she indicated how shallow the rise and fall of the man's chest had grown.

Everyone silently agreed the young man was running out of time.

"Please Djerah, stay with us," she lightly touched his bloated forehead, then looked back at Marai who reached for some more clean cloth.

A son, Marai reveled in the thought, *though a little goddess would be no less a joy*. He moved to her other side; his hands trembled as he sweetly cupped her chin.

"When we do this healing, I don't think you should give any more of your energy into it. It's too dangerous for the child, if you should draw some of the pain and hurt from him," he positioned himself on one side of Djerah. Naibe-Ellit's eyes flashed a different gold fire.

"No beloved. You'll need me. I'll just have to be careful," she contradicted him then adjusted the way she sat with Djerah's head in her lap. Ariennu settled at his other side and tried to relax.

"We'll have to put ourselves into trances. If you don't think you can because of everything else, follow me," he said. "We have to get started with whatever we can do for him."

Chapter 22: Interim

A helpless expression filtered over Deka's face. She slithered next to Maatkare, then lay her head on his arm as Marai left the dais area. He saw her eyes fill with purest hunger as her slim fingers played across his thick shoulder, down and over his chest. The prince knew she was trying to take his attention away from the sojourner and his gesture that released those inside from the spell of stalled time as he strode toward the women's tent. Maatkare knew the man's show of power had surprised even her. He patted her hand and stopped her seduction attempt.

"Let him go for now. Give him his moments with your sisters and the wretch who has stolen a few more moments of his own life. When he dies and nothing they do can save him..." He set down his bow, still puzzled that his skilled 'short-snap' shot had bounced off the man's cloak. He knew he had aimed well enough and his pull had been even. He grumbled a little, picked up the box, and opened it once more to look at the glimmer of the stones.

"Very well, Akkad, do what you will. I will learn the things my grandfather hasn't the energy to undertake. I can feel that he knows he has lost my cousin over this nonsense." He muttered under his breath, closed the box, and stepped down from the dais, leading Deka by the fingertips of one hand. "We'll just see about these now, while you're busy with the others." He spoke to the sojourner's departing back even though he knew the man didn't care about his words.

"Sit on the rug over there, Nefira," Maatkare's voice charmed again once he and Deka had re-entered the tent. He indicated a place on the soft carpet in front of his camp bed, but noticed her tearing at her hands in anxiety.

"You *were* different from your sisters in kind. I *meant* what I said." He sat, then reached forward to gently touch her hand. "Calm yourself. I have need of your strength." He placed the box containing the Children of Stone between them.

"You worry about this man Marai being alive, don't you; what it means; how I will be to you now. You ask yourself if I will reject you," Maatkare continued. "As I said to you on the first night we enjoyed each other, whether I do or do not depends on you. I see your strength and your openness to me and I respect it. You told me once this sojourner did not see into your heart and failed to meet your needs."

"I… I don't know what to say," Deka bowed her head. "My heart ached for him once. Now that he has returned the pain is still there, but my need is for *you*, my beloved."

Maatkare sat still, as if her words meant little, then opened the box. When he removed the wdjat which she had placed on top of the stones, he extended his upward turned palms to receive her hands.

"Good. Then say nothing more of him."

She placed her hands on his and sucked in air as his thumbs gently traced the tops of her hands.

"Here. You touch the Ntr stones for me. I've held one or two at a time, but I need you to show them I mean no harm to them." He turned her hands over and placed them down on the glimmering mass.

Deka felt the sensations of the crystalline bodies soar around and over her hands in greeting, but suddenly tensed when the ghost-words of her memory swarmed from them.

Ha-go-re! Akh-go-re Nejter Deka Nefer Sekht
My name is sung ever-present
Though I am here.
I fly to you, I come
On dark but burning wings I walk on air
Open the sky to me
Ha-go-re Ta-te

Deka heard her own voice singing in her stone. She closed her eyes lightly, distantly aware that the prince had moved his own hands so they would be on top of hers. He wanted to read the sensations through them. The song repeated. At first she mouthed it, then whispered it then began to sing it.

"Nefira…" she heard him call, but it sounded far in the distance. "What is this?" the faraway voice asked again. "Speak."

"I…" she started but couldn't finish "Ha-go-re! Akh-go-re Nejter Deka Nefer Sekht…" she sang aloud, sinking deeper into a trance. Something shook her hands and lifted them. She heard his determined grunt and an irritated hiss.

Burning him… she thought, then asked the Children of Stone inwardly: *Will you speak to my beloved Raem* she sang the second phrase of the song aloud. "My name is sung ever present…" She felt the voices whirl the answer through to her thoughts.

The wolf hears
But disregards
He touches, but does not feel
He is wise but does not know
He is not open.
He will not move.

I must help him, then. I must open him to the spirit of greatness he deserves. Is there anything else I must do? Would you come into him, Ta-te? she asked silently, hoping the sensations in the prince's hands had distracted him from reading her thoughts.

When she lapsed into her trance, Maatkare heard her begin to sing but realized she couldn't hear him or accept his judgements in such a state. He knew he had to rouse her before she went too deep and slipped too far away from his control.

"Nefira, what is this? Speak!" he shuffled her hands, lifted them and then placed his own hands in the box beneath them. A crackle of energy raced up his arms before he could think through the utterance *Eeen Nau, Eeen Tjoad...*

Wicked laughter sounded in his ears; then... a memory of something dreadful. *The afternoon Meryt killed herself. How can these stones know this?* He opened his eyes and stared at his hands resting under hers in the glimmering box. A rainbow pattern swarmed their surface. The energy of the Ntr stones tingled on his hands like small bits of lightning.

"Nefira Deka, wake. I need you in *this* world, teaching me how these things work," he ordered. The sojourner had told him he would get the demonstration he needed if he brought the box of stones and the Wdjat to the women's tent after he gave him a few moments to greet the other women and see the wounds on the traitorous man.

"I..." she started, then lapsed into the song again.

He'd heard her sing it before.

Ah. That Ta-Te character who governed you long ago then rose on a column of light. I told you he had died because it's been so long. He never returned for you. Your child by him died as you birthed it and you were so ill you knew not if it was a boy or girl. Happens, he thought to himself. *Now they bring my own memory forward. I can't allow this. This is enough for now.* He raised both of their hands from the stones and snapped the lid shut.

She also told me she believed I could be the new Ta-Te; that she had thought this man who brought her out of the wilderness, saw to her healing from her old injuries thus far was the god in new skin, but she fell out of that belief because he feared her. I didn't. The prince knew women and how one controlled them with a mixture of discipline and sex. If there was disquiet over any of these three, he had simply whispered the control utterance or used the "nau" loop and ring his grandfather had given him.

"Why did you close the box, beloved? Did you not feel them speaking to you?" Deka asked.

"I heard them and I felt them too, but I suspect a trick set up by your former friends. Perhaps I will see how he uses them himself. Ready yourself," he tried to read her expression, because for a moment he felt her blocking a thought from him.

Something's not right that this sojourner would let me have these stones so handily. There's a trick in this. She knows something is in the works and now she, too, is afraid to speak of it. This with her is not going to work until she makes a full break from them. He raised his arms and stretched a little, as if the brief touch of the stones had pulled his energy and resolve from him.

"They still think they can heal the man after I told them it's impossible even for a god to bring him back. I have seen the ghosts assembling. If he thinks…"

Her hand reached forward to still him and her eyes shone as if she had become a worshipping little girl in the throes of first love. She hadn't listened to a single word he said.

"My Ta-te. You are my only reminder of Ta-te alive, Raem. We should just go to them, then. If there's a ruse, I will know it."

The prince's lips pursed. He set the box aside and beckoned for her to sit on his lap… to embrace him.

And there it is. She adores me. She would give me all, he struggled to keep his pleasure at that thought quiet.

"A few moments more," Prince Maatkare smiled almost paternally. He had a daughter in Ineb Hedj, aged five years, but Sadeh had not let him do more than hold her briefly. She wasn't a warm and friendly child and neither were her vain little brothers. They were all spoiled by her indulging them. Maatkare shuddered and wondered why Deka on his lap felt better than his own children when they sat there.

And why do these stones stir my memory of Meryt when I've kept those thoughts away so well? Heka? Deka nestled in his arms and stroked his chest for a few moments.

"By the way," he asked one last question, "did they tell you anything else when you first placed your hands on them? Your head went back and your stone came forth again… right before you sang," Maatkare stroked her hair as if she was a favorite pet.

She didn't answer, but that was the only answer he needed. He knew he would have to watch her very carefully.

Chapter 23: The Fledgling

"We have to get started with whatever we can do for him."

Maatkare heard Marai's voice catch a little as his own guards lifted the side of the tent wall for him and Deka. He saw the sojourner moving to one side of the young man so that Naibe faced him. Ariennu held the injured man's head and chest up slightly, but froze when he came forward.

"Sit where it pleases you Your Highness," Marai greeted him, but did not look up. "Leave us room to work this."

The prince stepped forward, spied a sheepskin mat near the group surrounding the dying man and indicated he and Deka would sit there.

"Rutiy, Sutiy… you go," he quietly gestured to the new guards, "but stay close." Then he smoothed the fleece out for her and he sat beside her. The guards left for the outside of the tent wall but guarded it obediently.

Marai bowed his head as the prince and Deka watched, then began.

"Djerah bin Esai… I call you by your name and the blood of my sister Houra bint Ahu. Stay a while," his hand moved up over the young man's swollen and discolored forehead.

"Rest, young Djerah, we will heal you," he spoke aloud.

Maatkare shook his head. "Pointless. See his chest rise high? Struggle? Death comes, I tell you."

"We will heal you. The Children and I will heal you." Marai glared and repeated the phrase, apparently ignoring him.

"The Children and I will heal you…" Maatkare mocked as Ariennu and Naibe extended their hands near Marai's hand. "What foolishness is this?" He wanted to make them stop, but then stared intently at the way the women gently touched and soothed Djerah as if they were his lovers.

His chest fell and then tentatively rose again.

Maatkare thought about that for a moment. *Hmm. His breathing is easier now. They do have good touch techniques.*

"He suffers, Marai," Naibe spoke just above a whisper. "He still feels all of the pain. It hasn't gone into the night for him. When I touch him, I can feel it burning in him. He cries out but no sound comes."

The prince wasn't as fluent in Kina as he wanted to be, but sensed the young woman had said something about his pain.

See? See what you did, heifer? His thoughts grumbled.

The young woman paused, gave him a withering glance and looked to the big sojourner for advice.

Marai nodded and moved his fingertips to the young man's oozing temple, then nodded to cue the two women.

"Djerah, go into a deep sleep. Ari and Naibe will talk you through it."

"Deep sleep. Beyond the pain. Deep sleep... sleep deep..." the two women quietly chanted again and again.

Maatkare frowned, because that was the way of speaking taught to the healers. The difference was that these women invoked no god or goddess as they attempted it.

"Fools," the prince made a petulant grumble. "You cause him to sleep, and he *will* die. I read his thoughts. It's what he wants. He will just keep trying to go through the portal until he succeeds. You can't stay watchful forever."

Naibe's head bowed a little, a sorrowful expression on her face. She looked up at the prince, flashing direct black and golden wells at him.

Beautiful, Maatkare thought, but as he stared he felt a kind of terror. Her face didn't change, but her beauty and the sensuality suddenly frightened him. *She's drawing strength from this sojourner. She wasn't so strong when she believed he was dead.* He watched her glance at Deka and sensed her silent message to both of them.

If there is any good left in you, please help us.

Maatkare instinctively looked into Deka's feverish but sightless eyes when he felt her grip tighten on his arm. He knew she wanted to help with the healing but felt it would upset him. That she was afraid of displeasing him excited him, but he motioned for her to proceed. He decided to employ her worry for a moment.

"What is this?" Maatkare grabbed Deka's arm, yanked her close, and then whispered under his breath. "A moment ago you swore you were mine, but now you suffer to go to this man? You *know* my answer. You have always known it," the prince took her hand on his arm and flung it down. His face turned away. *Lying ka't. This is how it always starts.*

"Beloved… It's not that. *They* call to me. *They* ask me to come. I can't tell you how it feels, unless…"

"What? Unless I am one of your former little group? I can see this will be a worry for me then," he snapped.

Her hands quickly grasped the box of stones he had set in front of them and opened it.

"How many of them do you think you need?" her voice, hoarse with emotion, barely made a sound.

The prince read all of the pathos in the sojourner's eyes as the big man's thoughts joined in the chorus of voices that called from the box of stones. Maatkare couldn't heard the words well, but sensed Marai calling her.

Deka…

No. No more. I can't. Her inner voice faded inward, then whispered to him, p*lease beloved. Don't reject me. Just watch me help.* She waved her graceful hands over the gently purring stones. As if she had always known how to conjure them, Deka lowered her hand to touch them and slipped into a trance.

Maatkare felt her slip backward in an ecstasy, but just in time he moved behind her, then held her against his chest. Lights ran out of the box and up her arms, creating a triangular arc of prismatic light between the stones, her arm and the blood-red stone in her forehead.

Een… Maatkare instinctively thought, attempting to control and guide her trance. He felt the first unspoken word of his utterance bounce off of an unmistakable barrier, followed by agony in his own ears. Marai and Naibe's glance froze his thoughts, turning them into the pain his utterance usually gave them.

"Agh! You dare. You…" he released her and grabbed his ears. When the misery subsided he saw Deka entranced and half-floating as if he still held her.

She slowly raised her hands from the box after she passed them over the stones one more time. Three deep blue stones, shimmering and surrounded by light, followed. Fourteen others trailed up behind them. They rose, becoming weightless, shining little balls of light that zipped joyously about the tent for a moment like fireflies and then descended into Marai's upraised, cupped hands.

Little ones. It's so good to feel your strength again.

Maatkare heard Marai's welcome much more clearly, as if the onslaught of reversed pain had been a kind of initiation. He watched the warmth of their energy as it lit the faces of those around the young renegade.

Heka as I have never seen, he craned forward for a better look. *Nothing like this exists inside any of the sober studies of the different disciplines. So beautiful! It rises and evokes at his wish, yet I can't taste any of it.* He supported Deka's body again, then waited for her to rouse herself.

Marai turned Djerah's head gently to one side and placed three deep blue stones in a semicircle between his ear and eye. Pointing one finger downward at a place in the middle of the stones, he breathed out. A shimmer of heat formed between the big man's fingertips and the dying man's temple. Marai's face crinkled in a slight, almost pained grimace as if he were forcing out the last of his breath. Stopping that gesture, he beckoned and Ariennu followed in tandem. Naibe, sat slightly apart, with her hand resting on Marai's shoulder. She closed her shining golden eyes. Her lips whispered a chant of calmness and strength again and again.

Beyond fear, beyond pain.

In the middle of the shimmer, the prince saw a red and black light flash once and a new wound magically open on the man's swollen, purpled left temple.

He cuts skin without a knife? Maatkare scooted Deka and the box of stones a little closer so he could lean forward.

"Go on, Nefira. Help them. I'm curious now. Just remember what I said…"

Her head nodded, even though she hid a concerned whimper.

Thick, black blood oozed out of the new hole. As it did, the prince watched Ariennu gently dabbed at it with a folded clean cloth. Marai massaged the spot to get all of the old blood out, then pinched the lips of the wound he had made together. He chose one of the three blue stones and traced it over the wound until it sealed. He moved to another badly discolored spot and repeated this procedure. The same followed three more times on that side and two times on the other.

Stunned, the prince tried to mask his wonder. He didn't realize he had continued to inch closer, until Ari glared at him. An evocative glow moved up over Marai's hand and into his face. Maatkare shook his head in disbelief, his attention riveted by the seeming contradiction of a man who looked so powerful yet now appeared as tender as a new mother is to her child.

No. That's ecstasy work. My stupid cousin Wse works this gift, and Grandfather was his tutor. Could he have seen a talent and taught it to him, but for some reason denied me the training? he asked himself.

Slowly, the swelling and discoloration disappeared from Djerah's face. Marai and Ariennu very carefully, raised his limp form into an almost seated position so he faced the box of stones in front of Deka. Gently enough to not disturb him, they removed his stained and ragged loincloth so that he lay naked on the bedding with his legs slightly apart.

Marai and the henna-haired woman touched various places on his body to check his life.

"Goddess, it's too late." her face fell for a moment and she shook her head. She touched his throat for a moment then looked to see if there was any indication of breath in the ruin of his face. Her eyes appealed to the sojourner.

"No. Ari, we can still do this. Bring him back. Believe it," Marai urged. He stopped for a moment to touch her shoulder, but she insisted.

"No. He's dead, Marai. It's over. No heart, no breath. He has the one eye that fixes on nothing and stares. I've seen dead men before. I know."

"I could…" Maatkare almost wanted to check the young man himself, out of perverse curiosity, but stopped himself before he realized he had been ignored. Then, for the first time in ages, he felt a dull ache in his chest. He understood that feeling.

Which of these wretches is sending me remorse? Bastard shouldn't have come at me. I'm a trained warrior; a leader of king's men. It's my blood, damn you all to the nasty jaws of Ammit! You don't try to make me a villain in this, his thoughts growled.

Naibe gasped and looked up for a moment. She knew what he thought. Her finger went to her lips to hush his subconscious ugliness.

Maatkare stared again, completely astonished. He had seen adepts heal the sick and feverish, but he had never seen anyone care for a man's *head* so zealously. In some cases of injury, he had heard of small holes drilled in the bones of the head so that the fatty matter inside would not become corrupted with fluids and constrict the flow of blood to the senses. Wise men knew this stuff in the head had something to do with the regulation of the heart and breath, but was otherwise worthless.

Young Naibe had told him to be quiet.

No, woman. You don't you shush me, you failed sorceress. It's still your fault. He could be enjoying a hero's place in the afterlife for enduring all, even if it was ill-conceived and stupid, but for you, but for what I have made to grow in your belly, I might have killed you. Yes. I know your secret and knew it since the night I saved your worthless life. So you go on and lie to yourself that by act of the gods it is of this man Marai's seed, if it makes you feel better, he chided Naibe in silence. She lowered her open gaze, mortally offended, but the snarl he felt emanated from Deka.

He turned his gaze to Marai and Ariennu again, almost forgetting that Deka still lay in his arms governing the healing in her own way.

In his own irritation, he had bragged about impregnating Naibe to Deka.

So you see, then, he sent the woman in his arms a message. *How I am with you, depends on you. I have no need of a child from you for the next few moons. I have better plans for us. If she births successfully we shall see if it comes out howling.*

"So, Sojourner Marai. You intend to bring the dead back to life? Still?" he asked, but was once again ignored.

Marai cupped the base of the young man's skull in his warming hands, as he searched for signs of life. The prince observed the air near the big man's hands shimmer like distant sand in the bright sun. As he focused on anything he could learn, he saw Marai's hands pass over and shape the man's face, crushed nose, and jaw as if they had been made of wet clay. The fourteen stones that hovered like orbs of colored light, moved to hover above the lotus points on the young man's body without touching his flesh.

Alive? Still? I was certain I felt his spirit coming free. Maatkare wanted to demand an explanation, but knew no one would give one to him even if he ordered it. To him, it looked as if they were going to use the floating stones to attempt a full cleansing and regeneration of the body before them. In his own discipline, the preparation of the dead including placing amulets and scarab shaped stones on the body, as it was wrapped. It aided the spirit and gave it a good and protected passage through the afterlife. If a similar technique of placing stones worked on a man who was dead with the intent to *restore* him, it would be an unknowable miracle. It would be a step toward immortality for anyone who controlled the Ntr stones and learned the technique. It would also be dangerous in the hands of foes. If enemies could be healed and regenerated they might get up and avenge themselves for the inconvenience and the suffering they had endured.

Prince Maatkare Raemkai had been taught the thirteen points of light and color in the body, each corresponding to a god or goddess. Each could be strengthened and energized, to heal a particular ailment or injury governed by that region. It was considered impossible to work more than one or at the most, two points at the same time because each progressed through the other. Healings of this kind needed several sessions. Anything more courageous could kill the patient or drive the more empathic healers mad with the suffering they drew into themselves.

If he does *have enough life in him, these untrained fools will just…* he saw Marai raise a forefinger to one of the orbs, then speak a phrase. Ariennu and Naibe repeated it as a soft chant. A stone drifted downward. Naibe released her grasp and moved away from Djerah.

Hmm. She is protecting the child within then. How does that play if it's mine? She says it isn't. It might be. I should like to see her prove it is not, Maatkare mused briefly then muttered internally before turning his attention back to the miracle of regeneration taking place through the stones.

One stone, a red one for HetHrt, was placed at the young man's sack, an orange one just above the ben for Aset, yellow just above the navel for Sekhet, green at mid-heart for Bastet. Each time they placed a stone they whispered in the

Akkad language first, then his own Kemet tongue. They named the parts of the body each stone governed, as if they instructed the fallen man to pay attention and allow the healing to take place.

The way our own ritual is done for the newly dead. We *instruct.* He sat perplexed, then realized he still had a firm grip on Deka when she whimpered a little.

"Do you regret you are not with them, Nefira?" he whispered in her ear.

"No, Raem," she answered quickly.

Too quickly he thought.

She knew his doubt instantly and shut her eyes as if she was in pain.

As they watched, Marai placed the turquoise stone at the base of the man's throat for Nt.

The prince noticed that the stonecutter's nose was less discolored and had a better shape, but the blue stones rested around the nose and continued to leech out the old blood and discoloration. They darkened, bloated as if they were drinking the old blood, and then expelled the fluids so that they ran down the sides of the young man's face. Ariennu dabbed the gore with any clean spot on the cloth she found.

That's all? I haven't seen his chest rise or fall since Red Sister told this Marai he was dead. Then again, I've seen people deny someone's death out of grieving. Thank the gods I've never been slain with such mourning since the dog… Maatkare's thoughts grew solemn again. The deep purple stone was at his brow, the point of HoRa. The crystal one, NefertM floated above the top of his head.

Suddenly, the prince noticed the little crescent shaped stone Deka had found in the dirt near the ladder where this man had been tied. It floated up, the last in the group of fourteen, then paused a hands width above the stonecutter's head. A spark shot down to his forehead at the point between his eyebrows.

"Wait. I wanted that one. It's a fourteenth, but there are only thirteen regions. Who said…?" Maatkare objected aloud.

Naibe scooted back to include herself in the circle around the man. The sojourner and Ariennu hurriedly welcomed her and joined their arms to hers. A tone, part whisper, part music, and part whistle sounded in the prince's thoughts. At that instant, a wave of energy swept over him, knocking him backward and leaving him light-headed enough to lose his grip on Deka.

Dizzy. How dare they… He felt instantly drained as if the magic this sojourner employed had cut through every defense, attached itself, and had begun to pull his *own* energy from him. As the feeling grew into full-fledged disorientation, Maatkare fought to stay conscious. *Light. Light broken into colors,* he reveled in new visions. A band of prismatic light extended up from the three sojourner's brows and hearts, then extended out toward Deka who remained in front of his arms. When it reached her, it bounced back again. Her own light joined theirs. The tone grew in strength and volume, and a slight glimmer surfaced over the young man's head.

What the… No… not allowing this… Maatkare gasped, starting to position his hand in a defensive gesture. *You can't have her. You can't.*

A rush of a small whirlwind, spun between the three then returned downward into the stones as if they had breathed out. Banded color like a miniature rainbow glimmered upward from the stones poised over the man who still seemed pale and dead. A spark returned upward from his forehead and for a moment the prince thought he saw the man's chest rise. Then, an instant later he saw it fall, then rise again.

He breathes. Gods…

Maatkare stared, open-mouthed, and unable, by this time, to believe anything that had paraded before his eyes.

Deka trembled in an involuntary spasm as her own light burst forth. She fell back against the prince and hung, head thrown slightly back and open-mouthed as if she were a lifeless vessel for the force that had suddenly issued from her.

Force of Atum's dark! I command you to stop this! He incanted deliberately, but without any outward display of fear.

She didn't respond to his words, but inched forward with the box of stones in her hands.

Maatkare gestured the command with his fingertips, then lunged forward to grab her, but a bolt of black lightning tripped from the gently whirling source. It ignited her, encasing her in a flame that didn't burn or appear to hurt her. The fire seemed as ordinary as the skirt she wore. The fire arched to his thickly muscled arm, down his chest, over his belly, and into his loin, sensing and arousing him as if it had become a lover's touch.

Find the pain that makes your spirit hard
I could not, when I was walking

A small, low-voiced woman whispered inside his thoughts.

When you truly understand love,
You will live among the gods

Fire. Saw this before when she lay with me in ecstasy. Maatkare wanted to touch the woman; to hold onto her because he felt dragged away from the scene before him by forces he couldn't comprehend enough to counteract. He couldn't touch her or even sense enough of his feet so he could dig into the earth of the tent floor. Something didn't want him there. It filled his eyes and pulled him further away from his place on the skin. He growled and fought as Deka rose and slowly moved toward Marai, the young man, and the other women.

Faithless wretch… he thought for an instant that she was still trying to break free of him.

No, beloved, Deka's thoughts broke through his confusion, a coy expression in her eyes. *I am with them in this for the moment; to show you all that awaits us with the use of the Ntr children. I will return to your arm when it is complete.*

A spirit double of her body drifted in front of him while her physical form walked with the box in her hands to sit at the young man's feet. The spirit danced between his body and her hers, bathed in the illusion of flame. Her eyes slanted and ears rose slightly. Her teeth pointed.

Lion, he smiled and for a moment he wanted to say something but found himself drawn back into the world of healing.

Marai felt everyone who sat in the circle around the young man breathe in and out like wind as it rushed in a storm. That draft of air raced through their chests, went around the circle in one direction, then reversed, going out through their brows and the tops of their heads. Their breathing formed an encircling fiery ray. For a moment, his thoughts drifted back to his cave home at Wadi Ahu and to a mystical night when the Children of Stone greeted him from the firmament. He no longer saw Naibe's sweet face beside him, Ari's concerned expression, Deka's embarrassed humility, or Maatkare struggling with unseen forces on the nearby sheepskin.

Shine for one who begs to serve you
Return to the night…

His gentle tone lifted the words above the nearly silent melody. It made him ache for a simpler time but he knew he never really wished to go back to being that humble and ever-depressed shepherd who mourned a wife that had endured him more than loved him. This was the reality he wanted; his hands becoming beacons of light that worked as healer's tools.

The unlocking of the secrets, he shook his head, inspired again. *Energy to the Children. Our will from us to make him live. The asking of it, if it is possible.* He understood everything he needed for the healing of the young man, but on a level he would never be able to put into words or even remember once he broke deep contact with the Children of Stone. The tiniest components of the young man's physical body transformed into a map of the innermost parts of the symbolic flower of life. It looked the same as if had been when he had meditated on it and walked the spirit path into the center.

This time, the vague outline of the interior of the young man's head presented beneath the path. Some parts were dark and corrupt, others disconnected and painful. As he walked, he breathed and whispered to the places that looked damaged.

He whispered: *Be well, be strong.* The women joined the chorus and finally the masses of Children from all the far reaches of anything in the greater parts of the sky joined. *There are so many of them!* He almost distracted himself, then recalled the young man lying in the grasp of death. Each particle received sparks of renewal from the crescent shaped stone Marai had positioned on Djerah's brow. As it worked in concert with all of the voices, it sighed in sad pity and began to whisper.

He has waited too long
Just past the threshold.
There is still a way
Do you understand what I ask, Man of Ai?
I whisper to you that I am willing

The gentle whispers changed tone and by the end of the phrase the voice had become Djerah's. The stone changed to an oval shape and sank into his skull. At that moment the high pitched hum varied through the chorus of words that came through loud and then faint. The hum sounded like ears ringing, or wind whistling.

Marai hadn't wanted to give him a stone that way, but knew there was no other way to heal him. He had died. Marai knew he had been dead the moment he looked him over and saw that the bubbling froth at his lips had faded. Maatkare had stalled him too long, because he *wished* them to fail.

Ari is right. Houra told me it too. They knew. I just wasn't ready to let him go. And then, Houra told me he had a great purpose and that this was going to be his first day of a new kind of eternity.

He regarded the ongoing repair the stone made as it became familiar with Djerah's body. Their breath signal sighed like the opening of a lotus in the morning and its evening closing just before it submerged beneath the surface of the water.

It was why those in Kemet revered that flower. It died and rose again as much as they wished it to. Light opened and shut; spilling out multitudes of jeweled, colorful raindrops. Multicolored flames erupted from the places where the rest of the stones lay.

Gradually Marai's breath grew shallower and he began to detach from his deep trance. He opened his eyes tentatively to see Maatkare staring holes into Deka while he rubbed at his upper cheeks and temples to regain some stability after what the big man sensed had been some kind of spiritual struggle.

Ariennu and Naibe roused themselves and looked to him for further instruction.

Djerah lay peacefully on the slightly bloodstained linen. Other than some discoloration and greenish bruising on his face and newly built nose, he seemed to be dozing.

Ariennu stretched a little and frowned at Naibe-Ellit's expression of fatigue. Marai saw her start to slump and reached for her, but she straightened.

"I'm all right. A little weak," she stroked the very slight rise in her belly, then acquiesced and let him hold her. The healing had worked, but not without cost to everyone. The young man's brow pulsed slightly where the small white Yah stone had dug bloodlessly into his head. Layers of new skin already formed over it.

Marai's heart pounded in his chest. He closed his eyes again and touched the place where the Child Stone had buried itself. The images of healing raced through him. Smallest parts of the blood, bone, skin, hair, and bundles of sparking lightning received new messages as Djerah's new stone and the others still positioned on his body worked together.

Won't work. Djerah's too much like Sheb. He's far too sensible to do well as a host, he thought. *He wouldn't want to be like me. He said as much on the trip up here.*

It is something new
That never has been done before.

His internal chorus reminded him that Children had worked the first part of the miracle in an open, dusty tent.

We don't have to go to your vessel? You can just… He started, but they finished.

Uncertain.

OPENER OF THE SKY

Each one is new.
Quiet and rest for now
His chosen one struggles
More may be needed
From those who embrace him.

Marai knew he himself had been reasonably healthy when the Children of Stone improved him, but the women had hosts of physical problems. Djerah had been dead for a few moments. A gentle but instructive voice, part Akaru and part his own sound, spoke in the middle of his thought clearing process.

The Djerah you knew
He who traveled with you,
Becomes another.
The one bonded to him,
You name this Yah
Which he chose,
had made a wise choice.
He is strong enough to function,
When his path is chosen, he will rise
He must sleep now with the new one
You must protect.

Thought so, he nodded silently.

"Here, help me bind his head, but keep the bandages off his nose, so it won't mash down again. If it looks bad tomorrow I may have to brace it open with reeds as it heals." He whispered in Naibe's ear, then pressed and kissed her. "We need to keep him still and asleep for a while to let his own life force restart. It was already gone. Ari, you and your prince were right. He *was* dead. We just brought him back."

"My prince? *My* prince? I should slap you," she gripped her arms, vaguely nauseated.

Marai shrugged, but then noticed Deka had scooted back toward Maatkare. The sojourner was about to say something to her, but Naibe suddenly gripped his head and pulled it down to her breasts.

"Ohhh, my sweet love. This *has* weakened you. Come to me *now*."

Marai trembled involuntarily. He barely noticed the way she looked over his head at the prince. He gasped, trembling and panting, still dizzied from the expansion of his thoughts so closely after the spending of his energy. He knew she didn't realize she was using her command voice, but he was so spent from the transfer of life force that his thoughts couldn't organize themselves. He had no defense against her softness and gentle way, her intoxicating scent, the curve of her belly, her firm and exquisitely shaped legs. She held his head and wove her fingers through his silvery hair while Ariennu gently bound Djerah's head with the last of the clean linen.

The young man's breathing was still very slow and shallow, but even.

Almost forgot, Marai noticed Prince Maatkare had regained his seat on the sheepskin rug. The general grabbed Deka as if he owned her when she moved within his reach. The moment he touched her, her brown-green eyes popped open wide; but glazed in a combination of horror and delight. The closed box lay in her lap, but suddenly opened on its own. Sixteen of the seventeen stones that had participated in the young man's healing rose from Djerah's body. They hovered a hands breadth above him, shimmered and began to emit an orb-like light. It was as if they were waiting on Marai to instruct them.

"Thank You, little ones. You've done so well. I'll see he lives up to you; that we all do," Marai looked up, smiling through his weariness as the orbs rose and began to migrate toward the box Deka held. He watched the anguish filter over her face when she heard his words: *I'll see he lives up to you; that we all do.* When they had all returned, she snapped the box shut, set it down and turned to seek comfort in the prince's arms.

Marai turned his head to look at them for a moment, still unable to shake off the feeling of re-kindling rage. He returned his gaze to his own armful of Naibe and then over to Ariennu who wearily pulled some cool, clean sheeting up over the resting young man. Marai wanted to hold her too and let Maatkare find his own way out of the tent without even bidding him the slightest courtesy. They were all exhausted.

"You all right, woman?" He saw Ari blinking and weaving a little.

"Yeah, Marai," Ariennu whispered weakly, as if she was on the verge of collapse. "I *do* have to rest. You go be with Little One and I'll be with Djee here. If he starts to fail, I guess our stones will wake me up." She didn't wait for the big man to answer, but folded Djerah's left arm gently over his belly, then patted it affectionately.

How like a gentle mother she is, Marai thought for a moment. *Too bad she never got to really be one in her life. Maybe…* he started, but shook his head to stop the thought.

The woman lay beside the young stonecutter, then shuffled her position for a moment so she wouldn't accidentally hurt him if she moved in her sleep. Soon, she drifted to sleep.

Marai cuddled Naibe-Ellit, then turned to stare quietly at Maatkare for a moment before he spoke. He didn't know what possessed him to choose the topic other than his fatigue but all he could think of when he touched Naibe and felt her trembling in his embrace was how she had been mistreated by the man in front of him.

"You *knew* she carried a child, and still you…" Marai started, still dizzy and very weak, but in need of some kind of excuse or explanation.

The prince's face took on a stoniness he didn't expect.

"I've known *that* for a while… *and* that you presume much of goddess Tauret to think it's *your* seed sprouting in her," he affirmed, not wanting to look at Marai's expression. "Perhaps she put her gifts to work in your absence, knowing the son of a prince or even a king would have more value than the son of a peasant."

Don't… even… start that with me or I swear to all the gods you will choke on the next words that come out of your mouth before they finish forming in your heart, Marai's eyes silvered with evil.

Deka heard his thought and knew the prince must have heard it too. She sucked in a gasp and cautioned him, then turned and gave an apologetic glance back at the sojourner.

"If that, or whoever's child it was even *mattered* to you, you'd have treated her better, but I know you merely sought to rule her as you do anything in your sight." Marai continued, but added more quickly before the insult sank in.

"So, our demonstration of this 'power' and how the stone works has opened your eyes?" Marai's voice lilted sarcastically. "Us… it has weakened," he started, but noticed the sly smile that crept into the prince's mouth. He knew exactly what Maatkare was thinking.

"Very well. Go ahead and have your men kill us while we rest, if that's your wish," Marai saw the prince shrug slightly as if to say he didn't care if they lived or died. The sojourner looked in the direction of a jar that had held the women's daily ration of honey beer. Without looking in it, he guessed it was empty. Ari had always a fierce drinker. Being made to participate in some killings would have given her a thirst that would have taken her to the bottom of the urn some time earlier.

"I don't think you *will* kill us, though. We could use a little more beer, if one of your men could bring it…" he saluted, fully humble.

Maatkare rose with Deka in tow. An attitude of disgust radiated like a dark aura from him.

You will pay. Ask me for refreshment when you should be begging for your life? His thoughts hissed. He stuck his head out of the tent and motioned for one of the guards outside to enter and fetch the empty jar for him.

Child. Spoiled Child. Marai thought and knew the prince heard it because he paused and turned slightly, that same curled pout on his lips before he left.

In a few moments, the two guards placed the re-filled jar inside the tent. Marai tried to understand what Deka murmured to them in a language that was even further removed from the one the people of the Akaru used. She entered the tent alone and dipped a cup of beer for him, but blocked her eyes and her emotions from Marai as she served it.

Yet another tongue? Something she has remembered? Marai bent down to take the cup and sought her eyes again. He felt all of her torment instantly, but let her know he forgave her again. He still felt disappointed she had never tried to welcome him after he shied away from her in the Children of Stone's sleep pod.

Go where you will, woman, his thoughts gave permission once again. *Poor Deka, I wish it had been meant to be, but…*

Don't go from me, Man-sun. It's not over. I just don't know what's next any more. I knew I was to come here. I told you my reasons were not known to me. I still don't know, but without you I had to choose another way, her eyes flashed.

It's alright. I just want you to be happy, woman… that, and to stay beautiful as you are. He sighed and shook his head.

Nefira Sekhet Deka, he mentally repeated the name the prince had given her. *Beautiful Sekhet; Sekhmet the Goddess whose birth was in Ta-Seti or Ta Netjer. But not her, after all, are you? Blood is familiar to you. So is the hunt. Your men say Menhit, the lion.*

She shook her head "no" as if to say 'not yet, I cannot overthink. I must be silent and allow truth to come; for my and his purpose to be learned.'

Stay a moment, Deka, Marai touched her shoulder. *I always did know you were different.*

Her stone was one of the different ones in the original group. It had been special from the start. He remembered fishing it out and holding it up to the light to start a fire that would cleanse the corpses of the thieves lying in the sand below his cave porch. *It's as if the Children knew of her before I started finding everyone. Maybe they knew of Naibe, Akaru, probably Wserkaf, oddly they allowed Djerah… all lost sheep for me to find?*

The answer whispered in his thoughts below her recognition.

You have learned much
And we bear much sadness.
Remember, man of Ai
Whose race is of the stars
Learn from She
As she has taught ones in high places
Death is only part of a greater life.

Changes come to all,
Have great courage, and do not fail.

The prince interrupted the Children's transmission when he stuck his head inside the tent to check on Deka. Her stay had been too long to suit him.

Marai smiled his gratitude, sipped the beer from the cup, and then offered Naibe some. Next, he offered it back to Prince Maatkare, half out of expected courtesy and half to see if he reacted to possible poison in the cup. *That's Old Hordjedtef's trick, Sweet Horizon in the cup. But you would rather challenge me with your body and your heka,* Marai mused.

The prince put up his hand to show disinterest, still lost in thought over all he had seen during the healing.

"Problem is;" Marai began, "and what irks you the most, is that you want to see and know so much more. You want to learn what the priests were afraid to teach you. You know they were afraid you actually *might* be king past the chosen ones. I believe that has always been your elder's problem, too; that he was and is *feared* instead of respected. But, if you try to kill me and succeed..." his shoulders slumped.

Marai didn't really want to welcome the prince into another discourse. He wanted to sleep.

Maatkare blinked again, frustrated that any witty response had abandoned him and that cruel or terse ones had also become air. Uncommonly, he looked at Deka's downcast features and felt a strange sense of her aura beginning to surround and protect him with her power and grace. It drew him in like tentacles of need.

"So sleep. Don't try to leave or take your things, though. I have guards on this tent who will wake the camp if you do anything more than piss in the night," he towed Deka to his tent. Marai saw that her walk had become stumbly, but thought nothing about it for the moment. There was so much more he wanted to think about instead.

OPENER OF THE SKY

Part 4: Returnings and Revelations

Chapter 24: Regrouping

Marai drank in all of Naibe-Ellit's beauty. The straw and wool-scrap-stuffed barrier between the shabby floor rug and their bodies had become the most luxurious bed on which he had ever rested. They were both exhausted, but neither of them could sleep. As he lay facing her, his hands cupped her breasts. He felt how hot and firm they had grown in his absence. She felt so good to him after so many months of remembering and dreaming of her. He wanted her, but worshipped her too deeply at this moment to enjoy the limitless passion of her body; to feel so full of her that he might burst.

"Are you well, Sher-ellit?" he asked, worried that this glory of a woman who had his child in her belly might somehow be snatched from him the way Ilara had been taken eons ago. He inspected her glorious ripening nipples with his mouth and tongue. His hand traced her slightly rounded belly, feeling its new firmness and knowing how much it begged for more of him inside it. He wanted her as recklessly as she wanted him, but knew they both needed to rest. The bottom of her wrapped shift had pulled apart just enough to admit his hand. He gently stroked her mound, feeling the lips of her kuna open wetly like the dewy petals of a flower. She sighed against him, then held his head to her breasts.

"I missed you so very much," he whispered. That late afternoon, they both wept for joy, kissed, and held each other until they slept.

In the royal tent, Maatkare watched the woman Deka as she slept. He *sensed* she carried his child.

Perhaps it is her *child by me that I have sensed, but my thoughts placed it in young Naibe's body. Still, it would be good to claim a child of hers even though it could be my silly cousin's w help or, from what I understand, the king's or crown princes. There will be time enough for Nefira if I'm wrong*, he thought. *I know she has a fertile belly. She gave birth long ago, though she no longer bears the tattoos for it. She has the scent of a woman with a bud unfolding. These women, her and Naibe, seem to forget I am enough wolf that I can smell their changes, even through washings and perfumed oils.* He checked on her again. *Good... a nice deep sleep. I won't be stopped, then.* Even so, he spoke some words.

I have inquiries, gentle ones.
I must learn, if you would teach.

Maatkare sat cross-legged beside his bed, opened the box and studied the gentle shimmer that emanated from the stones. *This way, with everyone asleep and too worn out to speak against me, perhaps I can convince these little god-stones that I have respectful intentions.* He took two or three stones out at a time and examined them, then reflected on everything he had witnessed in the women's tent. That led him to consider one more thing: *Nefira Deka, though... I saw how she was when this sojourner showed up, suddenly alive and healthy. Is she safe from his influence now? Will she be drawn to return to him?* Maatkare's thoughts raced.

The other sojourners had worn themselves to their limit when they restored the life to his prisoner. His own reaction had been different. Maatkare felt oddly invigorated for having watched the process.

The distant squeal of sound from the tent where the prisoner lay intermittently reached his sharpened sense of hearing. It was evidence that the healing of the prisoner continued. The prince stuck his finger in one ear to wiggle it, but the sound remained the same.

Heka. It's just Sekhem. I studied this in priestly schools and used touch on the woman Naibe when she drowned. I know there is also healing Heka with light, color, and sound vibration, but this was so much stronger when these little ones boosted it through all of the others. They caused this worthless piece of trash to live. Whatever for? Their sense of mercy for him makes a problem for me now. My men will wonder if I let him go. He still killed my men and led a raid. Ntr stones notwithstanding, he must still pay for his crime.

He looked back at the sleeping woman sprawled on his bed, exhausted from her part in this. *They needed you, Nefira Deka, didn't they?* He considered that she had brought the box of stones when they came to the tent to watch. *If she had left these stones, or if we hadn't gone to their tent, would any of this have worked? Once I have learned what there is to know of them, I can deal with the other matters. She'll rest now. When she wakes, she will speak to me of the son she will give me. If not, perhaps I shall grow weary of her, as well.*

While he waited for her to wake, the prince picked up an impossibly good malachite patterned with some lighter waves. He'd been told his own eyes looked a dark olive green with amber lights although the clearest mirrors or water never reflected such a cherished color.

That green stone was the one the sojourners had first placed on the prisoner's brow. As if it hadn't been the right fit, they had moved it to his cheek to absorb the blood and fluid during the healing. The prince held it up to the light to see if it still held blood or did anything further on its own. When it remained silent, he whimsically placed it on his brow.

An immediate flash of light and heat, followed by coolness, assaulted the place where he touched it to his head. He fumbled with it in a rush of both fear and excitement. His breath quickened as he held it in place with his left hand.

When he chased animals in a hunt or even when he charged into a battle with his men, he felt the same thought-numbing feeling. At any moment, he knew he might make a fatal mistake. It was what the thrill of hunting on foot with bow and spear, just as the ancestors had hunted was all about.

Fear? he asked himself. *No. Not fear. This is more than that; a lot more*, he felt desperate. His breath came in hiccoughing gasps of joy that bordered on mad laughter. The stone settled, causing a slightly painful sensation in his brow, as if it was biting him. His eyes rolled back in his head from the combination of pain and ecstasy. The taste of blood in his throat filled him with ravenous hunger, but he choked on its thick salty warmth. Another fit of trembling left him feeling stronger, but intensely aware of sounds and smells. A growl that began in his throat and swept through his entire being formed. His lips slavered and foamed. The claws on his right hand went to his mouth to find that his teeth had grown sharp and long. With a silent howl he pitched backward on the reed matting covering his tent floor.

Wepwawet! Anpu Wolf! The Dog god. Son of Sutek. Animal within. My animal. My little one. My black dog, he breathed. He had tried to access that ravenous energy in every part of his life and study with only limited success, despite the warnings of his teachers against fully taking beast form, unguided.

Ha! Like telling a child who makes an ugly face that it might stick that way… Amazing! He plucked the stone, which had nearly attached itself, and flung it away.

In a moment, when he came to his senses, he sought it from under his camp bed, then gently picked it up and returned it to the box. He froze at the sound of an echoed, growling voice.

See… You see
Feel it
It is you
Taste it
Yourself in power
You become a god.

The voice spoke, but is sounded like a growl mixed with his own voice.

"I know," he whispered aloud to the internal spirit voice. "You'll teach me then?"

Learn…
You are your own teacher…
As all are…
You are opener of the way,
Open what is in your own heart
See with new eyes

The voice in his thoughts trailed away as the flesh on his face rippled back into its normal shape. The prince reveled in the momentary silence that followed, then checked to see if his rustling around on the mat and the growling had waked Deka. It hadn't.

Maatkare noticed the shimmer of the stones had changed after he handled them. The white, blue, and green light he had assumed were normal colors had become primal energy colors of red and orange the moment he ran his hands over them one more time.

At once, a surge of fire ran up his arms, engulfing them in the same kind of flame that had surrounded Deka when they had traded sexual energy. It warmed, but it did not burn his skin. Once again, his breathing sped up and his body drew on the energy of the fire image on his arms. Maniacal laughter came to his lips, but stopped in an abbreviated gasp just short of making a sound.

Something magically formed in his upturned palms that had rested on his knees in an opening pose. Maatkare took a deep breath to seize control of his thoughts and to slow the ecstasy of the moment. When he opened his eyes, he stared down at a beautiful dagger made of a strange crystalline metal. It had apparently formed from the few stones he had taken up in his fingers. When he turned it over, it gleamed like a sun-glass and metal combination; made of an ore he had never seen. It was not gold, copper or even bronze. The hilt was in the form of a crouching wolf with the blade extending from its jaws. He stared again, but the moment he focused on the wolf and the blade, it dissolved.

Snorting, growling, and panting filled his chest. He couldn't catch his breath again…

"Again? The wolf? Oh be cursed, een nau… nauu… you little bastards…" he hissed through his suddenly pointed fangs, knowing he couldn't risk waking the woman on his bed. Maatkare's struggle to free his hands now drawn to the rest of the stones became a war of wits. Part of him wanted to keep the box open; to continue learning, but his senses told him: *No. Do not open again. Enough for today.* He slammed the box shut, stashed it under his bed and scrambled, without even thinking about it, to Deka's resting form. Oddly comforted, he clung to her and held her until his breathing slowed.

OPENER OF THE SKY

Chapter 25: Djerah Reborn

Marai snuggled Naibe-Ellit, deep in adoration of her as goddess, woman, and as the mother of his child. Each time he woke, he turned to her, stroked her hair and then carefully touched her belly, still awed by her beauty. Remnants of the energy emitted by the Children of Stone had continued to rouse him throughout the early evening.

The prince is meddling with them, he commented to himself through tired-but-beauty-dazzled eyes. *Wonder why they aren't exacting some kind of punishment. There's another plan in this, damn them. Wish they would let me know more.*

At some point, Naibe turned to him. When he looked into her eyes and then into her soul he knew she hoped he could erase all of the memories she had took on during the months he had been gone. He was right.

You healed young Djee. Now you heal me, my Marai. She whispered into his heart, commanding him with her golden eyes and soft mouth. *I've waited for so long since I knew it possible that somehow you lived. Now, if I wait another moment, I will surely die.* Her thoughts hushed into the silver of his beard. He gathered her up quietly, kissing her, clasping her gently then draping his travel cloak over them. Soon they were lost in each other's tenderness.

Djerah tried to look through the crusted slits of his eyes. He had become aware of a dim lamp light that flickered nearby, but his eyelids felt glued shut. They itched mercilessly, but when he tried to rub them, he discovered he couldn't move his arms. Oddly, that sense of weakness comforted him. That he couldn't move didn't frighten him and neither did the prismatic shimmers that blurred his vision when one eye cracked open slightly. He felt safe. A vague whispering sound inside his head lulled him, taking all of his interest in movement away.

It's all right, he told himself. *Rest. I need to be still. Sleep.* He closed his partly opened eyelid and welcomed the red and black pulsing of the vessels inside it. A dull ache under the skin on his face felt like a sunburn.

Did I die? I remember fighting and shooting. I took an arrow, no, two in me. Yah, it hurt so much! Better now. Is this Paradise? He wanted to sit up and to see where he was, but the ache inside his head increased slightly as a warning that he should remain motionless.

Flashes of memory passed unmercifully through his thoughts as an ongoing explanation of *why* he should rest. A demonic face that resembled a slavering wolf merged with the face of a petulant cherub complete with fang-like teeth danced through his thoughts. He remembered that face.

Royal. Must be someone royal who hurt me. Looks like the royal family a little. Do they all look like the statues, or just the highest of them? He wondered at the sudden fluidity of his unspoken thoughts. *I am a craftsman. I can cut and polish stone.* He remembered both too much, and not enough at the same time.

Why am I thinking about my craft on top of some battle I fought? It doesn't make sense. Who was that man who hurt me? The hitting. The blood. Djerah recalled the horrid crunch sound the bones in his face made and that he felt agony the first time. He reviewed the numb but audible thuds that came again and again until the power to hear left him, along with the ability to see. After that, only a feeling of something pushing hard on his face twice more came before there was nothing left to feel.

Why did Yah not strip that memory from me along with the name of the man who did it to me? Why can I remember other men dying with me, but not his name? A twinge pulsed at the young man's brow, followed by a reverberating ache. Something in his head whined, and a higher pitched whisper that sounded like a child singing recited:

And one... And One... it pulsed.

Sigh in – hear the voice. Sigh out.

A higher voice, like a little girl's repeated the phrase this time.

Shhh. Djerah! Oh, Djerah... it called with a titter.

He felt more pulsing. Hearing other intense whispers, he tried to crane his head up just a little, but still couldn't manage it. He sensed passionate speech, lovers as they spoke to each other in a most gentle voice. The words swept through him like a warm touch so full of love that it filled the entire tent.

A few more horrible moments returned to his memory. The young man wanted to moan in rebellion, but only succeeded in gasping in a little more air.

On your knees, murdering wretch! His Highness will deal with you first, then I will enjoy finishing you. Some guard was jostling him where his foot had been shot and punching a sharp wound in his side to make it hurt more.

Made me watch. Highness. A prince, then. The men followed me here. Why would I waste good men's lives? Doesn't make sense. Savta Houra was here, but I saw her the way Marai showed her to me… young. He remembered the darkest of moments when it didn't even hurt at all any more. She had rushed to embrace him and perhaps guide him to the afterlife.

In that instant, he had known her entire lifetime of misery and trial; the way she had been raped by the slavers in trade for the lives of her husband and their boys. He saw her working so hard to lift him and his ancestors up from poverty in and around Ineb Hedj. The pall of his heartbreak and the regret that he had died so miserably and so young melted in the glow of an eternity of her love. They had been walking into the light when the whirlwind had forced them apart. He knew that force.

It's just cruel sport for anyone to keep me alive. I'm ruined. A blood fever will come. If I live, I'll be useless like father and grandfather were. Marai. My kin. Strange man who walks like a god… says he was Savta's brother. I remember that name.

He squeezed his eyelids tight, because the next thought that came to him was more painful than any wound this prince or his men could give him. The man named Marai was one of the loving whisperers. *He's lying with the pretty young woman from the market who made the honey dates… Naibe? I know her voice. She is his wife. How is she here? I have a wife, too. Raawa. No. Not anymore. A peacekeeper took her heart while I worked across the river.* Djerah knew he would never again feel love as passionate as the two people nearby felt now. *Perhaps I should have noticed that my wife was not so welcoming at any point in our marriage. I thought she was just tired from her work and from chasing the little ones.* Hopeless tears welled in his eyes. *It's no good. My heart is dead. Why must I live to remember that?*

A gentle hand touched him as if it sensed his trouble, then checked his bound head. He opened his eyes more successfully this time and tried to focus on something like brightly patterned fabric, open, but draped over ample, mature breasts then tucked into a wide leather belt.

A Kina woman wore that style back at our new home in Little Kina-Ahna sometimes. She was a healer. Said it honored her 'bastard father' out of Keftiu.

The touch, he thought, as pliant hands sent warmth and healing into the side of his face near his eyes. A woman gathered him up into her arms, gently easing his head as she lifted him up.

Know her too. Aree. The other one called her Ari. Why is she here? Where is here?

"Don't hurt yourself," her voice quietly urged. "You have to let the healing set."

"Ah," Djerah's voice whispered weakly. His throat was so very dry. He struggled, suddenly terrified that he was unable to raise his head higher than the woman was lifting it. He still couldn't bring his hand up to touch his face or to examine why it felt bloated, puffy and very much felt like something was crawling around under his skin.

My head, he projected thoughts tentatively. *Thoughts clear, but...* He was surprised at the sudden ease of his efforts. The noise between his ears; a whine-like ringing wrapped in whispers rose.

"He p..." Djerah tried to say '*He put something in my head*' but his words didn't work.

"Easy, Djee. It's Red Ari. You know me, right?"

He tried to nod, but only his lids flickered.

"And yes we did," She added. "We *had* to."

He closed his eyes. When Djerah thought of the woman soothing him and heard the gentle sighing from Marai and the other woman in the tent, he thought of home, remembered his discovery that his wife had abandoned him and swallowed hard.

"Why?" the air rushed out of his parched lips, but his thoughts screamed: *Why? Why save me? I do not deserve to live. I want to die; to hold my savta's hand again.*

"Djerah," he heard the woman call his name again, this time the tone purred and sang.

He felt the woman tipping a cup to his lips, then cursing a little that he couldn't drink yet. She dabbed at his lips with a cloth, but just the act of her moistening them felt wonderful. Her caress continued, spreading the coolness onto his intermittently aching eyelids. He felt her inspect a place on his brow that felt puffier and had its own peculiar pulse.

"The little stone you brought with you will help you heal more quickly than we could. It asked to be part of you now. It will teach and guard you. You were dead, but it wanted you to live. We nearly lost you."

He felt her put his hand to her mouth to kiss it, open-mouthed and fully passionate, then lick his palm and breathe on it.

"No," Djerah tried to resist. "I…"

"Oh, my," her voice laughed gently but sounded naughty. "Maybe not yet, but you *could* use it, you know. I won't force you. And Marai? He won't mind. He knows better than anyone that no man owns me. Prince just *thinks* he owns me, but he's about to learn…" She turned his hand and kissed the other side, her eyes gazing intently to see his expression. "We're all part of each other; one with the Child Stones inside. We know each other's thoughts more than mere friends or family might, but we are also free. In your own way, so are you now. He doesn't have to tell me, but Marai thinks of you as the son of his heart."

When Djerah strained to open his eyes a little more, he saw her face more clearly in the light. The rainbow shimmers had parted in the middle, allowing clear sight. She smiled, but when he saw her face it seemed like the image was both young and old at the same time.

"I should let you rest instead of worrying you." She smoothed his face, "Hmm. Your eyes…" she started, puzzled, and then shook her head full of hennaed curls as if she felt a shiver of sensual delight. "Makes sense, I guess."

Djerah wanted to frown but the puffy part of his brow forbid movement. Her words puzzled him and that gave way to worry. *Eyes. What does she mean? Things look like crystal is over them with the colored lights, but that's fading. I see better than I recall. I worked on the lime faces high up… polishing. Working like that in the sun will frost a man's eyes after a while.*

The woman had piqued his curiosity. He sensed she knew that.

"Umm…" she hesitated, still whispering. "I don't want to scare you, but when you get a Child Stone given to you, your looks start to change. I don't know how *you* will change or how much, but I saw your eyes get a blue cast to them, like day-sky over the black. You had to, uh… grow new ones. The prince put one of them out for you and the other wasn't good," she paused. "Now try to rest. I just didn't want you to worry when you saw yourself."

"I…" Djerah struggled to speak and winced. She noticed that, too.

"Damn. Too much." she muttered to herself. "Look, just don't think about it right now. Just rest." He felt the woman lie next to him again keeping her hand over his heart so that it slowed a little and began to beat evenly.

How gentle she is, he thought, then relaxed some more.

Naibe-Ellit drifted between laughter and tears. She trembled in Marai's arms, almost desperate for more of his touch, but saved by the thought of how much she was in love. The young woman traced the sojourner's gently closing eyes with her fingertips and cradled his radiant head to her breasts. Neither of them spoke, as if words would spoil the rapture they both felt.

"Marai?" she voiced a thought after long moments of silent adoration. She felt him nod for her to say anything she wanted to say into his bliss. "Don't ever leave me again. I wanted to die without you at my side. I *tried* to die, so no memory could come in front of those I had with you and so many tried. I could never forget this beauty we have together now, to look for it in other arms. It was only about you the whole time," she crooned.

"I'm here, now," he pulled her close.

Naibe thought she might vanish if he *didn't* hold her.

"My heart breaks to think I could ever be without you again, my goddess," he smiled.

Loving him had never been better than this. In his arms she could easily push away all of her troubles.

"You stopped time to keep Djerah with us. I felt it. I talked to your sister. Ari doesn't know," she whispered, then felt him tense a little in surprise.

"Houra?" he asked. "You saw? What did she say?" Marai suddenly worried.

"Shh. Don't tell her, or anyone else. I want it to be a secret way for us." She meant it. In those moments, she wanted to use all of her magic to stop time for both of them. If she could have frozen time the same as he did on his approach to the camp she would have chosen the quiet moments when they held each other after they had loved. It had always been her favorite time.

Another gasp of pleasure shuddered through her as he pressed her.

"Marai, oh my sweet love. When I die, promise to be with me in the Garden of Eternity where the still water flows. No more being apart. Never. No more." Her eyes widened, wondering why such a thought of death had come to her at the time of greatest joy.

"Yes, I promise," she heard him whisper. "Today and always, I will be with you."

OPENER OF THE SKY

Chapter 26: Ameny

Maatkare grew drowsy. The energy that flooded him when he examined the Children of Stone drained away as he came to his senses.

Odd that just touching these stones strengthens, then weakens me. It doesn't hurt me, though. He thought about all that had just happened. *That knife came back to me! It seemed made of nothing from the world of men. I know it must have been created by a god. Folly! It fit so easily into my hand, as if it had grown there, then it vanished! I still know they made it for me.*

He had seen a knife that resembled it when he had just been a child. It hadn't been as fine. It had been a rather crudely made relic he had discovered in a cache of hidden junk at his grandfather's Nekhen estate. The blade had been dark and corroded by the weather. He never spoke of his find to his elder or even his father, but he vowed he might have one crafted like it one day. Having safely re-hidden it, he was only mildly dismayed a few years later when he learned it had been discarded by some hapless servant. This evening, it had just appeared in his hands as if drawn from the ghost of his memory.

Maatkare gingerly eased himself to his feet, still shaky from everything he had experienced, but determined to appear strong to his men. Orders had to be given, so he straightened his clothing and exited the tent to request food sent to the women's tent. He told the men that no one was to concern themselves with the people inside unless it looked as if they were trying to escape. Then, after a brief inspection of the encampment, he trudged back to the tent.

The sun had lowered into the horizon. Deka had stirred by that time and was putting together the trestle board so they could eat. She had hammered her face into an almost expressionless mask allowing only her exhaustion to show.

"Tired?" he asked, a sly smile emerging as he sat on the edge of his bed again. *With child after all, is my guess, but doesn't want to say it to me unless she's certain.* "Now, eat the food the servants brought, unless your gut is sour." He turned away from her, sending her the clear message that he wasn't going to put up with any of her feminine troubles whether she decided to speak about them or not.

After a few moments of bitter silence, she tentatively reached for his arm; a signal for him to turn his averted glance to her.

"I have much crowding my thoughts, beloved one. I need time to sort them." Deka sought his eyes.

"I see you, woman," his voice seduced her again, but when he refused to look in her eyes, she lowered her gaze once more. He knew his blank expression upset her, but he needed for her to remain uncertain of her standing for the time being so that she would behave more submissively.

"You don't know your place with me now that I have the Ntr stones. You ask yourself if I will still desire you. I know that, because he who was dead has returned and now your heart confuses you." He paused midway his lecture and saw that one of her servants entered with the trenchers of food. "Do you trust your own thoughts or do they betray you, you ask yourself?" he seized her jaw in his hand and squeezed it until Deka winced in pain. The moment he released his grip, she threw her arms around him.

"I'm devoted to you," she lay her head on his arm but did not meet his gaze.

And she lies to me, too. So now that begins. Knew it would sooner or later, the prince mused as he shrugged her embrace, then eased from his bed to sit at table she had set. *We shall see how she fares in the morning.*

They ate in silence until finally, as if she seemed unable to stand the lack of conversation, she spoke: "I wish you didn't doubt me just because Marai has come."

Maatkare didn't answer.

"Raem... what must I do to prove it?" she spoke in a flat, but quiet voice.

"Do?" he raised a brow, slowly raising his eyes. "There's nothing, really, but I won't condemn you yet. You have told me you are on a different path than this sojourning man and the others. Time and your acts will tell me if that's true," he regarded her sadness, then decided to give her a ray of hope.

"Soothe me, then." His left hand took hers and placed it on his own left shoulder. Your little heifer of a sister wrenched my arm today at the discipline. I need the tightness worked from it before we move inland to the grass, so it won't catch on me when I draw my bow. You'll heal me won't you?" his voice slithered in a sweet but demanding way.

"I will. I promise to do *all* that I can," she replied, but the word "all" felt almost like a threat.

What you do, woman, whatever you think… I'm inside your heart, watching you, he thought.

Maatkare woke deep in the night with the feeling that something was dreadfully wrong. He had been so tired from the miserable day of combined defeats, and a big evening meal that he fell asleep as the woman worked his shoulder and arm.

This isn't my bed in the camp or the one in my home.

He sensed he was in a different bed; a high and stately-looking one with netting draped around it. *I know this place,* he remembered. *Damn! A dream that's so real it's like I have risen and flown through time into the past.* He began to sweat as he thought: *Not this memory. I'll wake myself. I cannot think of that cursed ka-reen,* but he was locked in the memory of the woman who had come to him that night long ago. She had been heavily veiled and disguised as a bed gift for a visiting and youthful prince. She had roused and aroused him, and with minimal seduction the two had enjoyed an incredible and insatiable evening that stretched into the dawning hours before they collapsed on each other, exhausted.

I don't want this, Maatkare tried to stir but nothing he did freed him from the memory. Merytetes, elder daughter of Menkaure, had been the woman in the veiling. His grandfather had suggested she seek him as a bit of a naughty joke, since she had been looking for a good consort. At the time he hadn't understood the manipulation, but in retrospect too much had become clear.

Grandfather did this to me, damn him and his ambitions, Maatkare recalled. *Princess Meryt's half-brother Kuenre had died. I had never met my own betrothed. I recall her name was Beni, but she had gone to Amenti, ill of a fever, just hours before I arrived to be joined to her. Grandfather whispered to me to not be sad, or to view it as an omen about my future with women. He had bigger plans for me. He brought me to King Menkaure and presented me so they could discuss my future. They set me up to be her plaything and perhaps, later on, a general.*

The prince stopped trying to wake himself.

If this dream-vision has such a fierce hold on me, perhaps it's a prophecy of some future event. He knew his waking memory had been muddled from the start. It had been necessary. *Meryt...* his thoughts spoke into his dream *if your ghost is doing this to me, know you did enjoy my bed as they all do. You, though, craved it to sickness, and taught me even greater skills. You cursed ghost-woman! I took away much for having been schooled in pleasure by you. For that, at least, I thank you.*

He saw in his dream-memory montages of couplings any time of day or night, most of them rough.

She liked it as rough as I could make it. My acted disrespect made her ravenous for me. Women say they hate it, but they don't. They fear the pain but love the pleasure of being slammed in two... deep underneath where their red soul buries itself. She insisted we marry, after a while... and that I be appointed Crown Prince, adopted as son by the King so that I would be her 'brother'. I should have known she merely wanted to own her prize.

He lay still now; drifting into a meditative trance of recollection.

She wanted me to quench her fire any time, day or night, but never concerned herself with my needs. He remembered he found Sadeh in the alleys of White Wall. *Sadeh. That girl would do anything; literally anything, so I brought her into my new estate as Meryt's "maid".* His laughter almost roused him. Sadeh viewed Meryt not as her superior, but as competition. The battleground was his bed and his body. Between the two, he wanted for nothing.

No. I will remember only when it was good, only when it was fun. The prince struggled again, but an external, ghostly force held him in that memory as it darkened and verged into the forbidden parts. *She miscarried... again. During her recovery and time of purification, I turned to Sadeh and other servants to ease the infection of hunger she had given me. She turned to strong drink to ease hers.*

As the dream continued, he saw the king come to caution him about the rough treatment of the divine daughter, urging him to take advantage of the concubines for such activities. Then there was another tragedy, a child born still. This time he recalled prophetesses coming to the king about a vision of great darkness that lay about my palace. In the next moment, he saw Meryt degenerate into an often sloppy but demanding drunk.

I drank with her, but I was coming to loathe the sex that bound us. Still, I could not drive her from me. The more I disrespected her the hotter she would burn for me. I would pretend to rape her. She liked that. He knew what was coming next. It was the day he had put from his memory nearly seven years ago.

Meryt, I curse you to Ammit, you wicked ka-reen. I don't want to see it. Release me, damn you!

They had argued briefly on the day she died. It was about his use of concubines and any other woman he could bend over. This turned to slapping and screaming and then to throwing and breaking things. It was the worst fight ever, but this time, he realized, it was not a game to excite his response. She drew a knife.

Servants scattered in terror to alert the king that the fighting and shouting were getting out of control.

I remember that, you crazed and moaning heifer. You told me you were putting me out and not naming me as your brother of heart if I didn't learn better manners in your house... if I did not submit and honor you properly. But, you had lowered yourself way below honor any honor I could give you.

"Oh, manners like *this*?" He had swept her off her feet to his room for some violent and reconciliatory sex with Sadeh thrown in as an added attraction. When they finished, he thought it was over. They downed more drinks and joked into the afternoon.

Then you started up again... still said all you had to do was say one thing to your father and I'd be finished... Bitch! I laughed, but you didn't and then I knew you meant it. Damn... I see it all now. I kissed you. You poked at my arm with your dagger and cut me a little. If I hadn't been quick...

I was so drunk I lost my balance avoiding your blade. More drinks. Called you a cow, but as an animal, not in your sacred role of Hethara, the divine one.

In his dream, he saw Sadeh and himself tying Meryt's neck to a lead on the rail and mocking her like a cow in a breeding pen. *She liked that,* he reflected, *when I yanked the lead at the right moment.* She always did.

He saw her struggle away this time and crawl up on the rail, turning to mock him.

"Monster! Demon! I will jump into my Amenti now, rather than squeeze out your disrespectful sons..."

Maatkare struggled in his dream but felt the ghostly influence gaining on him, demanding that he witness the rest.

I didn't believe she would say that.

He saw himself poke at her to scare her off the rail and into his arms, but saw she slipped. *I grabbed the leash to pull harder, but I was so drunk I maybe... I maybe... didn't... exactly.* The straps that fastened her shift and the lead around her neck caught on some of the decorative sculpture on the other side of the rail. He remembered he paused and looked, now. He hadn't remembered it before. She dangled. Her hands grabbed the straps from her silent throat as it crushed and she choked. He heard his youthful self shriek his wolfish victory howl as she struggled.

"O that din't take much... just a little push..." echoed through his memory and he saw himself sink dizzily to the floor for a moment.

I came to my senses an instant later... or was it longer? Sadeh was not there. She wasn't about to get herself executed over some drunken accusation. Stinking ka't.

The sound of mad scampering and crying out rose from the lower floor. He saw himself lean over to pull the rope, but by his time her mottled face and bulged eyes showed that she had accepted her fate.

Servants scurried up to cut her limp form down while others assembled below to catch her as she fell.

Drunk... I was worse than drunk he thought.

Someone helped him dress and eased him down the stairs. He saw her lying on the floor, neck choked and gasping weakly. He saw how the image had stunned him sober as he lifted her into his arms and tried to rouse her. The king rushed in. As if he had blacked out again and now saw it in detached memory, Maatkare remembered being thrown against the wall by his majesty. He struggled up and rushed to Meryt in horrid realization of what had taken place. The two men cried while they held her and watched her life go.

He lost his wits, the king did. He had a special carved bull-shaped wood and golden coffin created for her, then lay in it himself while she was prepared. He ordained that she would be worshipped forever in the arms of Atum.

He wanted me dead, Maatkare felt the sad memory almost strangle him in his own rest. *He should have killed me the moment she passed from us, but something stopped him. It* wasn't my begging or his blaming my drunk state, either. It was something far more powerful. Grandfather had worked his magic to convince the king that his dearest daughter had been despondent over the stillbirth of her child. It was despair of an unhappy life…

No, the bitch jumped. I called her dare. Maybe I did push her a little. Maybe I could have grabbed her and just didn't on account of being passed out. Doesn't matter. Don't know why her ghost wanted to tell me this after over six years.

Maatkare woke with a start. Nefira Deka kissed his tense shoulders and lay her head on his chest. He swatted her aside, instantly feeling…

"You! You brought this cursed dream to me," he sat up holding his head and shuddering in something between rage and horror.

"Dream?" she picked herself up. Her eyes glimmered just a touch of flame over their darkness. "Did you have a dream, beloved? Tell me it, so I may soothe you."

He *knew* she understood his dream. She sensed thoughts and if he had waked her wrestling with his demons she would have paid attention. At first he resisted, turning from her.

"Maatkare Raemkai," she whispered and placed his hand on her belly. "His name will be Ameny…"

Maatkare paused, gave a sick half-laugh that echoed. *Oh you have some skills to bring this to me now, you she-beast.* He took her in his arms, or moved to, but this time she lifted Wserkaf's wdjat up to the lamplight to see the image that formed. It was the text of a poem. When he recited it, he sensed that he was speaking of the near future but the scroll had been written much later in a distant kingdom as if it had recorded a long recited history.

Then a king will come from the South,
Ameny, the justified, by name,
Son of a woman of Ta-Seti,
And a child of Upper Lands,
He will take the white crown, the red crown

He will join the Two Mighty Ones
Akkad will fall to his sword,
Tjemehu will fall to his flame,
Rebels to his wrath,
Traitors to his might,
As the serpent on his brow subdues the rebels for him,
One will build the Walls-of-the-Ruler,
To bar them from entering Kemet

"See" she whispered, very lovingly by her eyes continued their mysterious glimmer as she put away the medallion. "Don't regard the past that can't be changed and how your life was steeped in these miseries."

"You did this," he sulked, turning again. "And because of that damned stone…" but she was already shaking her head 'No'.

"Only so you could bury it, then assume your greatness," she gently kissed one of his eyes.

He nodded, trying to understand, but still not trusting her as he turned to kiss her lips and stroke her dark belly. *Think of what will be, not what has been. I see you. I see your plan for me. I'll humor you for now, but I will watch you work this game.* He noticed her cryptic smile at that moment, but thought he had imagined it.

Chapter 27: Resolution Delayed

"What? No. For the love of… Goddess!! You just came right in here this morning and sat down to watch us? For how long? Bastard!!"

Marai woke with a start to the sound of Ariennu's scolding voice. Without looking, he sensed Prince Maatkare seated between his head and the opening of the tent; arms folded in self-satisfaction.

The sojourner raised his head and turned to verify his thought then sighed, disgusted. How long the prince had been seated in contemplation of his "guests"? Marai didn't even *want* to know.

Did you? Marai noticed the man's hand gripped his fly whisk and that it looked as if he had been about to poke or nudge one of then, just to be irritating.

Naibe felt him move, noticed who was there, and gasped. Marai hushed her alarmed squawk, covered her with his cloak and then sat up with her.

Ari threw her own arm over Djerah, to protect *him*. She knew all of the commotion the prince had just caused reflected in his entertained expression.

"Oh?" Maatkare raised one brow, then rose and took a step toward Ariennu and Djerah. "Disrespect from you, Red Sister? I see you sleep in *my* tent, loaned to you, are a guest in *my* camp, and tend *my* prisoner. Did it ever occur to you that your manners could influence my decisions? Seems I've gone this path with you before, haven't I? Still that mouth of yours rings in my ears as if it begs me to treat you and yours badly. You act as if you have come to long for the ladder again," he chuckled then turned to stare down his hawk nose at Marai and Naibe.

"And you," the prince stared down, then poked the big man's arm with his flail.

Marai felt the sharp dart-like point on the tip dig into his flesh, frowned, and wrapped Naibe in a protective embrace.

"Aw, that's touching," Maatkare nudged Marai's arm again and was about to move to Naibe's exposed breast when the sojourner snatched the flail, snapped it in two pieces with one hand, and tossed the halves aside in one fluid movement.

"Poke at me if you like, but not her," Marai spoke quietly, then spat "…Highness."

A growlish, dog-like snarl issued from behind the prince's throat. Maatkare's personal guard and the two guards assigned to Deka filled the gap in the tent flap, ready to assist the prince, but he waved them off. He re-folded his arms, stared down, and sent an ugly thought.

I will deal with you, sojourner. Just checking the baggage. He turned again and, as if pacing, returned to Djerah and Ariennu.

"So. He recovers then, but is still weak enough that there's no fight rising in him?" The prince flipped his hand at Ariennu "Back up so I can see him, ka't."

Ari hissed, but Marai gave a nod for her to comply.

When she moved, Maatkare squatted to examine the young man's wounds. He touched Djerah's discolored upper cheeks and saw the puffiness shift underneath his skin. A little serum oozed from a place where the sealed skin had been left open for drainage. The prince touched it and then tasted a little of the fluid. Satisfied that there were no signs of early putrefaction, he spoke.

"Wake yourself. I order you to open your eyes and look at me."

Djerah tensed, cracked open his eyes that still wandered unfocused, then struggled to raise the upper part of his body in apparent self-defense. He tried to push Ariennu's protective reach away but his strength faded and bewildered pain showed in his face.

"No, Djerah, don't…" Ariennu looked across him to snarl at the prince again. "Haven't you done enough, to him? Leave him alone."

"Hardly. He is *still* my prisoner and wants death for his actions. That he lives just means I ought to try harder next time. And I want no orders out of your mouth, either. *I* give those, understand?"

"He doesn't listen to people much, does he?" Marai commented on the exchange quietly, patted Naibe, put on his tunic, and began to get up. "Stay here," he stood, his head almost grazing the top of the tent.

Djerah tensed and struggled to rise, then gasped and fell back.

He's moving too much, too soon. Marai's gaze narrowed. It puzzled him that the Children of Stone hadn't thrown the young man into a deathlike sleep that would last for several months. *The poison I took at Hordjedtef's hands couldn't have been as harmful to me as this poor one's beating, but he can already move and even reason.* He moved closer then tapped his brow a little, hoping Djerah was able to receive his thoughts.

Be still. Know I am here. Don't move or let him upset you.

"Be still. Know I am here," Maatkare looked up at the sojourner but couldn't resist the mockery. "You already know I hear thoughts, fool. I showed you that yesterday and you're still not guarding them from me. And did I *not* say this man is still my responsibility and my prisoner because of his crimes? And as for my Grandfather poisoning you; was it not true that our gods in their ultimate wisdom led you on such a dance that you drank the harmful thing of your own free will?" The prince watched the big man carefully, tilting his head to the side in almost boyish fascination, then glanced at Ari.

"Oh you're not going to demand we let you keep him..." Color drained from Ariennu's face. She bent close to the young man.

"Oh, you're quite the tender charmer when you want to be, aren't you?" he smirked. "So gentle with him, like a mother. I know you, Red. He's just something *new* for you. Your man came back from the dead and went straightaway to your young honey sister. I have your other sister in kind eating from my hand. Checking your options and making new plans, eh?"

Ari's face reddened with ire.

"You think... you..." Ariennu stammered, taken aback and too furious to finish.

"You see, I know how you ka't conspire and think. I saw it plenty as a youth. One has her prize, the other plots to take it away from her or to create envy by flaunting herself for another where he can see."

"Your Highness," Marai spoke in very low and even tones, squatting a respectful distance from the prince. "She is my wife, as are the others, including the one you *think* you have swept from me. I'm asking that you respect that; one man to another."

"Have I not been respectful and honorable?" one of Maatkare's winged eyebrows raised. "I *could* have given you my entire regiment to deal with yesterday but instead I allowed you to come in, heal a man who *still* deserves death, and sleep with your former women, all because the one you wrongly call Deka asked it of me."

Marai blinked, suddenly awed by how much the prince reminded him of Count Prince Hordjedtef in a younger and perfected body: education, fitness, skill, and seductiveness. Yet he was, on top of all else, just as pitiless and ruthless as his grandfather and all of the kings of Khufu the Great's seed.

If he did do this at Deka's bidding, Marai thought, *he must have seen an advantage to it. I doubt he knows the meaning of the word love or devotion,* Marai mused, moving a little closer.

"But all good things change," Maatkare addressed Marai suddenly as if he had still heard the sojourner's thoughts. "You're here and would like to take everyone back. I've told you yesterday that isn't going to happen. And just so you know, I'm as learned as any of my cousins who feel entitled to these Ntr Stones. Perhaps in some ways I am moreso. I've been examining these stones. I've already learned how to make them do some fairly *amazing* things."

Marai hadn't noticed the prince had it at first, but at that moment Maatkare flourished a knife that had been tucked into his belt.

"You see? This here; I *dreamed* this knife and my very thoughts created it and formed it on top of the stones while I watched. First, it vanished, but when I rose this morning, I thought of it again and this time it retains its form."

Marai's eyes fastened on the knife. In that moment his world fell away and he saw a burly and grizzled raider challenging him at Wadi Ahu. It had been a lifetime ago. He had known so little about his new abilities through the Child Stone pulsing in his brow that early morning. He had been horrified to vomiting and fainting after he walked through thirty men snapping them in half, turning their own weapons on them and garroting them with their own clothing and jewelry.

That man, whom Marai later learned was the leader of a band of wilderness thieves, N'ahab-atall brandished a knife that day that looked like a cruder version of Maatkare's new blade. The first knife had a bone hilt carved like a crouching wolf that bit a bronze blade. This blade's hilt was solid gold and the blade was made of a metal that had an almost crystalline sheen to it. The sheath of the raider's blade had been wood carved as a naked woman with widespread legs receiving the wolf's mouth… an insult to the goddess. This blade, fortunately, had no obscene scabbard.

When Marai had recovered from the enormity of his deed that morning, he had taken the blade with the thought to destroy it in the fire, but then the world changed. He met the women. The knife had vanished and he had forgotten about it until now.

"You are fascinated by it?" The prince noticed Marai's pause, but didn't sense his memory flooding him or the sojourner's instant recall of a later dream in which he had seen a vain young prince searching for the Ntr Stones, based on his meditations of where they lay. All he had found was the burned encampment where a knife with a corroded blade lay discarded in the dirt.

"I've seen the first one… up close." Marai answered dully.

Ariennu heard the word 'knife' mentioned, looked at the weapon the prince was showing and froze.

"What the… It looks like N'ahab's old knife. Goddess. How did you…"

Maatkare smirked the sideways grin, then tittered a little too much like a jackal for Marai's comfort.

"I would say perhaps these little stones of yours like me after all. Or shall I say we just *understand* each other." He carefully tucked the blade away in his belt and added, "You don't like it, but you know everything that has taken place is all by the design of whatever race of gods pilot these marvelous little tools of heka."

Ariennu screwed up her mouth as if she wanted to scream, then decided to spit at his highness foot.

Marai sensed it and stayed her with a gesture. *Easy, woman. Don't provoke.*

Damn him, Marai. He's summoned N'ahab's ghost with that knife. I swear! I stole the damned thing for him when we were just children and he carved out the goddess legs for it to fit in. Do something to him before I get myself killed doing it for you! Ariennu bowed her head, then grasped Djerah's hands to keep herself from launching her fists at the prince.

"And that worries you, doesn't it?" the prince addressed Marai and Ari but at that moment…

Naibe hurriedly fastened her straps and jumped up from her bed to leave the tent. She froze when Maatkare spoke again.

"Go on, and when you've made your water, get your sister and the little ones in the box. I was just going to ask that she come join us this morning."

Naibe looked up at the guard by the tent flap and with a little hop speeding her step, she hurried to the blanket shrouded privy constructed for the women and then to the opening of the royal tent.

Marai saw Deka meet her, then silently return with her as if she had been waiting for a signal. As soon as both women entered the women's tent, the Ta-Seti woman took her place beside the prince.

Deka, Marai attempted, but she didn't respond. He knew she heard him, but understood she felt it was safer to wall her thoughts from him. Yesterday, when he had first seen her, the lack of response hadn't caused such a great ache in his heart. When she assisted in Djerah's healing, he had thought she was reaching out to him. Today, when he sensed the nothingness, something about it scared him.

Deka, Nefira Sekhet Deka. At least show *you can feel me, h*e tried again, because he had always been able to feel the women's energy unless it was being actively blocked by external forces. Their inner voices had always joined the chorus of the Children's voices as if they were speaking in a hushed, singsong cadence. Even Djerah's music had started to whisper faintly through his own newly implanted stone. A wall existed in Deka's heart when the sojourner sought any sort of feeling in her hard dark eyes.

Deka, please... his glance was at once desperate and sad. *How did I... how did we ever fail you so that you could completely cut us out? You know your stone weeps. I can feel her weep at the apartness from the rest of us. Know that.* He felt ill. Maatkare's self-pleased smirk didn't help. He felt his self-control over the rage that had been building inside him over the weeks of his journey erode even more each moment the prince and Deka remained seated near him.

Naibe-Ellit sensed Marai's anguish as she sat beside him again. She embraced his shoulders and lay her head on them in sympathy.

She hears you, my best love, Marai felt her thoughts solemnly whisper. I knew about it long ago; from the time you and I first loved... maybe even when I looked into the past that was hidden from her. She can't come with us now. Maybe she will come back to us one day and maybe not. She just needs to be apart from us now.

The prince sensed Deka's turmoil in the silence and grasped her hand firmly. That touch woke her for a moment. She reached into the air, even though her head stayed bowed. An affectionate little spark danced from her fingertips to Marai's stone.

"Would you *like* to go with him; to take the son of my body from us?" Maatkare noticed the gesture she had given. The lack of emotion in his steady gaze switched to a moment of glaring cruelty. An almost doggish whine became spirit and moved through the air.

Hurt Puppy? That's affection? Strange. And she's with child too? I didn't sense that one, Marai saw his surprise mirrored in Ariennu's and Naibe's faces.

A child? Naibe thoughts were happy at first, but Marai sensed that her second thought was about what kind of demon would come screeching from between Deka's legs in some months. She shuddered, patting her own restless belly.

Marai knew she was still worried that her own child might not be his, so he whispered: *It's* my *child, my goddess. Your little one sang it to me last night. And even if it was not, I would love it because you made it and brought it forth.*

Feeling her shiver in delight at that thought calmed his irritation at the prince for the moment.

Ariennu fussed over Djerah again as if he had become all of the children she had given up so long ago.

No," Deka's voice hesitated, but then moved ahead. "Nothing has changed in the night, as you have questioned, beloved." She answered the prince, then turned to Marai.

"My place is here with *him*, Man-Sun. So long ago I told you I wanted to know who I am. You *knew* this. When I am *his*, I know it. I'm glad you live for my sister's sake and even mine, but I am unchanged in my destiny." She looked for solace in Maatkare's face, but seeing it unmoved, opened the box of Child Stones and picked up the fine cloth wrapper from the top.

She reverently lifted Wserkaf's crystal Eye of Truth wdjat, then looked up once again into Marai's eyes. Her dark, slim hand gestured above the stones, summoning the seven that had been separated at one time. They rose and slipped into her cupped hands. The pulse from them as they nestled among each other on her palm caused her to shiver as if she had been gripped in ecstasy.

Marai knew they were sending her a private message.

"If I give these to you now, as a promise that we will all be together in time, will you release me?" she asked the big man plaintively, eyes looking directly at him. At the same time those eyes stared a thousand leagues away.

"If you *must* have three women, seek another, my sweetest Man-Sun. It was always the Children's intent that I be parted from you when I arrived in Ta-Seti. Did you not see it? I had hoped you would not grieve when that day came." Her mouth moved as if she recited something out of a ritual.

"It is why I could not allow you in my bed or to make me a child. I could not let you know the deepest part of my heart," Her eyes closed as if the words of her truth had been a kind of farewell.

Marai felt something in his thoughts explode. He knew Deka had said these things several times, but he had always thought it was her way of setting herself apart from Naibe's sensuality and Ariennu's brash attitude. He always assumed the four of them would come to her beloved ancestral home and then search for whatever she needed to know together.

This is wrong, Deka. You know it is. You let this man overtake you like a thief and now you swear by him as if your soul has died. I see that. But leave us? Always intended it? Then you should say out loud that you used *us and that you used the Children of Stone as well.* He felt the dark rage he had battled settle at the top of his shoulders and move up the base of his neck the way he had felt it grow when the shape of the war bull Bakha Montu moved through him in Hordjedtef's plaza and later at Wserkaf's home. It had lurked and whispered like a clinging evil entity. It patiently repeated for him to strike and murder all of the evildoers throughout his entire journey. It wanted him to see and act on everything this grinning and self-assured prince had done as it dropped the masks that the Children of Stone had kept over the worst of moments.

In one instant, he saw Ariennu released from the ladder on the prince's boat; the way she had crawled to him and begged for Naibe's life while he sneered at her. He saw Naibe in such dread of being drained by him that she decided to drown herself in an escape attempt. In all of the newly unmasked truth, he sensed Deka in the background, never opposing or defending her sisters in kind.

Marai lunged and knocked Maatkare backward to the mat-lined earth so quickly the prince never suspected him. The sojourner felt his own transformation roaring through perceived reality as he locked the man's head in the crook of his arm. His face went dark and the specter of the bull shape emerged. His other hand, now more hoof-like, pushed up and wrenched in attempt to snap the prince's neck.

Maatkare growled, fought and snarled, gnashing his suddenly sharp fangs and slavering jaws.

Go on! Be the wolf. But I have your throat, so it's just you. No cry for your men while I rip out your throat. He crushed the prince's throat and felt the gristle beneath the cords of muscle and tendon start to give way. *Too easy, but I want it to be slow so you will suffer and know the way you choked my goddess to draw her power. You can't breathe. You have to give up your power before you die,* Marai's thoughts hissed deep into the young general's conscience.

Maatkare dug his heels into the earth and sank his claws into Marai's arm. He hit, struggled and tried to free himself from the devastating grip as the defiant growls in his throat became hideous gurgles. His lips frothed and eyes blazed an angry gold.

The men's struggle spilled, thrashing and kicking around the woven mats as the prince bit, gnawed and tore through Marai's forearm like a mad dog. The sojourner barely felt his skin rip open as his grip tightened and crushed into his opponent's thrashing throat. Maatkare's wolf-image briefly fled then re-formed with greater power, as the fight continued.

"You stop this now! For the love of the goddess, don't do this, either one of you!" Ariennu screamed, leaping to her feet and darting in to the fray. She pulled Maatkare's head back and tugged on Marai's profusely bleeding arm but the men were locked in a struggle she had little power to stop.

Deka raised both hands in the defensive pose of an utterance, but stayed in her place on the mat, guarding the box of Child Stones.

"Don't you even think about it, or I will tear both of your arms out of the sockets." Ariennu whirled, then turned to press on Marai's collarbone to numb his wounded arm just as he made a final push on Maatkare's throat.

Astonished, Marai felt his grip loosen involuntarily. He noticed the pain and the blood that gushed from the torn and jagged skin on his forearm, then glanced at Maatkare who fell face forward on the scrambled mats. He clutched his crushed throat and gasped for air, unable to breathe or speak. Marai jumped up and began to kick him hard in the ribs and once under his chin that had begun to half-heartedly transform into a muzzle again. He was about to fall on him once more when Deka hissed and began to crawl forward, eyes glowing red.

Ariennu glared at her, then focused on a way to stop Marai herself. She leapt on his broad back and called into his ear:

It's over.

You've won.

You kill him and he wins

You shame him. That's enough for now.

Hardly pausing to realize that she had used something like her own version of a voice of power, she pulled the big man back until he sat on his heels and began to shake his silver head. He snorted and gave a softened bellow of acceptance, then settled into a more human shape.

When she saw that the worst appeared to be over, Ariennu slipped away and seized the wdjat as well as the seven stones that hovered nervously in midair above the box. She snatched them out of the air the way one might grab at flying insects, and put them in her skirt, then edged over to hold Marai away from any further challenges.

Maatkare sprawled back with his hands at his throat. He gasped from lack of air and his face darkened as if Marai still strangled him.

Deka reached the prince and gently licked Marai's blood from his lips and face, then held him and rocked him, until she felt his deep shuddering gasp, cough, and rasping breath begin again. Then, licking her own lips in joy, she placed her hands on his throat to warm and heal it.

Marai gripped the jagged edges of the wound on his arm together and winced. His stone had leapt into prominence and a shimmer of silver light cascaded over his face and down to his bleeding forearm. The bull form lurked in the corner of his conscience and projected forward intermittently over his human form.

Ariennu laid her hand on his wound and warmed it the way she had seen Marai heal Djerah.

Deka didn't even attempt to hide the thoughts she sent to Maatkare from everyone else.

You have prevailed against a god and been undefeated. You have the victory, she peppered his throat with little kisses until the prince stopped gasping and solemnly rubbed his half-crushed throat. *See. He bleeds like a man. Kiss my mouth with his blood, beloved. Give me his taste.*

"Ari. Let me go. You *know* he needs to die," Marai grunted and pressed the lips of his wound together so it could seal itself.

"No please. The Children don't…" by this time Naibe clustered near him. She soothed him in her own gentle way.

"Damn the Children, then! None of this should have happened," he grumbled. Deka looked up in shock.

Naibe and Ariennu gripped Marai and restrained him with all of their energy. He was more than ready to launch a thunderbolt of deadly will that would collapse the prince's throat without his even touching it.

Maatkare grabbed his swollen neck, feeling the tightness and choking resume, then hoarsely mouthed the words of control, "Een…" and coughed.

"Has no effect on me, wretch," Marai started but paused as the voices of the Children whispered in their own rhyme:

Cease and calm.
You will die
And he will die

OPENER OF THE SKY

But not today.

Marai felt the terse voice of what he thought was the Akaru filter through the subsiding stone in his brow. That shocked him, because he knew the elder, though chosen, was not a host of the Children of Stone. The puzzled expressions on the women's and children's faces showed him they all shared the recited verse.

Both men exchanged stares of dull hatred, slowly eclipsed by a kind of admiration for each other's strength.

"Very well…" the prince coughed, still unable to say more than one or two words at a time. He rubbed his bruised throat. Deka immediately comforted him, shooting a more than irritated glance at the sojourner.

You… If you care anything about me, Man Sun…

As Deka caressed and consoled the prince, Marai began to see a very different radiance of desire and hunger displayed in her actions.

Ari is right. She has changed. It's as if she feeds on our struggle, denies it to herself and then finds great joy that her words brought my wrath when I have always wished only happiness for my goddesses. He reflected; looked at the newly sealed jagged pink line on his flesh and then shut his eyes once more to think about the Ta-Seti woman.

Marai had seen the ominous darkness in Deka's face many times. Like the entity that hovered over his own soul that first day he emerged, it had stripped her of any physical affection for him when they first woke in the vessel. It had lurked just over her shoulder like some dark imp that whispered to her in a shared private language. When he and Naibe-Ellit had ripped the sky open with their passion, the night they lay beside the way station well, Deka had entered the young woman's ecstasy in a way that nearly frightened her out of her wits. The day Wserkaf had followed them to their apartment and pranked them with a love charm, that same energy had nearly claimed Naibe again.

So… it wasn't Hordjedtef or the priests who tried to kill Naibe. It was you, Deka. You said you couldn't remember your past. I think you lied, but most of all you lie to yourself every day. Now, your prince's heka just unmasks it for the rest of us. Does he even know? He thinks you are swooning over his position, his sexual skill, and his excellent appearance. What is it about you in reality?

Deka's face looked up, surprised and oddly innocent of the dire accusations Marai had heaped on her. Her finger coyly went to her lips and to her stone as if she was saying: *Shhh… don't tell…*

Maatkare sat, his expression defiant, as if he dared Marai to mention their scuffle to the mysteriously unaware men outside the tent.

Ari. You clouded this, didn't you? It's why you had to stop us before they noticed and came in to help. Marai checked the wound again to see if it was fully sealed then twisted his forearm back and forth to make sure he had its full use.

The two men continued to sulk and stare at each other in a kind of quiet respect.

Marai turned his attention to the Ta-Seti woman as she nurtured her fallen hero and shot the occasional hurt glance at her returned husband.

So, this really is a rift in us, Deka? Is it truly by the Children's design? Marai wondered.

Deka sensed Marai's thoughts, then turned her gaze away from the prince for a moment.

One day you will see. Brown Eyes was right about me… and you are very, very wrong about my beloved. We are born of the same spirit. Leave us to each other.

Naibe stared quietly at Deka as if she had asked her one more silent question. The woman shivered, then gazed at the prince as if her adoring glance at him could blot out any thoughts the young woman sent to her.

Marai bowed his head, still unable to process the idea that Deka had chosen to go her own way. He touched Naibe's arm as if to say: *You told me to leave her alone. Now I tell you the same thing.* He knew Naibe had opened another secret in Deka's heart and the woman didn't like it.

My Love. There are things… strange things in my heart. I had to provoke it.

Marai sensed her thoughts retract, just as a favor to him. He distracted himself from that thought and watched the skin on his arm assume a deeply tanned color. In the near distance, Deka caressed Maatkare's neck and throat in her own healing manner. The sojourner stood up and stretched a little, even though the prince had not given him permission to do so. He recalled too many moments when he had reached out to the woman of Ta-Seti, and was misunderstood. Now he moved quietly past the couple, turning only once to glare in disgust at the prince before he fastened his gaze out of the opening of the tent. Looking at them petting each other as they sat together was still too painful.

Deka rose, leaving Maatkare for a moment to join the sojourner at the tent opening. She took the box of stones with her, then placed her hand gently on his arm. The touch of her sensitive hand was almost too much.

"I can't believe you're really going to stay, but you are, aren't you?" he turned and looked down at her deep green/brown eyes. They softened for a moment. All of the coldness and hardness melted. *So gentle her eyes. It is too much, h*e looked away, feeling the pit of his stomach knot and sink.

"I must, gentle Marai, my only Man Sun," her sweet, low voice soothed him. "Believe me when I say there is nothing you have done to drive me from you. All of you have been so good to me, but this is what I have longed for. I wish to be here in the place of my birth. Don't you want that happiness for me? That peace? That I be happy and find peace?" She stared at her hands for a moment then looked up again. "You take the Eye of Truth to the priest. It's his. Take the seven and five more to lock a promise to it..." she handed five more of the stones to Marai. The five stones glimmered in the slightly concave shape.

"Just thought..." Marai shook his head, dismayed. Naibe came to him and threw her arms around him, understanding his grief. For one moment, he looked back and perceived the prince's expression as one of smug satisfaction.

Marai knew something was desperately wrong about her staying with the prince. The rhythm of the Children of Stone's music had suddenly hit a sour note that played into an irritating chord. *Deka shouldn't be staying,* he kept telling himself. *This is one journey, not five separate ones. She seems so sure of herself... more than ever and yet resigned to some invisible, uncontrollable thing.* He wanted to say a thousand things to her, to somehow wake her up from the strange dream-state into which she had fallen, but nothing he thought of saying made sense.

She moved back toward the prince, her statement to Marai complete.

"Your Highness" he made himself look at the couple again.

Maatkare rose to draw Deka away from the sojourner, then turned with more than a little disgust on his sullen face, as if Marai had been thoroughly rude to call after him once more.

"What now?" he snarled. Deka enclosed the stones that would remain in the box, then turned to regard him lovingly. "Don't congratulate yourself on a victory, sojourner," he looked back over his shoulder as Marai returned to Djerah's area. "The women pulled us apart… and we *let* them do it. If there's a next time…"

"I doubt there will be," Marai quipped. "It will still be up to you to treat your Nefira Deka, as you call her, with the best of care. You seem to think that just because you have her now, and because she feels she must stay with you, that you own her." He raised a forefinger and quietly winked at the woman on the prince's arm.

Deka shivered in delight, but froze, fighting Maatkare noticing the feeling of pleasure that swept her.

"It's just not true, Highness. She is *still* a host to a Child Stone and linked to us because of it."

Maatkare froze as if he hadn't truly considered what that might mean in the long view of things. His mouth opened in surprise, then snapped shut.

"You should go now, Nefira," he nodded. "You've said your piece. Wait for me in our tent."

Deka hesitated for an instant, but then slipped out of the women's tent and to the royal tent without pausing or looking back again.

No. Deka stay… Marai sent his own lament but it only stirred Maatkare into turning toward him; his hand gently caressing the wolf head pommel of the beautiful knife in his belt.

The sojourner shook his head at the implied threat, delighted that he had flattened the prince so quickly in the fight that he hadn't drawn the knife. He was suddenly inspired to add another layer of insult.

"So what will you want of her when you return to your home and to your wife and children? What becomes of the child in Deka's belly, who you already know will become mighty because of what *she* is?" He waited for realization to dawn on his princely adversary.

Maatkare's broad shoulders twitched as if he wanted to 'correct' the perceived challenge but thought better of it as Marai continued.

"Will those enthroned now welcome her as goddess, or will they conspire against her as they once did with me? Will you find you must turn usurper and unleash the Children of Stone you have taken to help you spill the blood of your *own* kin?"

The prince's face twisted in disgust, but he took in everything the big man said. He mulled over the last part, then shook his head and bent to pick up his nemes, which had come off during the scuffle. He put it on his head and answered:

"None of this is your concern… and… your welcome here has run out. I assure you that the stones I'm keeping will be given to my cousin, eventually." His eyes resumed an emotionless expression as he lifted the tent flap to leave, adding: "Gather your things and go… all of you, before my feelings on the matter change. My men will see you to the edge of camp without harm. If your man isn't well enough to travel, it's still not my problem because my wish for him was death and it still stands. He is still unpunished and will be turned in on my return if the lot of you are foolish enough to remain in our land."

Naibe scurried to Marai and half-clung, half-pulled him away from going after the prince.

When the guards saw Deka leave the tent with an anxious look on her face, they massed outside the flap to wait for the prince's command. He beckoned to his remaining personal guard and gave orders that by mid-afternoon, when the sojourners left, the men were to fell and reset the tent as an additional room for his own housing. Then, as an afterthought, he looked back into the women's tent at Marai.

"So it would seem that you are somewhat wise after all. In different circumstances I might have tolerated you. My grandfather misjudged you, except that he knew you were young to your skills and not one of you were seasoned. Still, you're not just some dust wizard to be contained or routed for daring upon the sacred mysteries. My advice? Turn in the Wdjat and the twelve stones you have and then leave Ineb-Hedj as well, because I'll speak to his Majesty on my…" Maatkare suddenly recognized Marai's eyes silvering almost imperceptibly.

"Dead? When?" he asked, suddenly pale and so internally upset that Marai heard his next thoughts:

I should have felt him passing by. These women must have known about it and blocked it from me.

"You knew, didn't you? Nefira did not, but I can feel you two had all manner of secrets, didn't you?" Maatkare glanced at Ari briefly, then toed the earth at the opening of the tent.

Ariennu had risen from Djerah, who had lapsed into sleep again. Marai scooped her into his other arm and looked down at her, amazed.

"Me?" she protested. "How could I know if *you* didn't?" her eyes sought Marai for a moment. "I didn't know *you* were alive, Marai… not until you walked into the tent last afternoon," her glance moved back to the prince, whose expression showed he didn't believe a word of her story.

"I believe that part," Marai spoke out. "I tried to contact them, but something or someone blocked me until I neared your camp," the sojourner affirmed. "Majesty died two days before the ten days of my journey here on the very night I awakened from my *supposed* death. They were already gone."

"Humph…" Maatkare began again, this time glancing at Ari. "I guess your healing powers were as dim as your otherworld sight too, then, if you and the young one working together could not lift the curse laid on him. I believe he had reached the end of the six year rule granted him by the oracle of Buto. There was likely little to do about it."

"Then perhaps, you should search the Child Stones you have for your answer." Marai absent mindedly rubbed Ariennu's arm, but shot a glance back at Djerah. "Be careful when you look, though."

"Meaning?" the prince asked but Marai found himself more interested in Djerah's symptoms than in adding barbs to his royal host.

He's too weak to get to Qustul, unless I carry him. No option really. Every moment I stay it gets worse… every word I speak, dangerous. Too tempting, though.

"You *do* know that it was your grandfather who brought your king down once he arranged for the women to go away with you, don't you?"

"I'm listening," the prince paused, but looked outside to see that his men were not idling. When he turned back, he fondled the hilt of the knife.

"Your Great One wanted my ladies out of Ineb-Hedj and away from King Menkaure because he needed to work his own design privately. They were getting too close to His Majesty and they knew about how his daughter *really* died. I'm sure he felt there was no choice left, if you were to ever ascend."

Marai felt a satisfied smile creep across his lips just as incredible darkness crossed the young prince's face.

"Last night, you even dreamt about it, didn't you? I can learn much through this, if Deka is with you when a dream comes…" The sojourner tapped the place on his brow where his silvery stone lay as he drank in Maatkare's slow seethe of rage and the pain of his sudden vulnerability.

"She couldn't send me a dream if she had no idea of the truth," the prince grumbled, but his eyes shifted downward, deflecting. "Princess Khentkawes has told plenty of lies about it in the past because some errant mouth opened to her, but she was not there either," he snarled. "The old ka-reen jumped. She took her own life just to ruin me after she discovered she couldn't command me *or* suck out my soul. It's known. It's recorded as a suicide."

Ariennu held out the twelve glimmering stones. She had taken the other seven out of her belt and perched them all in Wserkaf's wdjat.

"Oh, Really?" she chuckled.

The stones gently hushed at the prince. Their echo bounced off of the gold in his new dagger so that it glimmered and the slurred sound of his own very drunk voice echoed in everyone's ears.

Just a little push.

"Seems you were about to shout it from the rail yourself the night I was hauled out of there. You know it was, because you told me yourself what happened; not Wserkaf *or* his wife." Ariennu snorted, indignantly. "And Little One was taken because we worked as one through our Child Stones; a threat to your grandfather's plans for you because his Majesty liked us so much."

"Leave me…" Maatkare shaded his eyes. "Go back to Qustul and to the old man. You tell him, too, that I know of his plans for rebellion. He'd better put a leash on his men in two weeks when I'm ready to come through. If I see anyone coming here, they will be shot by my bow masters before they clear the ridge, no questions asked. I *should* arrive back in time for the funeral, but understand this matter between us is *not* finished. You both have assaulted and tried to murder a prince" he spun around with his back to Marai and the two women. "My men just have orders not to harm you as you leave, but I'm about to change my thoughts and have you chased down like bad animals. All I have to do is just to take your heads from your necks and you will die like any mortal. Then the stones will come out rather easily, don't you think? And don't think I won't be able to do it one day," he stomped toward the royal tent.

"Damn You. Not if I get to you first," Ari started to leap after the prince, but Marai stayed her.

"Don't. Just let him go. Like he said, it isn't over," the big man turned from the flap and went to check on Djerah.

Ariennu stood for a moment, in more than a little stunned rage until Naibe took her hand.

"We'd better see about him too," she indicated Marai who now looked up at them both. His eyes had grown sad, even though he tried to hide it.

Ari. Come here woman, his thoughts spoke as gently as a caress. *And bring the little ones we still have. See if we can give him some strength for the travel. He's not doing that well.*

CHAPTER 28: THE UNQUIET FUTURE

"Well that's that, I suppose," Marai rubbed the back of his neck, profoundly disappointed. "I still…" he started, but he finally began to realize along with Ariennu and Naibe that the attempt to free Deka from the prince's grasp had failed. They had only succeeded in causing Maatkare to evict them from his camp and Djerah was in no shape to travel.

"Maybe it's for the best; getting away from him *and* her for a while," Ariennu ran her forefinger over the tops of the stones resting in the cup of the wdjat. "I've known her longer than any of us, I guess. Old Chibale pulled her into my camp on a chain a life ago, but *he* was the one who was a slave. Maybe that's what's really going on with them."

"That would make as much sense as anything else," Marai shrugged. "I just thought we were all supposed to…" sadness filtered over him again.

"Then she'll be back," Naibe affirmed. "It works out. I was certain you were dead, my love, and the fates returned you. Djerah was dead and now…"

A sound came from Deka's old mat where Djerah lay. Three pairs of eyes snapped down at him.

"Let's just go." Djerah spoke just above a whisper. He struggled to raise himself up on his elbows.

"Oh, look at you, handsome man…" Ariennu instantly handed the wdjat to the sojourner, shocked at the young man's weakness even though he tried to sit. She looked up at Marai and solemnly shook her head.

There's no way, Marai. Moving him now will kill him for good this time. D'you think the Children could…

Marai knelt by the young man and checked his face. He knew what Ari was asking. 'Could the Children work a different outcome?'

No and no. he shook his head. *Nothing makes sense except leaving as soon as possible. You know that in your heart,* his eyes confided.

The edges of the black and red areas on Djerah's face had begun to turn green and yellow. They were still badly disfigured and fluids oozed from the corners of his eyes and out of one nostril. His nose had emerged from some of the swelling but it looked different; no longer as wide as it had been. His eyes glimmered a deep metallic bluish color with the dark centers shifting and contracting unevenly as if they were going through a routine of adjustments. His hair had thinned and some of his brownish black curls were shedding on the surface of the linen where his head had rested.

Wasn't the shape it was last night… or the one he came with. More like mine, not so much Kemet. Ari's right. It's too soon. He ought to be sleeping undisturbed. Marai set his lips and thought about the hot journey overland back to Amani Suph Qustul. Whether the young man was put on a drag or whether he was carried, it would be dangerous. He wondered if somehow another stronger healing session could take place before they had to move.

"Just go. Get ready, Marai. I'll rest at the lion master's. I can feel… can feel…" the young man faded and sagged to the mat, clearly weaker from his attempt to communicate.

"I'll read his thoughts," Naibe had joined Marai and Ariennu. Her hand extended to the young man's brow as if her touch could still him. "His stone has found out something. It's told him we *have* to go. What you said about the dead princess upset Maatkare, Ari." Her eyes sought Marai's next, then fell, "and now he knows about poor Menkaure Khaket, too."

Marai already knew they would have to move Djerah or deal with the prince sending the regiment after them. The longer the prince thought about letting them go, the more likely he would perceive his men thinking he had been defeated. When that thought combined with the sense that Akaru's men who would want revenge for the killing of the boys who had come with Djerah *and* the thought of his own future after the death of the king, he would feel much less in control of his life. He would predictably lash out at them in some way if they were still nearby.

Seek shelter by the water
But first under a hill

Then many circuits of your sun-star
In the King's peace
Healing proceeds

Djerah opened one eye again. He lifted his hand weakly and touched his brow to examine the edges of the puffy mound around his newly settling Child Stone.

"I think I can go," he whispered again, but his voice sounded weaker.

"Let me go talk to his Highness," Ari suggested, looking at the still flap of the tent. She heard men moving around outside.

As if he had heard a silent signal, the tall guard stuck his head through the flap. A haughty look spread over his face.

"What do you want?" Ari snapped.

"Checking to see if you are getting your things together, ka't." He used the common term for her, when earlier the worst he had ever voiced was a terse 'woman'. "His Highness wants an afternoon foray. You should at least *try* to give him some sport…" he chortled.

That implied their worries had been correct. He had openly considered giving them chase, perhaps just to finish Djerah and Marai, once they had been gone for some moments.

"Oh we *are* getting ready, but if it had been in my power our new brother would have brought *you* down, and not your partner. He was always the one who was nicer to me… and better with my body than you ever were… *tiny el*," she spat.

"I'm going to enjoy riding you with my spear when I catch up to you…" The man took a step to slap her, but Marai waved him away.

Ari. Walk away. Don't say anything to him, Marai projected his thoughts as the man left, then nodded to Naibe. "How long will it take to get everything rounded up?"

"We have our baskets. That's all. Deka's things are already in the other tent, except for her mat where Djee is lying. Maybe we'll make a drag with it for the parts that aren't so rocky." Naibe looked around the area to see if anything had been kicked into the far corners when the men fought. "He isn't setting an escape trap for us, is he?" her eyes widened as she gathered anything she saw and plopped it in any available basket. Things could be sorted later.

Marai remained at Djerah's side. He touched and continued breathing out healing energy on the various bruised and wounded places, in hopes of speeding up the process a little. He sensed re-doing a healing with the Children of Stone would be too much for the young man to tolerate in his weakened state. His actions now were to simply strengthen him for the journey.

"Prince Maatkare's fight is with me; pure and simple. He knows I almost beat him. He's tough though, and has some mighty skills… but he's not used to anything other than winning. He'd likely fight without honor if he felt there was an advantage to it," Marai looked Naibe in the eyes when she passed by him, then reached up to grasp her hand in a comforting gesture. "He just *might* be giving us time to move and then planning to tighten the circle and jump us once no help can come to us. I don't think he would follow us into Qustul Amani though… even fully armed. Metauthetep is seen as a holy man up and down the river. His warriors will be mad enough. He wouldn't be advised to lance *that* boil."

"I won't die. Won't risk…" Djerah's voice weakly trailed. His hand raised to beckon Marai closer.

Can you send a thought? Marai silently asked. *It should be easier for you than it was before you got yourself hurt like this.* Try not to speak aloud until you are stronger.

"They told me…" he spoke softly, as if he hadn't heard the big man. "I must go before the hot day. Rest under a hill. There's a cave there where we were waiting. I remember that now," his bandaged head fell back to the padding as if that many words had been more than he could bear.

He is stronger, Marai realized. *Child Stone is working fast, but it's doing strange things to him.*

"You rest. I'll put you on the sled with the baskets. When we get out of the grass to the hill, I'll carry you." He patted the young man's shoulder and turned to see if he could tighten the bundles the women were making.

The Children of Stone are opening something new, he thought. *Maybe Deka stays, then. Maybe she comes later. Don't know…* Marai knew that, but he couldn't shake the thought that something had still gone very wrong. *Even the Children*, he thought, must have taken a step back in wonder of these new lotus petals that have suddenly fallen away.

Prince Maatkare made certain Deka stayed in the tent while a heavy guard followed Marai, Djerah, and the women away from the camp. The five sojourners moved quietly into the grass before the sun was at its highest point. The prince watched her fidget, sigh, and once or twice he thought she might get up and chase after them. As they left the camp, he lay on his bed deep in thought, but didn't beckon to the Ta-Seti woman. Instead, he let her pace back and forth until his guard came back without them and stated the sojourners had passed the line of trees at the base of the hills he called the North Ridge.

Unless she can truly fly, she won't catch up to them now, he mused.

For a long time, he left her standing by the tent flap. After a while, he motioned for her to come to him. She turned, but when she did he noticed the quiet pain in her eyes.

"You've done the right thing. I'm proud of you, Nefira," his smile was sly and tinged with just the right amount of seduction.

She came to the bed and reached down to take his extended hand.

He held it for a moment, then tugged her closer. Bringing her hand to his lips, he kissed her knuckles tenderly. "You are so strong and brave; as a goddess should be…" he chuckled, pleased. "Now sit, rest your heart. When you have rested, go forth with me among the men as my esteemed companion."

She gingerly sat, then lay curled against his chest; her fingers spread out over it. For long moments, she smoothed his hard, deep muscles, but he said nothing. Whenever she started to speak, he hushed her with silent words, but on another level he grew increasingly worried about the things the man Marai had told him. Even though it was before the heat of the day, the men dropped the former women's tent and re-assembled it into a palatial extension with all of the accompanying racket of post hammering, rope strapping, shouting, and occasional laughs peppered with curses. He needed her to sleep so he could sort things out.

OPENER OF THE SKY

I sense your troubled heart, Nefira... your heavy choice. Een saphara, my sweetness, een saphara. All the layers of your heart must rest: ReKaBaSa all. He gently kissed her hands and waved his fingers over her until she fell into an exhausted sleep. *Good. Sleep now.*

He eased from beneath the woman, rose, and quietly drew a cool linen up over her shoulders. After he made sure the box of stones were stowed safely under the bed, he sauntered across the dark-but-warm interior of the tent, dipped up a cup of beer, and looked out to see if the extra tent room was being constructed properly. Nodding his approval, he sat in his camp chair to rest and think before going out to survey the hills. Other men would be returning soon from with news of any further trouble and a report on the counting of the dead from yesterday's failed coup. In the meantime, he could think about his future.

So Red Sister and young Naibe think my grandfather hastened the king's death? Wonder if anyone else suspects? Wse wouldn't dare! He's too loyal and he has too much to lose as rising Great One. Red Ari only thinks she heard me drunk-talking about Princess Meryt and she herself was almost laid out full that night, as I recall. No one can prove such a thing. The dream I had shows me it was a game gone wrong, anyway. Everyone in the Hedj knows my temper well enough and if they think hard about it they can just as easily remember how that ka-reen came to disrespect me and try my patience. He sipped his beer, pulled a little on his lower lip, and continued to think about how this man Marai suddenly being alive and the spirit skills the women had demonstrated might have the potential of up-ending his plans.

A temper I have, but, by the gods, people listen to me. When they don't... Why am I troubling myself? Meryt's been dead nearly seven years, he mused. *Now Menkaure has joined her, and what the dead have to say is only open to the best of interpretation.* Maatkare raised a brow, knowing he certainly had enough wealth to ensure good readings.

The king loved me once, because he knew I could put a fire back in his line and quench the one that burned in his daughter's belly at the same time. His own bodily son wasn't up to the task, before he died. And Shepseskaf, the concubine's son, always hid behind Bunefer and Khen's skirts. If this tale gets another round of telling and more believers, I'll be lucky if I even get Nekhen when the old man dies, or worse the title will go to my aunt's useless sons.

Grandfather Dede knew all of this. It's very likely some crazed fable from Wse's wife again. What did grandfather have to gain in ending the king? His own comeuppance? Madness... he crept to the bed, opened the box of stones, and found the small green stone he had handled before, then held it up to the light that streamed through the vent at the top of the tent.

What will you tell me if I ask you and your brothers something new? Will you sing to me of Nefira? Should I have turned her out with the rest, or does me holding her and the rest of you as well respected hostages insure for my greater future?

Two sons, a daughter…
More disguised as other's children

Maatkare pondered the sound of a small voice that had not come from the stone, as he expected it might. The green stone lay as if soulless in the palm of his hand. Deka slept soundly on his bed. He knew it couldn't have been *her* dream voice. His hand went up in a protective gesture.

I dispel you, spirit, he whispered into the air. *Don't pollute my thinking.* He didn't know what had spoken, but it manifested as a male and brought up another point. He *did* have children, claimed and unclaimed.

Nefira Deka carries my child too. Has even named it Ameny. She says it's a son who will surpass even my own deeds. I would love to see that indeed when I look down from my Boat of Stars one day. I have to think about placing this Ameny ahead of my young Senurepet, Sadeh's boy. Not a bad child… but she spoils both him, his sister Tena-maat, and little Raemetre rotten. She is a commoner. Nefira claims divinity, if we locate her family. It will still be hard any way around if I have no true claim to the throne. He glanced at Deka, tracing a symbol of pleasure in the air so she would know he wanted her to dream of him, when in truth, his thoughts were leagues away.

Wse's wife has the marriage pact with Shepseskaf. If something were to happen to him… he paused, suddenly enlightened. *Oh, well then… that's a plan.* Maatkare envisioned a naughty consummation of that marriage. *I would see old Princess Khen scream in joy of me just to spite the vanity of her dear, but straying Wserkaf.* He snickered almost loudly enough to wake Deka. *And then here are such rich fantasies that I giggle like a dim-witted maid catching her superiors in the rut. I need clarity.*

Maatkare crouched by the bed again and took the box that held the rest of the stones out from under it. He went to the front of the tent where there was a little more light, then sat cross-legged on the soft skin rug. As soon as he opened it, he felt Deka move to his side and gently whisper ethereal encouragement.

Beloved Raem… learn from these, her voice lulled and enchanted him sweetly.

He looked back at the bed, but saw she lay asleep in her spellbound nap. Even though she slept, her thoughts and memories were there in spirit, ready to join his vision. As he concentrated on the emptiness needed for clear vision, he saw her wandering in a grey mist, lost in her own dream as if she waited for him.

See me. See the goddess in me. Do you, mere man, bend your knee? She requested.

He shook himself and stared at the glimmering box of stones, caught between being taken aback and mildly insulted, but didn't answer the spirit voice.

She won't start putting on airs just because I chose her… he returned to his meditation.

Her wandering human form faded from his vision, then began to transform into some kind of bird…

Vulture, Maatkare whispered to himself, but the thought of her having *anything* to do with the goddess Mut, panicked him until his zeal for learning took over. As his vision continued, her spirit flanked him like his twin. She was lion to his wolf, like Sekhmet, or the Flame of Menhit, who danced for the First Ones. *Ta-Seti-ta-Netjer.* When he spoke the words, magic engulfed her. *Powerful,* his thoughts whispered as he brought to his memory their first night together.

I thought to take you quickly in the alley, leave you when I was done, but your body cried for me to go slow. I came to you as a wolf, attacking in the night, yet something about you made me like a docile pup, lapping your feet and begging for the sweet. He had wakened something in her and now she was returning the favor by waking him up.

Ha-go-re! Akh-go-re Nejter Deka Nefer Sekht
My name is sung ever-present
Though I am here.
I fly to you, I come
On dark but burning wings I walk on air
Open the sky to me

Ha-go-re Ta-te

They were flying, hand in hand. Her burning breath wreaked havoc on the earth.

I bear the standard of war before you, he whispered as if it was a prayer. *I rain my arrows down on the unrepentant… I am the slayer… to your Avenger… You, as high goddess promote me as king.* He fell to one side, gasping and faint from the dizzying thought of it.

"Raem? Are you well? You shouted in a dream." Deka was awake. She hustled to him in his chair, then nestled close to him and drew her knees up to her chin so sweetly, as if she was still a little girl. He looked at her, but suddenly saw a woman whose youth had been stolen far too long ago. The red and black shadows that had filled the tent slowly dissipated as his trance vision cleared.

She helped him sit, then showed him that the stones in the box had begun to glow red like a pool of luminous blood. Passing her slim cinnamon-colored hands over them, she turned her palms up in a receptive gesture.

Your face. Maatkare didn't notice her hands. He saw the way she smiled demurely as the fire of the stones ascended to light her face in a rosy glow, then shot a brilliant blue-turquoise shadow in hollows of her cheeks. Her hair fanned out like a dark cloud in an imaginary wind, glinting blood-red lights at the tips of its blackness.

"I have given *all* to you, my Wepwawet, for you have opened the way for me. Together we will open the sky and together we will ascend on the light to be part of the eternities," she spoke, but her voice sounded like the chorus of a thousand united in rustling whispers to the prince. Maatkare felt the blood draining from his head in horror and delight and his heart felt as if it had dissolved into steam before he collapsed in her arms.

OPENER OF THE SKY

Chapter 29: One is Missing

They watch

Waiting, extending love

Those who were here before

Transmuting light in to matter

At starborn level they came

Goddess and God walked on earth

In the body of fire and light.

Learning the passions of its many creatures

Creation subdividing from the starborn ones

became first gods born but now unable

to ascend, to return

Clothed in the substance of earth

they had become proud,

developed ego as they developed flesh

Children of the First ones

Had found a way

Lives ended as light and thought

encased in crystal,

Part fallen stars,

Part risen stones…

They watch

Waiting, extending love

It is time for the second ones to gather the remnants

of what went before

Passion is a seed of greatness.

OPENER OF THE SKY

Intellect the food of dreams
Love the synthesis of both
Strength and healing the key
…I am lonely and tired of waiting
Yet so reluctant that I cannot do
What must be done.
Will you dance with me?
Love me and distract me?
Walk with me?

The fact that he had slept very little since Marai arrived and even less since the sojourner had gone into the prince's camp didn't concern the Akaru too greatly. He knew the time for his preparations grew short and that he had so much left to do. During the day, he rested and often slipped in and out of trances. At night he woke from the power of his vivid dreams. He couldn't trust his revelations to a scribe, so he wrote every thought that came to him in open verse.

It's time. All the signs are falling into place. After all these years it's finally falling into place, he thought. He wanted to take all of his writings to the old king's funeral to show them to King Shepseskaf before the new year dawned. His most powerful thoughts had been about the solving of the mythical Children of Stone. Soon, with everything he knew, all would be answered.

He hadn't been to Ineb Hedj in several years, and had relied on Aped to bring him news of the royal city. Now the old man looked forward to the trip to meet his grandson's teacher, Prince Wserkaf, and perhaps see Old Hordjedtef himself before the Great One retired. If there was time outside the formalities, they might go over his findings, study the secret numbers, work on star calculations, and puzzle through mathematical mysteries.

At first, the elder Akaru reveled in the way he felt so alive and so radiantly happy. He thought of the way the big sojourner smiled despite his misery over his missing wives. He loved the way the man's great heart spoke so openly and unguarded. He truly *was* without any sort of hidden motive.

Marai bin Ahu! His very name seems magical! The elder felt as if his own inner voices had always known the strange man's name. They had sung it to him, even when he was a young boy.

Marai, Marai, Marai… his name is Marai… That was the name I heard that night the stars sang to me. A man walking as the sun; tall as the sky. There is so much more to learn from him, but why this year? The signs in the stars and in the weather had never lied to him.

I told young Maatkare to turn around and go home – quickly. I told him that his name favored badly, that even in the future when the divine woman was not so respected, it would be known as a woman's name, but he didn't listen to me. He insulted us with the rotten meat. Then, this Marai tells me the high king has died. After this, some foolish boys went with young Djerah the fledgling and now they have brought back the body of the youngest one killed as a message that the rest of them will not be coming home. They'll be burnt in the field and their souls will be condemned, unless I can go out and do a ritual over the places where they died. The littlest one was only thirteen summers old! Too young to die a captive. Akaru mused over the recent events, filled with awe and yet sorrow. He knew what his people would demand, even if it would be a disaster.

The people of Qustul were peaceful farmers, fishers, and cattle herders. The young men play-fought and sparred among themselves, practicing for the battles that never came. They organized hunting parties in the leaner years. Despite what they thought about themselves, they weren't seasoned warriors like Prince Maatkare's men. Sending men to answer for the insults and now the poorly led battle would be as futile as throwing more lambs at a rising slaughter.

The Akaru realized, quite painfully, that every moment of his life was grinding to a point. Soon, too much would be required of him.

I'm an old man, proud of my peaceful life! After the heads of the households left, he sat on his observatory porch in the Amani Suph portion of Qustul. He had felt their anguish and their weeping when he spoke to them. Many times that morning, he wanted to sit and weep with them too.

I knew these boys. I blessed them and sang in great joy with their fathers. Such hope for their future. I healed their fevers. Now I have to go to the places where they were slain. I have to go into the prince's camp to bless the spot where they were executed so they may rise up and not become roaming ghosts. It wasn't supposed to have been this way, he lamented, then recalled part of his sermon:

He paced back and forth in front of the gathered assembly that morning.

"If we send a hundred fathers, uncles, and brothers against so many, how many more will die? If you take the head of this prince and send it to his king, will not three thousand arrive to take our heads and bleach our bones in the cruel eye of Atum, with no one left to ensure our resurrection?"

Prince Maatkare had sent a note with the martyred child.

The evil energy from the linen scroll sent with the youth's body wanted to burn Akaru's hands when he tried to read it.

"Hear a small part of his words," he had begun, but the rabble of families talked over him and began to get up. They wanted to rush into the encampment, even if it meant certain death, despite his pleas. Akaru never liked using his calming spell to force his will on anyone. It had worked so poorly on Marai when he left that he almost thought it wouldn't work on the heads of households gathered in front of him until he remembered Marai was no ordinary man. He put up his hand and let the gentle wafting breeze of the first created day lull the men until they turned to listen to him.

"I order you *hear me*. Decide your course once you do. I will not stop you, then," he lowered his hand then held up the linen in the other.

"The men who came to die would not speak against each other and thus were heroic."

It meant Akaru would be allowed to slink into the camp unharmed, to humbly do his ritual.

"Will you still slaughter yourselves over vengeance because he tempts you?" He asked, judging each upturned face. "If you can be patient this last time, there will be no more of him and his bloodthirsty ways." He paused, checking the faces staring mutely back at him. "I will send my grandson Aped ahead of our delegation, with a writ to the king, and put this writ from the prince to place beside it. He will contemplate them both, and then as god will make his decision when I arrive for the burial. It is the sane thing to do," his voice rang over the populace.

I saw their faces. They wanted permission to avenge. They wanted to go up to the Island of the Elephants to burn his boats to the water, even though I told them he would know who did it and turn back to take us with unimaginable brutality.

The elder stood on his observatory porch and paced anxiously. Even the shady comfort of the palm trees inside his walls couldn't ease his worries.

I could blame young Djerah for this hot-headed mission, but this thing has been boiling so much longer. A blood feud has wanted to start for a long time because of this prince, even though I have gone out of my way to accommodate him. Maybe this is the storm I see in my vision. Maybe the stars predicted the rift that would divide the upper from the lower land once more, rather than predicting the return of something as unknowable as Apep or the wrath of Sebiumeker.

After long moments of silent contemplation, he held up his hands and moved them around in a circle to form a ball of light. He hadn't done this kind of heka since he was a child. If he sent the light to Marai and his party, he could get them to return and stay a safe distance. If Marai truly *was* the singer in the wilderness he would recognize the light, because with ones just like this one, he had led a ragged shepherd on a moonless night when his own very young body was wracked with fever.

The ball in his hands increased in light and became as visible as a small sun.

The singing. I couldn't make it sing the way they sang to me, but it's still important I make the statement, he thought and released the little sun-light orb. It danced away from his hands and toward the place where the prince was camped.

It's still too tragic, Akaru meditated on his actions. *Their blood, even though the punishment was justified, cries out for me to do something. My people demand it!* the elder closed his eyes and he silently prayed after the departing orb:

Go far into the grass, young prince, his thoughts whispered. *Go into the grass and don't come back for a moon. Better yet, go back home another way, before the gods take notice of your evil heart. If you are foolish enough to come through here in a week or two, there will be a war and I will be unable to stop it.*

I then say to my own, if the prince insists, let him pass through. The word in his heart he will remember is that we are men of peace but we will not be rolled over! We will await him in the next hunt, if the new king even sees fit to send him. This prince will know by that time to bring the entire army and the king as well. As of this hour, there is no Peace treaty of Amani Supf.

Akaru Sef palmed a small tablet that contained the image and seal of great king Khufu who had organized the treaty when he was a baby. He spat on the tablet and with a second gesture, snapped the tablet in half and whispered aloud: "The King Khufu has met a second death before the race of the Ta-Ntr, Ta-Seti."

Akaru turned once more before he climbed down to enter his small palace. *If his Highness fails to understand all I have done for him, I will just explain it to him the hard way. I'll wait for the little light I have sent to bring me word of Marai and those with him. After that, if all this that I've dreamt comes to pass, I can hide here for several days. This time, I have to stay. The goddess begs me to act and then to stay the course.*

The wind stirred the dust a little, whipping the length of his rope and lion cloak around him. A storm strengthened in the distance. Sultry, hot wind lifted from time to time as it moved closer. It searched for something or someone; inspecting everything it passed and then releasing it.

Akaru Sef rushed to the gates the moment his guards alerted him that they were being opened for Marai and his company. He hadn't realized so much time had passed since the sad morning assembly. In better days, one of his wives would have come out to the observatory to find him. At other times, he would move among his people and visit, picking up news and gossip. Now he spent much of the day walking and thinking. When the boy's body had been returned with the letter from the prince and the gold for the boy's family, Akaru spent time with them, conducted the meeting with the heads of households and then told Xania, his chief wife, he needed to be alone until he felt better. In times of conflict, he withdrew to meditate for longer hours in the observatory which would one day be his burial and ascension chamber.

At last they are here! He pulled on the tall cedar door to the left, then beckoned everyone into his enclosed estate. Almost instantly, however, the old man noticed their arrival pointed out disarray instead of triumph. Despite his alarm, he greeted the women as they passed him through his gates and waited for Marai to carry Djerah inside.

"Welcome to my home, beautiful one," he spoke to Naibe-Ellit first.

She shuffled forward less than gracefully, tired from her long walk across the countryside, but she magically mustered up enough strength to look pleasant.

Was there not a woman of our land with you? I don't see her. Akaru's thoughts echoed.

Naibe-Ellit bowed her head once, a sad expression in her large golden eyes, but the elder didn't seem to notice. He had moved to Ariennu.

"And you must be Lady Ari, your hair black with red like the hide of Sutek but bright and curly, curly." And under his greeting, his thoughts probed:

The woman of Ta-Seti… Where is she?

Ariennu looked away. She had heard and understood his thoughts but indicated, by her silence, that she didn't want to talk about it. She turned to Marai, who carried an ashen-skinned, semi-conscious Djerah in his arms.

"He's worse now, isn't he?" her low voice reflected the somberness of their arrival.

"A little bit. We just need to get him out of the sun and see if he can take some clear water. Cover him in the dark so his Child Stone can work on him some more." Then, in what seemed to be an afterthought, he looked back over his shoulder at Akaru's shocked face and said: "Good to be back, Honored One."

Akaru nodded and accepted the greeting, but noticed the young man's nose and ears were bleeding. Once again he battled his misery over Maatkare and that prince's usury of the treaty he had symbolically broken moments earlier.

Brave young fool! He was not supposed to strive yet, but now that he has, he has taken power from them too early… the elder grimaced. When he touched the young man's healing injuries, he sensed Djerah had been well enough to start on foot for the first part of the journey. As the heat and his thirst grew, he had become too dizzy to stand upright. Even though he had been carried by Marai the last half of the journey, it hadn't helped him much. Despite the setback, he had insisted on appearing strong enough to walk through the gates. He collapsed into Marai's arms after two wobbly steps.

"Here. Put him on your cloak just in the shady part of the courtyard. I can take a closer look at him there," Akaru Sef quickly gestured the two house servants who had come back from Buhen with him. "You men get your wives and put up a bed in the corridor behind the bathing area. It will be cooler there; quiet and moist."

Marai carried Djerah, who mumbled something unintelligible, but as he did he bent down so that Ariennu could unfasten his travel cloak. When she spread the cloak out in the shade and put a bag under one end so Djerah's head would be raised, Marai set him down and watched carefully as Ari hushed the stonecutter and settled by him. It was enough. Just her presence seemed to have a calming effect on him.

Akaru moved forward to look at him while Ari sat on her heels and turned to take a bowl of wine mixed with water from one of the servants. She dabbed the fresh oozing of blood to clean his still swollen face and shoulders, dribbled a little liquid onto his lips, then sat back satisfied that they moved a little.

"She wouldn't come with us," Marai soberly answered Akaru's earlier silent question. He stretched; then drew himself up until the flat of his hand pressed the rafters. "She chose to stay with the prince," he shook his head dismally then looked up at the support beam as if he might lift it for sport. "That, and it seems he has managed to plant a child in her belly."

Akaru Sef's head whipped around and his mouth gaped in horror.

"Huh?" he questioned. "That wasn't…" he frowned, grew silent, and then reflected on what he had just heard. *It wasn't supposed to turn out this way*, Akaru thought. In his dreams, he met the woman, learned what family she may have come from and together found a few relatives in the region. He sensed more about her now, and knew more of her reason for staying, but now he dreaded the truth on hearing this. He knew his prying about the reason had upset his guests as much as it bothered him.

The elder rose and turned to Marai, who clasped the younger of the women to his side. He knew she was exhausted, even though her smile charmed and her eyes seduced.

"I will show you where to stay," he led both of them to a niche near the open place where servants were stringing the bed for the young man. It was a small double chamber. "See here?" his eyes twinkled. "Each side for two…" he turned to look back at Ari, whose wide shoulders slumped in fatigue "…or three, or however you like to sleep and not far from the bath." He turned them around and moved them to the open courtyard to sit and enjoy some refreshment as the evening meal was prepared.

As soon as the big man moved the gear from his overland trek against the wall in the little room, he came out again, his arm slipped warmly around Naibe's back. He paused and pressed her again; swayed gently, and giggled a little when he touched her belly.

"She truly is all love and passion," Akaru beamed back at the young woman and then at Marai. "I hear you singing your song of long ago to the goddess when I look into her eyes," he grinned. "You love like lions! Who among men could quit her bed if she chose them?" Naibe-Ellit blushed a little before she moved forward to kiss the elder's brow, then returned to nuzzle Marai's arm.

Akaru noticed the servants had finished, then motioned to Marai, who carefully lifted the young man and carried him to the bed. He didn't stir, so the men checked him again. After that, Marai gathered Ariennu in his arm and returned to the open courtyard with her.

"I heard what you said about Baby One. You sound like every prophet up and down this cursed river, though, with your words all in fine verses. I'll bet you don't have anything so pretty for me," Ari snorted, pouring the beer the servants had placed on the low dining tables into five cups while the Xania came out of the other side of the court. Ari sat heavily by Marai's left arm and tipped her cup for a long, thirsty drink.

"You, lady? You want a reading? Well then..." Akaru shut his eyes and sighed, then quickly began to speak a customary praise. "Your treasure is in your warmth. You are a happy, laughing sunshiny day... a rainbow in the cloud. Courage is your passion and wisdom is your fire. You would not make a child long ago, because your life then was too hard. So now, are you *not* the wise mother of *all* the wandering children?"

He knew she had taken in the words and that they had cut her as well as healed her.

Ariennu dismissed Akaru with a wave of her hand. "They know me, alright. No secret. You're good though," she found Marai's other arm in time to hear the elder finish.

"It was wrong for the other one to stay. She should be here. She has something important to do in this place. I feel that very much in every bone. This *is* her place. She was even here recently. She should remember that night."

"You would think…" Ari added, refilling her cup with a frown at the way Marai's hand stayed her efforts to pour more drinks. "Ever since we started this journey she has talked about coming to Ta-Seti and that her place was here. Well, here we are and now she has stuck herself with *him*."

Marai shook his head again. The old man felt the rage in his guest coming to the surface again.

"So, am I some kind of coward to allow her to stay? Should I have killed him and made her come, even with his child in her?" he began. "I *had* the chance," he looked down at Ariennu, then at Akaru, "but Ari here knew there should be no more killing." He rubbed the stiffness out of his eyelids. The old man knew Marai wanted untroubled sleep more than anything.

"I was keeping you from getting your arm chewed off," Ari protested. "He was wolfing, or didn't you notice that through the blood in your own eyes? It wouldn't have ended well before he died."

"I saw him. I'm sure he saw the bull Bakha of my wrath while I stopped his breath, hoof to throat," Marai grumbled, finishing his drink. "I was looking for his heart so I could freeze it, but couldn't find if he *had* one." Sullen silence followed, punctuated by quickly tossed sips of beer from everyone assembled at the dining couches.

For several moments, Akaru thought about the exchanges between Marai, himself, and the two women. The women let Marai brood quietly. Each attempted to sooth him in her own way. After a while, the elder felt a slight ray of poetic inspiration begin to creep through the dark mood that had seized him when he discovered the Ta Seti woman had stayed behind.

Maybe this will help them; and me, he thought.

"And in the end, what *true* man takes away a woman as if she has no will of her own. If you had made her come with you, you would have been no better a man than this prince of ours when he seduced her, because you would have been deciding what was right for her," Akaru Sef suggested as he straightened up.

"True," Marai nodded. "I was just surprised his hold on her was so strong."

At this point, Akaru and the guest sighed in some relief as the first course of the evening meal; a soup and a bread, were brought out.

"Oh, now…" his slim fingers wagged with a sudden new thought. "Some women *like* a cruel man because it's a challenge to keep him even, to tame that wild heart of his. They think it is the fighting strength of the lion they are looking at; that he will protect them. They find out too late that such men care only for their own welfare and when a woman opposes him he will abandon her for another. I know this prince has wicked ways, but I have understood his needs. It is *not* born cruel as much as seasoned so. They may *indeed* have a journey together," Akaru let his words settle a little while he sopped his soup and sweetly fed his wife.

Marai fed Naibe and the young woman teased and fed Ariennu by poking the soup soggy bread at her mouth until Marai dipped and lifted her bread to her. They laughed, but Akaru added another thought.

"Your wives understand men like this… why not you?"

"He's right, Marai," Naibe remembered much of the pain of the past few months. "You know how I went to you long ago and got you to unburden your sad heart about your wife who had died? When you were gone from me I did so with other men. When I was on His Highness' boat the first day we met, I tried to reach out to heal him, but he craved every last bit of my energy and did not care if I became empty. Something dark in his soul drinks too deeply and too quickly like one near death of hunger. You can't stop letting it happen… I tried. It was killing my own heart to be with him," her sigh prompted Marai to press her tightly to his side.

Ariennu remembered and grabbed at another cup of beer. She covered a burp and snickered… *Yeah here I go. Drink to forget, but I could lay at the bottom of a brew vat and drink the froth until my guts ripped but it wouldn't take the thought away that it was me that got us into this mess with him. I'm the tough one. I can take this. Tough nothing. I showed myself that. I'm a good drinker and a decent squeeze, but there's nothing.*

Ari, stop. That's all finished now.

She felt Marai enter her reverie.

"Yeah? What about Deka," she looked to see the elder and his wife chattering about something else, then added in a whisper. "I never thought I'd care about that old Bone Woman, but it still hurts me about her. The old man's right. She *should* be here and she *is* in danger, but she has to come here on her own. It's not right for us to go and get her. I just hope she gets her fill of him soon… really soon."

Chapter 30: The Dark Balance

Ariennu took off Marai's sandals, washed his feet, and rubbed them with a sweet nut oil. Even though it was deep night when everyone finished their meal, she still wanted to pamper him. It had been too long. Much of her need was to get the feeling of Maatkare's hard sleekness, haughtiness, and petulant stare out of her thoughts.

Later, she thought. Maybe I'll have time for a nice, long bath myself. If he wasn't so tired. If I wasn't so tired, I'd drag him in with me for some sweet playtime. She hadn't bathed in deep warm water since that evening over a month earlier, when Maatkare allowed them to come here. *I like this place!* she thought. *Peaceful. Not noisy like little Kina Ahna. Not worrisome like the palaces with their rotten, spying little maids. It's just sweet and peaceful. Djerah will get well quickly here. Maybe the old man is right. Maybe Deka will come to her senses before too much longer. Meantime, it'll be good to watch Djee's strengths grow. Be like watching a child learning to walk.*

She saw Akaru, now quite animated from everyone's return and good conversation, press his wife close, then get up to take a lamp out to the observatory.

"I have to see if there is something I missed as to why she would wish to stay away. The gods of the wind will answer tonight."

Priests, holy men, scholars… all the same! she thought. *Maybe he'll make his way back after everyone's asleep.*

It puzzled Ari that the little crescent shaped Yah stone had sought young Djerah as a host. Naibe and Marai didn't seem to understand the reason either. It could have cured his wounds, but remained outside his body like the other child stones, but for some reason it didn't want to.

He had the child stone in his mouth and he was willing to die before he gave it up, she thought. *Maybe it was his loyalty. Maybe that's the connection. Maybe it was because he's Marai's nearest living kin, like a son. Why does he need a son, though, if Little One's going to have his baby?* She shrugged then looked at Naibe, who was curled near Marai, totally exhausted and asleep.

Wonder how that's going to be? One born to two hosts. And now Deka. Will those children be born with a stone or will they be given one at birth or when they grow up? She gestured to Marai, trying to distract herself with other thoughts.

"Come here, big man, let me soothe you," she whispered seductively, the way she often did when they were in Ineb Hedj, living the life of working peasants.

His silver-cast eyes twinkled.

"Sure," he flopped down on his face like a new youth anticipating something sweet. "I might go to sleep, though. It's been a rough few days."

"I'm tired too, Marai," she admitted. "Just so glad to be with you again."

He turned for a moment and sat to embrace and kiss her.

All of her lonely and desperate moments melted as his warm scent surrounded her. She had craved that closeness, and understood now, more than ever, the beauty of his love. It respected, but didn't need. It craved, but never sought to control or own. She wanted so much more in that moment; to disappear into his arms and become part of him.

"Missed you, woman," he whispered, then gently released her and lay flat on his belly so she could rub him with the oil.

"Treat you like a king, always, because you *are* my king." She thought of her brief moments with King Menkaure months ago and the way he would send for her to rub the tension from him. It didn't take long for her to ease the weight of the day from Marai's shoulders and back. After a few moans of joy, his reaction slowed, then stopped. She knew he had dozed.

Look at him, curled up next to her. Swear to goddess I wish we'd been alone. I suppose I'll check on Djee a moment. Then I think I can find a spot by that beautiful big back of his. Room for one more!

Wonder if Marai looked anything like Djerah before the changes, she mused, then reluctantly visualized a taller man; a big, ugly, old mountain of a man. *There I go,* she laughed inwardly at the thought as she smoothed his perfect back. *They* are *kinsmen after all. You stay right there. I'll be back.*

Ari eased up, then quietly took the lamp from the window sill. When she tiptoed to the slightly raised bed and pulled back the shroud-like sheeting, she noticed the swelling in the young man's face had gone down and the oozing had nearly stopped. Once again he looked like the brash and temperamental young man she remembered from the market who seemed as if nothing good had ever happened in his life. Djee was slowly returning to them, even though his former life, like theirs, would never be the same.

What are you going to be to us? she contemplated. *Now what will be left for any of us? The stones, once they're all together again, need to go into some "chamber of secrets," wherever that is.* That much she understood. There, they would become a treasure of learning for men of Kemet, and indeed, for men of the entire world. *Then what happens to us?* she asked herself. *Will we live out our long lives interpreting these secrets and teaching the brightest minds in the world? Boring. Grindingly boring! Marai and Naibe will have a child; maybe more after that. They'll bring up a bright and gifted family, so at home moving around these priests and kings.*

Ariennu knew a child would never come out of her own belly unless she re-invented herself again via the Child Stones, but what use would it be at this point?

Will it be something to ease my loneliness? AkaruSef said that. *I'm going to be the mother of the rest of the children who were chosen. I'll tag along like some wise but ageless crone and grandmother. Baby One and I will attach to one of the temples. Maybe I'll go with them, being a healer and friend to the men they encounter and gather up.* She felt suddenly that she would never be completely accepted by anyone. *I'm not from Kemet. I'm not their race and I'm not royal or magical. I'll be Marai's co-wife, but soon he'll be looking only at Naibe-Ellit and her baby. He's that kind of man.*

She thought of Maatkare by comparison.

Cruel man in need of love? Ha! What does Deka know about that kind of thing? Ariennu found herself daydreaming about the prince. *Didn't stop him from using me plenty of times, the disrespectful bastard! Still, that luscious body of his when it needed soothing and oiling… that line he could draw between torment and ecstasy. He could work all sides of it, depending on how he felt any given day. Made me want him to do things to me I never even knew about or thought I could allow, when I've already had a life full of the best and worst any man has to offer. He made me crave it, then sucked out the energy of my passion and wore it like a prize. I'm just a trophy he's hunted and conquered. I almost forgot how that should offend me. Men like that don't love, they take. Be nice to have another go at it… get him to be sweet and beg, for once… take joy in teasing and mocking him… Could make an old woman like me all twitchy inside.*

Ariennu felt a drop in the sensation of the air, as if an icy draft had blown its breath into the open room.

"Oooh. That *was* bad…"

She looked up to find Akaru had crept quietly back from his nighttime observation. He smiled tentatively up into a moonbeam that had filtered through the shady boughs that hung over his open courtyard. He spoke to someone or something. "Yes. I hear your cry. Let me open the sky for you so you can come to us…" he warbled. Ari saw him shape a little ball of light between the palms of his hands, then harden his peaceful face into a scold. "My wayward one, you have been naughty."

"Something's wrong," Marai flipped, suddenly awake. He sat bolt upright and almost disturbed Naibe's sleep.

"You? The orbs come from you? I thought they came out of the stars. How can *you* make them?" Ari's jaw dropped.

"Sometimes I make them. Did you see the one I sent today before you arrived?" Akaru asked. "I was just sending our missing woman one with a little message inside," the elder swirled his hands and another little sun-like object formed.

"No. Just this one," Ari answered, sensing the way the light warmed her face just before it took flight like a ball of fireflies.

"I always could do that, even as a child," the elder's face crinkled in mirth.

Ari chortled, mystified. She remembered Marai talking about the little balls of light that led him to the vessel in the wilderness that first night. *Connected? Of course he is. But what connects us?*

Marai hushed Naibe-Ellit, who had roused and tensed, suddenly aware of the curious sensation in the air. He hoped it had been a dream that was strong enough to wake him and that they both could return to sleep. He would have preferred to snuggle the women on either side of him, to think of Naibe's sweet love and to feel the joy of the child in her belly. That this time it would work and he would have a living, breathing son was almost too much joy.

A tortured cry, like the yowl of a forlorn animal or the scream of a strange bird, cut into their restful bliss.

"It's Deka, isn't it?" Naibe-Ellit asked. "Do you think she's calling out to us now?"

"Oh, I'm *certain* of it," the Akaru chimed in as he moved toward their sleeping area. A servant sleepily trailed the elder but stayed out of earshot.

"I wish she would…" Marai rubbed the back of his neck soberly then gathered Naibe gently into his arms and stared quietly, but somberly into her gold-lit eyes. He *had* been dreaming of his life and of his journey with the women thus far. At first the hours between the times when they held each other and loved each other seemed to have so little meaning. Now these in-between times were themselves the sources of limitless bliss. Everything was memorable, etched with Naibe's smiles and the way she shimmered like spangles when she walked; the way her voice lulled, like sweet golden bells.

And Ariennu? Though he felt no sense of goddess-worship in her presence, she had become a cherished friend in the way a man takes another man as a friend. She was a man in the flesh of a woman: cursing, hard loving, drinking, laughing too loud, playing dirty tricks, and not flinching a bit in the sight of danger. Prince Maatkare never broke her, but he took her far too close to that brink. Marai knew he had arrived just in time to stop the wounds they received that threatened to overtake their power. The prince would have to answer for all he had done.

When Akaru sat on the woven rush mat beside Marai's guest mat where he and Naibe lay quietly, his shoulders drooped wearily.

"I had a vision, while you rested, which has puzzled me… that's why you saw me speak," Akaru began. "I sent this woman another message and opened the sky for her answer."

"We've *all* been having those visions," Marai grumbled.

"At first it wasn't exactly about the woman," Akaru answered. "I meditated on why it should bother me so much that one of your women stayed with her captor. Then, my thoughts fell right onto why *anything* ever befalls us in our lives. Is it the gods? Is it some random energy we bring to ourselves? If it's that and nothing more, then why do we not have the power to change *all* things? One's looks, for instance…" his face grew dark and haunted.

Marai recognized a fine sharpness to the elder's features he hadn't previously noticed. A regal haughtiness drifted over the man's image as if the spirit of Deka had walked out of the ethers and had fluttered too near him.

"I haven't thought about it as a grown man for years," Akaru continued, but then restated. "No. I *did* discuss this with young Aped, my grandson, when he came home from Khmenu and first told me of you. It makes me wonder if I really *do* have the power to change hearts as old Djedi told me I would one day have."

"Djedi," Marai shivered in more than a middle of the night chill. "I hadn't heard that name in a while. He was the one who was supposed to take the Children of Stone from me when I started, but then they cast us into a sleep of fifty years so there would be no way for that to happen."

"Yes, Aped told me this. He had seen you in the marketplace when the Ta-Seti woman danced for him… that you had asked about it and became ill to find time as the flesh knows it had not stayed put."

"I see the pieces are *still* falling into place, even now." Marai was about to say that had been hard for him to realize fifty years had passed overnight and that Ariennu had convinced him it didn't matter that very afternoon with her own love… that they would just look for his heir. *This old magical man? After all this time and Deka was, in her own way, right to yearn for Ta-Seti*, he asked himself. *Why make me so gullible then? I thought it was Hordjedtef, then Wserkaf, but now here I am with this elder as if the third try is the best answer.*

Naibe maneuvered out of Marai's arm to the Akaru and took his hand in hers as if she had sensed his trouble and was drawn to soothe it.

"When I was little they would point out my pale color, my spot freckles, and how my eyes were different: Sorcerer's eyes, they said, because they reflected the green and the black water in the two seasons in them. When I was tiny, other children here were afraid to play with me. There were always whispers about me. I also saw you, just then, looking at my face to think where you have seen its shape and features," he quipped.

"My father *was* a warrior, but also of an old and noble house that traces back before the darkness. His second wife was a minor daughter of a minor wife of Great Khufu himself. She told me it was the look of my lion-mother I took, not *her* own family," he smirked.

"A daughter of Khufu?" Marai recoiled, surprised. "Didn't realize you were connected that high up. You're old Hordjedtef's nephew too… and even related to our nasty mannered princeling?" Marai felt mystified and amused at the way everyone was related who had anything to do with governing the red and black lands.

"No, more like a cousin, and Djedi was Elder Hordjedtef's uncle. I don't even think he has taken the trouble to recognize that I may be part of this… just how he can control me; hence these artificial 'forays' of our prince when the hunting is actually better in the western grasses near the Elephant Isle.

Great King Khufu appointed the man who took me as a son, because there was no strong king alive in Ta-Seti, Wawat, or Kush and the tribes were always warring. My 'father' was no noble. He was a soldier of fortune who had wandered in from the Wawat as a youth and worked his way into the king's favor. He singlehandedly put down the rebellion of Kush, though many were slaughtered by the kings' men, and began to work out the terms of the "Peace of Suph." Old Khufu knew how unstable the region was and didn't want to risk one of his own sons there, so he installed him at Buhen, and dispatched his daughter, Ko, by one of his Ta-Seti concubines to be a second wife and to form a peace bond which was re-instated by Djedephre, and later Kaphre and Menkaure. Because of our prince, and what he has done to my people for no reason other than to show his brutality and might, I am petitioning to his 'new' Majesty to either send another emissary, or consider the Suph finished. Anyway…" Akaru Sef continued, seeing his chatter was about to be interrupted by the servant bringing nighttime sleep tea.

Marai looked for Ariennu. She was in the darkened area with a lamp, checking on Djerah.

"The woman turned up barren, and she worried the treaty would be shattered if she had no child. When I was found, she became my mother. When father passed into the Reeds the rule passed to me," he shrugged.

"The people here never objected to a bright-skinned man as a sepat ruler in a dark brown land?" Marai listened carefully, trying to anticipate. "You're pinker than I am. Were there no other children to contest it?"

"Oddly, no," he frowned. "I thought it was because of the wife who served as my mother… her rank, and that on her death it would be trouble for me since there were half-brothers by other wives to contest me. Instead, they got me to come down *here* to re-build in the place of the gods where the old ones once walked and were happy to stay in higher lands and rule there."

Ariennu returned and flopped down onto the mat with the others, snickering and taking up the cup of tea offered to her.

"Gold. His hair wants to be twisted with gold just as yours is with the silver color," she giggled, then caressed one of the curls at Marai's brow. "Like the sun kissed it bright. Just a streak or two for now. His color is getting better, too. I think he's going to be a pretty one," she grinned, but her smile wasn't even close to one of maternal pride.

"Should we warn him about you?" Marai laughed and ducked as if Ariennu had reached forward to smack the back of his head. Instead, she brought forward Wserkaf's Wdjat.

"Maybe you should, or maybe it's time to look through this thing here while we still have our hands on it?"

"Oh?" Akaru craned his neck to look at the crystalline disc, shocked "I haven't seen that since I was a boy. It belonged to Djedi, but he told me he found it near here before I was born." He beckoned the servant waiting up to tidy the cups after they slept.

"A pan of water, would you? Then, don't worry over the clutter here. Go to sleep."

While the man dipped a pan into the pool, Akaru reached forward to touch it, then sighed. "It has made quite a journey. I wouldn't have thought…" he started, pausing to 'read' the surface. "Djedi to Great Hordjedtef to Neferhetepes daughter of Djedephre," his eyes twinkled, "to her son Wserkaf, to you, Lady Ariennu is it, to the woman of Ta-Seti, and now again you have it?"

"It was Deka. She gave it to us. His Highness didn't try to stop her, because he knew it belonged to Prince Wserkaf," Naibe quickly answered, but Marai finished her statement:

"The seven traveling stones and five more were part of a promise that he will bring the others. He wants to see their full power and knows he won't until all are together again. I don't know how he thinks the priests would allow it, unless Great One does and that's not likely." He stared at the mat where he had almost drifted to sleep while Ari massaged him. He wanted to lie down again. The relaxing tea was having the desired effect.

Ariennu yawned again, too.

"He definitely has something else going on under his collar and khat," Akaru shook his head. "Wonder what?"

"He believes he is one of the Children's chosen since Deka chose *him*," Marai shrugged, "or so he said before he kicked us out of his camp."

"Perhaps he *is*, then," Akaru nodded prosaically. "Perhaps this was the *real* reason why you couldn't kill him, handily and not due to any spell he may have used. Maybe it was why the ladies made you stop, which brings me back to the thought of my ability or *anyone's* ability to change hearts."

"Now *there's* a truly rude thought." Even though Marai had been carefully taught by old man Hordjedtef that every brightness needed something in the dark to balance it, Akaru's concept made him groan. "One of the basic truths in the world, I suppose. Evil is needed in order for our spirits to progress. I just wouldn't understand someone accepting that they *were* the evil side and embracing it."

"Ah yes, you know that then," the old man chortled, suddenly more animated. "Adversity is the seed to doing well. Without it, the soul would not know *how* to do well. It serves us the same way fire makes brass true. Without it, the brass wouldn't shine," Akaru smiled. "How can one be good without the knowledge of evil? How would you know what *not* to do if there was no evil example shown to you? How would you know not to kill, unless you had seen or known the horror of murder? It *has* to exist. Without evil, we would ascend and drift without a point of reference. We are not ready to do that. Here…" the elder pinched his flabby forearm skin and held up his own arm. "Here is where we prepare even though we may be stuck in the glamour of our physical lives. Our people fell so far into the abyss along with

Apep and the damned that when we rise up we will ascend to a place never opened before, higher than the one from which we came."

Ariennu floated the crystal disc gently on the surface of the water.

Wonder how it rides just below the surface, but above the bottom of the pan? It's cupped. Bubble under the surface? The design covers everything but I still see…

For several moments the four of them said nothing. They contemplated the images they saw. Then, in the distance to the south and east, as if an unknown thing had been listening for them, something in the wind changed.

Part 5: Wolves and Lions

CHAPTER 31: WEPWAWET

In the early morning, just as the grey of the dawn mist had begun to clear, Maatkare's personal guard and a patrol chief crept to the royal tent. They had a message.

"Fool," Maatkare's head raised. At the same moment, his hand curled around his throwing dagger and sent it whistling past his guard's right ear into a nearby post. "Tired of living this morning? At least you knew enough not to flinch and lose an ear or eye." He sat up further on his elbows as the startled man pried the blade from the post and sheepishly returned it. Maatkare laughed a little, then glanced to his left arm. Nefira Deka slept beside him.

Ought to sleep. And I ought to sing that one's praises for distracting me with her fire last night, too. I almost didn't hear the guard. Bad luck if the humps start making me too tired for proper command.

"So, what do you want?" he addressed the men.

The captain of the watch bowed low and backed up after he had returned the knife. Still mortified, he quietly stated: "A lion, Your Highness. It's in the grass not far from camp. It's an old rogue, maybe starving or wounded, some of the men said. No pretty trophy and a good tangle of tough meat, but the sport would be excellent and quick enough that no one will be overly tired before they bring him in," the man looked up expectantly.

Lion. Been waiting for a mean old boy like that. I'll name this one Marai the Sojourner and work some irritating spells on their leaving with his death. The prince threw aside his bedsheet, which woke Deka. Before she could ask or complain, he addressed her:

"Lion's been seen, old and past his prime. I'm going to bring him in by heat of the day. I expect I'll be hot and tired, so *do* be ready to soothe me," he scrambled quietly, belting his kilt and gathering bows and arrows. Then, in a surprise gesture, he brought his new fancy knife out of hiding. Stopping to stroke it and feel it purr in his hand, he stowed it in a temporary leather sheath around his waist.

Without even making eye-contact, he gave Deka a quick kiss on the face, then slung his equipment in various quivers and scabbards about his body before he left with the guard and the captain to round up men, spears, and nets.

Whenever Maatkare left Deka alone in the royal tent, she usually amused herself by singing, tidying, and straightening all of her possessions.

Highness is particular about cleanliness and neatness. It pleases him to see things well ordered, she repeated to herself, recalling his frequent rages over soiled clothing, a bed untidied and unfreshened for too long after he had risen, a shoddy bit of grooming. She wanted to be certain that his ill temper was never directed at *her*.

Today, after a final tour of their nicely put away room, she noticed the angle of the sun and chided herself.

Here I am, dreaming again. She had cleaned the plate that held a light meal of bread and date honey that reminded her of the confections she, Baby, and Wise Mama sold a long time ago when they had lived in Ineb Hedj. Her head bowed so she wouldn't think about them or guess what they were doing.

They let me stay, she contemplated. *Man-Sun didn't put up much of a fight for me. Did he never desire me? Part of my soul has always told me he did. Wonder what happens when Wise Mama realizes Baby One has always been for him, Men say they want more woman than one can meet, but soon enough they pick a favorite. Raem has picked me, even above wicked Sadeh at his home. I will free him from her and her dull spawn soon enough when we return victorious.*

Wise Mama will find a man. She always wrapped her legs around something, before, during, and after Marai. Shouldn't worry over her finding her way. She's that sort. I shouldn't be thinking of them. It has passed down the river from me, so to speak!

She belted her kala more securely under her breasts and adjusted the straps to cover her nipples. When she had painted her lips red and retouched the red color on her nails, she left the tent to wander the camp.

It was quiet outside. Her new guards Rutiy and Sutiy were out with the hunting party, so they didn't come to flank and walk with her. There was no speech lesson to teach them today.

Maybe they are not even mine any more. If they do well on the hunt today; prove themselves, Raem will want them as his own. Someone's already pointed out to him that for all of their muteness and dull wits, they are excellent trackers. They move like lions. Lions? I've never truly seen a lion up close except for the shape I take in my dream. I feel her energy more strongly now. Maybe they sense it.

Wawat slaves and black as night. Twins and mute... cast out as suspicious when my senses tell me twins are instead highly valued. They were a gift from this man who governs the sepat where we bathed. Still... why would they not be good at what they do?

She had at first regarded them as docile, until she saw the way they had obediently and without any sense of hesitation tortured and killed those boys who came with ill-inspired Djerah. Their cold and passionless administration of justice had proven them to be so much more than they appeared.

Will you take them from me, my Raem? They are not proper women's servants, but I was seeing if I might heal their voices. I know they have messages for me about Ta-Te and about what I may face soon. I can feel it when I look into their darkest eyes. They should be free, not bound. Their thoughts call me MaMa Menhit and it burns my ears. I need to know why.

When she returned from her walk, she began to grind up some powder and then mix it with a purified fat to make cosmetics for both herself and the prince. Later, she constructed a bead frame, threaded it, and worked on a new collar for her beloved as well as more jewelry for herself.

Bored again by midday, she rested then walked out to see the brewers draw beer from the fermenting vats. She paced restlessly. It was the heat of the day.

Raem. Beloved. Hurry back to me. This has gone on far too long. Am I nothing but your pet to come home to; a lioness caged? She sent her thoughts into the air, but knew it was pointless. *You are driven to be all your men need, but do not forget me. The men must have gone far into the grass,* she thought. Most of the time when the men hunted, the wind brought in distant sounds of animals crying in panic or men shouting. A cheer always rose toward the end of the hunt when the prince made the kill. Then, he would come home.

When Naibe and Ariennu had been here, there were more distractions. The younger of her "sisters" would grow anxious about what the prince might demand of her. Ariennu would simply posture and mock, then put her thoughts in the rudest place possible. Deka remembered just shrugging at them, trying to ignore them both and do her beading or needlework. Now that they were gone, *she* felt like fretting.

As the afternoon wore on, Deka knotted the row ends for the beading strands and pulled them loose from the frame. The remainder of the Child Stones beckoned to her from their box on the top of the trunk where Maatkare had placed them. She had steadfastly ignored them, feeling that if Maatkare had obtained them as a prize and had even had them make him a knife, perhaps it was best if she left them alone.

Then, she heard:

Deka… come and play with me.

The voice of a young child whispered, perhaps from the box of stones. Her fingers froze. Quietly, she put the handful of bead ropes away, sat on her heels in front of the trunk, and carefully lifted the lid.

When she opened the box, she saw nothing had changed about the unsorted remaining Children of Stone. They glimmered a little unsteadily. This caused her to worry that there would be some sort of anguish, regret, or even reprisal that would leap out of the box ready to accuse and scold her about her decision to stay with the prince.

She waved her fingertips over them without touching them, then stared at them again. This time, the glimmering stones found more words. She couldn't understand them and so she placed her hand over them.

Deka Nefira Sekht

The child voice whispered.

Do you hear me calling you?

"Who is it?" she asked the air and for a moment there was silence. Then:

Ameny…

Deka gasped, then frowned. Her hand found her belly instinctively as if to soothe the one newly sprouted there. *My child? I don't believe you*, she wondered.

Perhaps, perhaps not… but you refuse to see me, Ha-go-re!

The Ta-Seti woman jumped, startled. *You know that word?* She shut her eyes and let the music the child sent rise through her body. *Akh-go-re Nejter Deka Nefer Sekht.*

An impish giggle returned as if the small spirit was amused by this game.

Her hands gracefully stroked the stones, feeling their sigh evolve into more poetry. This time, they answered her fully.

> *Whisper how the heart is gentle*
> *Soften when the heart is hard*
> *Give birth again to something new*
> *Rebirth to what is old*
> *And ever was here before*
> *Heal the hurt given*
> *Give not your hurt in place of joy.*

It's true. I have been lonely. I miss them already, I guess, she reflected. *Can you send word to them that we will all be together soon? I just have to see something here, and Marai couldn't stay. It's just for me and I need more time to know what it is. I thought it was the spirit of Ta-Te calling me home, but now I'm not so sure… Perhaps reaching through these little ones here might be a way to ease that.* She waited, but there was no response.

Tell them we'll meet again in the north after the hunt is over. We will be at the funeral if the winds are good for the journey back. I will bear young Ameny in Ineb Hedj and begin to raise him up as a young god, while my Raem endears himself to the new king who has no child marked as his heir... Perhaps he will be a consort for his daughter in the fullness of time. And Raem has been out in the grass with his men all day! She knew it was a lonely dream.

A few of the men had drifted back with the first kills by early afternoon. There had been no lion, but there had been other game. They needed to process the meat before the heat spoiled the blood in it and worms came. Once again, she put away the Children of Stone and went out to walk among them. She shivered in jealous delight as they hung up and bled the carcasses. They laughed and cheered among themselves about her beloved's unflagging manly energy. Maatkare Raemkai was so like Anhur, the hunter's god, the men exclaimed. It was such a wonder and an honor to be on his elite hunting team and wonderful to run out with him, even in his most awful and tyrannical moments when things went wrong.

I want to go out with him. I should be with him, Deka grumbled as she moved through the clumps of men while they worked the hides and trued nicked and bent weapons.

Does he forget what blood runs in my veins? I'm no blossom of the back roads of Ineb Hedj like Sadeh... no pampered god's daughter like Meryt. I should be at his side like a sister, to draw a bow, to chase and fell prey; to drink the heart's blood of a kill. She paused, puzzled, and then returned her gaze to the men as they worked. *Does he pamper me? I've only just now told him of the child. I can still run and fight for many a moon yet. I am no plaything to be left and to be picked up on his return. If I show him...*

During these last days of the hunt, before Marai and the others had arrived, Deka had plenty of time to think of Raem. Two weeks ago, she had moved to one side of the royal tent. He still entertained himself with the others, but he liked to drink and fight with Ariennu and overpower Naibe until she cried for mercy. Gradually, he had begun to treat her as a kind of prophetess. Now that her sisters were gone, there was no such interplay.

Each day she would re-think and almost resent him by noon, but scramble eagerly to him by the time he approached after the duties of the day. When she was with him, the feelings of being in the arms of something strong and dark had only grown more intense. What Marai had awakened, he had multiplied in her. She felt a strange peace and sense of power when he would lay her down, despite the savage and almost desperate couplings that ripped her own sense of self away in a wash of never-ending eruptions of pleasure. He would take her until she begged to die, grab her and force her to take more until she was senseless. If he had ever stolen energy from Naibe and Ari, he now donated bits of it… just enough, to keep her barely conscious and able to yield even more to him until he was fully sated and allowed her to rest.

That moment of ecstasy they shared was like victory in battle. It felt as if she stood atop a hill to await a storm that would surround and consecrate them both. The moment any part of that subsided, he assured her he had just begun to give her pleasure. As she lay helpless and recovering, he lay beside her. He licked and kissed her. The instant her senses returned, he stripped them from her again and brought her into an agony of so much more.

Just thinking about being with him on his return left her gasping and squirming in delight.

Marai had caused her storms to well up, but was always too considerate to take them or to command them. She had struggled so hard to release them so that she would one day be able to partake of his love and gentleness, but it had never happened. Maatkare welcomed her storms like the scent of blood and matched them with his own.

The stones waited for her in the tent. When she returned, she watched their color ripple into redness and heat at her touch as they read her patterns of ecstasy. She ran her hands over the stones, then felt a moaning keen rising from her chest and escaping her lips.

Prevail, my love, and come to me.

In the back of her thoughts a wind had begun to stir. She closed the box, then took a spare bow out to practice.

The men paused briefly that afternoon, under the shade of a clump of trees, no closer to the goal than they had been in the morning. After a brief round of beer and dried beef, they tightened their sandals, re-strapped their armor and crept into the deeper grass.

Toward evening, when under usual circumstances he would have quit stalking any beast and returned to camp to sulk and drink, Maatkare decided the lion was almost certainly as tired as he had become. He was astonished that the creature had been able to outlast and out maneuver them all day long and almost wondered if it might be enchanted. They saw it had slowed and that it stumbled some of the time. Most of the time it faded out of sight into the grass.

Go into far the grass, young prince, Maatkare thought he heard a whisper. *Go into the grass and don't come back for a moon.*

"Eh? What?" he shook his head. "The heat..." he muttered under his breath, beckoning for one of his men to bring him a skin of diluted wine. *Won't be long before the old wretch gives up and lets me take him.*

The new men who had risen above being Nefira's guards were serving as trackers. They crouched back and glanced side to side as if they themselves were beasts in the presence of a superior animal.

Growling like big cats, too; like they know something. He must be near. Maatkare thought.

His remaining guard had taken notice of something else in the wind, just as the Wawati had, but spoke his objections through his teeth.

"Your Highness, it's enough."

"Wuenre, you amaze me," Maatkare snarled a little over his right shoulder as he crouched lower. "You get me out early with no manners and now you turn coward on me. And all this after I tore off more than a couple of rounds of that red-haired piece of trouble for you!" He focused his eyes on the perceived shift in the tall grass ahead. "She infect the nature of your balls? Make your rump sprung? I notice you haven't been much good to me lately, even let that Akkad ass-rider pick off Rekenre. Now *there* was a loss. Where were you when that happened?"

Dare he question me! Maatkare grumbled. He didn't care that the tall guard seethed in indignation. *This is worse than war fatigue over one dumb beast*, he was exhausted. *I should go home, get roaring drunk and ride a different animal, but I can't give that monster the satisfaction now, even if he just dies from the run we've given him and we see bird's circling in the morning.*

"Men," he turned and addressed the few in the hunting party he had not released. A double handful of men remained. Most guarded each side of the prince and brought up the rear. Porters of the refreshments had been dismissed to go ready the late night celebration. "I expect your best. Stand with me to the end and you will be rewarded in a double share of beer. Even some wine..." His voice urged over the sudden roaring cheer as the men resumed the serpentine marching through grass that had begun to lay flat under their feet.

When the sun gave way to the rise of the full moon in the early dark, the prince felt a twinge of power enter his hand as if it searched for the mystical blade stowed safely at his side.

Where is he? The prince's head orbited like the head of a hawk. No one had seen evidence of the lion since the dark fell on them. *Has he run off? Are we so sure he's weary that we've missed that? Is this a joke? If this is push-back from the lion man I will cut his withered hands off and cram them down his throat before I pull his head off and send it on a staff to his young priest grandson in Buhen. Dare he use his pitiful sorcery against me! Once he was a friend. Now he's just old and in my way.*

"Move, men! I see... There, moving in the grass, see him thrash!" Maatkare felt the energy suddenly leap through him.

Prevail, my love and come to me!

Deka's voice called on the wind.

Battle spirit Sekht, he felt her thoughts move through him in Deka's seductive voice. *We drink the blood tonight. We drink the blood.*

The prince pushed his men harder now that the end was in sight. Something was rising above them like dark lightning. The men lit torches and formed a circle around the perimeter, watching for the beast to move in any direction.

"Stay with me, men. You break now, I will kill you myself!" He screamed curses at them. They pushed inward, drumming and stalking in tedious steps around the confused animal as it crouched in the long, stinging grass.

At first, Maatkare thought he'd overdone it. He felt giddy, but ignored it. Something descended in a sheet of power then rose, taking the last of his wits. Lights flashed in front of his eyes.

Go into the grass and don't come back for a moon, it said. *Better yet, go back home another way, before the gods take notice of your evil heart.*

A little light? Has the sun blasted my eyes? See a little ball of light… What?

"Highness… there see…" the equally exhausted guard pointed.

"What?" he snapped. "Don't distract me. Push in, damn you! Get the net ready! Get the net…"

CHAPTER 32: LION

When the sun sank below the horizon and the purple of Nut's mantle followed from east to west, the men knew from many years of experience that it was too dangerous to continue the hunt. To break ranks and go against the prince, however, was fatal. Against all good sense, he ordered the outer perimeter of his men to light torches so they could tighten a circle around the beast and start the final advance.

Go. Go. I'm tired, you bastard; you ruiner of days. He gritted his teeth and cursed under his breath, more than convinced that he had been circling and chasing a demon from another realm that had taken the shape of a scarred old lion.

"He'll make a mistake, soon. He's tiring. I smell his old blood. We'll net him and end this day of nonsense," the prince convinced them. "Then, my spear will split his evil heart…"

He knew he needed to win this, even if he took home only a mere symbol. He wanted to enjoy the ritual of bringing the lion down and painting the faces of his men with its blood. They would cheer and dance as he joyously ate the animal's heart raw while it still beat its last. He owed them, and this beast owed *him* his life. He sighed, then rallied his men for a last charge.

Something barely moved in his sight line.

"Net!" The prince shrieked.

Men scrambled and flurried.

Out of nowhere, the beast leapt on him. He vaulted away with what he thought was a minor scratch. The lion pounced again, then turned to maul the guard who had frozen in shock beside him.

Maatkare sprawled backward in the grass, momentarily dumbstruck and breathless. He winced in pain and grabbed at his bleeding upper arm.

Torn. Gods. My hand goes down into the meat of my damned arm. It's bad, damn it! Then, he croaked aloud: "Wuenre, you snail… I will crush you."

The animal picked up the scent of fresh blood and grew strangely renewed. It rallied and turned.

Screaming. Who screams? "Wuenre!" Maatkare saw something thrash in the grass. "You take my curse to your Amenti, you gutless wretch. Cover me now... Redeem yourself... you didn't..."

He sensed nothing from his men, flipped, turned, and dug his feet into the ground to push forth on his belly through the grass. He reached the last place he had seen the guard.

"Net the bastard! For the love of the gods..." he squalled. Roaring and thundering filled every shred of his conscious thought. The lion was around, in front of, on, and behind him. Something gave way in his own heart that blotted out everything but himself and the menace in the grass. He was alone except for another screeching lump of humanity on the ground beneath the beast. It screamed, begged, and thrashed as deadly claws and teeth bit and tore.

Maatkare rolled away hard, knowing he couldn't save the man next to him, then focused on saving himself.

"Idiots!" the prince screamed at his men, his mouth paled. "Cursed cowards!! Get to me! Get to me!" He clawed and swam in the blood-slippery grass, then drew the strange gold dagger of Wepwawet from its temporary sheath at his belt. *This! Do the heka against this beast. Do it... Eeen Nauu Eeen Sekht een Anhur Saba... Oh Aanpu... aid me send this monster to the great nothing!*

He hadn't planned to use it. He'd taken it, as a battle favor to honor the coup over Marai and his anemic little attempt at a challenge.

Burns!

The prince felt the knife go weightless and transform as he gripped it. It acted as if it had fainted and fallen into his hand so that the end of his arm became a giant, rending claw. He wanted to see what had happened, but in the waving light of torches and the din of men shouting he couldn't.

Can't look now...Changing. His good hand gripped hard while, at the same time, he tried to ignore the fire that blistered his wound and paralyzed his left arm. As he seized the blade with his right, the thrill of his transformation into the great wolf dog swept through him. He felt himself leap into the air, suddenly wild, furred, and snarling. His last human thought was about his men. *The men. They can't see me do this...* then *Death!!*

Men screamed and cried out in terror. Feet slipped and pounded in wild disarray as they scattered through the grass in sudden panic. Maatkare seized the lion's mane as the beast pounced on him. He struck downward with the magical blade that had become a claw and reveled in the agonized roar followed by an unholy death-agony screech that filled his sharpened ears. He couldn't breathe. Blood filled his throat. The panic of strangulation became a very human thought.

Choking me out again, bastard. No!! I will live! The massive animal weight fell on him. Through gore-blurred vision, he saw the black lion face transform into a dark wolf and finally settle as the moonlike hide of the black-faced war bull. Once again a lion, its teeth and jaw clamped and bloody spittle slobbered down.

Cursed thing. Damned vision. Seize it. Still it and eat.

Red thoughts raced through his flesh and teeth. They itched to bite and snap. He wrestled from beneath the crazed and wounded beast, straddled it and began to rend and tear into its fur in savage glee. The hot, salty pulse of blood gushed in his face and streamed down his neck, but he craved more of it. The lion was dead. Some of the men may have been dead.

Another man cried for mercy somewhere, but no one came to help either of them.

Men? Come... He felt darkness swirl around him, suffocating him with delight.

Nefira, his thoughts cried. He fell forward on his prey, slipped, and almost fainted to one side as he gored at the breast of the twitching creature. He sank his jaws into the exposed and steaming fleshiness of its breast, and wagged his head back and forth with a strained growl until he felt the hair and skin rip and the wetness surround his face. He tore out more meat with his teeth, ripped with his claws that now only gripped the blade for assistance.

Eat. It is good.

The prince bolted down the sinewy tissue and lapped the blood. His head sank back to the carcass, exhilarated then he threw back his head and howled long and loud before he devoured his rest of his meal.

OPENER OF THE SKY

CHAPTER 33: OPEN THE SKY

In her vision, she flew away again. There wasn't much else to do.

Fly away. Fly away.

Deka knew she had gained the admiration of the few men in the camp who hadn't gone with the prince on the lion hunt. She read their thoughts and their impressed disbelief as she drew a bow heavy enough to wrench the shoulder of anyone but a trained archer.

They don't dare help or speak to me without my beloved present. At first it thrilled her that men feared her enough that they wouldn't assist or teach her. She was there for Prince Maatkare, now as the only concubine. Then, the thought that her companions had moved on struck her. *Am I your concubine, Raem?* She thought at the empty air, *or am I still caged by you, even though I will it?*

He hadn't returned. If the first hunters who trickled back in had been enthusiastic, the next men no longer praised his efforts in the field. Deka listened from inside the tent as men openly worried that the prince had taken leave of his senses in his zeal for triumph. Someone would end up dead before the foray was over, they said. The lion was no mere wounded animal; it was an elder god. His insistence on doing battle with it would mean nothing for any of them but doom.

Deka was worried. Maatkare had been distant after Marai and the others left, as if their departure hemmed him in and constantly accused him of failure. There hadn't been an easy victory in this hunt either. She knew he thought about losing his prowess, and wanted to encourage him somehow.

Raem. Be safe, beloved. Know when a challenge is too great. I will love you even if you fail to bring in this beast. Your men will still praise you. She sent a thought into the air but no response returned.

Concerned and bored with possibility of just waiting and doing nothing, she sat on the bed, took the box of stones from the top of the trunk, and opened it again.

Help me see. Help me go to him and give him the strength of a god. She placed her hands on top of the shimmering mass and felt the instant jolt of separation as a spirit walk commenced. This time, her flight felt different from the personal journeys and dreams she had undertaken most of her life. She felt herself rise up in the darkness of the new night sky.

I just wanted to escape from the boredom, the waiting for him to come home, but this is not the same. This is about me and proof of what I am. I can feel it. Tonight I learn! She exited her trance-swept shell of a body and flew by campfire lights in a circle below.

Is this the hunt? Is it finally finished? Will they be coming home soon? She took a deeper breath, relaxed and soared once out over the great river. Coming back into herself for a moment, she swooped down and back. *He will arrive soon! He will have me anoint him with perfume, after his men have bathed a day and evening of sweat and dirt from him. I will run my hands over him...*

She reveled in the memory of the raw power of his muscles; the way they never relaxed too much, as if his skin was packed to the limit with incredible, bulging strength. Just a touch from him always left her fainting with delight. It had been that way from the first night they were together, and was part of her desire as she waited.

She shut her eyes again because she had been determined to send her spirit out to follow him in. Once again as she rose, she found herself drawn to the small village on the waterfront where they gone to bathe that time shortly after they arrived.

Despite her efforts to return to the hunting party, her black overskirt transformed into smoke-like wings and carried her gently to Qustul Amani.

But I must go to him. Wait. Is that a fire burning? Where are the men? Why do they run and cry in terror?

When she received no answer, she shrugged. She continued to float to the little town where another force called out to her. A little light formed. At first, Deka thought it was the full moon on the horizon and that the fires below were lights like the stars. She focused on a dozen other lights that bobbed toward the licking fire but then felt wrenched toward walls and a porched building with Marai standing there. His moon colored hair framed his swarthy, copper face as he peered up into the starlit sky. He looked every bit the silver-hided and black-faced war bull in human form tonight. Three men stood with him.

Friends are with him now. Look... she felt a tug of loneliness and remembered the window in her apartment in Ineb Hedj. When she had been there, she had always stared at the very same stars to see if anything of Ta-Te remained in this world. In that memory, Marai was always with her, gentle as a father. He stroked her arm and pulled her backward just a little so she could look higher up in the sky without falling. She thought of the way they had almost kissed at the well before he left, and how much she had wanted that kiss, but couldn't accept it.

Oh but these are dead worlds now. Be happy for me Marai. I am finding myself.

Deka...come and play with me.

The child voice which had called itself Ameny, the voice of the child she would give the prince, whispered from inside the little moonlike light just as it floated in front of her.

Come down. We want to see you, pretty woman.

The voice transformed into the gentle warble of an older man. It led her closer to the men on the stone porch, then plunged down with her as if it wanted her to get a better look at them.

"Marai, my Man Sun" she breathed aloud "I *do* see you. Do you see me?"

He nodded, but didn't focus on her. A man who looked like the stonecutter her beloved had punished stood with him, but he had changed. His hair was lighter; his beard appeared smoother than she recalled. She sensed the pulse of something pale and moonlike on his brow.

You have a stone, now. You have replaced me to him. It heals you, but you are weak still. Deka felt a coldness envelop her heart because Marai and the others were moving on without her.

"Marai. Look. Do you see her; the spirit?" she heard the younger man ask and saw him point.

"It's her," Marai answered with a little laugh that sounded sad. "It's our lost Deka on a spirit journey."

"No," her spirit answered. "I don't *want* to be seen by you…" but she was distracted by the sight of a tall dark man who stood with them. "You. I know you," Deka gasped.

She remembered a hot and dusty day in the market and a tall young priest of Djeuhti who had evoked her dance. When she got up to move for him she had remembered the steps from a ghost of memory. That action had set everything else into motion. It was the day everything changed.

A smallish, older man pointed up at the sky and beckoned to the little orb of light that had led her to them. She sensed familiarity, but she didn't think she knew him until she felt the name Metauthetep Akaru Sef whisper through her stone:

Know him.

It said.

The man Marai was to meet? The Akaru Sef is supposed to be a mystic and leader of people in this sepat. My beloved says he is a worthless coward. But, she wondered, *do I know him more than that somehow?*

"Deka." Marai's gentle voice in a singsong question. "Are you ready to come to us?"

Of course he would know I was looking, but not that I was regretting. She looked away and was about to send another thought to him when the small old man beckoned to the orb, then dispersed it in a sparkly flash.

"Ah! I thought it was you. I *do* know you. You *are* the woman of this place who has been searching for her lost spirit. I have felt your call for so very long," the man moved closer to Marai and raised his hand as if he was pointing out her spirit-shape to the others.

Has this been a cruel game? Deka tensed. This was the light she had seen in her camp when the child's voice spoke from it. Now this old man appeared to control it.

Marai, stay away from him. He's dangerous, she rushed at the group of four men.

She saw the young man Djee stagger, then rub his eyes as if his head ached. He turned away, about to fall, but the tall dark priest supported him.

Marai turned to him and warned:

"Djerah. Don't. You're still not set inside. Make your thoughts blank. Go over there, sit down and practice that."

As Deka watched, the tall one moved the young man to one side and made him sit with his head down and hands crossed up over his shoulders in an attitude of self-calming. The young priest stood and frowned in his own sense of recognition.

"She's the one," he started. "…the same one who danced our women's dance for green growing, as I told you, Grandfather…"

Deka gasped, feeling a pulse of energy that she had been correct. Instantly, a wave and a distant music fluttered in her heart. The elder had started to hum a tune as he pointed at her floating image.

The music drew her closer to the older man. *Your old voice is music; music of a thousand rising out of the Land of Grass. How do I know you?* she asked, her wings settling into a quiet skirt again in her dream. *No, I do not. I cannot know you,* she turned away but felt his gentle thoughts push into her like early-season wind.

Oh, come to me, my pretty one. You are far lovelier than the woman in my dreams. You should not have stayed away from us.

She saw the elder's eyes lower then raise again. His hands suddenly went up to her.

"Sekhet Meri Netert, my memory's sweet voice calling to you above the battle. Is that truly who you are?" The Akaru spoke aloud and his words riveted the other men standing with him as if he had repeated an utterance. "Yes I *do* know you so well. I know how you want the taste of life now, how it marks you and burns your insides. But you must tell our father this one thing. Do not bring the storm today; do not bring it so soon or so many of his own creation will die. It is your sacred duty and why you must come back to us," the old man whispered his thoughts into the air. Deka felt so comforted by them, marveling that this old man she didn't know spoke to her so easily.

Sekhet Meri Netert…Sekhet beloved goddess he called me. Is that it, then? Our Father? Who? She never considered that she may have had a father. *A storm? He expects me to go to him and delay it?* She withdrew, but noticed a smiling face looking poignantly up at her, sadness and joy in his wrinkle-lined eyes.

"You know it is, and that you should come to us, sweet one. You should not be apart from your sisters and brothers, and yes, I have always been one of you, waiting here. I have been calling to you forever."

Marai reached up to shape the outside of his vision of her. She saw him bow his silvery head, then the smaller man grip his arm in support as if his utterance to her had weakened him.

Marai. Sweet Marai. I see I've hurt you so. But you see me now. You see how it has to be, you all do. She began, but something horrid drew her back like a screaming snap when as she noticed one of Akaru Sef's eyes had blazed green in a deep lowing howl of wind. Something else appeared, like a golden orb on his eyes. For the quickest of moments, she heard the scream of the wolf that merged with the wind. It howled at her back and yet a voice in the front still echoed:

Ha-go-re! Akh-go-re Nejter Deka Nefer Sekht Meri Netert

My name is sung ever-present

Though I am here.

I fly to you, I come

On dark but burning wings I walk on air

Open the sky to me

Ha-go-re Ta-te

Chapter 34: Fire in the Blood

When the triumphant howl drifted over the camp, Deka froze, roused from her journey. In all of the times past, the howl of a wolf or a jackal that rose in the distance meant there had been a final kill. Soon after that, the prince and his men always marched back to the camp. They celebrated and imitated his victory cry with their own hoots and howls. This time there was no sound of men on a joyous-but-weary return.

After an agony of quiet, Deka heard distant yipping and tittering of hyenas; these were real scavengers, *not* human imitations. She closed the box, put it on the trunk, got the lamp, and then went to the tent flap to look out.

Men had begun to stream back to the camp, but as they arrived they motioned for others to run out to the grass and give them some help.

Raem? Where is he? Deka's heart pounded in her chest. She knew something had gone wrong when she had been swept away to visit Marai. "What's going on? What's happened?" she asked the commotion of men who hurried past the tent opening. She wasn't answered until a stoic older man followed by an assistant squeezed rudely past her.

Neither man looked back to indicate Maatkare was following or apologized for their behavior.

"Excuse me? Why are you here?" Deka felt an uncanny amount of rage start to build in the pit of her stomach. "This is his Highness' private area. Has he *asked* you to be here? Where are his regulars?" she followed the men around the tent as they bustled with the setting up of healing supplies, then realized they had begun to remove the fine bedding from the luxurious padding.

"He's been hurt?" she asked, but neither man looked up from their preparations to verify her suggestion.

After long tense moments, while Deka watched and tried not to tear at her hands, Rutiy and Sutiy, the mute Wawati, shuffled out of torch-lit darkness. They carried the senseless prince into the tent and carefully deposited him on the bed, which was now draped with tanned hide. At the sight of him, her heart seized because so much blood drenched the prince's rumpled shendyt, chest armor, and greaves; he looked as if he had been skinned and laid open.

Dead! She felt a momentary giddiness at the sight of the blood, then a dread speculation over what force might have caused such grievous wounds. Her thoughts raced back to her flight to the observatory and the Qustul settlement. *The wind. The old man has done this. Why have you killed him? I knew he would do something and I warned Marai, but I should have been* here *at the hunt to protect my beloved. He distracted me with his spell of light!*

This man had been in the back of her dreams, she knew, but she had constantly pushed him out and away from her. He was a dream that became part of her reality the day the priest visited and cast his spell. When they were in his house on the way to the mines; when she and Raem had activated the Wdjat, he had lurked. He was there, but invisible. She had felt nothing that night in his house but an almost demented need for Maatkare to claim and then reward her. Tonight, the man had shown not only his face but so much more. He had answered her questions, but now she didn't want to know those answers.

Tell our father, he said? Lies! Our father? As if he is my brother? A brother? No. No. Nooooo No No brother. There was never a brother. Maatkare is my sworn brother and my love. Maatkare! Be well and defend us… she felt a sob catch in her throat *…dead? Oh no, not yet… not now, my sweet.* Her inner voice froze at the sound of a gurgling little cackle that rose from his body as the guards deposited him on his bed. He shivered and trembled in shielded agony. When she turned, she saw that he still clutched the golden dagger in a death-grip.

He's alive. Deka pushed her way back into the main area of the tent, then knelt beside his bed to cover his quaking form with passionate kisses. She lapped at the blood to clean him in her own way. *Oh blessed thrill, Maatkare, my hero. You are truly a god now.* She wept, touched him, and held him up, weak with joy. When his head lolled backward, she gathered it and pulled it up so she could kiss his eyes. He rallied slightly, but soon lapsed into senselessness. Blood steadily welled and ran onto the hide bed cover.

"You have to let us help him," the physician bent to her arm and urged her to get up.

"No. Not yet," she wrenched her arm away from him. "I have to see his wounds. I have to see how bad they are. He would want me to know how it is with him."

The elder shrugged, then ordered the big guards to get stilled water and salt. With a glance, she made sure he understood he ought to give her more time. When the grooms arrived with it moments later, Deka bid them sit quietly beside her while she bathed the prince's face and unbuckled his shredded armor.

It's bad. His arm and chest were torn open by that demon... but he beat it! He will survive. He has to. Her fingers moved quietly to the open gouges and tried to smooth the ribboned skin over his breast so the edges would lay straight. Tears of her joy dropped onto his heaving chest and her shoulders shook with sobs, overjoyed that he at least responded to her by tightening the grip of his right hand. She raised up.

"Let me take this, beloved one," Deka's hands grasped the sticky knife he still gripped in his left hand. "I will clean it and put it away for you," she whispered, then spoke to his thoughts: *I will respect it, because it saved you and brought you home to me.*

The elder physic returned and touched her arms gently.

"Let us help him now... we mustn't wait any longer. We will bathe his hurts and make him comfortable."

She looked up, as stunned as if she had been dreaming, then glanced back when she heard the prince make a weak grunt of pain.

"See? It's a long gash. He bleeds from many claw marks at his shoulder and arm, a bite tore his skin, but see how he fought until he was victorious! He will defeat *this* hurt, too."

She read the physic's thoughts far too easily and knew neither he nor his assistant agreed.

Poor creature. Her grieving has caused her thoughts to deny that he will die soon.

She sensed them thinking. A low growl issued from her throat. *Did they dare claim he would fail so easily. They are traitors. All of them.*

"You're wrong. I know your thoughts. If you haven't the skill to heal him, leave at once and I will do it," she focused an evil stare at the physician who froze for a moment.

Deka knew she had frightened the man, but despite her outward show of confidence, she worried. Maatkare's wounds bled steadily from a dreadful raking over his beautiful left arm and part of his upper chest. If the bleeding couldn't stop, he would continue to weaken. The cuts were deep. She bent to give him some strength with a kiss and tasted the blood from his feed in his mouth.

No. What? She frowned, recognizing the taste of a man's blood. *My love, what have you done?* The back of her hand went to her mouth. She moved back, gagging. *The taste is off. It's not the blood of a beast or an enemy. If he's tasted the blood of one of his own men he's brought a curse on himself!* She didn't know how she knew that, but at that moment she accepted it.

Tales of men of any rank being bitten by beasts and then inclined to take their shape sometimes against their own will were always bantied about watch fires of the encampments. It would be her duty to see such evil never took hold. *No, I won't let you be a slave to this. In our kind, it's a gift, not a curse! You taught me that.*

"Do what you can for him." She looked up and addressed the physician who hovered nearby. "When you have threaded his deeper wounds I will stay with him through the night." She faded into the background of her part of the tent addition to think about whose blood she had tasted on his lips. The big Wawati stood guard outside the tent. She hadn't seen the tall guard who used to annoy Wise Mama and preen for his Highness to allow him permission to use her.

Wuenre. Now where is he in all this? She frowned, then unable to sit still while the physician and an assistant worked on the prince's arm, she cut through the edge of the main room and exited the tent.

She moved to one of the guards, touched his arm gently and looked into his eyes so that he understood her thoughts. The other guard turned and followed both of them to a place just outside the main circle of the tents.

Talking fingers, she gestured, knowing that these men still might not understand her. She would send thoughts along with the gestures, hoping it worked. They *were* intelligent, she knew, but they were different. Deka was only beginning to sense what the oddness they possessed was about.

Because you are brave protectors, we understand each other. She gestured while pushing the thought to them. *I will reward you in ways you may not know once all is returned to me.*

MaMa, the first one addressed her. *Protect.*

What happened out there? Why do the men shy from me, yet wish his spirit to go free? She placed her hand on the big dark man's throat, giving him the thought it would help him speak.

Wounds kill the heart. His face turned away, but Deka knew the man was not sorrowing. He guarded a far different emotion… a kind of envy.

Let me read what your eyes saw in the battle, she looked into his eyes. Her other hand touched the second guard, who had been looking over his shoulder and attempting to sense and interpret some of the chatter in the camp.

When the window into their memories opened, she saw animals thrashing and screaming. Maatkare slashed and struggled under the weight of the beast, then emerged with something in his hand that looked like raw meat and glistened in torchlight.

He didn't walk as he held it. Suddenly on all fours, he crawled, growled, and snarled, curious that the bravest of men scattered. Then, he found a weak one, already injured by the beast.

The scene faded with his senses, but Deka understood through her Wawat spies that Maatkare had eaten his kills and drank their blood down hot according to his ritual. That was expected, but he hadn't stopped. Along with the heart of the beast he had eaten the hearts and lungs of the fallen guard Wuenre and started to take another of his men who was wounded but not dead.

Battle fever.

Frenzy.

Has taken a curse in his heart that will make him become a beast.

Better if he dies, than lives to remember.

Better we die than see how self is changed by the gods.

It shouldn't worry him, she thought on sudden impulse. *Blood is blood and it is life. Drink the blood of our enemies including those we see as cowards among our own. Are all of these men cowards to cringe at his justified ravage? His victory over his weaker nature? You have done well, my love. You, my two helpers,* she sent a thought to the men, know *that I understand you now and what is on you. Know that one day you will be free. Go run the camp and listen for more who may speak against us. They are afraid of us now. They will whisper loud and often.*

Deka blessed the two men when they bowed to her by gently touching their throats again before they took off running. She knew they would be back before they were missed. Her head turned at the sound of a gentle, almost pathetic whine that issued from the tent. When she looked inside, she saw the assistant and another burly man she had missed entering the tent holding the prince down while the physician sewed the deeper slashes in his arm closed. His head thrashed back and forth in misery and his lips drew back in a permanent snarl that showed more blood and darker matter in his teeth.

Be strong, beloved. Rise above the pain. You are mighty. It cannot hurt unless you allow it.

"Look." one of the men holding him called to the other who was wielding the fine copper needle and linen thread. "His eyes have become beast eyes. If highness lives, he will be foaming and mad. See the dog face he already assumes?"

Deka's thoughts trained on the assistant's words. *Is Raem in such misery he's becoming a wolf in front of them? He told me once not so many had seen it since he was a youth… that he had learned to control it. Poor man.* She pushed further into the tent and heard the doggish whine of pain. The men had finished with the tiny linen sutures and applied a wound gel of rendered fat and herbal infusion to his arm and chest.

"Finished?" her voice snapped as they wrapped his wounds. She made no attempt to soften her voice or to sound less anxious.

"We've done what we can. He no longer bleeds, but we expect there will be a fever and madness that follows it in a day or two. He could not possibly survive once the fire reaches his noble heart. We will come then to give him draughts for his misery and to pray with you. It is in the hands of the gods," the physician did not make eye contact with her. She sensed he was humiliated that his best medicine could not save his prince.

"Go, then." She drew herself as tall as she could, then pushed in to kneel at Maatkare's bedside.

When the men reluctantly left, Deka took up his left hand, careful not to disturb the bandaged part, kissed it and then licked his fingertips. She wanted him to suddenly rally, seize her, and possess her for hours but she knew he was too weak and ill. She didn't understand why his mighty sense of self-preservation or self-healing had abandoned him as he lay before her. He had never shown less than perfection to her.

"Beloved." She ordered.

His head thrashed and wagged on the pillow.

"Look into my eyes. See me. Look at me."

He panted, but then stilled for a moment to open one wildly darting eye. He pushed her away with his good right hand. "Go. Go away," he mouthed.

"No, beloved," she whispered gently. "You woke my heart with your power and made it rich when you punished the men. I have to give you a deeper awakening now and I tell you that you must live to triumph," Deka kissed his lower lip, taking it gently in her teeth and tugging it with a playful nip.

The heart remembers a long ago ascent.

The voices in her thoughts whispered.

"I know it burns, my love, but you opened me to power and I return it to you tenfold," her voice trembled with awe. She clutched his hand and clapped it to her cheek, then sank to him with a whisper. "Be at peace with it. Seize it as you needed me to do it not so long ago. Taste it."

The prince's eyes darted in animal panic for a moment, fixed on her, and glared. A sharp, green-gold light emitted from them. When he growled, she froze for an instant, confused. His eyes were different than they should have been. The aura of the wild, black wolf-hound *should* have left him after he battled. Even though his glance set her into a momentary panic, something in her heart thrilled at the look in his eyes. She'd seen that look in his eyes long ago… even before the children had crafted the knife and long before they had even met.

"I know you," he whispered.

"I know." She replied.

OPENER OF THE SKY

The first day after the hunt, almost as soon as he regained his senses, Maatkare demanded large quantities of beer be brought to him so he could slake his thirst. By the second day, he tried to drink himself to stupefaction. Each time refreshment was brought to him, he quaffed it heartily. Then, his guts cramped and nausea sent him sprawling to vomit with such force that his wounds began to seep again. He staggered back to his couch, weak and ill, then lay panting and gasping for long moments. It appeared to anyone who saw him that every part of his body ached and trembled like a demonic spirit had infected it.

His vizier brought the physician back to look at him several times each day. The men zealously changed the dressing and reapplied the gels to the stitched places to keep the thread moist, often making note that the gouges from the lion's claws were not as deep as they first expected.

Deka overheard them exclaim that she must have worked some kind of sekhem on his wounds.

"In a few days the threads will be clipped and you will be fit to command again, Your Highness. "I've taken great care so that you should have very little in the way of a scar by the time another year has passed. The gods have blessed you, truly!"

"No! Not good enough!" the prince screamed and cursed them. She listened, almost helplessly from her side of the tent, as he ordered them to apply more oils and bandages. He drank until he stumbled and careened around his side nearly senseless. When Deka tried to go to him, he bellowed: "You! You *know* something. I can feel it. You know I must be without flaw if I am to rule! No scars! No marks! And you think you have rights with me? I'll show you. You are now to be on the other side of camp. If I see your wicked face…" he screeched drunkenly, then lurched to the opening of the tent and ordered men to begin detaching her tent room.

"Raem…" she protested.

"Your Highness," he corrected, starting to slur his words from the drink and the rising fever. "You don't like your place under my heel then you just go running back to your Akkad devils and see if they will even want to take you back. I'm done with you!"

"He doesn't mean it," she repeated almost silently to herself, but secretly she wasn't sure. *How could he bring me in and then just cast me out? How could he wake me inside and not expect that I can also turn on him with a fierceness which will give him sorrow?*

For the remainder of the day, she shot arrows, worked beads, and dreaded being alone with her increasingly volatile thoughts. *If Marai or that old man did this to show me I made a bad choice, they will pay!* Then, she felt the uneasiness of nausea and remembered her child. *He* has *to care about me.* It was a sleepless night in both tents.

By the third day, Maatkare's guts had turned to water in addition to the black vomit, and his fever began to rage.

Deka heard the concern in the camp and ventured close to the royal tent but didn't dare go in.

"It is as I feared," the physician exited, shaking his neatly shaved head. "He has black water fever."

"Lie… he tells lies…" Deka heard Maatkare squall in the distance. "He's tryna kill me, Nefira… I know you are out there listening to this ugly bastard. You know there was no pond out in the field for me to drink. You *know*…"

"Beloved." She tried, standing just outside. "Calm yourself. Let me help."

"No. I will not see you like this. I cannot see you." His voice came back deeply despondent.

"I will heal you."

"No. You will not. Go Away. Go to your Akkad husband. I don't want you, sorceress."

He doesn't mean it, she sobbed inwardly.

In another day, dark, angry streaks moved into his armpit. His arm and chest, which had been healing well, developed an odor and grew septic. The physicians washed the wounds again and again, putting ash and honey salve under clean bandages several times a day. At last, Maatkare ordered the physicians to bring him no food or drink. He knew healing from his own studies and decided to sweat out the wound poison with only manna paste to help lower his fever. When it abated, he huddled under skins and shivered violently. The wounds had fewer odors but were bright red and some which had not been sewn opened and had begun to weep pus.

After pointless hours of his trying to bring the trembling fits under control and the sight of the foaming drool that occasionally spewed forth from his lips, along with the vile and hearty curses, the physician convinced him he would die soon. He relented, but didn't want to die alone any more.

"Nefira…" he forgot his vanity and demanded her company, in several soul wrenching screams.

When the grooms fetched her, Deka quickly gathered her things and followed them to the royal tent.

If my Raem is dying, I need to go to him. I need to try, even if he fights me, she decided, but couldn't avoid noticing the reactions of the men as she moved. They stared and many of them avoided her as she walked, she knew she had lost any friends she may have made in the camp. Men who had once respected and admired her now whispered: "She has cursed his Highness."

It was a long walk. She heard enough whispering as she moved through the camp that she wanted to rise above it like a fantastic winged serpent and ravage it, but she contained herself.

Fools. They don't know who I am. Raem, poor, poor Raem you must not know what I have recently learned of myself either. They whisper about me. They must be punished. Ah, but you taught me they are lesser creatures, not worthy of a spell or even a gentle reminder of their rudeness.

"What are you saying," she paused by one man. "I hear what you are thinking."

His response was the same as the rest of the men in the camp. He showed veiled fear and handled an amulet to ward off any curse she might hurl at him. She hated when they whispered, because she always *knew* it was about her and she wanted to retaliate; to raise her hand and cause a headache, stumbling, or a momentary blindness. Tonight, she knew she couldn't be distracted by those thoughts.

For the past three nights, she hadn't tried to seek Marai or the curious men in the riverside town. She hadn't *wanted* to seek any advice from Wise MaMa or Naibe. She just wanted her beloved to be well, but every hour he seemed to worsen. She meditated on all of the sensations of the land to see if there was an answer from her forgotten past, but only received the image of herself striding above the earth as if walking on air and among many men with her beloved at her side. It was like the song she had always chanted.

He has to live! I want my vision to live!

She overheard the men murmur about the lion hunt from time to time. What they witnessed had been nothing less than stunning. Tonight, as she crossed the camp, their whispers poured through her thoughts. Each group of men turned their heads to watch, and for a moment she thought they might come to accuse her.

"He transformed into the wolf the moment the lion leaped on him."

"So fast. No time for a spell to take hold!"

Another group argued: "He killed the lion, but he killed Wuenre, his captain? I think he did it before, to draw the lion, then ended the poor man's pain."

"No, it was after they were attacked. He killed with the magical knife that woman gave him."

"No, no you didn't see anything in the dark from where you were standing. You were with the ones fighting the torch fires that got into the grass. How could you see a cursed thing? I saw Highness change and bite both of them, then eat their hearts and lungs. Poor Wuenre did not deserve… Shh… here she comes…"

A third gathering was accusing their leader of murder.

"They were having words. Highness was shouting at Wuenre about slacking his duty right before. I think he was pushed in front of that beast."

"He became Wepwawet. That much I know."

"No, it *had* to be a demon. Once the lion was down, the god should have left him."

Deka sensed from everything the men whispered that once they realized the lion was no longer a threat, they were still afraid to approach the prince in his wolf form. He had growled, snarled, and threatened anyone who tried to approach or to stop the grisly feast until he had fainted with delight and lay, fully in the shape of a man once more. They had carried him back to the camp and fled to their tents, hoping everything about that day and night had been some kind of illusion or dream.

"It's that woman. Shh. There…"

Deka felt their opinions shift as she passed the physician speaking quietly to his own group of men. Bowing her head, she sharpened her own sense of hearing.

"She's done this to him. He should have left all three of those women home and taken the locals, but he got proud. Could he not see they were adepts in some worship? The one he calls for is from the goddess race. She caused him to form as a wolf. I saw it once when I came by the tent as they were in pleasure."

She paused in her step, about to speak, or fly over to the man and slap him, but decided to listen to the next man disagree in his defense.

"No, he has always wolf-like… Remember he is a priest of Wepwawet and I heard he has a good gift over the animal within. This is just a natural progression of things. He has finally gone too far by eating the raw flesh of his kill."

It's making him sick, though Deka thought. If I don't help him it just might make him mad. How can he rule all of Kemet in such an uncontrolled state? He sweats and gnashes human teeth while he lies on his bed. It isn't a shape shift, he suffers.

Deka nodded to the guards who brought her, dismissing them; a cryptic smile dotting her lips as she went inside the tent.

I know what this is. The last of his old nature is at odds with the new. If he fights it too hard, he will die. I have seen this before somewhere in a dream. Did my Ta-Te endure this? Is this what I recall? She looked at the cups of beer and medication that lined the table where the box containing the Children of Stone had been sitting. It had been moved to the trunk again. She sensed it had not been opened since she placed the cleaned dagger inside it. Before the physician left, he had refilled the brazier with herbs that made a calming, sweet smoke and placed several malachite scarabs at the prince's throat for protection against evil spirits because it was well known by healers that shadow demons could easily enter him in his weakened state. She sat by Maatkare's bed and grasped his hand in hers to calm him, then set his headrest aside. After she eased plump pillows under his head so he lay with his head slightly above his bandaged chest, she held him, kissed his hands, and pressed them to her cheeks.

He's so weak and trembly now, she paused, thinking: *Children of Stone. I'll use them the way Marai used them on young Djee. Certainly my beloved is worth it to the gods; worth more than an ignorant peasant boy. He is at least worth it to me.*

She started to get up to fetch the box of stones, but the prince seized her hand and pulled her down to him. His sudden display of might startled her so much that she sprawled over him. She kissed his upper chest above the wrappings, then looked earnestly into his face.

"The knife. Take it from me," he muttered hoarsely, then he realized he no longer gripped it. He remembered she had taken it and cleaned it the first night.

"It's in the box where they made it for you. Do you want to hold it?" she sought the expression in his eyes, gladdened that they had calmed and that he had recognized her.

"No. No. Don't get up, don't get up. Stay. I heard your thought, Nefira, that you said I am worth… augh, why am I to be marked like this?" his eyes were shot with horror at his own potential ugliness, but then Deka saw them fill with desire for her. His hand walked up her arm, then pulled her close so he could whisper. "Why does it burn?" he gasped. "I can feel a spectral poison burning inside me like curse. It never responds to my cleansing words, but keeps burning me."

"I know. I know. Shhh… shhh…" Deka consoled, her fingertips moving over his brow. "Yes, it burns in my heart too, my love. You gave me the taste and I accepted it. Can you not rise up higher yet because what's inside us calls to you?"

"Then you admit you did this to me, sorceress," his eerie laughter started as a low titter, then grew into a faint, but hideous cackle as he pressed her so close she could barely breathe.

She knew he understood, then raised up in a slight struggle to find his mouth so she could kiss him again and again. Deka's lips moved to his flickering eyelids and eased his fever for a few moments before his hunger for her rallied. Waves of passion started to course through him, but faltered.

"I did not cause this, beloved. I did not bring the lion to you, but I *can* heal you." Her lips made a fervent whisper next to his ear. She leaned into him, careful to balance so that she didn't hurt his wounds, then let him take her.

"Drink deep of my spirit," she spoke directly, then kissed his mouth in a deep kiss to give him all of the sensual energy he needed begin to heal himself. Soon, she had grown so weak with pleasure that she collapsed and lay her head on his bound chest, then gasped in delight that there was no strength of any kind left in her. It felt good to be depleted that way; to have given everything.

Her slim hand wandered to the box on the trunk and flipped it open. She closed her fingers on a stone by the way it felt and then held it up so they both could see it. It was the green malachite stone that had a deep olive undertone like eastern jades. It matched his eyes far more than the teal green scarab amulets perched at his throat. Deka took those away and set them on the table beside the box, then reverently kissed the stone. She touched it to her own brow where her blood red stone pulsed faintly, then put it to his lips, watching him become still as he studied its glimmer.

"Oh. You found the very one…"

She felt him sigh beneath her in a much stronger passion.

"Y-you want this one?" she gasped because she understood what this meant. "Inside, the way I have one?"

His hands tensed in a slight spasm. Prince Maatkare followed her hand up to his brow as she placed the stone there.

She felt the Child Stone sigh as if it had come back to a place it had always belonged.

The prince nodded, but whined in a little surprise as the green stone sank into him. He shut his eyes in an ecstatic gasp. "It's beautiful…" he faintly cried. "Beautiful… I can see… everything so clearly."

When he opened his eyes Deka saw that they glittered slightly.

He's already learning, she thought, a*nd this* has *happened before in my dreams.* She had seen the same wildness of heart that she saw in Maatkare. Some vague part of her memory stirred at the way he had raved. Somewhere in time, so long ago, someone else had transformed, but it hadn't been into a wolf. It had been seamless and flawless, unlike this evening. Her Maatkare had asked for the Child Stone, and had received it well, it seemed that the Children had agreed to translate him into a god; a real one – into Wepwawet, the Opener of the Way to the other gods.

It's what the Children wanted all along. It's why we were allowed to see Man Sun healing young Djee; why we could take part. It's why they allowed themselves to be parted from each other and to make him a golden knife that grows rich with blood in the same way we do when we taste it, she sensed. *He'll be one of the wise, but this time the learned men of Kemet will respect him. He will open their hearts, so to speak. It will be so much more fitting than the image dressed in Marai's lighter skin and eastern tongue. Marai is a foreign peasant. My Raem is a prince. He was born to the magic, the sorceries, and the wisdoms of his land.*

In her dreams, she saw legions of warriors, led by a wolf-headed god or carrying *his* standard on shield and flag.

This time, it will work. I will be with him every step of the way. Something's still wrong, though, her thoughts insisted. *The transition still feels too wild,* she sensed he had no desire to control the animal spirit raging in him. *It's not going restive.*

The spirit of the wolf-dog appeared to pace back and forth, uncomfortable in its human prison. Deka knew it sensed something. She was aware of it too, even though she tried to blot it out. Ta-Te was in the wind, and he was watchful.

Deka watched Maatkare sense and learn the strengths and personalities of the stones as he moved his hands gently over them. He'd been much stronger today. His fever was gone and his wounds had healed with only a faint scar that had begun to fade into the luxurious brown color of the rest of his skin. His eyes brimmed with a light of ferocity that bordered on madness. As he continued to feign illness so he could study the stones in the seclusion of his tent, he and Deka heard men were talking about what had happened to their leader and what it meant.

"It's not right, what that woman is doing to him. She is using her heka to heal a man who should have died from infection. Those wounds were deep and no amount of fine suture could close those hurts!"

That was the head physician.

"His Highness would not wish to live a cripple. Hunting and warring is in his blood."

"Oh but he would let a sorceress fix him. This is a matter for the king to decide when we go north."

Those voices were the man next in line after Wuenre to be Captain of the Hunt and his Vizier.

"Well you need to keep that thought to yourself around them. I think he would be best sending that woman back to the Akkad giant who was here and to those other women who went away with him."

"Ooh!" Deka squirmed, distracted from her study of his hands as they absorbed the reddish glimmer. "Raem are you hearing this?" she wondered why Maatkare wasn't paying these suspicions any attention. "Should we make an example, beloved? Don't let them have these thoughts of us! You should show your might to them."

His hand went up in the air as if he dismissed her thoughts. He never looked up from the box of stones, but quietly reassured her.

"I hear them. As long as it's talk alone, it's not conspiracy. It shows they fear us, and from that comes respect. It will only increase their obedience once I am ready to show my might to them. If it becomes something else, I'll deal with it."

For Deka, that was not reassuring. By evening, the murmurs had increased. She paced like a beast in a cage. From time to time she glanced at the prince, who still sat cross-legged on his bed and who had only infrequently looked up from the box of stones he studied.

"Call a council. I want them to see I have recovered," he suddenly spoke the evening of the second day. His voice was svelte and slippery, as if he was sleepy and meditative. It didn't have a fierce and powerful sound. It wasn't even growlish as she expected it would be, it was *pleasant*.

"Something is wrong, beloved?" Deka frowned. "I think you chose the wrong stone."

"Really?" Maatkare leapt from his bed energetically, grabbing her by the waist and whirling her around. "Now why is that, Nefira Deka, Nnn?"

"You…" she began, struggling a little. She didn't recognize this playful creature in the tent who had taken harsh Maatkare's place.

Am too peaceful? he corrected her, then added aloud: "Perhaps *they* teach me where you *cannot* because of your own unquenched fire, eh? I know you. What could you possibly know of that subtlety which is in itself taming. Grandfather will indeed be impressed if I choose to let him know of this gift you have given me… out of your great love."

Deka sizzled inwardly at the resurgence of one of her fears – that he might have used her as a means to get the Children of Stone for Great Hordjedtef. She kept a calm face over her thoughts and handed him his khat, but noticed as he placed it on his head that his hair was puffier but still tightly curled enough to fit under his headgear. She saw him smooth his quickly darkening face, but decide a slight beard might be acceptable when…

"Quick healing and now quick hair growth. My grooms will have to stay quite busy keeping me neat," the prince commented.

Deka felt his arm fasten and tug her outside the tent to the dais.

"Men," he stood and began to pace a little, giving a kick at the end of each row just before he turned. "I have recovered. Great Anhur has seen fit to preserve his scion and way-shower, and to heal him."

Deka felt his words rising through her in a different way. Now the force of his words caused her to tremble.

"While I lay in misery from the harrowing battle with the wickedness sent by Apedemak Aker; in the form of a demon lion who forced me to sacrifice one of our own," he paused.

She saw the faces of the men, all rapt as if they had suddenly found something to worship instead of conspire about.

I see how this works, she nodded.

"While I lay facing my own death I sadly realized my mighty cousin His Majesty King and God Menkaure Khaket was passing by. We spoke…"

Pauses at all the right places, like a rising king, Deka listened intently. She wondered if he truly felt any emotion at the death of the king or if his reactions were merely *calculated* to show him as a wounded-but-recovering son.

"We will return to the North in some days, but we must make certain the borders are filled with secure guardianship. I am tasked to finish any business in the Wawat lands and then in Buhen and Qustul."

Deka ignored the rest of the conversation, distracted by the thought of the way the stones had reacted differently to him.

As soon as the council finished and Maatkare dismissed the men to their evening patrols and duties, he took her back to the tent and began to study the stones again. As he sorted through them, a turquoise spark appeared at the tip of her fingers, guiding him. She thought of the differences between her beloved and Marai again.

When Man Sun and Wise MaMa handle the stones, they turn silver and gold, or several shades running from blue to pink. Little One never touches them. Something has changed now that we have these. She sat beside the prince and encouraged him to explore the various stones. Even the sweet, ethereal voices she remembered hearing when the Children spoke had changed into low, half-chanted susurrations; as if they had adapted to their new host. The new sound they made resembled a strange invocation instead of children singing – It was darker.

Eeen Nefira, Eeen Suenakhna... he repeated, over and over.

She couldn't dismiss the words as made-up gibberish anymore because she inwardly understood the language. Suddenly worried, she stayed his hand when he dug into the stones and let them flow through his hands like precious gems.

This happened once. Someone was destroyed by this. Is it Ta-Te I remember? Is this why I hesitate?

The blood-colored light spiraled up into him and through his eyes. It spattered him in a strangely lit, gory baptism. His look of exhilaration changed to one of horror mixed with delight as if he was swept up in a horrid storm.

Too much, beloved... too much... she begged him to stop. Then, when she thought his heart would burst from the strain, he shrieked, cackled, wept, and fell into an exhausted slump over his own crossed legs.

"Beautiful! Beautiful, by all of the gods..." he whispered almost feverishly. "O you foul witch," he tittered like a wild dog. Though his words degraded, they were filled with love, lust, admiration, and something even beyond that. "What have I let you do to me?" he cried, then extended his arms to embrace her.

As if she had become an arrow fired from a bow, Deka scrambled into them. She tried to calm what she thought were agonized spasms of dread. Seizing his hands, she kissed his fingertips again and again.

"I'm with you, my Wepwawet, my own lion Anhur. This is what you have always wanted. Grasp it. You open the way. You stand between worlds. Seize it and be mighty."

His arms surrounded her and although he kissed her naked breasts in unequalled passion, she noticed him tremble.

OPENER OF THE SKY

Chapter 35: Settling In Time

They lay in each other's arms, stunned. Deka wept in joy as she and the prince caressed each other's faces. Something in her memory had broken through both of them. Maatkare sensed it as all of her worries through the bond of their stones swept through him. Suddenly, he felt the urge to weep too.

That had *never* happened when he lay with a woman. He wept in grief as a boy when he was forced to shoot the black hound, Raemkai. That had been the last of his sorrowful tears. When the woman who first touched his heart was killed, his tears had been in rage over her murder, not in her loss or even the loss of his child her husband ripped from her belly. He never *met* the girl he was supposed to marry for status, so he couldn't even *force* his tears when she died. When his father and mother died he made some quiet tears form, but his grief was never deeper than his eyes.

They had lived complete lives, so why would I sorrow over their passing?

When his wife, the princess, was buried, he wept again in anger because it would be nearly impossible for him to ever be king. He made that look like sorrow too.

A different feeling rippled through him tonight. It wasn't sorrow or joy, but he still fought back tears and begged the gods that the woman didn't see his emotion as some kind of vulnerability.

Has my heart had been exploded? he asked himself as he lay panting and sighing. *Feels like it's melted in my chest and then that drifted like a pod of seeds about to take wind. Has it become part of her? Has she become part of me? I can't allow that. I need to pull myself from this. I need balance.*

Tonight, he regained more than his health. He thought he had begun to understand the Ta-Seti woman Deka. He thought he had seen the odd dark power that formed around her while they were enjoying each other. It was like his dog form, but not as fully forming. Now that the green stone was in his brow he had seen the missing parts.

He had envisioned Nefira Deka in a young, lithe form, standing high on a wall with a headdress like a strange upper lands crown: Tall white plumes issued from it, just as they did from the crown of Amun the creator. She drew a bow the length of her hard young body, demonstrating a skill for some great spiritual entity who stood behind her. His skin had an odd, deep red color that took on a black hue in some lights. Big red hands touched her arms lovingly. She whirled and danced.

That spirit. I know who it is, but his name escapes me. I've felt him before. Maatkare remembered a study and trance when he had been in priestly training. He had toyed with a dark energy wave and wanted to make black lightning arc from his hands. His teachers, generally annoyed and suspicious of his tricks, had warned him about summoning such power.

They didn't want me calling the power into myself before I had controlled my rage and my inner disquiet. I never listened to those old men who claimed knowledge of the animal and the guidance of war spirit but knew nothing of the beast himself. I knew what I was doing. I was calling down Sutekh as the storm and the wind. I would open the sky for him so that he would lay waste to those who had saddened me. The king, the princess, Red Sister, Brown Eyes, and even you sweet Nefira. You, my grandfather, who wanted to kill me after Meryt died. I knew you alone could get me. I went into study. I hid myself in Sokor and in the temples in the city of the wolf until I was more of an opponent... so you'd think I was improving myself.

Maatkare lay snuggling the Ta-Seti woman and thinking of a plan. No wisdom was needed; just timing. First things first, he would be the perfect noble at the funeral, appearing properly grief-stricken. He would discuss the matters with his grandfather and appear to be a staunch support to Shepseskaf and even to his poor cousin Wserkaf who was doubtlessly twisting in the wind now that his wife had been elevated as presenting sister and queen. He paused in his thoughts for a moment.

No, Wse will have to be either kept at arms' length or embraced so tightly he wouldn't be able to flinch. I'll ask the king to assign my return to the south, telling about the small uprising with Marai and this stonecutter. Once I am there, I will build, exert myself properly and march north.

The implications were huge.

He had been a man with no options other than time-wasting duty in peaceable lands. With a little more provocation, he knew he would be set up to usurp the throne in an excellent style.

Maatkare felt the stone in his brow tweak a little. He reached his hand up to touch the place where it lay buried, then noticed Deka had fallen asleep over him. He wiped her tear-stained cheek, then stopped himself.

This is foolish. I need to think and plan. The new plan would require much thought and organization. He sat up, gently easing her down, and noticed that it was already near day. *I must have dozed longer than I thought*, he heard the men already milling near the center of camp. *I need to go outside for a few minutes to encourage them…*

When he slipped on his open kaftan, he felt what he assumed was a bead of sweat on the side of his head. He dipped his fingers in perfumed oil and raised them to smooth it, but his fingers paused. *Hair.* It should have been stubby and short… just a five day growth from the flat trimmed style he normally wore. He kept it close to being shaved, but had planned to let it grow a little for funeral purposes so he could place a "lock of sorrow" in the king's tomb. It was supposed to be a tight curling tress about two fingers wide in length, when he pulled it straight.

What madness is this? Better not be wolf tails growing on me. He whirled around, seized a mirror and groped at what felt like tight, short-sheared wool. The lamp lit reflection showed him the image of a smooth, curled cap of obsidian black tresses. He put the mirror down, patted it, and grew almost pleased. It was human hair and it felt good to touch.

Maybe, when I ascend, I will start a style among manly men, if it continues to look good. Maybe I'll have it grow chin length or shoulder length so I can braid it without yarn extenders. He chuckled as he thought of the wind in it as he ran, of women running their fingers through it when it was unfastened. *The stone is doing this… and I feel good this morning.* Teeth… he checked. His shiny doggy teeth were still there. He looked at his arms and saw that his skin was smoother. There was less body hair to shave and no scar at all from the wound he received from the lion. The thing in his head was improving him.

He felt confused and childlike… almost happy. Still, it was time for his men to bathe him. He turned and lifted Deka into his arms, noticing once more how nice her body felt to him. For just that moment, he wondered if his having a stone would change the dynamics of his controlling form of lovemaking.

I'll work with it. Some things I'd rather not change though. You sleep, Nefira, and thank you for all. I can't promise you how I will thank you, but you will be praised for doing this for me. He carried her to her secluded side of the tent, which had been re-assembled, set her down, and waved his fingertips over her in an enchanted whisper so she would stay asleep. Then, he poked his head through the tent flap and whistled for his grooms.

The new captain went to fetch his grooms, but couldn't stop staring back over his shoulder at the prince's hair. Maatkare snickered at first, but then adopted a quiet and resolute face that implied he knew nothing at all had changed.

During his bath and massage, he sensed the thoughts of his grooms for the first time. The old sepat chief had handed them off to him when he first came through Qustul. He claimed they would be a good asset and no harm at all to him. When the rebellion had been stirred in the sepat, even though it was led by a deranged sojourner, he thought of making an example of them.

That was why… I used them as punishers. But, they hadn't hesitated or flinched. They worked excellently and without passion. He knew Deka read their thoughts, but for some reason he *couldn't* read them. At first, he had assumed the men were not very intelligent with their hulking forms and shambling gait, and assigned them to be imposing looking guards. Very quickly, he learned that Rutiy and Sutiy, as Deka called them, were as quick as any of his men. They were excellent trackers and fighters in hand to hand battle. Something was still exceedingly strange about them when he sensed their thoughts.

Do you see this? Lady Menhit does this to him. See her overtake him? It will be soon, one of them anticipated.

No, he answered their thoughts. *I can hear your thoughts now. For now, I am pleased.*

He silenced his own thoughts as they bathed him, and contemplated the reasons why men like his grandfather would go mad for the Ntr stones.

The stones are god-makers. They enter the bodies of mortal men and women and transform them. I agreed to take these "Children of Stone" to the temple at Per-A-At. There, they could be used as intended. First, however, as I told the sojourner Marai, I will examine them. No… he paused as the men shaved his face. *I will drag every bit of knowledge out of them myself.*

Nefira, because she saw me when I suffered… because I let her partway in… just opened the door for me, he mused. Suddenly, the thought came to him that if Hordjedtef got his wrinkled old claws on the stones, he could become young and pose a different threat; even a rivalry. Maatkare knew that at that point the Great One wouldn't need him at all to fulfill his unrealized dreams. He decided to keep his thoughts quiet and let the men finish.

After they dressed him in clean hunting gear, he rose and went to Deka. She lay sleeping sweetly on the spare pallet from her separate tent.

Should I thank you, woman, or should I curse the day I first saw you? he quietly bent to kiss her cheek. That broke his spell, and she startled because it wasn't like him to show unprovoked tenderness. "The men are spoiling for one last thing," he announced. "Back by dark this time. I want to test my new skills. No madness or fighting with devils this time."

Deka's eyes flew open and she spoke without even thinking of what she said.

"But, you need to take *me*," she jumped up and began to tie up her hair. Maatkare took a step, folded his arms and studied her. He was a little shocked as she bravely found one of his kilts to wrap around her hips so she could run without tripping on a long skirt.

"And I should take you, because…" he started, but saw the flicker of fire starting in her eyes. He wanted to laugh and to give her a little tap on the face to return her wits to her but at this point he merely shook his head.

Two of us with god-stones, eh? he thought, *and already I am staring at you like competition.*

"Your men told you I can shoot and I can run. I know you saw me draw a war bow in a dream," she moved close to him. "I want to prove it to you today… then I won't ask again, until the child is born," she trailed him into his segment of the tent. Her eyes focused on a large quiver of arrows.

"Nefira Deka, my Sekht…" he tugged at her arm and she almost shrugged him away. "You want to run with me so badly? No," he paused, shaking his head. "My women don't run with me. They wait for my return."

"Am I just that, then? One of your women?"

The prince frowned. The Ta-Seti woman had been quiet and had seldom spoken to him above a seductive whisper or a tart request for him to stand up to someone at the most. This was different and spirited. It was what he might expect from Red Sister Ari, but not Nefira.

"You *are* just that. One of many. You have my child in you, but do see it doesn't make you proud of yourself." He helped her tighten the straps on the quiver until it fit, then handed her the spare bow. "I just didn't expect you to speak up to me as if you know me… yet." He eyed her up and down and thought of the images of ancient goddesses, but tried to keep the urge to take her in his arms once more at bay. He paced as she stood near him, suddenly calm and humble – the old Deka Nefira.

"Perhaps," her voice grew quiet and restrained as it had always been. "Perhaps I've allowed myself to become… excited."

Maatkare knew he had hurt her. On any other day it wouldn't have mattered. His own eyes cast down and a feeling of blankness filtered over him. *She shouldn't have said anything to me*, he thought. *This is too soon. It's making me feel…* but then he stopped. Going to the tent flap, he looked out for a moment to see if his morning repast was being brought.

"One rule," he turned and took her by the hand, drawing her along with him outside to the dais where they would eat. "You stay with me. You keep up. You keep back. No mistakes."

Chapter 36: Peace of Amani

For a short while that morning, Marai thought it would be good to stay in Qustul Amani for a few more weeks. With the majority of the people of Qustul gone to the new city or up to Buhen, it was peaceful here. He thought he might offer to watch over the Old town while The Akaru and his wives went north for the funeral.

Marai knew they needed to go to the funeral too, however. If Deka hadn't given up on her prince by that time, he and Djerah would find ways of speeding up a boat with their combined skills and perhaps arrive with Naibe and Ari at the same time everyone else reached the white wall by traditional method.

For now, Marai watched Djerah move around the villa as if he was lost in thought. A week had passed since the young man's wounds had healed, and the changes in his physical form had begun to accelerate. He had begun to observe his surroundings and conduct an inner dialog with his Yah stone. In that manner, he trained himself to use his new skills.

Marai remembered his own early lessons had been very different. They had come more as a series of shocks: his looks, the magically appearing food and clothing on the vessel buried in the sand, the orbs that guided him, the fight with the thieves and the way he met the women. Djerah was learning differently, as if the Children of Stone had paid attention to the way wisdom was taught in the mystery schools.

The young man looked at and examined everything as if he had never truly seen it in his former life as a stonecutter or basketmaker. He stood reveling in the sound the leaves on the trees made as the wind moved through them or the reflection of the sun as it made star patterns on ripples of water. Sometimes, he took one of the twelve remaining Child Stones out of the bag Marai had given him to examine it more closely.

That night, as everyone still staying at Akaru's palace in Qustul Amani sat around low stone tables in the torchlit plaza and enjoyed their evening meal and conversation, Djerah suddenly held up the wdjat and spoke as if he had been talking in the sleep of deep reflection.

"It faces one way for HoRa and if you turn it over, it stands for Djehuti; one vision, one truth?"

"Wserkaf used it that way, why do you ask?" Marai nodded, pausing in his gentle stroking of Naibe's upper back.

"Well," the young man hesitated, "because he missed something only a stonecutter would notice, unless he just never told you about it." He showed the group a barely visible rough edge on one side of the crystalline roundel. "Anyone who's worked in stone can tell you this has been cut. Then it's had the edge softened or polished down so it looks like it was made of just one piece. Once there was another. Maybe it was even attached to it, like a clamshell," he thought for a moment. "I think this is where the child stones stayed once… inside both pieces, closed like an egg."

"The two wouldn't be big enough for all of the original seventy-eight," Marai turned his head and let Naibe poke a bit of melon into his mouth.

"Maybe it was bigger then, and shrank down when it knew it was going to be worn as a jewel. Maybe it changes size when it's with its mate," Djerah mused, then shrugged as he handed the wdjat to the sojourner and began to hungrily sop up the soup that had been set before him.

"It knew…" Marai leaned in to take the wdjat and ran his finger along the rough edge. "Hmmmm… I've only seen this one, but you're right. So this is the Djehut wdjat for truth. The other, the HoRa… wonder where *that* is?" he sensed what Djerah would answer in the next instant.

"The next part of the journey, I guess. Maybe this is the real reason why we have to go north again and not just for the funeral and to turn over what stones we have… gods know I'm not sure if I want to go back now. I'd be tempted to make Raawa and SeUpa's life a complete misery. I sense through my Yah stone that he got her and the sisters to go across the river after I never could, so there's no one at all left in Little Kina Ahna that we knew. They have an apartment in a fair neighborhood. They got me declared dead. I still think that if I showed up, looking better and stronger…" he started, moving over to the spot where Ariennu, who had gotten up for a moment, had been sitting."

"Sometimes it's hard to leave the dead with the dead, young man," Akaru raised a finger into the air, "but you *have* to."

Marai wondered about that too. All the way to Qustul he had thought of little else than creating misery for Hordjedtef and the prince for their acts against himself and especially the women.

"The Children didn't seem to mind helping me destroy the thieves when I returned to Ahu Wadi so many years ago." He remembered something that silenced that thought. It had been part of a vision while he and the women slept in the crystalline pods. The memory rushed into his, Djerah's, and Naibe's combined thoughts as a verse.

> *While we lay sleeping,*
> *Not long after some were slain*
> *A prince searched the wilds for us*
> *Guided by his vision,*
> *He found all consumed by fire.*
> *If you had not seen and slain them first,*
> *He would have killed all the women too.*
> *The legend would be one of loneliness*
> *And not of joy.*
> *We learn from you*
> *Man of Ai, Man of the sand.*

"So that priest you told me about, Hordjedtef, was on his way to Ahu Wadi just the same way his grandson parades about up here now? Why?" Djerah asked.

"He was hunting and looking for the valuables from the stars that his mentor Djedi had described, even back then. He was looking for the Children of Stone. His meditations brought him to the right place, but we and they were buried in a dune," Marai added.

"And if you ever wonder how Prince Maatkare came of such a hot temper and poor behavior…" Marai looked fondly at Naibe, then pressed her to him. "His men would have cleansed the wadi under his order, found three wretched and sick women there and finished everyone. So, I became the tool of my ladies salvation more than the instrument of the thieves' deaths. It was just their day to die, whether at my hand or Hordjedtef's." Marai kissed Naibe's forehead, then watched Djerah's face grow a little slack, yet frustrated.

"Exposing her would have been nice, though… and taking my little ones so they could have a better life," he shook his head.

"Days and nights like this, though," Marai kissed Naibe again, "make me want to forget all of this, get a few sheep or cows, and settle down here if you could find a fallow piece for me to turn into something."

"Up at Buhen, there's more grass and year round too. The cows do well and make thick cream milk," the elder smiled, looked at all of his guests, nodded to Xania. Changing tones, he added: "Tell me, though, how you'd ever be at ease, knowing what you do," he tapped his head, "and hearing them speak of what *they* want you to do." He laughed. "Maybe *that's* the blessing of being one of them, but not having a teaching stone. I know when my time is done I want to rest with my ancestors, not wander endlessly on some task of making the world a right one. I would leave that task to the gods."

Marai contemplated that. Despite the gifts they gave, the Children *did* nag. He thought of Wserkaf down in Ineb Hedj, with no life of his own. He thought of Deka following an entirely different plan. None of it made sense. He had always thought the women would find their own strengths. He would love them and make them feel more loved than any mere mortal man whenever they faltered because of his lonely years in devotion to his Ashera.

"Well, we already have one more and one less in our band," the sojourner quipped. "A long time ago I was told to see that the heir of Djedi received the Children of Stone. I thought it would be old Hordjedtef. Then, I thought it could be Wserkaf, but he refused. You told me, Akaru, that you were chosen as a child, yet you are pleasant here. And Djerah-Djee, you're just a surprise all around, but now I feel it was right for you to be a host."

Djerah laughed a little and devoured more bread.

There. That's a little more like it, Marai poked at the young man's arm. *We'll get you through the rest of this,* he lay back on a pile of soft pillows scattered around the dining couches.

"So we'll just leave Deka here?" Naibe's voice mirrored disappointment.

Marai looked up into her eyes helplessly. He didn't want to think about it, but Akaru spoke for him.

"Oh, I know you worry over that; but my little one is still with *her*… in the box you left with them. Perhaps when they come through, and they will do that," Akaru's face misted when he thought of the woman who had visited his observatory and the prince. "She is still so very unfinished with me."

Once again Marai and Naibe were about to ask a question, but Djerah, lost in his own myriad of topics, piped up:

"I would like to see the place of my ancestors. Whenever I lie dreaming, and this little thing in my head is working on me and teaching me things, the voices tell me need to go *there*. I need to see the place in the sand one day where the small craft lies; to see how it works inside." He shook his dark-but-sun-kissed hair. "Remember how it was easy for me to steer the boat on the way here, even though I had never done that before?" he asked Marai.

Marai remembered how well Djerah had taken to steering while he rowed, and how they never hit silt or high spots the whole way up, even though they kept fairly close to the river bank. He hadn't even needed to help him navigate at the Island of Elephants or as they approached the first cataract. Djerah had never been anywhere *near* a boat, except when he crossed the river to get to the stone workers city, but he instinctively knew how to steer one and how to get the best speed out of it.

"My steersman?" *If he finds the children's vessel in the sand, he just might be able to teach it to fly again.* Marai sat up again and shook his head in wonder at the way every mishap seemed to be part of the original master plan. It *was* like a marvelous game someone was playing. Who monitored it and what conclusion the game might have was something Marai couldn't answer.

"Well…" Marai started, at once lost for words. "Well…" Naibe leaned across Marai to hug and kiss Djerah before she scrambled back into Marai's arms. The young stonecutter started giggling, his warm brown skin darkening in a blush.

Akaru saluted him gently, with a grin, and poured more beer for everyone to toast.

"So you see," he said, "a happier night. Every leader needs a good *boatman* and one day perhaps a *star-boatman*." He raised his cup. "A toast to the first flight of the prophesied fledgling – the first to change while mostly awake."

When everyone laughed and raised their cups, Marai noticed Ariennu was still missing. He assumed she had risen to visit the privy, but that had been quite a while earlier. She had been keeping to herself more than usual since they left Maatkare's camp, which wasn't like her at all.

When everyone had come to Kemet from the wilderness, he had always sensed when she was apt to wander off and have an adventure with a man then cause him to lose his memory of it. He found it comical and not only gave her room to do that, but teased her about it. She had told him if he wanted her at all he would have to understand that, so he let her do as she wished. When they finally became intimate, she never stepped out after that.

He cursed himself. Marai knew he'd been so lost in the idea of Naibe having his baby that Ariennu had slipped further and further from his thoughts. Now that Djerah was adapting to his new role as a host, she knew she didn't need to stay around to create healings for him and he was still too wounded in the heart for anything more than disinterested sex.

Ari's gone. His thoughts rang out among everyone assembled for dinner. *Gone. And damn us all, celebrating while the poor budge sits on the side not even being missed. Now she's run off.*

"Should I go with you?" Djerah started to get to his feet.

"No, I need to do this alone," Marai tipped his cup then drained it, patting Naibe's arm and getting up from the dining couches. "My fault anyway."

"But I thought…" Naibe's voice grew small again.

"Don't worry, Sweet One. I'll find her," he bowed his head, sensing exactly where she was and knowing he was to come alone.

Chapter 37: Flower of Life

Marai guessed Ariennu was at the observatory. As he approached, he saw her standing alone on the wide porch roof of Akaru's temple where the men had seen Deka the other night. She stared out over the plain and into the direction from which the four of them had struggled just a week earlier.

As quietly as he could, and because he could sense her abiding self-disgust, Marai climbed hand over hand up the rope ladder to the top and then sneaked behind her.

I'm here, pretty lady. He sent a thought, wanting to touch her, but stopping his hands an instant before they made contact.

She startled a little, sighing tiredly, but didn't turn to face him.

"Knew you'd come," she smirked. "Sometimes I have to run off somewhere to get you, don't I?" She looked a little bit over one shoulder as he took both her arms in his hands and pulled her backward to him. Her sigh told him the rest of the story. He knew why she slipped away, but tonight he was counting on her to say its name.

"Yeh. I *am* jealous," she let him touch her, turn her, and hold her firmly to his chest. He tousled her frothy dark red hair.

"Sorry. I just…" he started to apologize.

"Yeah, I know. You always wanted to have a *real* child, and now…"

Marai noticed the sad look in her eyes. "You think Naibe's having a baby is pulling us apart, don't you?" Marai pressed her head, reassuring her. "It's not. That you can believe."

She sighed into his chest again. Marai knew why.

"Damn me, and you too, Marai. You always make me cry and here I go again,"

"I know why, Ari. It's because you are the tough one," he kissed her forehead gently. "It's the way you were when I found you, and the way you had to be again when I lay sleeping," he ran his fingers through her hair. "You know you're my back, my rod, everyone else's strength. It's what you've always been."

"I'm not so strong now... crying my eyes out on you..." she wiped her eyes with the back of her hand and looked up into his eyes. The neat, dark cosmetic lines had been smeared around her eyes and onto her cheeks. He took the edge of his cloak and touched some of black mark to clean it. "Sometimes I make myself sick with this..."

Marai grabbed her arms and shook her a little, then held her and rocked her warmly. "Sick with what? Lady, let me tell you something," he began again remembering the image of her lounging on the top of a sarcophagus, inviting him. "When I lay suffering, I kept seeing you, helping me be strong enough to keep trying to live. You were filling me with your rainbows; a sunny day after the storm." Marai smiled. "You were strong for me even then, even though you thought I had died, part of you never gave up."

Marai felt Ariennu wanting to melt into him and to feel his warmth around her.

"I just never wanted to believe what he told me; that snake-hearted priest! That there was nothing left of you. Gods, I was ready to turn myself into their goddess Aset for you and to run around searching heaven and earth for your body until I could have it and breathe life back into it. By El, I wanted him dead. I don't know what it was, but I just felt *weak* around him, like I couldn't do *anything* to defend myself. He made me do things..."

"But that's his power, don't you see?" Marai shook his head. "It even worked on me," he paused to revel for a moment in her look. He wanted to stop her from talking so he could just stand there holding her. "He puts the thought in your heart that he's not so evil – that he means well, then speaks into your dreams at night and tells you over and over that you're nothing and that he will defeat you. But, you knew the truth that you were strong." Marai shrugged, then began to sway back and forth with her. "And look! You beat him! He didn't break you, not my strong Ari." He kissed her gently, but her arms flung around him holding him tightly and desperately.

"You kept the Children of Stone and warmed the hearts of all the royal men," Marai let her hang gently in his arms. He continued, whispering and reassuring her. "You got Naibe calmed down. You told them how it would be different to be dancers and kuna women, to be good concubines to them who asked for it, even though it was killing you to admit everything bad that could also happen and go on happening forever…"

"But…" she protested. "I was just doing what I'd done before. Why praise me over that?"

"But nothing, sweet lady…" he stared down into her eyes again. "Do you know what miracles you worked to get up to the king in just *days*, past all of his viziers and physicians so that the old man realized he *needed* to stop you? That's strength. You looked right into a real god-on-earth's eyes and fed him tea; touched him… Even if he was a kinder one than his forefathers, people *don't just come up to* a king!" Marai felt all of the love and pride for her fill his heart.

"I bet the old man didn't even realize at first that it was *you* who put it in his heart all along and even convinced Wserkaf to show mercy to all of you." He quipped. "*I* was the threat! They could have turned all of you into the street or had you killed."

"Oh Goddess, Marai. You make me feel so…" she kissed his throat a little, looking around as if she wanted to find a place to ravish him "Powerful" and then thought to herself: *Dammit, everything's brick or stone around here!*

"And you fret over the *strangest* things," he smiled, walking her to the entrance of the empty burial chamber. He slipped down the inner ladder below the surface, then turned to look up "Come on. Hop down. See if you like it…"

Ariennu's laughter pealed naughtily as she descended and swamped him in an embrace almost before he could slide the heavy stone door above them in to place.

Found Ari. We are together. We are safe… He smiled a thought to Djerah, then turned to hold and kiss the wine-haired woman.

OPENER OF THE SKY

Epilogue: Opener of the Sky

Shortly after everyone heard the thought from Marai for them to "not wait up", the Akaru bid his wife goodnight and suggested Naibe go for a long walk with Djerah.

"Oh, I *would* like to walk with you, Djee," Naibe's eyes shone in helpful sympathy. "I know you are still torn inside and I *do* remember how it was when I was reborn. At least you are seeing the changes as they come, not being stunned by them on waking as it was with the rest of us."

"Go. Go on. Take a walk, but not to my viewing place." Akaru rolled his eyes in his own naughty mirth. "I need some space and quiet while I do my evening ritual, then I too will sleep."

The elder saw Djerah's genuine laughter and knew the young man's heart had become so much lighter. If he sent Djerah on a walk with young Naibe, he could journey among the stars, and perhaps to the mysterious woman who was now with the prince, without distraction.

"I'll wait by the entrance to the gated place," Naibe blew a kiss to him.

Djerah rose as servants removed the empty plates, helped Naibe to her feet, and then draped her little shawl over her bare arms. She folded her needlework and put it in her sewing and weaving basket. When she had put her things away, he offered her his arm.

Akaru noticed how happy they looked as they exited the plaza and chuckled as Djerah positioned his knife and sheath so he could grasp it quickly if there was trouble.

Trouble? No you won't have any, he thought, then called out: "Stay by the wall, you'll be safest there." *Fledgling.* Akaru thought, *and soon he will take his first flight. He is getting incredibly pretty, too, like Marai…like he really is Marai's son. Marai will have a son soon, and later more children, so why is it important that Djerah be his 'son'? Wonder what all of this means. If I consult the spirit tonight, perhaps I will learn the answer.*

He carried his lamp to the center of the open plaza. Once he set it down, he crept into the room where Marai and his other guests were staying and brought out the wdjat Djerah had handled and the twelve stones still in the leather bag the sojourner had left with his things. After he set the bag down next to the lamp, he went out to the center and pulled back rush mats that had covered an etched design of the Flower of Life. He found a broom and swept the dust out of the grooved tracks of the pattern so it was easily visible.

For him, it had always been a place of special conjurations and a contact point of greatest strength since before he was born. Legend had it that the design had been there since ancient times when the gods walked as men. It had been drawn in the sun brick surface by fire from the sky. Most of the time, Akaru meditated in his observatory. Tonight, he needed to make a stronger attempt to call the woman of Ta-Seti who had not returned with the others.

She had asked him to come, in her own way; Akaru knew that. When she had come to the observatory porch several nights earlier, he had suddenly known her name and mentioned it to her. *Sekhet Meri Netert*. She reacted and was about to say something, but was distracted and vanished. She had not returned, but he sensed her thinking about him at different times during the week.

When he lit the little pots of incense, he took the wdjat and twelve stones, placing the crystal medallion in the center of the flower and the twelve in double rows of six placed equally around the perimeter.

Oh, you are so curious about me now, aren't you, Sekhet Meri Netert whom they call Nefira Deka. He called you that as well, because you were pleasing. Akaru sat near the wdjat and closed his eyes. *But there are things you do not know. Our friend young Maatkare Raemkai distracts you and wakes your hunger, but doesn't know how to control it. Neither do you. You play with a hotter fire than you can know.*

He knew it would be up to him to distract her into leaving the prince and coming back to them. That way, she could evolve into her full form. Her return would need to be before the prince and his men came roaring though Qustul Amani to gather travel supplies and to go to their boats. That venture, he knew, would have to be swift or they would face battle with any men left in the newer town. Despite the elder's efforts to calm them, they wanted revenge even if they would lose.

And young Djerah. He thought as he began to clear his worries and lapse into a trance. *If the men from New Qustul return, someone will recognize him as the scruffy creature from down the river and wonder what sort of sorcery is animating and changing him and why their own relatives had not been resurrected along with him. Soon it won't matter if the dark portion of Sutekh arrives. Storms will already be here. I feel them brew and boil every day. I have to see what I can to do convince her to return.*

"I must speak to you who are lady of this land. I would learn your ways of heka. Allow me to fly to you." Akaru had the gnawing feeling that the woman was a true goddess walking and was close to the spirit and identity of Sekhmet, Tefnut, or Menhit. Maybe she was the reality of all three… She had passed the tests.

And that poor bastard Maatkare doesn't know she could disintegrate his soul into the prison of five thousand years just on a whim.

In the quiet, his thoughts rose and the smoke that rose around him formed into a giant ball of light that lifted his soul from his seated form. The orb wafted by the observatory, entertained for a moment's bliss by the thought of Marai and Ariennu immensely enjoying each other in an empty sarcophagus. He sped a little faster, pausing to see young Djerah innocently cuddling Naibe, as they sat counting the stars outside the wall. He saw the young man touch her slightly swelling belly and feel for kicks as proudly as if the child was his own.

He soared over the encampment. A celebration was going on below. Akaru sensed it. There had been a successful small hunt earlier in the day. The skins were already stretched on drying frames by the campfires. Other things were being gathered and tightened as if the group was preparing to break camp soon.

Planning his move to the boats in the morning? If that's so, I need to return to myself, because there will be ugliness. Still, I need to speak to her, out here, first. I need for her to be away from him. Akaru sensed blood and killing as he neared the royal tent. For a moment his thoughts froze, because he felt death, too. *Has she killed him? Have they killed each other?* He asked himself.

Outside the tent, the two black lions stood guard, but they looked like men. Akaru nodded to them that they were doing well. His shadow sensed her cleaning him, lapping blood from his throat in a strangely erotic tongue kiss. His head was thrown back in joy; his chest heaving. The prince was alive, but something other than drink and sex intoxicated him. Akaru felt a sudden numbness cut through him that was so powerful it almost hurled him back to his meditation area in Qustul the moment he saw her.

What is that astride the prince? What thing is that? What had at first impressed him as the cinnamon skinned woman mutated into something else. A blue-black, blacker than the darkest Kushite, alien creature that looked like the night sky come to life, bent over him. She was bent-shouldered, eyes red with fire… hair like flame that became golden and rippled into tawny skin that was no longer brown as spice. Her face looked up and, in a brief flash, he saw it wasn't even human, but caught somewhere between starry night and lioness.

The prince had become wild and dark in the same way. His black hair fanned out to his shoulders now. He was mad to almost screaming with desire, his fangs bared like a wolf or dog. The illusion of fine black fur coated him. Her stone blazed forth like a drop of glowing red blood. She was a lioness and he a wolf or dog, transformed in the midst of lovemaking.

"Feel it beloved," she whispered. "See how good it is. You are great. You are above all men. I worship you as my Ta-Te reborn."

Sekhet… voice of heat and dryness. I call you. Akaru Sef whispered, weak, because what she said about "Ta-Te reborn" had struck him like several knives. The name she recalled for the god she conjured was just wrong.

Daughter of the Eastern wind raise your face to me. One of the names you seek is Sutekh-Sebiumeker, raise your beautiful countenance…

Deka paused, raising her face. There were haunted shadows in her cheeks and an expression of horror mixed with delight.

Yes, he affirmed, going to her and embracing her with spirit arms. *You have found your lost self. See who you are? I have felt the same pain of loss, and so has he – but not like you. Do not cling to him any longer. Your place is among the stars. Come to me instead.* He continued, trying to convince her.

Akaru Sef's thoughts froze as Maatkare's eyes slid open in the realization that there had been a break in this strange wedding of two magnificent creatures. His eyes were glowing green. The stone in his brow was green too.

The governor lay on his side on the Flower of Life pattern in his open courtyard, numb. He didn't know how long he had been lying there, or that he had cried out loudly enough to wake his wife Xania. He knew she was there now and that she bent to check on him.

"Mtoto Metau-te, my Ameny… say you are well," she gasped. "Oh…"

His instinct, however scattered it was at that moment told him she realized she had breached the sacred space. He wanted to tell her it was alright, but couldn't.

"Too late. It's too late," was all he could say.

GLOSSARY

Pronunciation note: the pronunciation guides are purely speculative and written in common American English pattern.

Akh (Ahk) – Intelligence after death, memory.

Akkad (Ah-cad) – Ancient name for the area of modern-day Iraq; a person from that region.

Amenti (Ah-men-tea) – Also known as Duat land of the Underworld – The West, Field of Reeds. The place of the dead.

Ammit (Ay-mit) – "Devourer" or "soul-eater"; also spelled Ammut or Ahemait, was a female demon in ancient Egyptian religion with a body that was part lion, hippopotamus, and crocodile.

Anhur (On-Her) – The Nubian Lion god.

Apedemeketep (Ah-ped-eh-meh-keh-tep) – Grandson of Akaru.

Apep (A-pep) – A huge serpent (or crocodile) which lived in the waters of Nun or in the celestial Nile. Each day he attempted to disrupt the passage of the solar barque of Re. In some myths, Apep was an earlier and discarded sun-god himself. Also called Apohis

Ariennu (Ah-ree-in-oo) – Similar meaning to name Arianna or Ariadne in Greek meaning "most holy".

Asar (Uh-sar) – An Ancient Egyptian deity of the underworld and resurrection. Name of the Nile. Also called Osiris.

Ashera(h) (Ah-sher-ah) – A mother goddess who appears in a number of ancient sources "Queen of Heaven", consort of the Sumerian god Anu and Ugaritic El (both bull deities) the word 'elat' is used to describe her as "goddess".

Bakha Montu (Ba-ka-mahn-too) – The meaning of his name was "nomad". The warrior nature of Menthu made him a bull god Menthu would also be represented as a man with the head of a bull. There were at least three great sacred bulls of the Ancient Egypt called the Apis of Memphis, Mnevis of Heliopolis and Buchis at Hermonthis (the Bakha).

Buhen (Boo-hen) – Town and sepat south of Qustul.

Bunefer (Boo-ne-fur) – Prophetess for Shepseskaf, bodily wife, possible mother of his eldest daughter.

Buto (Boo-toe) – Ancient coastal city near Alexandria. The goddess Wadjet was its local goddess, often represented as a cobra. Her oracle was located in her renowned temple in that city. King Menkaure received a tragic prediction there, according to legend.

Deka (Deh-kuh) – Means "One who pleases"

Djedi (Jed-iy or Jed-eye) – Historical Djedi son of Sneferu. He was the first recorded magician.

Djehuti (Jeh-hoo-tea) – The Egyptian God of mathematics, writing, and scholarship. In some creation myths He is the voice of Ptah (the word or logos that appears in Christian and Jewish creation myths) as Ptah Emerges from the Cosmic Egg. Also called Thoth.

Djerah bin Esai (Jair-uh –ben-ee-sye) – Djerah son of Esai, Marai's great grand-nephew.

Djin (Jin) – Spirit, often demonic.

Dumuzi (Do-moot-see) – Is a shepherd god who represents the harvest season but also became a god of the underworld thanks to the goddess Ishtar (Ashera).

El (Ell) – Cannanite for penis. One of the male deities.

Haboob (Ha-boob) – Dust Storm.

Heka (Heh-kuh) – Magic, sorcery.

Heru (Hair-oo) – Horus Hawk deity.

Hethrt (Heth-uroot) – Hethara Hathor Mistress of Life, the Great Wild Cow, the Golden One, the Mistress of Turquoise, Lady of Iunet (Dendera, Egypt) Beauty, happiness music & dance.

Hordjedtef (Hoar-jeh-tef) – Also seen as Hardaduf or Djedephor in ancient literature. Son of Khufu, Count of Nekhen. Prince, Scholar, Author of the "Wisdom Texts" faded into semi obscurity after his brother Djedephre became king, but name appears as a living person throughout the rule of Menkaure.

Houra bint Ahu (Hoo-rah-bent-ah-hoo) – Marai's half-sister.

Iah (Yah) – Egyptian Time God Iah-Djhuty.

Ibu (Ee-boo) – The tent of purification. This is the place where mummification was performed.

Inanna (In-ah-na) – Sumerian pantheon in ancient Mesopotamia. She is a goddess of love, fertility, and war.

Ineb Hedj (In-eb-Hedge) – Earliest name for Memphis (Men Nefer) later Cairo means White Wall.

Kalasaris (Ka-la-sah-ris) – Woman's sheath was held up by one or two straps and was worn down to the ankle, while the upper edge could be worn above or below the breasts.

Ka-reen (Ka-reen) – Kemet-ized word for qua-reen – a succubus.

Ka't (Ka-tea) – Woman, vagina, used as a derogatory term woman good for only one thing (Egyptian).

Keftiu (Kef-tee-oo) – Land of People of the Sea; Crete.

Keleb (Kay-leb) – Sexually submissive male or dog position in M/M pairings – a Canaanite term.

Kemet (Kem-et) – Ancient name for Egypt.

Kentake (Ken-tah-kay) – Title for "queen-mother" of the ancient Kingdom of Kush in the Nile Valley.

Khat (Koht) – Simpler men's head scarf, covering.

Khmenu (Khmun, Hermopolis K'men-oo) – Worship center for Djehuti Thoth.

Kina-Ahna (Kina Land – Kee-na Ah-nah) – Canaan (Israel & Palestine).

Kuna (Koo-nah) – Canaanite version of the word Ka't (see above).

Kush (Koosh) – Sudan.

Maatkare Raemkai (M'yat-kah-ray Ra-em-kiye) – The names mean "Truth in the soul of the sun". It also means "the sun is my life force".

Mafdet (Mof-det) – Mafdet was a goddess who protected against snakes and scorpions. Mafdet was also seen as a feline goddess.

Malak (Ma-lack) – Semitic word for "angel".

Marai bin Ahu (Muh-rye ben Ah-oo) – Marai son of Ahu.

Menkaure or Menkaure Kha-ket (Men-caw-ray Ka-ket) – King associated with the 3rd Giza Pyramid.

Merytetes (Mary-te-tees) – Common princess name. In this case name of an unknown, speculated daughter of Menkaure.

Monthu (or Menthu-Ra Mahn-too) – A solar god (hawk or bull), associated with Amun and sometimes paired with Set.

Mtoto Metauhetep Akaru Sef (Muh-toe-toe Meh-t'ow-tep Ah-kah-roo-seff) – Regional ruler of Qustul Amani and Qustul.

Mut (Moot) – A primal deity, associated with the waters from which everything was born through parthenogenesis.

Naibe-Ellit (Nah-ee-bay El-it) – Name means "Calls My Lady" or channels the goddess Inanna or Ashera.

Nefira (Neh-fear-uh) – Beautiful one from the word Nefer.

Nemes (Nim-mess) – The striped headcloth worn by pharaohs in ancient Egypt.

Nit or Neith (Neat) – Goddess of Weaving, War, Hunting and the Red Crown, Creator Deity, Mother of Ra.

Ntr Stones (Nit-ur) – Kemet name for Children of Stone.

Nut (Noot) – Goddess of the Sky, Stars, the Sun, the Moon, Light, Heaven, Astronomy, the Universe and the Winds woman or cow covered with stars.

Oya (Oy-ah) – Goddess of the Wind and Storms.

Per-A-At – Heliopolis. Worship center for Ra.

Pyr akhs, pyr mer – Both terms for Pyramid.

Qustul (Kuh-stool) – kingdom seat in prehistoric Ta-Seti or Nubia.

Ra-Kedet (Ray-ked-et) – The ancient name for Alexandria.

Sadeh (Sah-day) – Maatkare's wife & former concubine.

Sanghir (Sang-hear) – Ancient Middle-Eastern tribe.

Satet (Say-tet) – Was the archer-goddess of the Nile cataracts, fertility goddess, due to her aspect as a water goddess and a goddess of the inundation, and a goddess who purified the dead with her water. She was a goddess of the hunt who protected Egypt and the pharaoh with her bow and arrows.

Savta (Sav-ta) – Granny, great granny (Semitic).

Sebek (Seh-Bek) – Human with a crocodile head. Sobek was also associated with pharaonic power, fertility, and military prowess, but served additionally as a protective deity with apotropaic qualities, invoked particularly for protection against the dangers presented by the Nile river.

Sebiumeker (She-boo-ee-meh-kur) – Nubian God of Procreation in human form. He was translated into Atum through Egyptian Influences.

Sekhem (Seck-him) – Healing magic.

Sekhmet (Sek-met, Sek-het) – Also spelled Sakhmet, Sekhet, or Sakhet (among other spellings) was originally the warrior goddess as well as goddess of healing for Upper Egypt, when the kingdom of Egypt was divided. She is depicted as a lioness.

Sepat (Seh-pat) – The Ancient Egyptian name for the regional divisions of the country.

Sesen (Se-sin) – Lotus Points; Chakra.

Shendyt (Shin-dit) – A kilt-like garment worn in ancient Egypt.

Shenti (Shin-tea) – A loincloth under-kilt.

Sheol (She-oll) – Underworld, Hell in Canaanite.

Shepseskaf (Shep-ses-calf) – Last or second to last king of the 4th dynasty.

Shinar (She-nar) – Babylon.

Sokor (So-core) – Modern day Saquarra place of the dead. Has to do with rituals for the dead. God seen as a mummy with a hawk head. Also spelled Sokar.

Sutek (Soo-tek) Set or Seth – A god of the desert, storms, disorder, violence and foreigners in ancient Egyptian religion Dark balance of Ra.

Ta-Ntr (Tah-nit-ur) – Land of the Gods.

Ta-Seti (Tah-se-tee) – Land of the Bow, Nubia.

Tauret (Taw-ret) – Hippopotamus-goddess of pregnant women and childbirth.

Tefnut (Teff-noot) – Goddess of moisture, moist air, dew and rain in Ancient Egyptian religion. Sister and consort of the air god Shu.

Tyre (Tear, possibly Tire) – Phoenician ancient trading outpost Lebanon.

Wadi (Wah-dee) – The Arabic term traditionally referring to a valley. In some cases, it may refer to a dry (ephemeral) riverbed that contains water only during times of heavy rain or simply an intermittent stream

Wawat (Wa-Wat) – North Sudan.

Wdjat (Wu-jot) – The Wadjet or Eye of Horus is intended to protect the pharaoh [here] in the afterlife and to ward off evil. Also called Udjat.

Wepwawet (Wep-wah-wet) – originally a war deity, whose cult centre was Asyut in Upper Egypt (Lycopolis in the Greco Roman period). His name means, opener of the ways and he is often depicted as a wolf standing at the prow of a solar-boat. Some interpret that Wepwawet was seen as a scout, going out to clear routes for the army to proceed forward. One inscription from the Sinai states that Wepwawet "opens the way". Also possibly spelled Upuwat.

Wserkaf (Oo-sir-kaf) – First king of the 5th dynasty formerly a High Priest of Ra and Djehuti. Also spelled Userkaf.

Yaweh-Sin (Ya-way sin) – Semitic lunar deity living atop Sinai, later shortened to Yaweh and disobedience of his law is Sin.

Made in the USA
Charleston, SC
17 October 2016